Jenna Kernan
and
Doranna Durgin

THE SHIFTER'S CHOICE

AND

SENTINELS: ALPHA RISING

D0473913

H HARLEQUIN® NOCTURNE™

Recycling programs
for this product may
not exist in your area.

ISBN-13: 978-0-373-60125-7

The Shifter's Choice and Sentinels: Alpha Rising

Copyright © 2015 by Harlequin Books S.A.

The publisher acknowledges the copyright holders of the individual works as follows:

The Shifter's Choice
Copyright © 2014 by Jeannette H. Monaco

Sentinels: Alpha Rising
Copyright © 2015 by Doranna Durgin

HARLEQUIN®
www.Harlequin.com

Printed in U.S.A.

CONTENTS

THE SHIFTER'S CHOICE   7
Jenna Kernan

SENTINELS: ALPHA RISING   291
Doranna Durgin

THE SHIFTER'S CHOICE

Jenna Kernan

For Jim, always.

Chapter 1

Private Sonia Touma's helicopter touched down on the landing pad at a marine base that didn't officially exist. Her orders read Oahu, which lay just past Maui, but instead she'd been rerouted here. The copilot slid the door open wide enough to heave her duffel and foot-locker to the tarmac then motioned with his thumb that she should get out. The pilot cut the engine. The rotors slowed as she hopped down.

She kept low and moved out of range of the blades, then straightened to glance about. Beyond the landing pad lay a dirt road. Parallel to the road stood a twenty-foot-tall security perimeter fence that stretched as far as she could see in both directions. *Keeping folks out or in?* she wondered. The cameras and other electronics topping the fence posts indicated in.

The hot, humid air rose from the tarmac and the yellow grass surrounding the landing pad. Sweat already beaded on her brow and she wiped it away with the sleeve of her uniform. October sure was different here than in Yonkers, New York.

Why was she here? It made no sense. She didn't have one single solitary skill that she could think of that would lift her above her fellow marines for a special assignment, unless you counted a criminal record, hitting people and a proclivity for telling people in authority to fuck off.

Her ears pricked up at the sound of an engine. She stared past the dry grass dotted with monstrous yucca plants until she sighted an approaching Jeep.

She eyed the driver, spotting the captain's stripes on his arm, and snapped to attention. The Jeep rolled to a stop beside her.

"Private Touma?"

She replied as expected, "Sir. Yes, sir."

Sonia waited until the captain's hand touched his forehead below the brim of his hat and then snapped her hand back to her side.

"I'm Captain MacConnelly. You'll be reporting to me." He looked her up and down, his brow etched with wrinkles. Whatever he'd been expecting, she had the feeling that she was not it.

He thumbed at the empty passenger seat. She lifted her duffel.

"Leave it."

Sonia dropped the heavy bag beside the footlocker and glanced back at the helo. The pilots peered past her to the captain who lifted a hand ordering them to wait. Her skin prickled as she faced the captain. It looked like there was an entrance exam.

"Get in," he said.

She did. Sonia eyed her new superior officer from the passenger seat. The first thing she noticed was his left hand on the steering wheel and the shiny gold wedding band there, so bright and new it glowed. The second was the tight coil of muscle at his bunching jaw. The captain looked ready to grind nails between his teeth.

Her supervisor cut the engine, shifted in his seat and stared directly at her.

"I believe in getting right to it, Touma," he narrowed his eyes on her. "I've read your file."

His words sent a chill down her spine that cut through the tropical heat. She glanced at her belongings broiling on the tarmac and then back to the captain.

"Thick file." He showed her the width with his thumb and index finger. "Mostly just reports of you quitting. You a quitter, Private?"

His summary of her life hit her like a slap. "I finished basic and I'll finish my service, sir."

He snorted. "Like you had a choice. Back to the wall, right? Well, just so we understand each other, let me assure you that if you quit this time, you go back to prison."

And there it was. The reason she was a marine in the first place. Not by choice, but by picking the lesser of two evils, while this man probably enlisted in the Corps. That was obvious by his distaste of her. Right now she needed to get her gear in this Jeep and that meant being whatever he needed her to be.

The captain swept her with his cold blue eyes, his lip curling at what he saw. "Wearing the uniform doesn't make you a marine. You don't have the first idea of the code."

She was not going back to prison. "Duty, honor—"

"Oh, stow it."

She closed her mouth before saying country.

If he thought she was such a screwup, why was she here? It occurred to her that maybe it wasn't his choice. That he might be following orders he didn't like any better than she liked hers. That would make this just a show of strength. The thought gave her a glimmer of hope. But she had to be sure in order to know how to play this.

"Our security check didn't turn up one person who knew you well enough to complete a simple question-naire about you. You have any explanation for that?"

Let's see whose orders she was really following. "If I'm such a substandard marine, sir, why am I here?"

His brows shot up as if this was the first thing she'd said or done that surprised him.

"You aren't here yet, Private. And you don't get on base until we finish our chat. You're a contender for this assignment, that's all, and only because you have the necessary skill set and because my wife thinks you can do this despite all evidence to the contrary."

She didn't have any skills. This was a mistake. Wait…had he said his wife picked her? Was that who was calling the shots? She must be a general or some-thing. Well, that would explain why he looked so pissed. "But you don't, sir."

"I think you'll last about thirty seconds."

She pictured herself in an orange jumpsuit and set-tled into her seat. She'd make thirty seconds, all right, and she'd make it past this guy. Sonia stared at the cap-tain. "I'll have to agree with your wife, sir."

"Your assignment is to teach an injured marine. He's depressed and occasionally suicidal and he is disin-clined to learn sign language."

Warning bells rang in her head like church bells on Christmas Eve. An injured marine, likely deaf, angry, suicidal and possibly in denial. *This* was her assignment? Oh, she *was* fucked.

"I don't think I'm qualified to deal with someone with those kinds of emotional issues, sir."

"You don't?" The captain's cool eyes regarded her and he held her gaze a moment before flicking his attention out at the empty road. When he spoke his voice was sardonic. "Well, I'm sorry if I gave you the impression that I give a goddamn what you think, Private. You are a marine, at least that's a U.S. Marine's uniform. That means you follow orders. Maybe you didn't understand how that works."

What if her assignment was an emotionally shattered, unpredictable time bomb, like she was?

"Sergeant John Loc Lam had two teachers just this month. He chased them both off."

Did he say Lock? What kind of middle name was Lock?

"It's your job to make him want to learn how to sign."

Sign language? She'd never even considered she'd be asked to use that as one of her skills. She'd learned to sign right alongside her sister, Marianna, who was born deaf.

"My wife suggested I hire a woman this time."

Sonia wondered how many others had tried and failed at this shit job before they scraped the barrel and came up with her? Now she was frowning right back at the captain who hadn't missed a beat.

"I think you'll fall on your face or run, just like always. Might shit yourself first. But your assignment is to do everything and anything to get him on board."

She wondered how the hell was she supposed to do that. But she said, "Yes, sir."

MacConnelly made a sound that might have been a laugh.

"Despite his appearance, Lam needs sympathy and understanding. What he doesn't need is a woman who is going to hit and run. You understand?"

Appearance? Was he scarred?

"I do, sir." Of course she didn't understand.

"You run and he's won."

"I won't run, sir."

He made a sound deep in his throat. "That's what the others said, too. Both made it up the mountain to meet Lam." He reached to the seat behind him and retrieved a laptop. Sonia's stomach tied itself in progressively tighter knots while he booted up his computer. What was wrong with Lam that made the other's run? When the screen glowed a vivid blue he turned his attention back to her.

"Everyone here on base knows Sergeant Lam's situation. But every word I'm about to tell you is classified. Off base, you tell no one. This goes with you to your grave. Any violation will result in a court-martial and I will personally see that you go to prison for a lot longer than six years. Got it?" He lifted his brows so they disappeared above the rim of his hat.

Sonia's insides went icy as she nodded her understanding.

"I need to hear you say it out loud, Touma."

"I understand, sir."

He opened a presentation titled Sergeant John Loc Lam. He set the computer on the dashboard between them and adjusted the angle of the screen.

"Can you see this?"

"Yes, sir." She could also see her duffel on the tarmac. Somehow, she needed to get that bag into this Jeep.

The first slide was of a young, thin soldier grinning as he leaned on the hood of a Humvee. His helmet obscured most of his face. "This is what Lam looked like when he was in my command in Afghanistan."

So the captain had skin in the game. Sonia braced for what she expected next, the deformed face of a man struck by fire or lead or jagged bits of metal. Instead the next slide was the traditional graduation photo taken after boot camp. Lam was in full dress blues. She stared at the rich brown eyes, narrow brow, full lips and the short-cropped black hair, and her stomach did a little drop as if she'd looked down from somewhere very high and a little bit dangerous. The man was a knockout with film-star good looks, she decided. What had happened to that handsome face, she wondered as she braced for what was inevitable.

She pressed her lips together and waited but he didn't change the slide. She noticed suddenly that the captain was staring at her, instead of the screen.

"Problem?" he asked.

What could she say, that she was taken by his good looks? She glanced back at the image before she said the first thing she could think of to avoid admitting her physical reaction to Lam.

"He's Asian."

"He's American," said the captain, not hiding his annoyance at her observation. "His mother is naturalized from Hong Kong. His father is also of Chinese descent, but he is third generation, born in California. Mother is alive and father is deceased, heart attack. His dad ran a restaurant in San Francisco. He has a younger sister named Julia, legal name Joon. She's seventeen now."

Sonia wanted to ask what happened to Lam, but now she was afraid to find out. Had the other teachers quit because their student was unwilling or because of his current appearance? If it was his appearance, that was just wrong. He couldn't help what had happened or the results. But what *had* happened?

"Lam entered a building in Koppel at night under my order."

Here it comes, she realized, gripping the dashboard as if preparing for a crash.

"Two fire teams had already gone in and all died. Lam and I entered with the last team. We were the only two survivors. This is what attacked us." He pressed a button and there stood a huge gray animal standing on hind legs like an ape. But the body was elongated, wolfish, with a pronounced snout and back feet that more resembled paws. The hands seemed like a bear's with wicked curved black claws. She gaped for a moment and then laughed. The captain didn't even crack a smile.

She pointed at the image. "That's a joke, right? You're kidding me. Photoshopped it?"

Her captain shook his head. Her breath caught and she peered at the screen taking careful note of the creature's yellow eyes and the dangerous fangs.

"That's not a real animal," she said, trying to assure herself more than inform him.

"It is. I saw it when it attacked Lam and this is the result." The captain pressed a key and the image of a black-furred monster's face filled the screen. "This is John Lam today."

Sonia glanced at the screen and then the captain and then the screen again.

She didn't recall scrambling out the passenger side but found herself standing on the tarmac clinging to the doorframe. The heat rising from the tarmac baked right through her thick-soled shoes. She stared at the captain realizing he'd been right. Her stubborn side kept her anchored for a moment like a shipwreck survivor clinging to a piece of waterlogged debris. Then she pushed off.

"Hell, no." Sonia backed away from the Jeep.

"Touma!"

She kept walking toward the helo, running away from the captain, that monster and her very last chance.

When she reached the closed door of the helicopter her brain reengaged. The pilot and copilot stared at her through the thick glass. She stiffened, with one hand on the lever. What was she going to do, order them to fly her home to Yonkers?

Hit and run, that's what the captain said. But no one would blame her. That thing was a monster. She glanced back to see the captain now leaning against the fender staring at his watch.

"Thirty seconds. And you didn't even make it onto the base. Have fun in prison, Touma."

She turned and swayed on her feet. The captain lifted his radio making a call. Sonia walked to her gear and hoisted her duffel to her shoulder as if planning to hitchhike. She needed to go. Somehow she needed to get out of here.

A second Jeep arrived and two burly MPs climbed out. Sonia dropped her bag as the reality of her situation hit her like a punch. Her stomach pitched and she thought she might throw up.

The captain held up two fingers. "Two choices, Touma. Do the job or do the time."

Sonia stood with her chin raised in a stubborn attitude that had rarely brought her anything good. He couldn't make her. She'd appeal or something. But it was top secret. She couldn't tell anyone. Not even a military court.

"Fine," said the captain. "MPs! Take her to the brig."

Seeing the two marines approach, with jaws set in determination, knocked the stubborn right out of her. She pictured the cell. Felt the walls closing in around her and her mind slipped to that terrible place in her childhood, dark and smelling of plastic and urine, her urine. She recalled her cold, wet clothing chaffing her skin until she pulled it off, waiting in the dark like an animal.

"No!" She lifted her hands in surrender. "I'll do it. I'll meet him. I'll teach him."

Her captain pressed his lips together, hands on hips. Finally he pointed to his Jeep. "Get in."

Sonia lifted her duffel and placed it in the rear seat. The captain said nothing to this as he climbed back behind the wheel.

Once she was seated, he said, "If he doesn't like you or if you run off, you're back in the brig."

"But I can't keep him from chasing me off."

"You better."

She recalled the mention of the teachers before her and wondered what Lam had done to make them quit. Sonia wiped the sweat from her upper lip. Whatever he did, it couldn't be as bad as prison.

"What if he hurts me?"

"He won't. I'd stake my life on it. But I can guarantee he'll try to scare the life out of you. So...you ready to meet your new pupil?"

"I'm not a teacher. I've never taught anyone anything."

"That's not quite true, Touma. You taught your sister,

Marianna, her first signs and you took out that library book so you could both learn."

Man, somebody was scary good at research.

"Do we understand each other, Private?"

She saluted. "Yes, sir."

He returned it with a definite lack of enthusiasm. "Great. You meet him this afternoon at fourteen hundred. I'll take you to your quarters, but I wouldn't unpack just yet."

Sonia eyed her duffel bag wondering where it and she would be by nightfall. She'd made it to the barracks, but barely had time to wash her face before a young woman arrived to give her a tour. Her footlocker was delivered before they left their quarters. Her guide was chatty and asked too many damned personal questions. The private was a nurse, so once she reached the medical facility she felt the need to introduce Sonia to a lot of people she didn't have the first inclination to get to know. As a result, she brought Sonia back late. The captain was waiting outside their quarters, drumming his fingers on the steering wheel.

Sonia climbed in the Jeep and they were off on a road that led through the base and then scaled the mountain in increasingly harrowing switchbacks. Sonia clung to her seat like a monkey on her mama's back as the vehicle jostled on the unpaved road. The low dry scrub lining their way reminded her of West Texas where she'd first been stationed. As they continued upward, the yellow grasses gave way to tall, spindly pines rising eighty feet into the air. The Jeep trail cut through the giants, revealing the exposed red earth, dry as the dust cloud that rooster-tailed out behind them. Through the pine she could see the perimeter fence continuing parallel to their route. That was a lot of fence through a whole lot of nothing. Questions buzzed like flies in her mind.

She welcomed the shade but not the rush of air through the open window that played havoc with the neat knot of her hair. She kept one hand on the crown of her hat as they bounced through ruts and climbed into the tropical valley. The land folded back on itself like a ribbon. Ferns now clung to the red earth, growing in bunches, some so impossibly high they looked like trees. The landscape seemed a primordial forest and she could imagine prehistoric creatures roaming among the primitive plants. The pines had disappeared to be replaced by trees she couldn't name. Moss hugged each branch like a fuzzy green coat and the air hung thick and heavy all about her.

"Rain forest," said the captain. "On the top it's grass and rock, but in between the ocean and the mountain peak we have this. Outer perimeter is five square miles. UV cameras, motion detectors, electronic sensors throughout. Inner perimeter is higher with deterrents in addition to surveillance. Plus a lock-in facility down below."

Deterrents could be anything, landmines, machine-gun towers, gas, patrols.

Sonia wondered what they were protecting. Was this all for Sergeant John Loc Lam? She considered the possibilities as the captain continued on.

"Nothing gets in or out without us knowing." He eyed her for a moment and then returned his attention to the road.

Sonia nodded at his additional warning that running would not work. Her back was to the wall. She was going to teach John Lam or end up in jail.

"Where are we going, sir?"

They switched back again and again until she was looking out at the Pacific Ocean's deep blue water. She could no longer see anything but the narrow tracks of the Jeep trail and the encroachment of lush greenery.

The jungle grew in a green curtain right to the edge of the path. It seemed that if she took one step to the right or left she might vanish forever. Why did she want to take that step?

She tried to penetrate the foliage with her gaze and found one shadowy break. Something stared back with wide-set yellow eyes and a face surrounded with shiny black hair. She startled backward against the clutch and pointed but it was gone.

"What?" asked the captain.

"A-animal," she managed. "Big. Black." But not any animal she'd ever seen. It had a caninelike mouth complete with long saber-toothed tiger fangs. *Was that Lam?*

"Shit," said MacConnelly, and then, "We're nearly there."

She could see the foliage moving parallel to the Jeep. Whatever it was, it could run faster than they could drive. From the safety of the vehicle, her fear tipped toward fascination as she caught glimpses of its black hide in the forest. What else could John Lam do that a normal man could not? She supposed she was about to find out.

The captain slowed to pull into a drive that she had not even seen.

Without warning the path opened up and the sunshine they had left behind in the valley poured down on them. Sonia blinked in the brilliant light as she looked out the window. The house took her breath away. The exterior was painted a pale blue-green with white trim. A wide porch with white lattice work circled the second story. The roof had just the slightest pitch and peak. Of course, no snow here, so why have an angled roof, she thought. Still, this placed looked about as far away from Yonkers, New York, as one could get and that was exactly why she loved it on sight. It wasn't attached to other apartments, it had a yard, sort of, and privacy. She remembered the perimeter fence. It sure did have privacy. Her gaze shifted, searching for John Loc Lam.

"These are my quarters. My wife wanted a look at you."

Sonia's stomach dropped as she prepared herself for this next inspection.

His home resembled a two-story boathouse perched on stilts above a small stream that meandered past a brook that reflected the sky and trees. A small arched bridge allowed a visitor to cross from the path over the water to the house. She glanced at the bank of windows that covered the entire ground floor and saw a face. As quick as she could blink the face was gone. Had she seen it? She could have sworn there had been a woman there with long wavy hair as red as a new penny. That creepy feeling slithered down her back again.

"She won't come out," he said. "She has agoraphobia."

"Fear of spiders?" Sonia asked.

"Open spaces. She doesn't go out and you don't go in." He put the Jeep in park and exited the vehicle. "Wait here."

Sonia rolled down the window and stared out at the flower boxes spilling over with exotic pink blossoms. The porch had a swinging love seat, a metal fire pit and several comfortably padded chairs.

The deep sorrow that bubbled up inside her took her completely unawares. How could she miss something she'd never had? A pretty home of her own, with a swing and a garden. It had always been just a fantasy. But here, a man in uniform had it. The fantasy now seemed almost possible.

"If you stay out of jail," she muttered.

Something hit her door with enough force to tip the Jeep before the vehicle thudded back to earth. Sonia screamed as the tires bounced beneath her. She turned and there he was, filling the gap in the open window. Big and black and foaming from his snapping jaws. He lifted a clawed hand and reached for her and Sonia found herself on the driver's side with her back pressed up against the door.

He snapped his teeth. They locked with a horrible clicking sound as he went still and his strange yellow eyes went wide. He looked frozen while she had stopped breathing.

She released the latch and tumbled out onto the ground and took off for the house, running faster than she'd ever ran before. Behind her, she heard him coming after her, jaws snapping, the ripping sound of the grass as he tore it out by its roots. She scrambled up the steep stairs to reach the front door and bolted through it, throwing herself back against the solid wood frame. The thing pounded up the stairs and thumped on the door sending vibrations clear through her body. Sonia flipped the lock and stumbled back to land on the floor where she cowered for many long minutes.

Finally the pounding stopped and the silence descended around her, more terrifying than the beating of his fists against wood. Where was he?

He might have killed her. But he hadn't. Somehow she'd escaped. One thing was certain. She was not teaching that thing.

Her heart slammed in her chest, jackhammering against her ribs until they ached. Finally Sonia recovered enough to stand. Her mind began to tick again. She recalled seeing John Lam running beside the Jeep at twenty miles an hour, at the very least. Yet he had not been able to catch her as she fled. And he had reached for her, but not succeeded in grabbing her when she was trapped in the Jeep even though he had taken her unawares. He'd nearly tipped the thing over. Could have, she was certain. But didn't. If he'd wanted to grab her that would have been a good time to do it.

But he hadn't. The truth filtered through the fear. He hadn't caught her because he wasn't *trying* to catch her. He was trying to scare her.

What had the captain said, she might shit herself? Well, she nearly had.

Was this some hazing? Did the captain know this would happen?

Sonia's anger rose within her like lava, clouding her judgment with great plumes of black smoke. *That asshole!*

"Damn them both!"

She unfastened the lock and threw open the door. John was gone. Why hang around when he was sure that she would run back to the captain and quit. Well that is exactly what she would have done if she could. But she couldn't because despite how frightening John Loc Lam was, prison scared her more.

Sonia tugged her hat down low over her eyes and marched back outside. She was not going to let that overgrown wolf pup scare her into a jail cell. Not now. Not ever.

Chapter 2

Johnny heard the Jeep pull out. Why the hell hadn't Mac told him that this teacher was a woman?

He might have given her a heart attack. She'd had her head turned to look at the house when he charged the Jeep and he already had his arm in the window when she turned around. He'd never forget the look on her face for as long as he lived. There, reflected in her big brown eyes were all the things he knew he'd become. She'd been terrified, of course, and she'd run. He'd run, too, at first out of instinct. The flight of prey triggered something deep inside him now. Then he'd slowed to let her escape. He was ashamed. Even as he pounded on the door he wanted to beg her forgiveness for what he'd done and for what he'd become.

But he couldn't go back. He'd chased her away and that was best for them both. Maybe now Mac would give up this stupid idea and let him train for a combat mission. Johnny knew he could be effective in the field if they'd just give him a chance.

He headed up the trail that led from Mac's home to his quarters wondering what it would be like to have that woman as his teacher. Like she'd ever come back after the way he'd welcomed her. She'd have to be crazy.

Mac would give him hell and Johnny would let him because this time he deserved it.

When he reached his quarters, Johnny was surprised to hear the Jeep engine. He didn't understand. Mac hadn't had time to take the woman back to base. The first prickle of unease lifted the hairs on his neck. He loped the remaining distance to his yard. There he found his captain disembarking with the woman. Mac's mouth was set in a grim line but he did not look pissed, certainly not as monumentally pissed as Johnny expected after the stunt he'd pulled. Johnny's gaze flashed to the woman, surprised to see that it was she who looked pissed. Her pretty face was flushed pink and her pointed chin was raised like a dagger. She stared directly at him in an obvious challenge. Now this was unexpected. Johnny took a step in their direction, anticipating she would retreat or move closer to Mac. Instead she scowled as if she'd figured it all out. He didn't know if he should run at her again or beg her forgiveness.

The involuntary growl started in his throat. She was upwind so he lifted his nose and breathed deep. He did not scent fear. More like fury. He'd watched her run. So why had she come back and why the hell hadn't she told Mac what he'd done?

He could tell by Mac's hopeful expression that his captain was clueless about his trying to scare her away. This was so weird. Johnny felt unbalanced, as if *she* was hunting him. He felt a rush of blood and a tingle of excitement.

This woman interested him.

But learning to sign did not.

Maybe he'd take the seat out of her trousers. He crossed to them both on his hind legs, clenching and un-clenching his fists as he came. She didn't retreat which showed a distinctive lack of self-preservation.

Instead, she snapped a salute and Johnny frowned.

Mac pointed at the woman's hand. "I think that one is for you, Sergeant."

Johnny straightened and returned a sloppy salute, now ill at ease. She was messing with him. He was certain now. He didn't like playing the fool so he bared his teeth.

"Sergeant Lam, this is Private Sonia Touma. I've briefed her on your condition and she's anxious to teach you the communication skills you lack. She is fluent in sign language."

Johnny tried to imagine what Mac had over her to make her agree to this. She'd been right the first time. Better to run and take the consequences. He didn't want a teacher, especially one who smelled like rose petals.

Sonia Touma stood at attention like a good little sol-dier. Johnny eyed her. She was short, curvy, from what he could see beyond her uniform. Slender wrists showed she was on the thin side. He studied her heart-shaped face finding her eyes angled and set wide beyond a nose that was slightly hooked, bringing an ethnic flare to her features. When he'd chased her, her hair had come loose from its moorings, but now it was all tucked up beneath her cap again. Certainly she had a lovely mouth, full and pink. As he stared, her mouth quirked and John-ny's pulse kicked like a jackrabbit. Oh, hell, this little female was trouble. Their eyes met and she held his stare, issuing an unspoken challenge. That glimmer of determination and the flaring of her nostrils intrigued the hell out of him.

Brave, stupid or suicidal? he wondered. But, of course, he couldn't ask.

"I've got supplies in the truck. I'll set them up on the porch," said Mac, just plowing forward like always.

Mac was so sure that this was what he needed. If she tried to teach him one thing he'd chase her down the mountain because he was not learning to sign. But still Mac kept pushing.

Johnny glared as his captain returned.

"I'll just put the easel up." Mac walked around the house and paused at the fire pit to take in the number of discarded and crushed beer cans. They both knew that alcohol didn't affect him. Mac must have realized that drinking beer on the mountain was a nice perk for his new buddies. Only they weren't buddies. You didn't have to assign buddies or pay them. But that's what Mac had done and then he couldn't figure why Johnny wouldn't hang with them. The only one he even liked was Zeno because he could tell a story complete with punch line. He made everything seem funny. Only sometimes they weren't.

The easel creaked as Mac placed it in the shade on the right side of the porch. He pulled two markers from his pocket. One red and one black. The eraser came from the opposite pocket. Then he dragged a single chair before the large, blank dry-erase board and dusted off his hands. Did he have a pointer for his new teacher? Johnny folded his arms and lifted a brow at Mac who ignored him. The woman had already stayed longer than the last two combined and Mac obviously took that as some kind of encouragement.

"I'm leaving the Jeep and walking down to see Bri. I'll be back in an hour." Mac pointed at his Jeep and then shook his finger at him issuing a silent warning to Johnny not to mess with his ride.

Johnny still considered rolling his Jeep again.

Mac handed over a phone to the woman. "Private Touma, if you need help just press dial. It calls the MPs directly. Otherwise, I'll see you in sixty."

The MPs? Johnny stared from one to the other as questions rose in his mind. Was this some trick, some setup to get him so curious he wrote on that damned whiteboard?

He glanced at Touma and decided that no one was that good an actor. Something was going on because the woman was shaking now, shaking like she was scared and not of him. What did Mac have over her that made her willing to stay?

Johnny could only wonder because he'd be damned if he'd lift one of those stinky dry-erase markers.

Mac gave Touma a hard look and headed for the trail on the opposite side of the yard. It led down past the waterfall and grotto to the captain's house, half a mile away.

A new scent came to him and he turned toward the woman. Now Johnny smelled fear. He glanced at Touma noting the strain on her face as she watched the captain depart. Was she dismayed at being alone with the big bad wolf?

She should be.

Mac disappeared down the trail and Touma blew out a breath. The smell of fear ebbed. Then Johnny realized something odd. She wasn't afraid of him. She was afraid of Mac. But that made no sense at all.

Had she thought that Mac's glare had something to do with her? He wanted to ask her and then was instantly annoyed at himself. He didn't need to ask anything. What he needed was to get rid of her before this got any worse.

The woman cleared her throat. Johnny emitted a low growl. Her eyes flicked to the hated easel and then back to him.

He wondered if she was stupid enough to pick up that red marker. She turned to the board and dropped the cell phone into the tray. She wasn't calling for rescue. Strange. But he found himself impressed with her bravery.

She met him with a direct look. "You want to show me around?"

Johnny stared at her for a long moment. She stared back with dark soulful eyes that seemed a little sad to him. He wanted to ask her what she'd done to get this shit job, but he didn't know sign language. If he learned he could speak to her. But that would be giving up. Sometimes he thought that all he had left was the daily fight to hold on to his hope. Learning sign would kill it.

"Listen," she tried again and this time, when she spoke she accompanied each word with a sign. "I'm stuck here for an hour and I'd like it very much if you didn't eat me while I wait."

Johnny exhaled in a short blast that was his laugh.

"So, do you want to show me your home or do you want me to go sit over there for the hour?" She finished signing and pointed at a bench facing the treetops and beyond that, the blue waters of the Pacific. Johnny spent a lot of time looking at those waters…imagining.

"Sit or tour?" she asked, making the signs for both.

He continued to stare, refusing to imitate her signs.

She smiled. "Great. My choice, then."

She walked to the bench and folded stiffly into the far corner. He remained where he was. She sat gazing out at the vista, a slight smile on her face. When fifteen minutes passed it became obvious that she was quite happy to sit there and wait him out. He worried about her. Why had she stayed?

It was one thing for him to give her the heave-ho but another for her to ignore him. He wasn't used to being ignored and didn't like it.

Johnny grabbed the dry-erase board and broke it into a manageable size, then retrieved the black marker and then returned to her.

He wrote one word. *Quit.*

She glanced at the board and crossed her arms, glancing back at the water. "Fat chance, furball."

He blinked at her. Had she just called him furball? He could snap her in two like a twig. He could throw her fifty yards like a football. He could…

He pointed at the word. She uncrossed her arms, lifted the broken piece of board from his hand and then threw it like a Frisbee over the edge of the embankment. Was she demented?

She started signing as she spoke. "Listen, I can't leave. You got it? I'm stuck here for—" she glanced at her watch "—thirty-one more minutes. So run along if you want to but quit bothering me."

Johnny growled and leaned in so that his nose nearly touched hers. She turned her back on him. Johnny stomped around in front of her and gave her the finger before jumping over the embankment.

Her voice followed him, a shout and a challenge

filled with fury and dripping with a mocking sarcasm that twisted him into an angry knot. "Oh, so you already know how to sign!"

Johnny tore through the undergrowth using his claws as his own personal machete against anything unlucky enough to get in his way. He could slice through metal as easily as he used to tear through paper so the foliage stood no chance.

What the hell was that? Furball? Run along? The woman must be suicidal or crazy. Maybe both. Where did Mac find these people?

Johnny slowed as he thought there might not be a waiting list of people willing to tutor a surly werewolf. He swung at a tall fern and greenery fell about him in tiny bits.

Beside him the dense, wet jungle clung to a cliff so steep that even he had trouble holding on. On more than one occasion he'd imagined just letting go.

"Johnny!"

He recognized the voice. It was Mac heading up the hill to collect his tutor. He sounded pissed.

Johnny took another step in the direction he had been going.

"I can hear you, damn it! Turn around or, so help me, I will take a chunk out of that tough hide."

Johnny knew Mac could do it, because his captain was also a werewolf. Bitten the same night as Johnny and in the same fight. Neither of them had known what they were up against, but their commander had.

Johnny turned back toward his captain. He turned for the same reason his friend hadn't given up on him—duty. Duty to each other, duty to the Corps, duty to himself, duty to his departed father, his struggling mother and the little sister he swore would go to college. He was so damned tired of doing his duty—but still he held on.

Nobody but Mac could keep up with him when he climbed this volcanic rock. Was it Johnny's fault that his new set of playmates couldn't keep up? Not that it was their fault. They were good guys. But they were still human and slow as shit.

Johnny crawled from the undergrowth a moment later. Mac met him, wearing a frown. You'd think being a newlywed living on a lovely tropical island would make his former squad leader happy. Johnny knew, if not for him, Mac would be.

Mac exhaled heavily as he rummaged in his pack withdrawing a black slate. Johnny snarled and Mac met his eyes and then scowled. Johnny didn't like writing because he couldn't really control the pen. It made him feel stupid, so he revealed his three-inch canines to no visible effect. Mac was one of the very few who could meet his gaze without turning away. That was saying something because Johnny knew what he looked like. In his werewolf form, he was nine feet of hideousness that could easily step into any number of horror flicks or out of every child's nightmare.

So Johnny avoided looking at himself. His long snout and black wolfish nose disturbed him nearly as much as the deadly claws and the thick canine pads on his feet. His eyes were no longer soft brown. Now they were as yellow as the rising moon. He still had black hair, but it covered his entire body, right up to his pointed ears and the knuckles of his distended fingers. Once upon a time in that old life, he'd kept his nails trimmed short. But he'd given up on that along with other things. So many other things.

Mac had gray fur when in werewolf form and his

eyes were blue. Johnny wished Mac would run with him instead of sending his substitutions. His captain withdrew a broken nub of chalk from the depths of his pack. The bag and its contents had been his new wife's idea. Brianna knew that her husband transformed naked from wolf to man and that he and Johnny had an ongoing communication problem. So she'd modified a bag so it would fit around his wolfish neck. Then when he reached his destination he could transform and get dressed which explained why his clothes were often wrinkled.

Bri said she would make Johnny the same pack one day. But so far he didn't need it. They'd been here six months. A year and four months since the attack and still Johnny had to use shampoo on his entire body and had no need for clothing since his fur was so thick it covered his junk. Johnny picked the twigs and bits of moss from his furry shoulder and smoothed his glossy coat.

Mac held out the slate to Johnny. He took it and briefly considered throwing the thing as far as he could.

"You ditched her?" asked Mac.

That answer seemed obvious.

"Why not give her a chance?"

Johnny growled.

"Why do you keep ditching them?" asked Mac. "The guys, too. How can I help you if you keep running off?"

He meant the wounded warriors. Johnny's own private trial-by-fire team. One member was even a double amputee, as if having the name Dugan Kiang wasn't handicap enough. Dugan could really run on those kangaroo legs, as he called them, but none of them had experiences that quite matched Johnny's. They could all visit their mothers, for example, and go on leave and walk into a bar without people screaming. And they could talk to each other and they'd all had women since returning Stateside. All but him.

He shrugged.

"Are they bad company?"

Not bad. They were good guys and good marines. Better than Johnny. At least they still followed orders. While Johnny had been second-guessing orders since they'd entered that building in Afghanistan.

His new comrades talked about what most men talked about. Sports, getting laid, work, drinking, getting laid. But alcohol no longer affected Johnny and as for women, the only ones who had seen him since the accident were the medical professionals with top-secret clearances. None of them touched him unless absolutely necessary and he could smell their fear as clearly as he could scent the wild pig that had tracked past here last night.

There was one woman who didn't avoid him but she was taken. Mac's wife, Brianna, had some very special circumstances of her own and that gave her an understanding of Johnny. At least her friendship did not stem from duty or pity or guilt—like Mac's.

"Johnny?" Mac extended the chalk.

He didn't like having friends assigned to him like the most unpopular kid in class and he didn't want a teacher that ignored him. He accepted the chalk, holding it in his large hands with difficulty. It twisted in his fingers, breaking the unsteady white line he scrawled but he managed to write "They're young" on the slate.

"Twenties. Same age as you," replied Mac before Johnny had finished writing. "Touma is only twenty. On her second assignment."

Johnny released the chalk and dusted off his fingers

on his hairy thigh. The fine motor control required for moving the chalk was a real pain in his ass. His hand-writing had once been a source of pride. Now his words looked as if they had been penned by a preschooler. Johnny scowled at the slate.

"They're all learning sign language. They want you to start talking to them. But you have to learn first."

He shook his head. It didn't make any sense. By not learning he could only listen to the guys' conversation. By not learning he was keeping himself apart. But he still couldn't do it even though he knew that his refusal hurt and confused his captain.

"Aren't you sick of answering questions with a yes or no?"

Johnny answered no.

"Now you're just being a pain in my ass."

He was. And if not for Johnny, Mac could spend more time with his wife and less with his guilt. But Mac couldn't walk away—not ever, because Mac had been the second werewolf that had attacked Johnny.

The scientists said it was Mac's bite, that second at-tack, that now made it impossible for Johnny to change back into human form.

Johnny wiped his words from the slate and tried three times to pick up the chalk before succeeding. Then he wrote "Combat duty?"

Mac shook his head. "They said no. Christ, Johnny, you don't follow orders. You come and go as you please. And you want them to trust you in a combat zone? Not gonna happen. Stay inside the perimeter, follow orders, stop acting crazy and maybe you'll get an assignment."

Johnny threw the slate.

Mac watched it disappear into the foliage. "Damn it," he muttered. Mac's gaze flicked back to Johnny, hands on hips. His captain looked like his mother when he did that. "Give her a chance. Learn to sign and maybe then you can have a field assignment."

Johnny raised his lips, showing his teeth. Mac blew out a breath.

"I have to go get Touma. She better not be crying. I hate crying women." He stepped past Johnny and then paused turning back. "Bri wants you at dinner tonight."

Johnny shook his head. He hadn't been to Mac's place since reassignment from the mainland, even though his quarters were only a half mile away. A new couple needed privacy. While he missed his friend, Johnny was happy for him; though, adjusting to life without his captain as a bunk mate had been hard. Nobody understood him like Mac.

"Yeah. She said you'd say no and said to tell you that if you don't come she's coming to your place and cooking supper there." Mac waited.

Johnny glanced toward the rain forest feeling the urge to run again. That pig was upwind.

"She thinks you're mad at her for taking me away. I told her that's bullshit."

Johnny met his gaze and held Mac's stare. The pain and regret was back in his friend's eyes.

"Is it bullshit?"

Johnny picked up a stick and scratched his answer in the dirt. "What time?"

Chapter 3

The following day, Sonia's escort to Sergeant Lam's quarters was Corporal Del Tabron who was missing his left arm from the elbow. He said he was part of the squad that worked out with John, though she'd come to think of him as Johnny since everyone referred to him that way, every morning and sometimes hung with him at night. Each of the five members was missing something. Sonia asked what Johnny was missing and was met with a blank stare.

"He's a werewolf," said Tabron, his brow knitting as if just now considering that she might not know this.

Yes, she'd been made aware of that she assured him, but it seemed that these men were all dealing with loss, while Johnny was dealing with change. The two seemed very different to Sonia and assigning these men to Johnny seemed comparable to giving a gorilla a kitten. The gorilla might love the kitten but the kitten didn't really get the gorilla.

Del didn't know why Johnny didn't want to learn sign but they all agreed that nobody except the captain could ever get Johnny to do anything he didn't want to do. But lately, he admitted, the captain had struck out a few times, too.

Sonia said nothing to this as she was already familiar with the captain's charming powers of persuasion.

Del gripped the wheel with a claw that looked like a bent pair of kitchen tongs. Despite her apprehension, he was a competent driver and he delivered her all too soon.

Sonia stared across the open ground to his quarters. She really looked at the building closely for the first time. Nothing about it said military. She wondered if the home was here before the base because the lovely bungalow was set on stilts and surrounded by banana palms and ringed with greenery covered with tiny orange blossoms.

How much rain did they get up here that they needed to put all the buildings on stilts? The angle of the hillside put the second floor at ground level in the back, but from her seat she could not see the rear. The house was all stained wood with a wide porch facing the ocean. There were several chairs on the porch. The roof was tin and painted red. A stream snaked along beside Johnny's yard and then dropped down the hillside and out of sight. *The same stream that threads past the captain's?* she wondered. She must have jumped it yesterday, though she didn't even remember. Or had she used one of the large gray rocks set as stepping stones across the gap?

She lifted her attention to the small house. It looked

like an adorable honeymoon cottage instead of quarters for a surly werewolf. She recalled his chasing her yesterday. He was all huff and puff, she decided. She had to believe that or she wasn't getting out of this Jeep.

Del called for Johnny who did not appear. "Sometimes he does that."

"What?"

"Ignores us. Takes off."

Good, she thought. *Stay away.*

"He might not be home," said Del. "But my orders are to leave you here either way." He gave her an expectant look and she wondered what he would do if she refused to get out of the Jeep. They stared at one another.

"Fine," she said and threw open the door, sliding to her feet. She slammed the door and stared at Del through the open window. He handed over the bag that included another set of smaller dry-erase boards and markers, paper, pens and a book of sign language. Del scratched his chin with his hook and put the Jeep in Reverse, but kept his foot on the brake and his eyes on her.

"He might come back."

Sonia didn't care if he stayed away for hours. She'd sit on that porch and stare at the Pacific, breathe the warm, tropical air and pretend she was here on vacation with a husband who adored her.

"Oh, and the captain said that he is picking you up and that he wants to see some progress."

"Progress?"

He shrugged.

"From the invisible man?"

"He's probably around."

Sonia stepped back as Del turned the Jeep around and vanished down the road.

Her heart rate increased at his leaving, but not from

fear of the werewolf. The captain wanted progress. Johnny was screwing with her freedom. That made Lam's disappearance a problem.

Sonia's search of the grounds yielded nothing. His quarters were locked. She had one lesson to teach an oppositional werewolf some signs and she hadn't even seen Lam.

"Maybe I shouldn't have called him furball," she muttered.

Sonia was shaking now with a dangerous cocktail of adrenalin and fury. This monster marine was not going to be the cause of her going to a military prison. She'd rather die right here on this mountain than end up in a cage.

"So you want to play hide and seek? I'm good with that." Sonia dropped her bag of supplies on Lam's porch, squared her shoulders and crossed the stepping stones over the rushing water, aiming for the place she had last seen him yesterday. She knew she couldn't follow his trail. She could barely read a bus map and had completely blown orienteering in basic. Three steps into the deep cover of the tropical canopy and the temperature dropped, the air turned damp and the smell of rot mingled with the fragrance of jasmine. She paused to look about. The birdsong was everywhere, but she could not see a single bird.

"Johnny?" she whispered. He didn't answer of course. Though her surroundings were inviting they were also unfamiliar, so she turned around and walked back to the clearing. But after six steps she didn't find it. A little jolt of panic popped inside her, but she held it down. She'd only taken a few steps. *Think, Sonia.*

The water. She listened and could hear the sound of the running stream. She blew out a breath and then headed toward the sound. It was farther than she expected and on the way it began to rain, a soft patter on the leaves above that didn't reach her. She crept under vines and between wide palm leaves that were stiff and sharp as razor blades. The rain fell harder, dripping off the greenery and plopping down on her hat with giant droplets. The patter turned to a drenching. Her teeth began to chatter. She glanced up at the sky and spotted a lovely white orchid growing from the notch of a tree, bobbing in the falling rain as if it was laughing at her.

"That's why they call it a rain forest," she muttered and eased over a mossy log.

One moment she was standing and the next she was falling. Her hands went up as her butt struck the ground with a jolt that rattled her teeth. She landed on a dangerous angle and slid on her backside as the world blurred into a sea of green. Vines and leaves slashed across her face and she lifted her hands to protect herself from this new assault. She stopped abruptly by striking something solid and folded over a log losing all the air in her lungs. At least she wasn't still moving, but she was dizzy. Had she struck her head? Sonia opened her eyes to see she was lying with her legs on one side of a slippery, moss covered log and her torso dangling over the other side with nothing underneath her but treetops and hot tropical air. She stared at the cliff's edge where the steep incline fell away. The tree trunk, that had saved her life, grew perpendicular from the cliff.

Sonia tried to scream, but the fall had knocked the wind out of her and breathing took all her energy. The dizziness increased and she knew if she passed out she'd fall and if she fell, she'd die.

Below her, silvery sheets of rain fell from the black clouds sweeping up the mountain.

Instinct took over and she grabbed her knees, holding herself about the mossy trunk like a ring on a finger. How long could she hold on?

Something grabbed her by the back of her jacket collar. She gripped the log tighter but was torn loose. A moment later she was thrown over a broad shoulder. Her hands braced on the man's back only to discover it was covered with soft thick fur. Sergeant Lam! He'd rescued her.

She groaned and relaxed, falling limp against the sable-soft hair that covered him. He gripped her legs and easily swung her before him, carrying her like a bride over the threshold.

Sonia trembled as rain streaked down her face. She was scared, but not of Lam. She'd almost fallen to her death. If not for him, she would have. She threw her arms about his neck and clung to Lam as the relief shuttered through her. Sonia nestled her face into his chest and tried not to let him see that she was crying as he climbed the incline that had nearly killed her. He moved with slow steady steps as if in no hurry to be rid of her. She was grateful because she needed a moment to pull herself together and here in his arms she was warm and safe.

The beating rain ceased as if someone had turned a tap off, leaving only the steady dripping of water through the canopy. The sunlight streamed down in bright ribbons through the gaps. The Sergeant stooped, bringing her back to her feet and she lifted her head from his shoulder forcing herself to release his sturdy neck. Sonia shielded her eyes against the glare and looked around. She was back on the opposite side of the stream where she had made the cosmically stupid move of trying to follow a werewolf into the forest.

Lam stepped away. When her gaze met his, he just looked her up and down as if searching for injury. He lifted a hand toward her. She glanced at it but did not flinch. If he meant her bodily harm he had only to wait for her to drop off that log. Instead he had rescued her. His attention moved to her head as he pulled a stick complete with leaves from her hair. Her neat bun was now a tangled mess of tendrils that frizzed in all directions around her face and neck. She touched her head, realizing she'd lost her hat.

She lifted her hands and began to sign as she spoke. "Thank you for saving my life, Sergeant Lam."

He nodded his acknowledgment.

"I owe you one," she said while signing.

He nodded his agreement that, yes, she did. Johnny dipped a finger in the stream. He used the water to write on the flat gray stone, "Sorry."

She made a fist and then moved it in a circle over her heart. "Sorry," she repeated as she made the sign again.

He mimicked the sign perfectly. *Sorry.*

Johnny cupped a handful of water and used his opposite hand to gently tug her down to her knees beside the stream. He dabbed cold water on her cheek and she felt the sting of a cut. His touch was warm and tender. It made her throat ache even more so she took over using both hands to splash water on her stinging, scratched face.

A Jeep horn blared. Sonia shot to her feet, her face hot. She spun toward the drive, obscured by the house.

"Fucking motherfucking fuck!" she said, still signing out of habit. She glanced at Johnny. "That's the captain and just look at me!" She held out her arms to show him the whole muddy, bloody catastrophe. "*And* he's going to want to see your progress! I'm screwed."

The captain called. "Johnny? Private Touma?"

Johnny headed for the Jeep. Sonia looked back to the jungle staunching the irrational urge to turn and run the opposite way. She glanced down at her soaked clothing, torn muddy trousers and the scrapes that covered her hands.

"There you are," said the captain clearly speaking to Johnny. "Hour's up."

Sonia wiped her face and realized she'd likely just smeared more blood on it. She trailed around the house lifting one foot after the other. She couldn't manage to raise her chin until she cleared the house. She looked to Johnny as if for another rescue but he stood still as stone, his jaw locked, his big hairy arms motionless.

"How did it go?" asked the captain. His smile died a moment later as he stared at her, his eyes going wide as his gaze swept the entirety of her appearance.

Demerits she thought and then giggled. She slapped a hand over her mouth to stop the sound. Johnny looked at her and raised one tufted brow. He had long hairs growing from his eyebrows, like a sheepdog's.

"Not so well, I guess," said the captain, scowling now. "What happened to you?"

Sonia signed as she spoke. "I slipped."

"Are you all right?"

She nodded, although every muscle in her body ached. She hadn't felt this bad since basic training.

"Did Johnny have a lesson?" he asked.

Sonia's heart sank. For just one instant she thought her injuries might have caused a delay in sentencing but this judge had no mercy in his heart. She drew a breath to answer the question honestly when Johnny began to sign, perfectly and in quick succession. He signed, *Slipped. Sorry. I'm screwed. Fuck.*

The captain blinked. Sonia braced for the explosion. Then the captain smiled, a grin really. Wide and bright and some of the tension eased from Sonia's neck. She looked from the sergeant to the captain.

"Well, well," said Captain MacConnelly. "Looks like you learned a lot." His expression seemed to glimmer with relief. That's when she realized he had fully expected her to fail. "Good work, Private. I'd say you've had enough for today."

He waited for her to deny it and, to her shame, she didn't.

"Okay. Let's get you checked out and cleaned up back at base." He walked her to the Jeep with Johnny skulking along behind them as if he knew he wasn't welcome. But he was. She'd rather stay here with him than go with the captain and that realization made her gasp. Johnny noticed it. The captain didn't.

Johnny pointed at her and then lifted his brows and made the okay sign.

A question, she realized and smiled. His first question. She nodded then signed back without speaking, *Yes. I'm okay. Thank you.*

Johnny nodded and the captain had not even noticed the exchange as he swept into the Jeep and started the engine. "I'll bring her back tomorrow afternoon at thirteen hundred."

Sonia held her breath. Johnny gave her a long stare and then a single curt nod.

Sonia released her breath in a long sigh. She was coming back. Thank God. She had gotten another reprieve.

Sonia reported to the medical unit for a check. Nothing was broken but the bruises were everywhere. They'd let her shower there and got her a new uniform. She was discharged and returned to quarters to find her foot-locker had been placed at the end of one bunk.

Progress, she thought.

She glanced at the concrete bunkerlike room. Her new home, courtesy of the U.S. Government. It didn't look a lot different than a prison cell. She glanced at the windows. No bars, she realized. That was one important difference. Still, leave it to the government to make a tropical paradise look like a group home. Sonia unpacked her belongings that were not really hers. Everything she now owned had been requisitioned. She reached the bottom of her bag and her fingers grazed the one personal item she still possessed. A photograph of her and her sister, Marianna, when she was six and Marianna four. Her sister's hearing aid looked gigantic back then and made her ears stick out. The image was made worse by the short pixie cut that matched her own, a result of the lice they had both had. Her mother had been told they had to stay home until the medication killed all the lice. Instead her mom had shaved their heads and sent them to school. Marianna had earned the name Dumbo that year and it had stuck until middle school.

Sonia stared down at the two skinny kids they had been, with arms looped over each other's shoulders like two vines growing together. Marianna had gotten out, though. Gallaudet University on a full ride. A whole college for the deaf. It was just amazing. And with Marianna taken care of, Sonia didn't have to steal anymore to keep them in that crappy apartment. Her mother came and went like the tide. Back in jail, back on the streets, back in her bedroom with money in her pocket that she'd spend on booze. She wasn't dependable. Marianna needed dependable. Maybe Sonia could get through the next four years, be honorably discharged and go live near Marianna. Maybe even with her sister. Get their own place. She'd find a job to help Marianna again, if she even needed help anymore.

Sonia kissed her index finger and then pressed it to her sister's image. Then she tucked the picture frame back in her empty bag. Someday, she'd have a bedside table or a mantle or a bureau of her own.

Something.

Someday.

She sat down to write Marianna a letter and then realized that she could not include anything about Johnny and that her letter would be inspected by strangers. So she described the scenery and all the annoying habits of her bunkmates. She didn't like sharing a room with a group of strangers any more than she liked sharing her private letters with censors. But then who would?

The following morning she tried to take a run before breakfast, but her muscles were too damned sore so she opted for a long hot shower and lunch with the perkiest and most irritating member of her quarters before reporting to the captain for transport to Johnny's home.

All the way up the mountain she told herself how immature and childish she had been. She couldn't call him furball or swear at him. It was so unprofessional. Today she'd do better. She'd set the guidelines and her expectations. They'd begin with the basics. Who. What. Where. When. She'd teach him the signs for time. Yesterday. Today. Tomorrow.

The captain did not get out of the Jeep this time. "I'll send Zeno up to get you in ninety minutes."

"Ninety?" she stammered. The sheer number of minutes between then and now stretched to the horizon. "I thought… I thought…"

But he already had the Jeep in Reverse.

She stood rooted to the spot as the vehicle disappeared. Sometime after the Jeep had vanished down the road she snapped herself out of her daze and turned toward the adorable house that happened to belong to a werewolf.

She called for Sergeant Lam repeatedly but got no response. Belatedly, she realized that he might not appreciate being summoned like a dog. If he were not a monster, how would she approach him? Sonia decided on the front door, climbed the steep steps and knocked.

Johnny opened the door. His dark visage filled the frame and this time she did not back up at the sight of him. Instead she snapped a salute which he returned and then stepped out onto the porch. It seemed she would not see the inside of Sergeant Lam's home today. Sonia found herself disappointed. She was curious about him and about how he lived.

He motioned her to the porch as she remembered how he had carried her to safety while she'd wept like a child in his arms. She followed him across the spotless wide planking that had been stained a natural color. The railings were also wood.

He motioned to a table under the wide roof. Who had hung wind chimes from the beam above the rail? she wondered.

He sat on a long bench before a coffee table that fit him much better than the two adjoining chairs and made the sign for her to sit. She removed her cap and placed it on a chair and then sat beside him on the bench. He instantly moved away as his eyebrows lifted.

Sonia spotted the bag she'd left yesterday and busied

herself removing the small dry-erase boards and markers of various colors and lining them up on the table. By the time she placed the eraser Johnny groaned. She was losing her audience.

Sonia was determined to keep control today. No swearing. No temper. Just cool professionalism and a lesson that she'd stayed up half the night going over. She tried to channel Mrs. Kappenhaur, her seventh grade music teacher, the only one she'd ever liked.

"Today's lesson is ninety minutes. We will be covering time and some words to express needs. For example, 'What time is the meeting?'" she signed.

Johnny signed more obscenities.

"Yes. I'm sorry I showed you that one. Let's begin with these." She signed as she spoke. "Who? What? Where? When?"

Johnny grabbed a board and uncapped the green marker. She sat fidgeting with her own board as he wrote with an unsteady hand. It was painful to watch and when he finished she could barely make out what he had written.

"Y R U here?"

Off topic already, she realized, hurrying along. "To teach you."

"Y U stay?"

Sonia scowled. "We aren't talking about me. I'm here to teach *you* to sign. That's all you need to know."

Sergeant Lam threw his dry-erase board off the porch.

They scowled at each other.

"You do not have the right to poke around in my private life. I'm your teacher." There. She'd been decisive without swearing at him and she hadn't lost her temper. But she could feel her pulse throbbing in her temples and Johnny was baring his teeth. She dug in her heels. This would only work if he kept his nose out of her business.

He lifted a blue marker and wrote "Trust me."

She laughed. "Trust? Why should I? Listen, Lam. You are not my therapist. I'm here to teach you sign. That's it. You don't get a free pass to all my secrets. Got it? So take it or leave it."

He gave her a hard look. She didn't care. This was nonnegotiable.

"I'll keep coming back and I'll teach you. But no personal questions." She signed as she spoke. "Understand?" She then lifted her eyebrows to indicate it was a question, repeating the sign. "Understand?"

He nodded, stood and then jumped off the porch. By the time she reached the rail he had disappeared into the green curtain beyond the yard.

She watched him go. "Well, that went well."

Sonia descended the steep stairs and crossed the yard, staring down at the jungle below her. She was not going back in there again.

"Sergeant Lam!" she called. She tried again and received no response. After several minutes she gave up.

"I'm going to keep it professional," she muttered in a mocking tone. "I'm going to set ground rules." She gave a mirthless laugh and began signing as she spoke. She threw her hat and felt no better.

Sonia waited twenty minutes. He didn't come back. She returned to the porch and replaced the caps on the markers.

She stared at Johnny's board. *Trust me.*

It was impossible. She didn't trust anyone but her sister. That's how she'd survived. It wasn't a fair request.

She walked to the edge of the clearing realizing that

he didn't have to be fair. Life hadn't been fair to him. Besides who could he tell? And what secrets did she have that weren't already in that damned two-inch thick file the captain had? But it was different saying them aloud. So different. Besides it was a sucky story. Depressing and humiliating. She'd be sparing him by keeping her mouth shut.

Or she could tell him whatever he wanted to know and get his furry butt back in that chair.

She could keep her secrets or her freedom.

She gave a cry of frustration. This overgrown furball was going to get her locked up. If she didn't get him back here then the captain would find out and... Sonia marched to the porch rail and gripped it tight as she leaned out toward the yard and filled her lungs with air.

"All right!" she shouted to the jungle valley. "I give up! I'm here because if I don't teach you sign, I go back to jail. Do you hear me? I'm an ex-con and you learning sign is all that's keeping me from going in for six. Johnny! Damn it, do you hear me?"

Johnny opened his front door. She whirled to face him as he fixed her with a long steady look. He'd been in there all along, she realized. From his place in the door frame, he lifted his hands as if gripping bars and then lifted his brows.

"Yeah. Breaking and entering. Stupid. I tripped a silent alarm. Cops got me and locked me up. If you don't learn sign I go back there."

And there it was, the reason he couldn't run her off and the reason she'd come back.

"Can we start over?" she said, signing in synchronization.

Lam placed one fist on top of the other and lifted them as if preparing to swing an invisible bat. He made a smooth strike, his big, gnarled hands sweeping in a wide graceful arch from one shoulder to the other. Then he held up two fingers. She understood.

"Two strikes."

Their eyes met and this time she nodded.

"Okay, but how is this going to work? You just ask me any damned personal, prying question you like and I have to answer it?"

He nodded.

"Well, I don't like that plan."

He shrugged and stepped inside his threshold. The door began to close. She hurried after him.

"Wait!"

He did, but he kept one hand on the door, ready to slam it in her face. Behind him the television blared. Football, she realized.

"Okay, okay. Goddamn it okay!"

Lam made his fingers and thumb form a circle in a quick mimic of her sign of okay. There was nothing wrong with his brain. But those claws! Damn, they looked like tiny bayonets. Her shoulders sagged as she accepted yet another defeat. She was not going to be able to keep Lam at a distance. She was certain this werewolf was going to try to unlock every embarrassing secret and forbidden memory. Like Scheherazade, she was here only as long as she interested him. But unlike her, the stories would all be true. Sonia glared up at him with all the hatred in her soul. He'd trapped her the same way the U.S. Marines had trapped her. The same way the captain had trapped her. She was getting tired of being trapped.

Four years. That was what stood between her and a new life. Record expunged. Fresh start. Useful training.

She wondered where she would be able to fit "tutored a werewolf" on her resume. She snorted.

"All right, Sergeant Lam. What do you want to know?"

Chapter 4

Sonia waited as Johnny returned to the porch, scooping up a red marker and a board. Then he walked past her and into his house, turning to motion her in. She crossed the threshold and her breath caught. His place was spotless and lovely as any magazine spread. The rattan couch looked as if it were never used. The low chairs and ottomans were way too small for Johnny and she couldn't picture him eating on a glass dinette with royal-purple place mats, cloth napkins and a green glass vase filled with several sprigs of orchids. Beyond the breakfast counter a spotless kitchen sparkled with natural wood cabinets and slate tiled counter tops. How did he keep it so clean and where did he eat? Better still, *what* did he eat?

"Do you even use this kitchen?" she asked.

In answer he opened the freezer to reveal it stuffed with frozen meat.

"Fruits and vegetables?" she asked.

He gave a shake, no.

So he ate meat, possibly raw, alone in this empty kitchen.

Suddenly the spotless house seemed as sterile as an anonymous, impersonal hotel room. From the outside it looked like a home. But from in here it seemed a different kind of prison.

She heard a football game and realized the living room had no television. She glanced toward the hallway that must lead to the bedrooms. Was that where he lived? Because he certainly didn't spend time here. He motioned to the couch and chose to sit on a leather ottoman that she thought might collapse under the strain.

She turned her attention back to Lam to find him watching her.

"Okay, Johnny. What do you want to know?"

He wrote "jail" on his slate.

She sagged into the hard, new cushions. "Oh, damn. Really?"

He continued to stare and she knew she wasn't weaseling out of this one but she tried. "I broke into a house. I got caught." She shrugged. "Arrested, fingerprinted, court date, a deal to serve four years with the U.S. Marines. That's it."

She waited for some reaction. He blinked and shook his head and reached for the board and wrote. He turned the board around and she read, "Why B and E?"

Sonia blew out a breath from her nose, a blast like one from a fire breathing dragon.

"Because I just was a bad kid. I got into a lot of trouble." She stopped talking and set her jaw as the burning started in her eyes. She didn't want to think about that now, but he was making her. She glared.

He motioned for her to continue.

"What do you want me to say? I'm not the good little soldier, John. Not even close."

He sat forward and nodded his encouragement and touched the word "why" on his board.

She showed him the sign and he copied it. *Why? Why? Why?*

Her head bowed and she looked at her hands laced and locked up tighter than her heart. She wasn't answering. She'd keep her fingers still and her mouth shut. Johnny stood, heading for the kitchen. When he reached the back door she realized he was leaving again and shot to her feet.

"Stop!" she ordered.

He did.

"Come back." Sonia admitted defeat.

Johnny resumed his place, staring at her with his eyes big and yellow and his expression placid. He still looked fearsome as hell but Johnny was nothing if not a good listener, she realized. He lifted his chin as if encouraging her.

Sonia signed slowly now as the words were coming from somewhere so deep she hardly recognized her own voice. Her fingers danced along with each sign as naturally as breathing. "Okay. My mother, she drinks—a lot. Been in rehab. Been in jail. For drinking mostly and for the crap she did when she was drunk. Driving, fighting, stealing, causing accidents, bringing home men, pissing in public places, passing out in public places, getting fired, getting pregnant and forgetting about the two kids she already had. Me and my sister, we don't look much alike, if you know what I mean." She couldn't look at Johnny now, not with the shame rushing up to burn her face, so she focused instead on the magazines fanned across the coffee table, all Martha Stewart and all five years old. "A mean drunk, that's what the landlord called my mama to her face, before he called protective services." She stared up at Johnny, feeling the burning in her eyes but she would be damned if she'd let him see her cry. She widened her eyes and willed the tears back.

Sonia kept signing. "So I wasn't a good kid. I got into fights. Kids made fun of Marianna, that's my kid sister, so I kicked the shit out of them. Then some parent advocate got ahold of my mother and said that the school district wasn't meeting my sister's needs. That Marianna had rights and Marianna needed a special program." She met his steady gaze. "My sister is deaf, Johnny. Born that way. They said it was because of my mom's drinking, but mom was in jail when she was carrying Marianna, so that wasn't it. Anyway. She was either born deaf or maybe she got sick and that made her deaf. Nobody ever bothered to tell me. So my kid sister is smart, but she can't really talk. Sounds funny, you know? When she was little we had our own signs. Then I found a book and taught her some real signs. Later, when she got in that special program, she taught me. Marianna got into a residential school, but it was up in Elmsford and that's like twenty miles from where we lived. They said I couldn't go there because I wasn't deaf. I didn't think she could get along by herself, so I cut school and took four buses and I found her. You know what? It was the best damned thing that could have happened to her. She lived in a big dorm. She got regular meals and had friends like her. She was wearing clothes I'd never seen before, clean clothes. The school officials called my mother and she came to get me. But she came drunk, of course, so the school called the cops and, long story short, Marianna graduated with honors and I went to a group home, for good that time. I dropped out of high school and ran away. I was a regular rebel without a clue. When you turn eighteen you age-out. That means no more foster care."

Johnny sat next to her on the couch, turning to face her. She shifted so he could see her sign, even though the words she formed didn't mean anything to him yet. It gave her comfort, like she was talking to her sister.

"I was on the streets for a while until I got assistance with housing. I even got my GED. Then I applied to community college and got in under probation. I didn't make it through the first semester. So, if you're not in school, you lose the subsidy. I got a job but it didn't pay enough to cover the bills so I…" She rubbed the back of her neck. "I robbed that house. Took a bus to a nice white neighborhood, picked a house with a nice private yard and threw a nice little cement rabbit through that nice shiny glass window. And you know what? I wasn't sorry. Why did this family have a house like this when I couldn't make rent? And the food they had in their kitchen. It could have fed me for six months. But they also had a silent alarm. Cops got me still in the house because instead of taking their cash and getting the hell out of there I stopped to eat a bowl of cereal with milk. I made a shitty burglar. But I wasn't a minor anymore and this was a felony."

Johnny lifted the board and wrote "You wanted to get caught."

"No, I sure didn't." She pressed her fingers into her eyes for a minute then went back to signing as she spoke. "Well, maybe I did, but I sure the hell didn't want to go to prison. What I did was stupid. I'm not a thief, I'm just…angry. Or I was. So my lawyer worked out a deal. Go to federal prison or join the U.S. Marines. Seemed like a no-brainer." She lifted her hands and then dropped them. "So I'm a marine. Wouldn't be if I didn't have to be. Wouldn't be here now but the captain said he'd lock me up again if I didn't teach you sign. I can't go back to prison, Johnny. I just can't."

The silence stretched.

"I'm sorry. I'm not like you. I'm not a good soldier. I didn't sign up to serve my country or protect people. I signed up to avoid a prison cell. So what do you say? Will you learn a few words to keep the captain off my back?"

He signed, *Yes.*

She blew out a breath, feeling somehow lighter than when she walked in. All that armor was heavy and he'd made her set some of it aside. She smiled at him and he lifted his brows. "Okay, then. Hey, Johnny, why didn't you want to learn? I mean it will make things so much easier…"

He stood up so abruptly that the ottoman slid back several inches. Whoa, what was that about? she wondered. Seemed Johnny had a few sore spots of his own. She recalled him breaking the first board and throwing the second and leaping off the porch and walking out on her. Johnny *really* didn't want to learn to sign. Her curiosity prickled and she watched him stare out the front window. Her not wanting to teach him made a lot of sense. Her not wanting to talk about her rotten childhood, she understood. But this confused and intrigued her. She walked over to stand beside him. He didn't look at her, but his ears moved and he turned toward the road.

A Jeep horn blared. Sonia jumped. He'd heard that way before she had, she realized.

She signed, *Time to go.*

He nodded and walked her to the door. For some stupid reason she didn't want to go, which made no sense at all. So she lingered inside the open door. The horn sounded again. Sonia stepped out onto the porch and realized it had rained again. The mist rose from the earth in tiny wisps. She was about to descend the steep steps, but Johnny took hold of her arm and walked her down. At the bottom she turned to the Jeep and found the driver was a dimple-faced man she'd never seen before. Her relief at not seeing the captain was palpable and she blew out a breath.

She used the wide stones to cross the stream and realized Johnny didn't follow her. She signed, *Goodbye* and he signed back, *See you tomorrow.*

She paused, impressed. Had she taught him that? She glanced at the bag she had left on his porch yesterday, recalling the book on sign language. Sonia considered the possibilities. Had he been studying?

The driver met her halfway and waved at Johnny. "See you tomorrow morning, buddy." His grin lasted only until he turned around and then his expression turned somber.

"I'm Carl Zeno," he told her offering his hand. "One of the Den Mothers. That's what we call ourselves. Beats Wounded Warriors, don't you think?"

Sonia murmured a greeting as she released his hand and climbed into the passenger side. The corporal set them in motion. She glanced back to see Johnny lifting a hand in farewell. She waved back.

"Say," said Zeno, "were you *inside* Johnny's place?"

"Yes."

"He doesn't let anyone in there. How'd you do it?"

"He invited me."

"Just like that?"

She shrugged.

"What's it like?"

Somehow talking to Zeno about Johnny seemed wrong, so she opted for telling him it was nice.

"Maybe it's because you're a woman. He's never had a woman teacher. I was talking to the guys about it. They think it's a really bad idea. He's moody, you know? You might want to be careful in there. So, you got off-base permission yet? I could show you around."

She put on her seat belt realizing that she felt safer with Johnny than with his den mother. "Not yet."

Zeno nodded as he kept his attention on the road. "Did he attack you yesterday? Because a guy at the medical center said you were pretty banged up. The guys were saying that maybe we ought to be there when you're with him."

"Johnny didn't do it. I fell."

He gave her a look that told her that he didn't believe her. "Listen he's taken a swing at all of us. Threw a full can of beer at Dom once. But he never actually hit us. If he did that to you—" Zeno pointed at her bruised cheek and the scratch that she knew crossed her forehead "—then you should tell the captain. They've got ties but I think he'd listen."

"He didn't do anything."

"I think they should lock him up instead of locking us all up in this half-assed zoo. Lam's just a mess. Won't talk to us, ditches us nearly every day. The guy's not human anymore. I don't know why the captain doesn't see it."

That third lesson set up the pattern. Not the falling down the mountain and nearly dying part or the sitting on his pristine couch part, but the prying into her past part. Sonia had to endure a series of personal questions on whatever popped into the sergeant's brain and then he'd endure her lesson and learn a few more signs. He threw in a few she hadn't taught him so she was certain he was reading that book when she wasn't around. By the end of each lesson she was exhausted, wrung out emotionally, but at least she was not in the brig and the captain was off her ass.

But what would happen when she no longer interested Johnny?

He was such a good student. She still didn't know what the big fuss about not learning sign had been. A power play maybe or a pissing match. Men were funny about their pride and dignity and Johnny *was* a man, despite what those Den Mothers thought.

Over the first week he'd learned where she grew up and that her sister was at Gallaudet University outside of Washington, D.C. And she'd taught him colors, numbers, the alphabet and a series of action words, like walk, run, come, go, listen, do. Lam was now using both the board and sign language to communicate.

Lessons took place outside in nice weather and inside in the rain. It rained a lot here, but not for very long. Today they were on the porch and he had a pitcher of lemonade for her and it really tasted like he'd made it from fresh lemons.

She signed to him a question without speaking, *Did you make this?*

He asked her what the sign for make meant.

When she finger spelled *M-A-K-E* he flopped his arms, unwilling to answer.

She kept signing as she spoke. "Because this is really tasty. Just the right amount of tart with the sweet. You made it, didn't you?"

He rolled his eyes and nodded, admitting that he'd made it. She grinned, pleased at his efforts. Somehow she suspected that he didn't make this routinely for himself.

"Fruits." She smiled. "You having some?"

He shook his head and finger spelled *O-N-L-Y M-E-A-T.*

"That get boring?"

Does fruit? he signed.

She laughed and lifted the glass, now beading with condensation. "It's great. Thanks." She took another sip and set the glass aside.

The early lessons had been very difficult for her. His questions were like having dental work done. But like dental work, she found if she just relaxed, it wasn't quite as painful. Still, Sergeant Beast, as she'd come to think of him, was a whiz at finding her soft underbelly. He would have made a great interrogator.

"So what is it today? My sister. My mom?"

He signed, *Day off.*

"Great. So how about you give me a question."

He nodded.

"Why didn't you want to learn sign?"

Lam shook his head.

"Oh, come on!" she said. "I told you about my mom."

Don't like, he paused to finger spell the last word, *S-C-H-O-O-L.*

She sensed the lie in the quick reply.

"That's bull. I answer your questions and you don't tell me anything about yourself. If you want us to be friends it has to be a two way street. Otherwise I'm just your...your..." She struggled with the right word, coming up with "lab rat."

Lam straightened and she knew instantly that she'd said something wrong. She just didn't know what. He rose and walked swiftly away

"Sergeant?" She followed him. He allowed her to keep up but kept rubbing his neck and then his long wolfish jaw in turns. "Did I say something wrong?"

He turned and signed, *Lab rat,* then lifted his brows to make the words a question.

"Well, yes. I don't know how else to describe it. Or maybe like a criminal investigation with me playing the crook. Or a psychiatric appointment. You know, 'tell me about your problems,' but shrinks never share their own." She was babbling and her hands could barely keep up. At last she sighed and dropped her hands to her sides.

Lam's stare was mournful. He began signing. She tried to understand but his gestures were wild and fierce as his emotions spilled into his words.

No. Lab rat. No.

"One way street?" she tried.

Ask something else, he signed.

"Okay." She thought for a minute. "Everyone on this base is here for you, aren't they? They all know about you. And with all the security and the fences and stuff. Are you a prisoner, John?"

He nodded and then shook his head.

"I don't understand."

He lifted the pad of paper and wrote while she sipped her lemonade. "Everyone here is trying to find a cure for me to change back."

She lifted her head and gaped at him. "Is that possible?"

He nodded and then shrugged.

She continued reading. "But fence is not to keep me in but to keep intruders out."

"I don't understand."

He lifted his hands in exasperation as if to say I can't help you with that. Then signed, *Finish.*

"What's finished?"

Lesson. Today. Finish.

"We still have thirty minutes."

He signed, *Walk you down. Need meet woman.*

She didn't understand but agreed. "All right."

He waited by a trailhead that she had not noticed in her first and only excursion into the dense undergrowth.

"We aren't taking the road?"

Long, he signed. *Two many long.*

She wasn't sure if he meant it was too long to walk the road or if he meant that it was twice the time to walk the road. Either way she was dubious about stepping into the jungle again. Most of the trails she had taken in her life had sidewalks and street lights.

"Is it safe?" she asked.

With me. Safe. Yes. Come.

She nodded her acceptance. "You're not going to ditch me in there, are you?"

He frowned and looked disappointed in her again. It was a look she was getting used to.

"Okay, I'm sorry. It's hard for me to trust people," she signed.

She motioned to the green wall of ferns and palms and a multitude of plants and trees she didn't know the names of. "Okay. Let's go."

Lam hesitated and her stomach tightened. He got that look when he was preparing to drill particularly deep into her past and if he went there she knew he'd hit a nerve, so she just started walking, somehow finding the trail. The path angled down sharply and she had to lean back to keep from falling. Lam nudged past her, taking point. The jungle here seemed a perpetual twilight because the bright sun never found the forest floor. She could hear water dripping from the leaves about her and occasionally was hit with a large droplet. The birdsong filled the air but she also detected an occasional worrisome rustling in the undergrowth. Johnny turned his head often to check on her. The sound of water began to increase, gradually drowning out her plodding steps and the birds.

Lam followed the switchbacks so they zigzagged in manageable steps down the embankment that she nearly tumbled down. When the trail leveled off it also branched. Lam pointed to their left and made a swimming motion, sweeping his arms in graceful circles. She heard that waterfall again. The one she'd glimpsed from an inverted position. The hairs on her neck stood up.

"You swim there?"

He nodded.

"I don't swim."

A-F-R-A-I-D. His fingers spelled the letters perfectly.

"Yes. I sure am."

Of water?

"Of drowning."

I teach you, he signed.

"No thanks. I'd rather fall down the hill again."

He shrugged and headed along the main trail. It didn't stay level for long. As she walked she tried to imagine Lam teaching her to swim. He'd probably just throw her in the deep end and see what happened. Swimming seemed to be a big form of recreation on this island, which only made sense. She hadn't had a leave day yet, though Zeno kept pestering her about going to the beach which she might enjoy, but not with him. She imagined she'd go to the shore alone, lie on a towel and when she got too hot just wade into the surf to her knees and splash water on herself as she used to do all those years ago at Orchard Beach in the Bronx. What would it be like to dive into the waves?

Terrifying, she decided. Like slipping from her mother's arms at the pool and just making it to the edge. Mom laughing, clapping, drunk. She shivered. But the swimmers on the Long Island Sound seemed so happy.

Sonia was so busy imagining herself diving into an oncoming wave that she didn't see Johnny stop and so, when he did, she bounced off his broad back and fell to her butt in the trail.

He turned and regarded her as she sat in a heap. Then he extended his hand. She accepted his offer without thinking and without flinching finding his palm warm, dry and rough as the pad on the foot of a dog. She had to tug to get her hand back. Man, his claws looked vicious. She wiped her hand on her thigh and then saw him stiffen. Had she insulted him?

She glanced up at those unnatural yellow eyes seeing the hurt she'd caused and feeling her cheeks grow hot.

"Sorry," she murmured but he just kept staring until she felt a hitch in her breathing that surprised and confused her. His look told her without question that he was unhappy with her and for some reason that troubled her. Her instincts told her to move away. What was happening here?

"Why did we stop?"

Lam signed, *I stop for you see captain house. You stop because I stop.*

He made a joke. His first sign joke. She nodded,

proud of his accomplishment and complete, if awkward, first sentences.

"Good one," she said, smiling.

He grinned in return. A grimace really, that disconcerted her because it showed his very dangerous-looking fangs. He noticed the direction of her gaze. His teeth disappeared behind black wolfish jowls. She tried to picture the man he had been and failed.

"Did you say the captain's house?"

He nodded.

"But that is twenty minutes or more from your place."

Lam pantomimed that he was driving a car and then walked in a circle.

"Faster on foot than driving. I see."

Lam practiced the sign for driving and walking.

"Can I see it?"

Lam took her to the edge of the clearing. Sonia paused seeing the place where she'd first met Sergeant Lam from a different perspective. Who kept the trail between the two properties so pristine and how often did Lam or MacConnelly travel between their places? Sonia stared up at Lam wanting to ask the question about his relationship to the captain and decided not to pry. She had the uneasy feeling someone was watching her and turned to face the back of the house. A woman stood on the porch above them.

"That's her!" whispered Sonia, in awe.

Lam lifted a hand and waved. The red-haired beauty waved back. She was by far and without question the most beautiful woman Sonia had ever seen.

"I saw her that first day. Or I thought I saw her. She was at the window and then she vanished. They said she never leaves her house. Is she really the captain's wife?"

Lam nodded. *She R-E-A-S-O-N for F-E-N-C-E.*

"She? Why is she a prisoner?"

Johnny shook his head. *P-R-O-T-E-C-T.*

The woman retreated to her home. Sonia felt inexplicably bereft. Suddenly she wanted to follow her. "Can I meet her?"

He shook his head.

"Why not?"

He didn't answer and Sonia stared at the place where the red-haired woman had been.

"I thought she never left her house."

Lam regarded her for a moment. She had the feeling he was considering his response. Finally he lifted his hand and spelled out three letters. *L-I-E.*

"So I did see her?" she motioned to the house. "But it's impossible. She disappeared right before my eyes." At some point Sonia realized she was explaining this impossible feat to a nine-foot werewolf. Sonia pressed a hand over her racing heart and dropped her tone to a whisper. "What is she?"

Johnny shook his head and turned to go. Sonia followed but she took one look back at the house. The captain's wife was now standing on the far side of the stream. Sonia was startled at seeing her so close, so fast, and then hurried to follow Lam. That woman was creepy as hell and she suddenly did not want to meet her.

Sonia turned and ran to catch up with Lam. She pressed a hand to his shoulder and he stilled then turned to face her. He stared at the place where she touched him and Sonia drew back her hand.

"Is she like you?

No.

"Is she the one who did this to you?"

No. She is V-A-M-P-I-R-E.

Was he serious? She gaped at him and he held her gaze.

"Holy shit. Really?"

He nodded, grim as a mourner at a grave. Sonia felt a shiver travel down her spine. She stared at him in shock.

Her thoughts exploded with denial and then horror. It wasn't possible, but when she looked at Johnny she knew that it *was* possible. Anything was possible. She wobbled suddenly unsteady, but Johnny caught her elbow and held on until she nodded to him. She looked behind them, now having another reason to fear this jungle. There was a vampire living here.

"She was out in the daytime."

He nodded yes, as if this were nothing unusual.

Johnny glanced back toward the captain's home and then continued on down the incline. The dripping on the leaves got louder as the humidity rose. Her shirt stuck to her back and arms. Lam grabbed at a broad leaf and tore it from the plant by the stem but never stopped. He twirled it as they continued on. A few minutes later they broke from the jungle and stood at the edge of a gentle slope covered with narrow-leaved plants that grew waist high on her but barely brushed Lam's knees. The trail cut neatly through the center. She paused beneath the cover of the foliage as she realized it was pouring. Johnny motioned past the incline to the U.S. Marine base and the barracks where she lived. She recognized her surroundings now.

It seemed the entire mountain was fenced, for they never crossed through a perimeter.

"Johnny?" She didn't know what to say. She was frightened and didn't want to cross the fifty feet to her barracks alone. He handed her the leaf and motioned that she should use it as an umbrella. She held it over her head. Johnny took her elbow and continued on, seeing her to her door and then signing his farewell. She watched him until he vanished into the wall of green.

A vampire, she thought, and they were protecting her. But protecting her from what?

Chapter 5

Burne Farrell waited as his chaser, Hagan Dowling, finished checking the abandoned concrete bunker within the Marine Corps Mountain Warfare Training Center in California. The two male vampires had made no progress tracking Brianna Vittori since they lost her trail eighteen months ago. So Burne, the elder hunter, had resorted to returning to her last known residence. The female's disappearance with two werewolves nettled his professional pride but more importantly her absence had prevented him from making her his personal property. His eagerness to have her only increased his annoyance at his best chaser's failure to produce her. Each day Brianna remained free was like a growing blister on his plum-colored ass.

No female vampire had ever evaded him for so long. But Brianna was not your typical female. Like all vampires, she was descended from the fey. But Brianna's mother was a fairy, a true Leanan Sidhe. So unlike him, any male child born of Brianna would look normal enough not to draw immediate notice.

It was Burne's disturbing appearance, and not any reaction to sunlight, that kept him, and his fellows perpetually in the shadows. He had been told that his great-great grandfather once walked among men. But Burne was sixth generation and with each new legacy, their form departed farther and farther from their human parent. The most pure vampires he knew were fifth generation. Brianna was first.

Her male offspring would not turn purple as ripe plums and be ugly as the back end of a pig. So he wanted her first male child to be his. The females of their race already walked freely in the light, when he let them. No females drank blood and all were visions. That was why they made such good assassins after training was complete.

Burne's skin was becoming more discolored by the day, dotted with purple patches like an octogenarian's. His chaser, Hagan Dowling, still had the white cast of a corpse. It only made his blue veins more prominent beneath his transparent skin after feeding but that would change with the decades and his veins would leak like Burne's until his skin was cold as death and he could not hold the blood he drank. And then he would die. They all ended that way. Being a vampire did not make one immortal. Despite the legends, vampires were mortal, even though they carried the blood of fairies in their veins.

Hagan breathed deeply. "It still smells like dog in here."

"Wolves," corrected Burne.

"Yes."

"Where would you go, if you were trying to keep her from discovery?" Burne asked Hagan.

"Outside our territory, if he knows what that territory is."

"Exactly. That's why you haven't found her. She's not here to be found. Perhaps her mother told her that we do not like to cross water.

"There are U.S. Marine bases throughout Europe, Africa, the Middle East and the Pacific," Burne continued.

"We need to search each one. Start with the Pacific. Go island by island. Meanwhile, I will check with our colleagues in Europe and the Middle East."

Burne stared at his chaser. Hagan's lips were the ruby red of a vampire just fed. His fangs had grown so long that they no longer fit in his mouth. They didn't retract like a snake's, nor were they hollow like straws. Their purpose was to tear through flesh and rip open major blood vessels so they could drink.

Hagan stared at him through milky-white irises. They were already fading from their birth color. Burne smiled. It always started with the eyes. He knew Hagan's vision was perfect, but this discoloration made him look like he was quite blind or quite dead. One look at him and the human flight crew would panic. He needed to get them across the ocean, a dozen preferably, without any of them being seen. Night was their usual disguise, though for this journey, that would not be possible. But it was worth any risk to find Brianna. Still, if they were discovered it would mean their lives, not from the humans, of course. But to expose themselves to humans was one of the great unpardonables. Some heads of state knew of them, took advantage of their services for a price. But being detected by such a large group as the passengers and a flight crew on a commercial airline would mean their death. Of course, if they were seen on the plane, it would be necessary to kill all witnesses.

He thought of Brianna, with her waves of copper hair and eyes as green as a birch leaf. His loins tightened at the memory.

"Return to our base and assemble a team. I will arrange transport."

"When do we depart?"

"Forty-eight hours."

"And the humans will not see us?"

"For their sakes, I hope not."

"Yes, sir."

He stared down at a photo of Brianna, taken from her apartment last April. Her face could be that of an angel, she was so lovely, her skin smooth and pink. Burne felt his heart pitch and his loins twitch. If he could catch her, he would keep her for himself.

"I want this one," he muttered.

"Yes, sir."

Hagan's reply was too quick and far too eager. Burne cast a sideways glance at Hagan and caught him ogling the image Burne held. His eyes narrowed on Hagan. The younger vampire forced a smile and the sharp tips of his fangs grazed his lower lip. It was possible that Hagan had similar ideas where Brianna was concerned.

Perhaps it would be wiser to accompany this team and see to her capture personally.

The next day, Sonia waited for her ride. She was unhappily surprised when the captain pulled up and motioned her to get in. She saluted and climbed into the passenger seat. They rode through the base. Everything seemed so normal out here with marines drilling on the rifle range. She turned to watch men scaling the wall on the obstacle course, using the twin nylon ropes to reach the apex. But things weren't normal. Johnny was a werewolf and the captain's wife was a vampire.

"Johnny tells me that you are teaching him a lot."

She turned back to the captain. "I'm trying my best, sir."

"He also asked me to tell you about what happened to him in California. I'm not sure why he wants you to know this, but I agreed."

Something about the captain's tone brought her to complete attention. He pulled to the shoulder so she had a view of men crawling on all fours under the cargo net.

"When we came back from Afghanistan we were shipped to the Marine Corps Mountain Warfare Training Center in the Sierra Nevada Mountains. We were told that they were trying to find a cure for Sergeant Lam. They did medical tests, oxygen levels, CT scans, blood work, but they did other things, too." Her captain covered his hand with his mouth and stared out the window.

Sonia watched him. Tension vibrated from him so clearly she could almost hear it. He dragged his hand over his mouth and then glanced at her, then quickly returned his attention out the window. She instinctively braced for what he would tell her next.

"They used Johnny for target practice to test the durability of his hide."

Sonia gasped. Now she understood part of the sadness she had seen in the captain's eyes. Lam was his friend, his comrade and a member of his squad. And his own commanding officer had done this.

"They shot at him?" she asked.

"Yes. He's bulletproof."

Sonia shuddered.

"They also used grenades. He almost lost his hearing. But that's not the worst of it. They took…" The captain wiped one hand over his mouth before continuing. "They took Johnny's sperm. Trying to make more werewolves."

"What!" Sonia's fingers went wide as her arms braced as if she were warding off something thrown at her face. "Who did?"

"Our commanding officer. We thought we were to undergo training and testing to make Johnny human. The truth was quite the opposite. They were trying to reproduce werewolves."

"Why?"

"Classified."

"How could they?"

"They did. And used his sperm." The captain rubbed the bristle on the back of his neck with his knuckles. For a moment he seemed unable to speak. "We found this all out later. There is at least one child as a result. A boy. So far he is completely normal and two other women, both marines, are pregnant. The boy has been adopted by a very nice couple in Northern California, the husband is retired military and knows the deal. We're keeping an eye on the child and the other fetuses, of course. Johnny knows. He wants to see his son, but…"

But he couldn't, of course. Not as long as he was a werewolf.

"This is terrible."

"Yes, so you'll understand why you shouldn't tell Sergeant Lam that you feel like a lab rat because he actually was one."

Sonia sank down in her seat. "I had no idea."

"But we are trying to make him human. This whole place, is all here for Johnny." The captain lifted his arms indicating the compound. "Everyone here. It's our purpose."

They weren't all here only for Johnny, she thought, remembering what she knew about the captain's wife. She wanted to ask him about her, but didn't have the courage. They sat in silence for a time.

"Something on your mind?"

"Why the fencing? Johnny says he's not a prisoner and I'm sure he could jump it or tear it down."

The captain said nothing to this.

"Is it for your wife?"

The captain's eyes narrowed to slits. "What about my wife?"

"Johnny says that she's a—a vampire."

"He shouldn't have told you that."

"Is the fence for her?"

The captain looked away. "In a way. She's a target. I'm protecting her."

"From what?"

"Male vampires."

"A fence can keep them out?"

"No. It can alert me when they arrive. But only a werewolf is strong enough to kill a male vampire."

The realization came first and then a rising wave of indignation. She beat her fists on the dash.

"I knew it! You're keeping him here—like some guard dog, to protect her?" Her fists were clenched on her knees. She wanted to strike, but she held back.

He stared her down, matching the fury with a glare that made her stomach twist. The captain looked pissed and dangerous as hell.

"That's not his job," he said. "It's mine."

"You said only a werewolf could protect her." She meant the comment as accusation, but the moment she said it the captain's expression changed and she understood the truth.

They'd been together in Afghanistan, Johnny and her captain.

"You," she whispered.

He didn't deny it.

Who else? she wondered. The wounded warriors? The MPs? Who else were werewolves?

"Touma. For once in your life, follow your orders and stop thinking so much."

She sat back, sagging into the seat. She should have known all along.

"No lesson today. We need Johnny to come down to medical but after what happened in California he doesn't like to come in for tests."

"That's understandable."

"This is different. We've made a breakthrough. He needs to see." The captain pulled the Jeep back out onto the road. "I don't care what you have to promise him, just get him down here as quick as you can. That's an order, Private. Your ass if he doesn't show."

Now how exactly did he expect her to accomplish what no one else had been able to do? He gave her a lot more credit than she deserved. Johnny only learned the signs as payback for her little revelations. She didn't have a secret big enough to get him off that hill.

Her head sunk. Yes, she did. But damned if she'd talk about that to him when Marianna didn't even know.

Sonia set her teeth and hissed at the captain. He didn't seem to notice.

Her superior had no qualms about using her to get Johnny to do what he wanted. She didn't like being a tool, but she liked her other option even less. She responded as expected. "Sir, yes, sir."

When they passed the turnoff to the captain's home a dozen questions sprang on her like hungry tigers.

She danced around the subject that so occupied her. "Does your wife like living up on the hill?"

He glanced at her out of the side of his eyes and then returned his attention to the rough road. "She does, yes. And she's very protective of Johnny. They became friends in California. If you hurt him, I'll be the least of your problems."

She definitely did not need a vampire pissed at her.

The captain dropped her off a few minutes later. "Call for a pickup. Sooner is better."

Johnny greeted her on the porch and invited her inside to the immaculate living room that he never used. She sat and Johnny perched on the adjoining ottoman like a tiger on a toadstool, waiting with folded hands for her to begin the lesson. But there would be no lesson today. So did she just blurt it out or try to ease into the topic of the medical center? Subtlety was never her strong suit.

She drew a breath preparing to dive into deep water.

"Johnny, the captain told me about what happened in California and at the lab. I think it's terrible."

His brow descended and his posture went stiff. She reached for him and laid a hand on his forearm, giving a little squeeze but he wouldn't look at her.

"Thank you for asking him to tell me."

He glanced at her now, but his muscles remained rigid under her light touch.

"I understand you not wanting to go back to a lab. But the captain, well, he says he needs to show you something."

He started to rise but she pressed down on his shoulder, as if that could stop him, but it did. Instead of knocking her hand aside, he placed his over hers and looked up at her with wide yellow eyes that were as foreign as the surface of the moon.

"It's not a test. He told me it's not a test."

Johnny shook his head as his eyes asked her to understand.

She slid her hand free to allow her to sign. "He also said it's my ass if you don't show."

Johnny slapped an open hand on the coffee table and all four legs snapped as the top hit the floor. He rose like a wave and paced through the dining area to the windows that led to the back porch. There he pivoted and paced back, coming to a smooth stop before the collapsed table. Grace in motion, she thought.

"What are you going to do?"

He signed his answer. *You come?*

She nodded. "If you want me to."

He finger spelled *T-R-A-N-S-L-A-T-O-R.*

"You'll go?" She barely kept herself from wilting with relief. "Thank you."

Johnny did not look pleased but he nodded.

"May I use your phone?"

He nodded and pointed to the one mounted on the wall.

After calling for their ride she asked to use his bathroom. He led the way and she trailed down the hallway that bisected the other half of the house. He had a guest bedroom. She peeked in there as they passed and saw stereo equipment, a wide-screen plasma TV with surround-sound speakers mounted on the walls. Instead of carpets, the floor was covered with two very large futons. One spread like an area rug and the other folded in half and leaning against one wall like a headboard. Both showed the indentation of a large body and a prodigious amount of black hair. This, quite obviously, was where Johnny relaxed. His man cave, she decided as they passed by the door.

He stepped aside to allow her to pass before him into a room to the left. There was a king-size bed that was still not long enough for a giant. His coverlet was a tropical garden of interlacing bamboo. The pillows, all four, had the same matching design. He was either very careful at making his bed or he didn't sleep here.

The bedside table had a clock but nothing else. No photos, no electronics. The walls had paintings that you might see in a hotel, a palm tree, a spray of orchids. But unlike a hotel, there was no bureau and the walk-in closet was empty because, she realized, Johnny did not need any clothing.

Did he live in the movie theater room or in the forest? She wasn't sure. But she was sure he didn't stay in this room.

He halted at a narrow door and pointed, then turned and left her, closing the door to his bedroom as he went.

Sonia opened the door to find a huge bathroom that seemed to have been constructed in what would have been the third bedroom. Everything was adjusted for a nine-foot tall man. She turned in a circle, impressed that the military could get this right. Had Johnny chosen the modern fixtures or had the U.S. Marines done that? What about the overlarge towels and the woven rattan floor mat?

The toilet was so tall that, when she sat, her feet didn't touch the ground. After she finished she washed her hands in the sink, and realized that it was set so high that she had to raise her arms to shoulder level just to reach inside. The mirror gave her a perfect view of her forehead.

There was no soap on the sink, so she opened the medicine cabinet. The inside had a mirrored back so she could still see herself. She could also see the contents of the bottom shelf: mint mouthwash, dental floss, a toothbrush, whitening toothpaste, a bottle of liquid drain cleaner and a .44 Magnum. She frowned and lifted the drain cleaner. This didn't belong here. It should be under the sink, not near his toothbrush and mouthwash. Her gaze flicked back to the gun. That didn't belong here, either. A werewolf did not need a handgun for home defense.

So what were they doing in his bathroom?

Her eyes rounded at the realization.

They said his skin was bulletproof. But Sonia thought if Johnny put that drain cleaner or the muzzle of that gun in his mouth...

Her skin flashed cold and gooseflesh rose on her arms as the truth hit her. Johnny wanted to die.

On the day she had arrived the captain had said Johnny was depressed and suicidal but she hadn't really believed it, until now.

Sonia stared at the evidence she could no longer deny.

She sensed him behind her. The moment she met his gaze in the mirror she saw him take in her horrified expression. His face went tight and his jaws locked. Then he lowered his snout and glared a challenge at her. She didn't pretend she didn't understand but met his cold stare.

Her heart hurt and she pressed a hand over the ache. "Oh, Johnny, no."

He reached past her and slammed the medicine cabinet door closed, removing the handgun from her line of sight. Then he took the drain cleaner from her trembling hands and placed it under his sink. Finally he grasped her wrist and pulled her from the bathroom.

"Johnny. You can't," she babbled. "You mustn't."

He kept walking and didn't stop until they were outside on the porch. The warm sunshine streamed down on the yard making everything look idyllic. It made what she had seen even more surreal. She tugged and he released her. They stood facing each other and then she threw herself at him, wrapping her arms about his middle as she burst into tears. He went still at that and then lifted his big heavy arms and patted her back. They gradually came to rest on her shoulders.

"Johnny!" she cried. "You can't kill yourself."

Wouldn't she if she were in his place? She didn't know. Her first thought was of Marianna and how hurt she would be. Johnny had a family, didn't he? What had the captain said? "You don't want to hurt your family. Your mom. Your sister. Julia…Joon." She rushed on, babbling now. "We have to go to the lab. They have something to show you. Maybe…" She didn't believe what she was about to say but she said it anyway. "Maybe they know how to fix you."

He blew out a breath. The air was a hot blast on her neck even in the warm sunshine. Then he peeled her away and stepped back. He descended the stairs with a heavy tread. At the bottom he looked back, with brows raised, as if to ask if she were coming or not.

Sonia charged after him. She had to get him to the captain.

Sonia and Johnny reached the back door of the medical building twenty minutes later. This entrance had an enclosed tunnel from the mountainside that allowed Johnny to come and go without drawing any notice. Johnny didn't like being the center of attention, according to her bunkmates. As the captain said, they all knew of Johnny, though not all had seen him. No one spoke of the captain's wife which made her wonder if they did not know what she was.

"Are you ready to go in?" she asked.

No. But go now.

The moment they passed the doors they received an escort through the facility and down into the basement. They passed several swooshing doors and signs that said Restricted. Finally they were led into a viewing room. Beyond the glass panels was a series of nine stainless steel doors about three feet square. They reminded Sonia of the dumbwaiters she had seen in a movie except these were three across and three down making a strange metal tic-tac-toe pattern. She noticed each door had a corresponding number painted above it.

Three men stood before the doors around a stainless-steel table that looked as if it were used for autopsies. The first was Captain MacConnelly. The second was the base commander, Major Paul Scofield. She had met him briefly on the day she arrived. She didn't know the third but he wore a lab coat. He was a paunchy clean-shaven man with a captain's bar on his collar, his double chin made more noticeable by the angle of his head. She glanced at Johnny who now rocked from side to side. Was it the lab coats or the place that made him uneasy?

"Just in there, Sergeant," said the shorter of their companions. The two marines clicked their heels and saluted. Johnny returned it and then headed for the door beside the glass viewing panels.

At the sound of the door opening MacConnelly's

brow's lifted. Sonia wrinkled her nose at the odd combination of odors. There was antiseptic, bleach and the smell of urine. That last smell made her stomach cramp and her mind leaped back. It took a few moments to stop shaking. She glanced about in discomfort but all eyes were on Johnny.

"John." The captain extended his hand and Johnny shook it. There was no salute between them. Johnny did salute Scofield who returned the salute with a smile and a clap on Johnny's arm.

"Good to see you, son," said their commander.

Sonia held her salute but no one seemed to notice her. Finally the major turned to Sonia, flicking a quick salute and ending her misery. "I hear you've got our boy learning sign. Good work, Private."

He made it sound like she was training a pony to count. She forced a tight smile and wondered if she'd have a moment to speak to the captain about that gun in Johnny's bathroom.

MacConnelly extended a hand toward the other man as he spoke to Johnny. "You remember Dr. Dimitrie Zharov. Zharov has been experimenting with the blood you provided."

The two regarded each other warily. Sonia could see the tension between them. Was there history here or was Zharov just anxious around an unpredictable werewolf? Sonia understood it but realized she was no longer frightened of Johnny. Now she was frightened *for* him.

Johnny shifted from side to side, one arm across his middle as he gripped his opposite elbow. His nerves were understandable after what he'd been through.

Did the captain notice the horror in Johnny's eyes or the slow unconscious shaking of his head? She moved closer to him and grabbed his arm at the elbow, giving a little squeeze. He glanced down at her and she felt some of the tension ease from his muscles.

"We've given your blood to several types of animals," said Zharov. "It killed the rats, mice and rabbits. But the dogs tolerated it."

She felt his tension return at the word blood.

He signed, *How?*

She spoke up, interrupting Dr. Zharov. "He asked you, 'How?'"

The doctor cast her an annoyed glance then looked to MacConnelly.

The Captain motioned to her. "Doctor Zharov, Private Sonia Touma is Lam's translator."

Zharov looked down his nose at her and Johnny's arm went tense under her fingers.

"Please answer Sergeant Lam's question," said the captain.

"How what? It doesn't make any sense."

She turned to Johnny. He signed his question and she relayed it to Zharov. "He asks how his blood was given to them."

"Oh, well, by subcutaneous injection. The dogs changed immediately into a version of were...uh...species. You will see here." He walked to a panel of buttons, laid out like a telephone keypad and he pressed number nine. A perfectly adorable dog with short wiry white hair and deep brown eyes greeted them with a stretch that looked like a bow.

"This is subject number nine. It will receive the newest variation of the strain today. He should have had it earlier but I was instructed to wait for you."

And he didn't sound at all happy about that, thought Sonia.

The doctor turned to the panel and paused, finger

poised above number eight. Sonia felt her stomach tighten in dread as she realized what was behind that next door.

"This subject received the last serum one week ago." The eighth small door slid open and Zharov stepped back. The creature inside leaped to its feet and began growling and throwing itself against the cage in a futile attempt to reach them. There were teeth marks on the steel, like punctures in soft wood. Sonia's mouth dropped open. The jaws where enormous and they snapped like a bear trap. The yellow eyes were familiar and the clawed front feet looked a lot like Johnny's. But there would be no mistaking it for anything but a were-creature. It spun in circles, biting the bars, vainly attempting to set its teeth into something, anything. It seemed mad.

Johnny signed, *Crazy.*

"Yes, I thought the same thing," she whispered and then raised her voice for the others. "He says it seems crazy."

Zharov answered, "Yes. They are all like that. Abnormal brain pattern. They attack anything they can reach. So I'm to show you the derivative of your blood that I've isolated. I've made two serums that show some promise." He pressed the second button revealing the next cage. Inside sat a mutt with a black muzzle and sandy fur. He trembled as he looked out at them with sad and hopeful eyes. "This is number seven. Received the first serum strain three weeks ago and I will be injecting number eight with the second serum, returning it to its original form. And I'll be using the first serum on number nine to create a were-dog. So, a very busy day."

He glanced to the captain who glared. The man acted as if informing Johnny was a nuisance. Zharov returned his attention to Lam. "We have mastered making were-dogs. Once in the were-form they stay that way without this." The doctor lifted a hypodermic needle filled with a clear orange liquid from the drawer beneath the table and then replaced it in favor of the shot that made were-creatures. Zharov hit the button to shut number eight. The were-dog made a final lunge for the bars before disappearing behind the descending door. The doctor then approached number nine, opening the cage and grabbing the dog's scruff to lift the skin from the body. When he raised the hypodermic Johnny grabbed Zharov's wrist. Zharov blanched. His fingers extended and the needle clattered to the floor. Johnny released the doctor and stooped to look at the dog. Why would the captain want Johnny to see a poor little dog go through what he had?

Johnny's hands flew into words.

She turned to the doctor. "He says, 'Change me back.'"

"Yes. That is what we all are working toward and I'd be one day closer if not for this interruption." The doctor massaged his wrist and then retrieved his needle, tucking it away in the drawer. Then he focused his attention on Johnny. "The captain wants you kept in the loop, so I've stopped my research to show you my progress." His tone radiated contempt. She wasn't sure if that was for the captain or if he resented having to show the lab rat his work. Either way she didn't like Zharov. The doctor regarded the panel of buttons and closed the gate to the ninth cage, trapping his subject again. That left only number seven. The gentle little dog that had apparently been a were-creature, though he showed no indication of it. Sonia glanced at door number nine and shuddered, knowing that sweet little dog had only received a stay of sentence and not a reprieve. But didn't they have to do this to find a cure for Johnny?

Zharov returned to the panel and faced them. "So here is my little dog and pony show. Would you like to see number eight injected and transformed? As you know, Sergeant Lam, I cannot inject the serum through the skin of a were-creature. So the injection goes in the mouth. It's not pleasant to watch. But you may stay if you wish." He turned his pale pitiless eyes on her now. "You might want to step out, Private."

She wanted to. She hated the cages and the needles and the smell of this place. Fear roiled in her stomach. She couldn't look at the cages without breaking into a sweat. Johnny noticed and grasped her elbow, giving it a squeeze. His brows lifted as he stared.

"I'm all right. This place…bad memories," she whispered. She wondered if the dogs were in the dark as she had been. She was trembling now, but she lifted her chin and met the doctor's gaze. It was his smile that tipped the scales. He expected her to run. She blew out a breath, still feeling nauseated.

"I'll stay." She spoke with a determination that she did not feel. She inched closer to Johnny who wrapped an arm about her.

She glanced at the captain who was staring at her with a strange look on his face. Zharov lifted a metal stick that had a short needle in the tip. He approached the were-dog's cage and opened the door. The dog lunged. Zharov was fast and efficient making a quick thrust with the pole which the dog immediately bit onto. Then he jabbed forward. Blood and saliva foamed from the creature's mouth. The animal fell back and went slack. The foaming got worse and the creature began to writhe and shake. The movements became less organized and grew into full-fledged convulsions. Sonia covered her mouth to stifle a cry.

"I warned you," said Zharov.

The creature went slack.

"Is it dead?" she whispered.

"No. Transition phase," said Zharov.

The dog now began to twitch as if in the throws of some bad dream, but its eyes had rolled back in its head showing white bloodshot balls. The fur began to change with the size of the dog. It was shrinking before her eyes, deflating like a helium balloon. The claws retracted. The teeth drew back into the pink gums. Johnny stepped forward, peering at the dog that now seemed just an ordinary brown mutt. The whimpering started next and the sound broke Sonia's heart. The creature was obviously suffering. Johnny leaned so close he nearly pressed his head to the bars of the cage.

"Careful, Johnny," Sonia whispered.

Johnny reached in and touched its foot. The dog startled and its eyes popped open. It struggled to its feet and wobbled as it turned to bring its face near Johnny's.

"Step back," ordered Zharov.

The dog licked Johnny's face. Johnny reached a claw between the bars and scratched behind the dog's ears. He turned to MacConnelly, signing fast. The captain looked to her. What's he saying?

"He says, 'Now. Give me, now. Shot. Now.'"

Zharov threw up his hands and turned to the major. "I told you. What did you expect him to say?"

The commander stepped forward. "No, son. Not today. But soon. Mac here thought you should know how close we are, that all of us are working to bring you back. But we need a little more time. Can you give us that?"

Sonia held her breath. Did they know? Did they all know about that gun in his medicine cabinet?

All eyes turned to Johnny. His shoulders slumped and he signed to her.

"How long?" she repeated.

"I estimate a month," said Zharov. "Transformation is still unstable. I have variables to control, dosage amount to calculate. Too little and there is no effect. But too much damages the—"

"That's enough, Doc," said MacConnelly.

The doctor nodded. Damages the what? Sonia wondered. The nervous system? The brain? The heart? The possibilities were endless and each carried a different horror. Her stomach churned and she glanced to Johnny. But he did not seem to hear.

Johnny pointed to the other doors.

"Seven has remained transformed for three weeks," Zharov pointed to the next door as he continued speaking. "Six for four weeks and so forth."

Ten weeks of experiments, she realized.

Johnny stepped past him and pressed all the buttons.

"No," said Zharov.

"Johnny, wait," said MacConnelly.

But it was too late, the doors whooshed open. Number seven stood and stretched as the neighboring doors opened. But her attention passed over to the reclining creature in cage number six. The animal seemed to be barely breathing and blood leaked from his ears, nose and mouth. The rest of the cages were empty. A shiver went down her spine. Where were the dogs from weeks one to five?

"Damn it," said Zharov.

"Cover them!" ordered Scofield.

Mac scrambled to close the panel. All the doors swept down, dropping with the finality of a guillotine.

"Zharov, my office." Scofield stormed away with the good doctor trailing past.

Johnny stared at the closed stainless steel doors and then he looked at his captain.

"We'll figure it out, Johnny. We're close now. You have to believe me."

Johnny growled and lifted the steel table cleanly from the floor as easily as she might lift an aluminum folding chair. Then he threw it with such violence that it sailed across the room, crashing through the glass panels. He turned to cast one look at Captain MacConnelly before bounding out through the gaping hole he'd created and pushed open the door without using the knob. The panel sprang from its position taking part of the frame along with it. And then he was gone.

Sonia turned to her commanding officer. She wanted to shout at him for his stupidity but instead she did what was best for Johnny.

"Captain," Sonia said. He turned to her and she spilled her secret, about the drain cleaner and the gun. The captain's expression darkened and he nodded grimly.

"I've been seeing the signs. That's why we brought you in. Hoping a female could reach him." He dragged a hand over his cheek. "What a mess."

They stared at the wreckage Johnny had left.

The captain's voice was quiet now. "He won't even talk to me anymore. Does he talk to you?"

"Yes."

"Good. Go after him. You know the trail to his place?"

She nodded.

"Get a radio from security before you leave and call me on channel four if you find him. I'll follow in the Jeep."

"Yes, sir." Sonia hurried from the facility, stopping only to collect a new radio which she latched to her belt. Then she set off up the hill along the trail she knew. She pushed herself to hurry, praying that Johnny did not do anything to hurt himself.

Chapter 6

By the time Sonia made it up the hill in the damp, humid air of midday, she was slick with sweat and puffing like a steam engine. At the first turnoff she headed to the right, thinking Johnny might have gone to the swimming lagoon to cool off. But she had miscalculated and instead of breaking out onto the large green grotto and the shimmering cascade of silvery water, she stumbled into the private yard of Captain MacConnelly and his vampire wife.

She staggered off the trail and found the woman in question on her mobile phone on the bridge that spanned the stream. Sonia now realized that the stream was the runoff from the swimming area that lay between the two homes. Brianna's gaze went to Sonia like a heat-seeking missile and Sonia heard her say, "She's here."

Sonia stilled as that prickling warning lifted the hairs on her neck. She started to back out of the yard as Brianna held up a hand to stop her. Sonia disregarded this and retreated to cover. When she turned to run she found that the captain's wife stood on the path before her.

"Johnny told you about me, then." Brianna regarded Sonia with a furrowed brow and a tight expression. Was that grief shimmering in her leaf-green eyes?

Sonia felt a trickle of remorse that she didn't understand.

"I can see it in your eyes. Well, better that you know, I suppose."

Sonia swallowed hard as her gaze flicked to the trail and her escape and then back to meet Brianna's open stare.

Sonia's skin prickled a warning, but she remained still, suddenly unwilling to run. She couldn't out distance a vampire, that much was certain. Sonia had forgotten how beautiful this woman was. And now, at close range she could see the pure opal radiance of her skin and the sparkling clarity of her eyes. She'd pulled her fiery red hair back into a ponytail. The casual style only served to better reveal the perfect structure of her high cheekbones and heart-shaped face. Her lips were lush and full. Sonia stepped nearer.

"Close enough," said Brianna.

Sonia jolted to a stop having just realized she was creeping forward as one does with some beautiful wild animal they do not want to frighten but are desperate to touch.

"You're Sonia Touma, Johnny's teacher."

Sonia nodded, thinking Brianna's voice perfect for speaking. She should be on television or the radio.

"I'm Brianna. They told you I don't leave the house. That I don't like company."

"Yes, ma'am."

"A lie to protect humans, like you. I do like company and I work with humans, but for their safety my only contact with them is electronic."

Sonia began to wonder if Brianna was really that pretty or if this attraction was one of her powers. Sonia stared at the slight flush on Brianna's cheeks and took another step in her direction.

Brianna backed away. "You're doing it again."

Sonia stopped. "I'm sorry. I didn't realize.

"Happens all the time." She lifted the phone. "Travis just called. Asked me to search the mountain. Please wait here. I'll be right back."

That made no sense. It would take hours to search the mountain. Sonia opened her mouth to say so and Brianna disappeared right before her eyes. One moment she was there and the next, gone.

Sonia turned a complete circle and found no sign of her. Finally she lifted the radio and called her commanding officer. When Captain MacConnelly picked up she explained that someone named Travis had called his wife and that she had vanished.

"I'm Travis."

Of course he was. His real name wasn't Mac Mac-Connelly, she realized.

"Permission to continue to Sergeant Lam's quarters."

"No. She would have searched there by now. Just wait. Out." The radio when dead and she returned it to her belt.

Wait. Where? Should she go in and fix a sandwich or sit in the inviting hammock? Sonia crossed the bridge and had just set foot onto the grass on the opposite bank when Brianna MacConnelly reappeared.

Sonia clutched her heart and the bridge rail simultaneously. "Holy Mother of God!"

Brianna smiled. "Yeah, I get that from Travis, too. It's jarring."

"How do you disappear?"

"I don't. I just move too fast for you to see. So I found Johnny. He's at his place. He's upset. I asked him if he wanted me to stay with him. He said he wanted you."

Sonia felt that attraction for this woman stir again, the insistent pull to move closer. This time she resisted and it faded like smoke.

"He listened to me and nodded when I said you were on the way. He was signing but I can't read sign, only the alphabet. Maybe you should teach me and Travis, too. Especially if they can't change him back."

The realization struck Sonia so hard she jolted. Brianna stopped speaking and stared with concern. Of course! That's why Johnny didn't want to learn sign language. Learning sign was an admission that he wasn't turning back.

"It was so obvious," she muttered.

"What was?"

"If he learns sign, he won't turn back."

Brianna shook her head. "That doesn't make any sense."

"Yes, it does, because Lam only needs sign if he's a werewolf. His captain's insistence that he learn must have seemed like an admission that they can't help him. But he's stubborn. He's not giving up even if everyone else is, so that's why he has been so determined not to learn."

Brianna nodded. "Mac should have figured that out."

Sonia thought of the way the captain looked at Johnny when Johnny wasn't looking back. It was an expression riddled with such guilt it made Sonia wince just recalling it. "Why is the captain so pushy about this?"

Brianna drew a long breath and then released it, turning on the bridge to stare at the water flowing below them. "Is that how he comes across?"

Sonia didn't answer as she watched this vampire sweep a strand of copper-red hair from her pale face.

"They're alike, you know?" said Brianna.

"Alike?" Her earlier assumption regarding her captain returned to Sonia and she hugged herself and hunched bracing for Brianna's next words. Confirmation was quick.

"They are both werewolves."

Sonia shook her head, denying what her gut told her was true.

Brianna waited until Sonia met her gaze before continuing. "The thing that attacked Johnny also attacked my husband. At the same time. It bit him, too. He still has the scars." She made a circular sweep about her own shoulder and chest. "After that he began changing into the same thing that Johnny became, only his fur is gray like a timber wolf's. Oh, and his eyes are blue, not yellow."

"He's changing into a werewolf, too?"

"He *is* a werewolf. That's why he can be near me without suffering harm. He's no longer human. But Mac can change shape at will. All werewolves can, except Johnny."

"There are more of them?"

"Many. But none here. Just the two of them. The others work with various government agencies. Make perfect body guards as they are the only ones that can stop vampire assassins."

"Vampire what?"

Brianna blew out a breath. "Assassins. I thought you should know. I don't have security clearance to tell you things like the others, but you are up on this hillside and that means you're in danger, too."

"From Lam and your husband?"

"Not from them."

"They're after you? Male vampires?"

"Yes. They're called chasers. They capture the females. Usually they know where to find them as the males are required to register any sexual encounter with human females that don't result in a human's death. But I'm unusual even by vampire standards."

"Why do they want you?"

"They train their females as killers, too, though a different kind entirely. They're all mercenaries, hiring to the highest bidder. A female's kills are undetectable since the energy draw shows up as a stroke or heart attack. Sleeping with me is deadly, unless you're a werewolf."

Sonia found herself backing away.

"I know it's terrible. Unlike the males, we are hard to spot. They are ugly as vampire bats. But we have some vulnerabilities. Werewolves for one. Wounds inflicted by shifters don't heal. Neither do injuries caused by anything iron until the metal is removed. Then we regenerate zip-zap. I think that's where the folklore about stakes and crosses started. Really what you need is an iron stake, like a section of rebar."

"Why are you telling me this?"

"Because they're hunting me and they feed on human blood."

"Do you drink blood?"

"I'm a vegetarian."

"But you feed on energy."

"Not exactly. I don't need it. The draw is involuntary on my part. Just happens, like, uh…" She wiggled her fingers and glanced skyward as if searching for something. "Like oxygen. You don't intentionally draw it from the air. You just do. Same with me and a person's life force."

"That's terrible."

Brianna's smile faded. "Yes. It *is* terrible."

Sonia wondered why Johnny wanted to keep her alive? Then her earlier thought returned to her.

"So Johnny's up here to protect you?"

"No. That's my husband's job."

"Then why doesn't Johnny live down below with the rest of us?"

"He prefers it here on the hill."

Sonia admitted she did, as well.

"Johnny's mission is to keep fighting until they can get him to shift back voluntarily. Then he can have a more normal life, visit his family and…" She looked away.

"His son?"

"Johnny would like that. But he can't."

"They'll make him into a bodyguard?"

"Assign him, yes. He wants that. It's a prestigious post. Protecting the president or other vital American targets. He told me he'd be honored. And I know he hates vampires. It's instinctive."

"All vampires?"

"Yes, well, initially. He's made me an exception, thankfully. Now you'd best go check on Johnny."

Sonia was about to agree, but Brianna disappeared.

Sonia reached Johnny's home a little after twelve-hundred, hot, thirsty and worried. Upon entering the clearing about his home, the first thing she noticed was one of the patio chairs lodged in the top of a palm tree at the side of the yard. The second thing was the eerie silence.

"Johnny?" she called but received no answer. Brianna's earlier assurance did not relieve the tiny heartbeat of panic in her throat so she crossed the yard at a run. Her mind filled with terrible images of a pistol placed in Johnny's mouth and liquid drain cleaner eating away the lining of his stomach. She hit a dead run as she charged up the porch stairs.

She heaved open the front door and stumbled in to find Johnny in the kitchen lifting a glass to his lips. Sonia charged across the room and slapped the glass from his hand. The plastic tumbler bounced as clear fluid splashed over the wide boards of his kitchen.

He lifted both his palms up with a clear question on his face.

"What is that?"

He reached for the faucet over the sink and turned the stream on and then off.

Water, she realized. Sonia grabbed the counter and dropped her forehead to her hand. "I'm sorry. I thought... I thought..." She turned her head and stared up at him. "It was horrible, wasn't it?"

He nodded.

She told herself not to, but somehow she needed his touch. Sonia stepped forward arms extended and he opened for her, gathering her up and rocking her as she clung tight. She started talking, babbling about the dogs and the empty cages. But how they were making progress. They needed more time. Johnny held her close and rubbed her back.

A voice came from the open door. "Johnny!"

Sonia sprang from Johnny's arms as if pulled by a bungee and snapped a salute. They both turned to see the captain standing in the door.

"Oh." His eyes swept from her to Johnny and back to her again. He returned Sonia's salute. "At ease, Touma. You both all right?"

"Yes. That is, I think so." She deferred to Johnny.

The captain came forward. "I had no idea those dogs were dying. But Zharov says that it has something to do with their anatomy which is different than a man's. I don't know." He rubbed his neck. "Anyway, we're close. Really close. You have to hang in there, buddy."

Johnny nodded.

"I'll stop back if I have more information." The captain turned to her. "You're staying awhile?"

She wasn't sure if it was an order or a suggestion but she nodded. "Yes."

"I'll tell them not to expect you. Call for a pickup if you need one."

If?

Sonia's brow furrowed. It wasn't an order, but she got the impression the captain didn't want Johnny left alone. "I'm heading out." He thumbed over his shoulder and backed from the room as if it might be rigged with trip wires. Seeing him flustered made him seem more human to Sonia which was ironic because now she knew that he wasn't human at all.

Did it hurt to change forms?

Johnny lifted a finger to her and then followed the captain, snatching the whiteboard from the counter as he went. He was gone long enough for Sonia to realize she had been hugging Johnny and the captain had seen them. She felt sick to her stomach wondering what would happen next. A reprimand at least. She was blowing it again. She felt it—getting too personal. Sonia looked to the back door and wondered if she should just leave. Johnny seemed all right. But what if he wasn't?

Sonia grabbed a roll of paper towels from under the sink and began sopping up the spill. The door opened and closed. Sonia hoped Johnny was alone. She heard his huffing sound and realized he could not see her behind the counter.

"In here."

A moment later he was squatting before her, dish towel in hand, helping her clean up.

"Is he gone?"

Johnny confirmed that with the sign for yes, rather than a nod.

"Am I in trouble?"

Why?

"He caught me hugging you."

No trouble. More lab tomorrow at noon.

"Both of us?"

Yes.

She was squatting there before him when she spilled her other worry.

"I met her."

Johnny fixed Sonia with his steady gaze and nodded. Had Brianna told him, then?

"She told me about the chasers. Johnny, do you think the captain is trying to help you or keep you like this as a watchdog for his wife?"

Johnny's eyes went hard and he shook his head. He signed, *I trust Captain.*

"All right."

"What do you think about the experiments?"

Sad. They try.

"Yes. And they can change them back but…" Best

not finish that train of thought. "But I'm sure they will figure out what went wrong. I hope it's soon." She drummed her fingers on the counter and then recognized what she was doing and stopped.

"This is impossible. All of it."

Johnny cocked his head as if to say, *really?* He scratched beneath his furry extended jaw as evidence that it was all happening, all real.

"So the captain is a werewolf, a gray one, who can change at will." Her eyebrows lifted as she gasped. "Is he naked when he transforms?"

Johnny nodded.

"Does it hurt?"

He signed, *Don't know. Think so. Look like pain.*

But Johnny couldn't know himself because he had never changed from this form. He'd been this shaggy fearsome looking creature since he'd been attacked in Afghanistan. Where had the creature bitten him? She could not see any scars, but then his shaggy coat covered him from nose to toes. She wouldn't dwell on this. If she expected Johnny to move past it, she needed to, as well. But it wasn't fair. She breathed deeply. *Let it go.*

Sonia folded her arms around her middle and stared out the kitchen window at the dense jungle that flowed up the hill.

After a moment, she realized she was searching for movement. Were the vampires out there right now? If they were would she even see them coming? Brianna moved too fast to see. What if they killed Johnny? She found that prospect brought a sharp stab of pain to her heart.

"I'm frightened for you and for the captain."

Johnny left his seat and rummaged in the kitchen junk drawer for a pen and pad. Then he wrote, "Natural enemies. We kill them. I'm a marine, Sonia. I might not look it but I'm a marine and marine's protect people."

"Yes. I know you are."

He was a werewolf and his neighbor was a vampire. But what Sonia had learned about the mercenary males, it made her skin go cold. Her smile faded.

"Brianna said the males are ugly."

Johnny nodded and then drew a quick sketch of a thing with pointed ears, slanted eyes. Slitted nostrils and needlelike canines. She stared in horror at the line drawing and then at him.

"Really?"

He nodded.

"No wonder they only come out at night."

He shook his head and signed, *Any time.*

She stared back at the drawing. Johnny nudged her and she had to take a fast side step to keep from falling over.

Don't worry. I keep you safe.

"Yes. I know that." She set aside the sketch and rubbed her hands together. "Are you hungry? I can fix you something?"

Not hungry.

"Johnny, they are going to figure it out. And when they do you are taking me out for dinner and dancing."

His gaze snapped to hers and his brow lifted as if he was checking to see if she was making fun of him. She wasn't.

"I'm serious. When you turn back, I want you to take me out."

He nodded slowly. *A D-A-T-E.* Then he lifted his brows.

"Yes. A date." She took his hand, happy to see the hope in his eyes and feel the warm reassurance of his big, strong hand. "And Johnny? Learning to sign isn't going to keep you from turning back. It will just make the waiting easier."

He did a double take at her words and straightened. His jaw bunched but he nodded his understanding.

They stared at each other. That's what this was about really. Overcoming fear. He was afraid of waiting for a cure that would never come. She was afraid of screwing up again.

"I'm going to stick this out and so are you."

This time he drew her into his arms and held her. She closed her eyes, feeling safe and hopeful. How ridiculous, she thought. She'd never been in more danger in her life. And then one of those moments from her past sprang into her mind with the subtly of a popping jack-in-the-box. She shoved it back down, acknowledging that she'd been in real jeopardy then, too. Not all monsters had fangs and fur. Some came in a bottle.

She pushed away as she muttered that she was hungry. Turning to Johnny for comfort was just a bad idea. He wasn't some overgrown teddy bear and she knew she was blurring the lines between them again. Maybe Johnny needed comfort as much as she did but that wasn't somewhere she was willing to go.

They busied themselves fixing a meal and then eating it at the counter. After that she made a call to the captain who sent a driver to pick her up. A few minutes later the horn blared. Sonia said goodbye hesitant now to leave him alone.

"You'll be all right?"

He nodded, keeping his moonlike eyes on her. She hesitated wanting to go, feeling the need to stay. The horn sounded again.

"Damn it," she muttered. "I'll see you tomorrow. Right?"

He looked weary as he nodded again and guided her out. He stood on the porch as she descended to the driveway. When she looked back she could not see him in the dark, but she could see the strange green glow of his eyes. They glimmered like an animal just outside the circle of light. A chill went up her spine as she waved and jogged to the comfort of glowing headlights.

She knew how long the nights could be. Would he be all right alone?

The next day, Sonia called for a ride before breakfast. She hadn't slept thinking of Johnny alone with that damned gun. When she got to his place it was to find his house empty. She pounded and called and peeked in the windows.

Why had she left him alone? Why hadn't the captain sent someone to stay with him last night?

As she grabbed the phone that called the MPs and flipped it open, she heard a familiar huffing. She spun and saw Johnny striding across the yard.

She pounded down the stairs to meet him halfway and then started shouting at him like a maniac.

"Where the hell were you? You scared me half to death. I thought you were dead in there." She pointed toward his home.

Johnny lowered his snout and his brow simultaneously as she finally stopped yelling. Her lower lip began to quiver. He patted her shoulder and she sidled closer resting her forehead on the massive hairy plane of his chest.

Finally she drew back and signed that she was sorry.

Johnny blew out a breath that made his gums flap. Then he signed that they should go swimming.

She began shaking her head before he even finished the sign, her skin flashing cold in dread.

"I don't swim."

W-A-D-E.

She didn't want to, but she agreed just to please him. Damn she didn't even have a bathing suit.

Twenty minutes later she was up to her neck in the lovely deep pool which seemed less serene with her flapping about in the water like a whirligig.

Somehow over the course of the morning, Sonia learned to keep the water from going up her nose as she made slow, steady progress across the pool. The water had become a cool refuge from the tropical heat. Her olive green tank top and bikini briefs made an acceptable bathing suit and paddling in a grotto sure beat waiting for an open shower at the barracks. Johnny was a patient teacher and in just one morning had straightened out her kick and taught her the arm motion for the breast stroke.

She reached the volcanic rock that edged the pool near the falls. Puffing and gasping, she laughed at the sheer joy of her accomplishment. Johnny had kept pace with her on the journey, but this time she had not clung to him midcourse. She'd made it all the way without help.

He lifted a hand offering her a high five. She slapped his hand hard.

"I did it."

Again.

"No way. I'm going to soak my sore muscles in that waterfall and then I'm going to sunbathe. Lesson over."

Johnny offered a hand and then helped her into a

spot where the water gently cascaded over her like a warm shower.

"All I need is soap."

He grinned. The horror of yesterday seemed to have faded for them both. The water worked its magic massaging away the soreness from her neck and back. Johnny swam as she enjoyed the falls. Afterward, she stretched out on the towel Johnny had given her and gazed up at the patch of blue sky. He left the pool and lounged beside her, water running in rivulets off his wet coat. It took a moment to realize what she was feeling, it had been so long.

She was happy. She felt secure and did not worry where her next meal would come from or if the cops would be at her house. She didn't worry if her little sister was safe or if her mother had drunk their rent away. Everything was all right.

It was an unfamiliar feeling, light and airy. She thought she might float right up there into the blue sky.

Something brushed her arm. She turned her head to see Johnny lying on his back. The sun made his wet black fur glisten with a glossy gleam. With his fur matted to his skin, it was easier to see his form. His musculature was more gladiator than average Joe, but he did not seem animal to her until she looked at his face. In profile his snout, nose and canine jaws were startling. He did not look human, but she was becoming more accustomed to his appearance. As if sensing her scrutiny, he opened one yellow eye.

He patted his chest with both hands in the sign for happy and then lifted a tufted brow.

"Yes. Very. I'm afraid someone will come and snatch it away again."

Again? His brows lifted.

She rested one forearm across her brow and glanced at the sky, letting the sun warm her damp skin. She held back a moment longer and then let it out. She'd never told a soul. But she already knew that she'd tell Johnny. The decision made, she rolled to her side, propping herself up on an elbow. Sonia thought back and the tension crept back into her joints as she wondered if he'd use this later to humiliate her.

She rolled to a seated position, folding her legs like a meditating yogi so she could use both hands to sign.

"All right. Remember when I told you I was in foster care?" She didn't wait for an answer, just kept signing and speaking, the signs flowing as she forced herself to release this secret. He nodded that he remembered. She didn't want to look at him when she told him, so she stared at the falls and the water cascading in ribbons onto the rocks as she spoke. "Well, I want to tell you why."

Johnny stretched out on his side. It was hard telling him that her mom had not been a very good mother. Sonia had learned from birth that this was not a topic that was to be mentioned, so she danced around the problem like a matador sticking the bull a few times to weaken it. Her mention of not having enough food caused one of her eyes to twitch. She glanced at him to find his jaw locked and his gaze steady. Sonia looked away again, speaking to the pool before her and then taking a quick glimpse at him when the anxiety grew too much. When she told him that she'd often eaten her Cheerios as her mom poured herself a tall glass of gin, no ice, Johnny tapped his front teeth. The gesture seemed unconscious. She pressed her lips together then watched the water falling and falling. Letting go at the top, regrouping into calm depths below. She let go, too.

"She wasn't too bad when I was little. Mostly just coming home drunk and falling asleep on the sofa. But she wasn't really asleep. You know?"

Johnny's nod was barely perceptible and there was a tension in his shoulders now, a quiet, deadly stillness.

"Then she got fired. That first time really upset her and she said she'd stopped drinking, but then I realized she was just putting it in her juice. I got Marianna up and dressed for school because Mama wasn't ever up at that hour. She got work in a bar. Well, she got worse. Child services came a few times. Marianna and I tried to clean up, but they saw the bottles on the curb in the recycling. It was the wrong day for recycling. That was the first time they took us."

Johnny reached over and grasped her hand. The warmth and the pressure gave her courage. She held on a minute and then thought she'd just stop right there. The rest seared her insides. But Johnny released her hand and signed for her to go on. She didn't want to but she did.

She continued to sign. "But it wasn't the last. Mama got us back and then showed up drunk at school. I was in third grade. She tried to pick up Marianna, too, but she ran and Mama couldn't catch her. When we heard the sirens, Mama left her and took me. I found out later that the school called the cops but they didn't have the right address because Mama had moved us to a hotel. It was a bad hotel. Not the kind you stay on vacation but where people live all the time. The room smelled like cigarettes and there was stuff in the dressers that wasn't ours. It took them two days to find us. Mama…" Sonia's voice broke. She swallowed, forcing the lump down with the shame. "It took them two days." Sonia looked away. "I was screaming that she couldn't leave

Marianna at the school. We had to find her and she said if I was going to tell the school counselor that she was an unfit mother then maybe I didn't need a mother anymore." Sonia bowed her head. "She locked me in a dog cage that was in the room. The big kind that you keep animals in at night. It was cream-colored plastic on the sides and the front and back had a grate that you opened from the outside but I couldn't reach the latch. She left me so I tried to claw through the plastic." She looked at her own fingers remembering the ragged nails and bloody tips. "And I was screaming. It smelled like a dog in there and I got…well, I still don't like closed spaces. I can't stand them. Then those dogs at the lab were in those little cages and I could smell them."

Johnny lifted a finger and scooped a tear from her cheek. She rolled against him, her back to his front. He held her tight, just tight enough to make her feel safe.

She stopped speaking, sharing this part only in sign. She felt him bend to look over her shoulder, focusing on her hands.

They smelled like piss and fear, just like me…. The police found me. I don't remember all of it. I was kind of a mess. Still am, I guess. So I don't tell people about it and I don't let people get inside. It's too risky. But then, you've had a rough time, too, and I decided…

Johnny finished the sentence for her.

He signed, *To trust me.*

Sonia gave a shuttering sob and nodded. She spun to face him, speaking in a strained voice as she signed, "I didn't know you when I came here. I was just afraid. Anything seemed better than prison, even teaching a werewolf. But you're not a werewolf. Not to me. But when I think of that cell, I can't breathe. I get dizzy and sick. It's like I'll never be free of that damned cage."

That's why you stayed.

"Yes." Sonia smiled. "But not why I'm staying now. The captain knows. I'm sure of it. He must have seen it in my file and knew I couldn't quit. Anyway, my mama lost us for the second time then. We became wards of the state of New York for almost a year. Foster care sucked but no one forgot to feed me. Mama cleaned up and they sent us back to her again, but that didn't last. The next time she showed up drunk at our school, Marianna got a golden ticket out of there and I got placed in a group home 'til eighteen. I wonder what she'll do after college. College." She sighed at the wonder of it. "I thought I'd be out of the Marines the same time she got out of school. We could get a place together, like a home. Just an apartment, but ours, you know? I don't know. It's hard to make plans. Life is unpredictable, right?"

Yes, he signed. If anyone knew how unpredictable life could be it was Sergeant John Loc Lam. *Won't let you go to jail.*

Gratitude squeezed her heart and she stared up at his big, lovable face. "I believe you." She lifted a hand and stroked his cheek.

His eyes drifted closed.

"And you're still taking me dancing?"

His eyes opened and they seemed sad and she realized in that moment that he didn't believe it would ever happen.

"We *are* going dancing, Johnny. Believe it."

Okay.

Her fingers slid down his strong neck and came to rest in the soft hair of his chest. She remembered something Brianna said and drew back to sign as she spoke.

"Hey? Have you seen the captain's scars from the werewolf attack?"

He nodded, his expression curious now, as if he didn't know where she was going with this.

"So where are yours?"

He frowned and he stared at her a long silent moment before signing that he didn't know.

"But you must have scars. Where did it bite you?"

Johnny lifted his index finger to his chest.

I, she read.

Then he crossed his hands at the wrist and swept them in opposite directions.

Don't.

Now he had his thumb at his forehead an instant before he swept it down to contact his other thumb, tapping them once.

Remember.

"You don't remember?"

Chapter 7

Hagan Dowling sat before his laptop's web camera as his superior's face came on his screen. Burne Farrell lifted his chin, revealing the distended blue ropelike arteries branching out over his throat. Their engorged appearance showed that he had recently fed.

Looking at his own hands seemed preferable to looking at his superior's slitted nose and spiny rodentlike teeth punctuated by two menacing fangs protruding from his liver-colored lips.

Hagan tried not to stare at the new purple blood spots that had appeared on his superior's neck and forehead since their last meeting only two weeks ago. When they had met ten years ago, Burne Farrell was in his prime, his skin an admirable lavender shade that seemed preferable to the white cast of his own dermis. But now that middle age had taken a firm grip on him, he grew more hideous with each meeting.

"So you have arrived," said Burne.

Hagan nodded, superstitiously checking his own hands for any sign of the dreaded purple stains before reducing the size of his superior's image to that of a matchbook. "Yes, sir. We are on the main island of Hawaii. The team's initial sweep located one female."

Farrell rose so quickly his face disappeared from view and the camera now relayed a view of his mint-green dress shirt and the black belt with gold buckle that held up his gray trousers. "Vittori?"

"No, sir. Just an ordinary female. Vampire. Tenth generation from her scent."

Farrell sank back to his chair, his expression peevish now.

"She is perhaps two years past her womanhood. Her father reported her conception but at the time of her first bleed, her mother went into hiding. She was easy to track."

"Then why the two years lost? She might have had a babe twice already."

"It is the backlog of missing vampires. My MV list is growing longer because of the hunt for Brianna Vittori." He glanced up now, not wanting to be obvious in his distaste. Burne's condition awaited them all unless they fell to the brutish werewolves.

His superior smiled, showing his two rodent incisors. "But she will be worth the trouble. First generation. Who knows what her male children might look like?"

Hagan knew from the obsession that Burne Farrell showed for Brianna Vitorri that his supervisor wanted her personally. But Hagan planned to be the first to locate her and first to impregnate her. If he was virile and she fertile than they might make a son whose skin did not speak of death and whose face that, if not comely, might not be so hideous that he was condemned to walk only in darkness.

"This latest capture is secured. I ask permission to let my men have this female capture as it will be some weeks before they can report to the training facility and several days before she can be safely transported for formal indoctrination."

"Granted. See that they don't feed on her. Such entertainment needs preparation. Just sex. You understand?"

"Of course, sir."

Farrell aimed a blotchy finger at the camera. "Find me Vitorri, Dowling. Find her."

His superior clicked a button, swore and then disappeared from his computer screen.

"Oh, I certainly intend to find her—for myself."

Over the next ten days, Sonia taught Johnny to sign in the afternoons and stayed for supper most evenings. Johnny had kept her secret and had not mentioned her disclosure again. He also rarely used his compliance as a weapon to get her to tell him personal information, which was a relief.

She might have actually begun to feel comfortable here until she recalled they could transfer her in an eyeblink. It was wiser not to lower her guard. Johnny liked her and that was good only because it ensured she could stay a little longer. But this was no more permanent than any of her other living situations.

No more permanent than anything had ever been in her life.

Still, he was a good student and his progress made her proud.

His sign vocabulary was progressing very fast now and he could carry on a conversation without breaking to finger spell words. He finally admitted that he was using the book and the websites she recommended to study at night after she had gone. When Johnny discovered that nicknames were common among the deaf community, to keep from having to finger spell out their names, he took to calling her Kitten. Kitten was the sign for baby and cat combined. At his suggestion, she called him Wolf, the sign that involved drawing her fingers outward from her face and nose to simulate his long snout.

On some occasions Brianna appeared in the late afternoon, seeming to enjoy chatting with Johnny now that he had a translator and their conversations were no longer one-sided. The captain's wife even started picking up some signs herself.

He had not told Sonia anymore about the werewolf attack or why he could not remember, but he wanted to talk about her. She permitted his questions glad that they no longer seemed an inquisition but simple interest in her.

Today, as they sat side by side on the mossy bank of his swimming spot, Johnny asked about her mom's current location which was in Fishkill Correctional Facility in Upstate New York. Sonia did not write her mom but her sister did and kept her abreast of more information than she wanted to hear. All Sonia wanted was to pretend she had a normal childhood that didn't involve her mother putting her in a dog carrier. She'd told Johnny as much and he said he thought she should talk to someone about it.

"You are someone," she reminded him.

When he pressed, she said she would if he would and he let the matter drop.

They had made their way back up the trail as the afternoon crept toward evening. Tomorrow was a big day. The doctors wanted to show Johnny something at the lab again and she'd been ordered to get Johnny to the medical facility tomorrow. She planned to walk up to get him and he'd agreed to go with her but after the last time, they were both dreading what might happen. She knew this because they were both avoiding speaking about the appointment. Perhaps that was why Johnny chose the walk back up the hill as the time to tell her about his family. He had a sister, Julia, which Sonia knew from her briefing, but she didn't know that Julia was planning to attend the University of California, Berkeley, come fall and Johnny was worried about the cost and strain to his mother's shaky finances.

He also said his mom was a widow who had tried to manage their family's Chinese restaurant after his dad's heart attack, but had failed, nearly losing the house with the business. He'd used his signing bonus to settle that debt, but their house was still underwater and there was no money for Julia's schooling. Sonia began to see why Johnny was so eager to get back in action. Combat duty came with more pay.

Too many D-E-B-T, he signed.

"So I'm a marine because I broke into a house and you're a marine because you wanted to help your mother keep hers."

And serve my country.

"That makes you a saint and me…well, not a saint."

He gave her a little pat on the shoulder that she found comforting. He had a way of making her feel hopeful. As if it would all be okay even when she knew better. This was one of those plateaus that came before she fell back into a valley. At least this time she saw it coming.

She was sick of thinking things would be different because they never were. Not for her, anyway.

On the walk from the swimming spot to his home, he looked out for her, helping her where she needed and letting her alone when she didn't. She'd never had someone who listened as intently as Johnny or who seemed to understand her quite so well. He accepted her, she realized, warts and all. He might not be all human, but he didn't have the fears that she carried about like some thorny armor.

When they reached his house, he convinced her to stay for supper. That wasn't difficult as she was tempted by his gentle presence as much as the chance to skip another meal served on a tray. Three square meals the military promised and they were square, unless you were in the field and then they came in sturdy little plastic packets.

Back inside his quarters, they found themselves to be ravenous. She rummaged in his cupboards, taking out plates and silverware. She excused herself to use his bathroom and could not resist looking in his medicine cabinet. No gun, no drain cleaner. Where had he put them?

She was tempted to search, but instead she returned to him. His quarters were so cozy that all she needed was her kit and she could move right in. Sonia stilled at the thought. This wasn't her home. It was Johnny's. She didn't have a home. Had never had one.

Johnny gave her a toothy smile and pointed to the grill. He had a whole fish on there that had turned red with the cooking.

"What in the world? It's still got its head."

He flipped the fish in one smooth motion.

"I've never eaten a whole fish on the bone before. Just fish sticks."

Johnny made a pained face and shook his head in disgust.

"I know, you learned to cook from your dad, right? He must have been something."

Johnny had a nostalgic look in his eyes when he nodded this time.

"Never knew my dad. Marianna and I, we have different fathers. I asked to see a picture of mine once and, oh, never mind, it's too sad."

Johnny motioned for her to continue.

"She didn't have a picture. So I asked her when she was drunk and she said she wasn't sure who my father was. But she knew Marianna's and he was a mean son of a bitch. Trucker, she said. I was just an accident."

B-L-E-S-S-I-N-G, he signed.

She gave a mirthless laugh. "To who?"

To me.

She felt herself warming up inside like a flower coated in frost when the sun is finally strong enough to melt the crystals. The warning bells sounded next. *Don't get attached. It will only make it harder when they transfer you.*

He lifted the wine bottle.

She shook her head. "I don't drink. Too many drunks on my mother's side for me to take a chance."

He set the bottle out of sight.

He explained with sign and finger spelling that he couldn't get drunk since the attack. Something had happened in the change. After supper, Johnny suggested a movie. He had an online video package and he let her pick. She hadn't been to a movie in months.

"We should go to a movie, too. Do they have a movie theater in town."

He nodded yes and signed, *Off island.*

They settled in, she on the couch while he sprawled on wide cushions on the floor, his broad head propped up against the couch just a few inches from her. He lay so close that she could have reached out to stroke his head from where she lay on the sofa and she found it a struggle not to do so. Why did she always want to touch him?

The movie she selected popped on.

She grinned. "So much better than fighting for computer time."

Write sister here. My computer.

The movie was a romantic comedy with that blonde actress who had such great comedic timing. She felt warm and peaceful and happier than she could remember. Johnny had given her something that she had been avoiding for so long she hadn't even realized she was missing it—friendship. But she didn't make friends. Too much risk. She yawned. Still, it would be nice. She hadn't planned to doze off but she did and the next thing she knew the sun was in her face and she found herself stretched out under a coverlet on Johnny's couch.

She threw herself upright and scrambled to her feet. "Holy shit!"

A moment later Johnny charged down the hall looking frightening as hell. He glanced past her and she realized he was searching for whatever it was that made her yell. She stilled, realizing he was searching for vampires. She'd actually forgotten that there were monsters out hunting for the captain's wife.

She lifted her hands. "I'm fine. It's okay."

Johnny skidded to a halt.

"But I fell asleep! I was here all night. Oh, God. What are they going to do to me now?"

Johnny signed, *Nothing. You with me.*

"I don't have permission to come and go as I please. The captain said I could spend the day. Oh, I have to report in."

She asked to use Johnny's phone and failed to reach her sergeant. *Screwed,* she realized as she made quick use of the bathroom before reemerging a few moments later, her face wet from the water she's splashed over it.

Breakfast? he asked.

"No. I'll see you at noon, Wolf, at the lab. If I'm not there come find me please."

Sonia hit the trail and headed back to the base at a full out run. Once there she could not find her supervisor and knew she'd catch hell later but she had to get to the lab for Johnny. She missed breakfast and had time only to grab a shower and change into her uniform before it was time to report. When she reached the medical facility it was to find her captain waiting for her like a one-man firing squad. Her stomach turned a full twisting somersault as she realized he had been looking for her. She snapped to attention.

"Where is he?" he asked as he returned her salute with a slashing motion that reminded her of a machete slicing through the air.

Her stomach dropped an inch as she realized that Johnny was a no-show. She'd been so caught up on her unplanned sleepover that she'd forgotten her job was to get Johnny's furry ass to the medical facility.

"He said he'd meet me here." Had he? She wasn't exactly sure what he'd said beyond offering her breakfast.

"Do you not remember me telling you yesterday to bring him along, Private?"

"I'll call him, sir."

"He won't answer," he muttered as he reached for his cell phone and dialed. And he was right. Johnny didn't.

"He might be on his way." Or she might just be done for.

The captain stared her down. As she studied her toes waiting for whatever consequences the captain might deem appropriate his phone jangled. He snapped it on and lifted it to his ear.

"MacConnelly," he barked. His gaze flicked to her as he listened. "Got it." He disconnected the call, his eyes still on her. "He's here." His tone changed, not friendly exactly but more respectful. "I don't know how you do it."

Neither did she, but he seemed in a mood less likely to result in him tearing her a new asshole. Now the captain's gaze turned speculative.

She shifted under his scrutiny. Sonia needed to get something off her chest. Johnny's revelation about the attack troubled her and she was pretty sure there would never be a good time to tell her captain about it. So she could either keep her mouth shut, which was better for her or she could speak up, which might be better for Johnny.

"Sir?"

"Touma?" His tone became cautious and his eyes narrowed.

She swallowed back her uncertainty and ignored the voice that warned that she should just mind her own business.

"Johnny told me he doesn't remember the attack."

His familiar frown deepened the lines on his face.

"Of course he does. He was there."

"He doesn't, sir. He told me he doesn't."

"Amnesia?"

"I don't know, sir. Just wanted to bring it to your attention is all."

"I'll look into it. Now meet Johnny at the lab. He's on his way. I'll see you there."

She saluted and when he returned it, she did an about-face but did not get far before his words stopped her.

"Thank you, Private."

She glanced back, surprised to see the sincerity of his expression.

"Yes, sir."

She reported to security and was guided to a different part of the facility and directly into one of the lab's examination rooms. She'd expected to find Johnny but the room was vacant. It could have come straight from any doctor's office except there were no windows. The heavy metal door swung shut behind her. The moment the door clicked she felt trapped. Cold sweat covered her as she tried to breathe, but the walls seemed to close in on her and she found herself panting like a dog.

She pounded on the door until her arms ached. Finally the door swung open and a marine stood there, one hand on the latch and his eyes on her.

She flung herself at him and he wrapped his arms around her while she shook like the last leaf on the tree.

"Hey," he cooed. "What's wrong?"

She gasped as the tears welled from her eyes and streamed down her face.

He made a shushing sound and stroked her back. She pushed back and felt a moment's resistance before he let her go.

Sonia heard the growl first. An instant later the ma-

rine flew away from her and landed on the opposite side
of the examining room, crumpling in a heap. Johnny
glared at her and she shrank against the wall, suddenly
afraid of the fury she read in his yellow eyes. Johnny's
gaze flicked back to the young man.

A lightning bolt of terror went through her as she
realized that Johnny was out of control. She knew in
her pounding heart that Johnny would kill that marine
because he had touched her.

"Johnny, no!"

Johnny stopped and turned to her. She signed as she
spoke. "It wasn't him. I was scared and I threw myself
at him." She had to get him to believe her. Had to stop
him from hurting this man. "It was me, do you hear
me? *I* did it, not him."

Johnny stilled. His body trembled and she read the
betrayal in his eyes. The marine scrambled to his feet.
Johnny turned and ripped the steel door from its hinges
and threw it toward the marine but it went wide. Intentionally, she thought. The marine ducked and then ran
for the opening, streaking between them and tearing
down the hallway, screaming as he fled. "Help! He'll
kill her. Help!"

She turned to face the angry werewolf. Then her
blood went cold as Johnny's gaze flicked from the retreating marine to her. She tried to speak but the look
he gave her froze her blood and her larynx all at once.
She lifted a hand and signed, *Sorry.*

Johnny roared. Sonia clamped her hands over her
ears. It was a sound she hoped never to hear again, a
long agonizing cry, full of anguish. Then he turned to
the table bolted to the floor and ripped it from its at-
tachments before hurling it against the concrete wall
opposite her. He threw the stainless-steel side table.

The wheels exploded from their casings on contact with the wall and the frame collapsed as if made from aluminum foil. The counter fell next, torn from the wall, sink and all. Water now poured onto the floor and out the open door. Sonia watched Johnny attack the large surgical light as if it were a serpent. He paused a moment to look at her and then lifted the door, throwing it halfway down the corridor.

Just like her mother's rages, she realized, curling into a ball and whimpering. Sonia looked at the open door and Johnny lifting the ruined examining table over his head to beat it against the floor again and again.

Sonia ran. She ran from her past and from her future and from Johnny's pain, but got no farther than the hall before her legs gave way and the shaking started. In her heart, she had known that what he felt for her was more than friendship. She'd let him give her comfort, disregarding the warning signs, so she could have dinner in her make-believe house with a man whom she didn't have to fear would get too close. But he had. What had she done?

She'd crossed some line, screwed this up, too. Now the captain or Johnny would send her away.

This was why she didn't let people in. She couldn't save them. Not her mother or her sister or Johnny. God, she couldn't even save herself.

The captain rushed past her and she rose to follow but Scofield grabbed her arm, halting her.

"What's going on?"

Captain MacConnelly charged down the hall at a run.

"I've never seen Johnny lose control," said Scofield. "What set him off?"

It grew quiet except for the pounding of her heart

slamming into her ribs. She knew exactly. Her eyes met Johnny's and she saw the question in his eyes.

"Touma. I asked you a question. What happened?"

They'd blame her. She knew it and she knew they'd be right. She had turned to another man for comfort. No, that wasn't it. Did his rage stem from knowing that comfort was all he could give her, all she could accept while he was a wolf? He knew it. She knew it and…oh, she had to get out of there. Before the captain found out and called the MPs.

The major's hand slipped from her wrist as he turned toward the crashing coming from the examining room. She saw a flash of gray fur, the captain, she knew and then Johnny's black coat as the two spun in circles like all-star wrestlers.

She couldn't stay to see how she had disappointed one more person. She never meant to hurt him. But she had.

She kept going, out of the lab, the hall, the waiting area and out of the building. She kept moving, a walk at first and then finally a full-out run. She had to get away.

Johnny wanted to kill Webb for touching Sonia, for doing what he had dreamed of doing every day since he had met her. Last night, when she was sleeping on his couch and he had covered her with a blanket he had leaned over, wanting to kiss her. Only he couldn't kiss anyone. He couldn't because he had a snout instead of a mouth.

Mac had him from behind. It didn't stop him from lifting the table and throwing it again, taking out a row of ceiling tiles.

Mac's growl rumbled through him. Johnny's arms

when slack. His shoulders drooped. Mac released him and stepped back.

He couldn't have her, not as long as he was stuck like this. He had to face it sooner or later. They were teaching him sign because he wasn't coming back. They all knew it. All these tests and research, it was just to keep him busy. They didn't have the first damned clue.

Mac watched him. Johnny punched both fists through the cement wall which collapsed into powder. The rough edges of the hole did not even scratch his skin. It didn't even hurt. He couldn't break his hand or cut his skin or put a bullet through his temple, because his hide was too damned tough. He could still put the barrel in his mouth, pierce that soft palate and then on to the squishy tangle of his brain. Sonia had forbidden it. Then she had turned to a stranger.

Johnny threw back his head and howled again, pouring out all his rage and pain.

Since Sonia arrived in his life, he hadn't thought about putting that pistol in his mouth. He hadn't thought of the poison that he had kept beside his mouthwash. Instead, he occupied his mind with Sonia, what she looked like with the sun on her face or the ocean mist beading on her dark hair. He spent his time away from her trying to learn as many signs as possible so his conversations with her might flow naturally. He'd cooked for her. He'd taken her on walks, gone swimming with her and watched movies into the night. But she didn't see him as a man. More like her pet Cocker Spaniel. He was crazy for her. But now she'd seen what he really was and she had left him, too.

He knew his father hadn't left on purpose. He'd died, but he was still gone, leaving Johnny to pick up the pieces alone, care for his mom. Johnny dropped to his knees. Care for his sister.

His dad was gone. He couldn't see his mom or his sister or that baby, the one they'd made from his sperm. Now Sonia was gone, too, and he was here, alone, a monster. Still. Always.

He covered his face with his hands, hating the long wolfish slope of his snout.

It wasn't her fault. Who could blame her if she turned to a man for comfort and it wasn't him? Because he wasn't a man. Johnny felt sick to his stomach. He wrapped his arms about his middle and let his head sink. Mac draped a long furry arm about him. Johnny did not resist as they sat side by side.

He'd thought she was different because Sonia had managed to look past the beast he had become and see him there underneath. He'd let her in and she'd let him in. It had been a battle and he wasn't proud of his tactics, but he'd cracked open that tough shell. She had been closed up tighter than a walnut and now he understood why. She'd been through a lot.

Johnny dragged his claws over the floor again and again in a restless repetitive motion and only stopped when he realized he'd ripped through the floor tiles and a half inch into the concrete subfloor.

She was gone like a lovely dream that fades in the light.

The captain's arms fell away and he gave Johnny's back a pat.

Johnny made a fist and rubbed it in a circle over his aching heart. *Sorry. Sorry.* So damned sorry for all of it.

But the captain lifted his brows in confusion. He couldn't understand him. Only Sonia could do that.

Chapter 8

Sonia kept running. Acting on instinct now, using her lizard brain, she called it, as she did when things got too frightening. Her lizard brain told her to run. So she ran. She didn't plan or notice what direction she headed. Somehow she was outside while her mind played a video loop of that marine crumbled on the floor. Just like her mother, Sonia thought, picturing her mama sprawled out drunk on the floor of the kitchen or the bathroom or the hallway and once on the front steps. She'd run then, too. To the park or the library or the YMCA. Somewhere, anywhere where she could blend in and act as if she was there for some benign purpose other than escaping her miserable, drunken mother and her own miserable sober life. She'd run many places but she'd never run to the bottle.

Sonia's sprint ebbed with her energy. She glanced behind at the way she had come, trying to orient herself, trying to think. She couldn't go back. They'd lock her up if she went off base. But if they blamed her for Johnny's outburst, then they might send her back to prison anyway. She hurt Johnny, her fear becoming his pain. She knew something like this would happen. Nothing ever worked right for her. He'd gotten attached, so had she, but what was she supposed to do about it?

She was just his teacher, wasn't she?

And perhaps his only friend. Sonia swiped at the tears.

Johnny obviously saw their relationship as something more than friendship. What he wanted, she could not provide. Had she given him mixed signals? Was this her fault, too?

She'd screwed it up, as usual. Like with her mother.

She knew her mother didn't drink because of her. Her mind knew it. But in her heart she always felt that she had never been enough. Not enough to keep her sober. Not enough to fill those holes—in her mother and she sure the hell was not enough to fill them in Johnny.

Sonia didn't get far. She didn't even make the main gate before a Jeep with two imposing, chisel-jawed marines with MP bands on their arms cut her off. The one in the passenger's side swung gracefully out of his seat and strode to her. Only her wobbling legs kept her from turning tail and running again.

"You Private Touma?" he asked.

She nodded, trying not to fold in half and grasp her thighs as she sucked in the oxygen she lacked from her run. Instead she placed a hand on the hood of the Jeep for support and burned her hand before retracting it.

"You're to report to Captain MacConnelly's office ASAP," said the burly MP.

Sonia glanced toward the road. The closed gate and

guard booth did not stop her from looking beyond to the open road. How many times in her life had she thought of running away? How many times had she actually gone? And how many times had her situation gotten worse as a result? She frowned, recalling being returned to her mother in a squad car. The cops had taken one look at her mother wobbling on her heels, wreaking of booze and called protective services. Two months in foster care that time. Worse. Run—caught— worse problems. Not this time.

Sonia dragged her feet as she walked beside the Jeep. Her silent companion tipped his seat forward and indicated that she should crawl in the back like a child. On the short drive to the captain's office, she rehearsed several ways to explain. Maybe if she set it out correctly he'd give her another chance. Then she thought of all the damage to that room and grimaced.

She had just enough time to wear a groove in the rug in the captain's office before he arrived. As she held her salute she wondered where he kept little stashes of clothing. He bared down on her, leaning close and scowled so hard that the furrows in his forehead turned white.

"You want to tell me what the hell happened in there?"

She really, really didn't.

Finally, he returned her salute and she dropped her weary arm to her side, but remained at attention as the captain began to add to the groove she'd started. He spun and marched and spun and marched.

"Start talking, Touma, because I'd like to know why Johnny, who has never shown violence without provocation, would suddenly go crazy and trash an examining room."

Sonia's throat went dry as she opened and closed her

mouth like a goldfish who suddenly found herself on the kitchen counter instead of in her bowl.

"Webb said Johnny threw him across the room. If Johnny had bitten that marine, Webb would be turning werewolf right now. And Johnny would be responsible for that forever, for changing a man to a monster."

She'd never seen the captain look so fierce. His eyes were changing from sapphire blue to the ice blue of a wolf. The tint rising to overtake his natural coloration. Was he transforming?

It occurred to Sonia suddenly that the captain had unintentionally changed Johnny to a werewolf and that this situation must be striking him close to the bone. She started backing toward the door.

"Do you know how difficult it is for a werewolf to control the impulse to attack when angry? So I'll ask again, if you know what provoked him, you had better speak up."

She didn't. Instead she clamped her lips together as her chin began to tremble.

The captain folded his arms across his chest. To Sonia, he seemed to be holding himself in. When he spoke, his voice seemed different, harsher, like a growl.

"Was it Webb or you or Johnny, because someone is responsible. Start talking, Touma."

Sonia considered saying that she didn't know what had set Johnny off because the captain was intimidating as hell on a good day but when he was angry, like now, and the veins in his throat and forehead pulsed with blood, he was positively terrifying.

But if she tried to pull that, then they might think that something was wrong with Johnny. They might put *him* in the cage and she absolutely could not let that happen.

"Sir, they told me to wait for Johnny in exam room

one." There, she'd gotten that part out and her voice only trembled a little. Maybe he didn't even notice. "Then the door shut behind me and I couldn't get out."

The captain's scowl deepened so that his brow was so furrowed that she thought she might want to plant some vegetable seeds along the rows.

"Locked in?" He shook his head in confusion. "Those doors work with a panic button so they can be opened without using your hands. Didn't your escort show you the red button beside the door?"

Sonia went still. "Button?" Why hadn't she seen a big red button beside the door? "No, sir."

"Was Sergeant Lam trying to get you out?"

"No, sir, Corporal Webb opened the door from the outside." She lifted her hands to glance at the bruises and cuts there from her efforts to escape. Why hadn't she seen that button? "I wasn't thinking and I just threw myself at him."

"You attacked Webb?"

She dropped her head to stare at the rounded toe of her shiny shoes. "No, sir."

"Ah. What happened then?"

"Webb held me and I was crying and hugging him and…"

Her captain made a sound that fell between a groan and a growl.

"Johnny dragged Webb off me. It was my fault, sir. It just happened and Johnny moves so fast. But Captain MacConnelly, sir, I didn't understand how Johnny felt. I thought we were becoming friends, but I never knew how he…"

She lifted her head and saw the captain's face flushed with blood.

"I wasn't thinking and Johnny saw us."

"Holy shit." The captain raked a hand over the stubble at his temple. "You're saying he did this because he was jealous?"

Sonia lowered her head as she fought the tears at facing yet another failure. She'd really wanted to help Johnny deal with this but it was too much. Instead of making his life easier she was complicating it and as much as she liked him, she was not prepared to take their relationship any further. He knew her well enough to know that sticking to anything wasn't her strong point. Why he even wanted her was baffling; she was such a screwup.

"I've failed to keep our relationship professional, sir. Johnny is lonely and I'm female and he seems to think he has feelings for me, which he might very well have." This was so embarrassing. "I'm not helping him, so I think I should go."

"True to form," muttered the captain. He pinned her with a gaze so cold she shivered. "Private, we are a hair's breadth away from fixing this mess. But we need Johnny's cooperation. In the last month he has been ordered to the lab a dozen times but he only showed up twice, both times with you. You haven't failed. He'll get over it. So will you."

"Sir, he could have killed Webb."

"That might just keep me from doing so." He rested the knuckles of his right fist on his desk and leaned toward her. "The day you came I told you that your file said you were cautious about entering new relationships. Well, Touma, let me be the first to tell you that you are in one. You have managed to reach Sergeant Lam when no one else could and you have kept him from doing anything to hurt himself. So I don't give a shit about the exam room."

She blinked at him.

"The day you arrived I also told you that Lam needed understanding and not a woman who would hit and run. So this time, Touma, you are not running."

She swallowed before she spoke aloud her other reservations. "Sir, Sergeant Lam sometimes cooks supper for me."

"So?"

"And lunch."

He gave her a look that showed confusion blended with irritation.

"And breakfast."

The captain's brows shot up. "Are you saying you are sleeping with him?"

The shock straightened her spine. "No, sir. But I did spend last night on his couch and we watched a movie together."

"On his couch?"

"I fell asleep during the movie. But, sir, I didn't report back to base until oh nine hundred. But I couldn't find my supervisor, sir."

"She noticed your absence and she reported it to me. How I proceed depends a great deal on your actions moving forward, Touma."

Her stomach squeezed and twisted as if being consumed by a boa constrictor. "Sir, I've screwed this all up. I don't know what I'm doing. I can't tell if I'm teaching him or he's teaching me."

"What exactly is he teaching you?"

How to trust. "Swimming."

"My wife told me you spend downtime together. Also that you eat meals together."

A shiver went down her back as she thought of Brianna, not just appearing to talk, but also sneaking about without either of them knowing.

"I asked her to keep tabs on you. Johnny knows. He can smell her whenever she enters his territory."

"I'm not a good teacher."

"Really?" The captain rounded his desk and sat in his chair. "So your complaint is that you are getting to eat really good food, swim in a lush tropical paradise and watch movies. What, is the couch lumpy?"

Sonia was not letting go so easily. "It's not a professional relationship. I tried but…" She let her insecurities pour from her with the perspiration. "He knows signs that I never even showed him. He's learning on his own from the book I left him so I don't even know if he needs me to teach him. I didn't tell you because I like Johnny. I tried to be firm and professional but it didn't work. The only thing that did work was if I answered his personal questions. If I answered, he stayed. If I didn't, he took off. I've mismanaged everything. That first day when he showed you his signs—" she lifted her gaze to peek up at him as the fear made her stomach ache "—those were curse words, sir." She dropped her gaze to the carpet. "That's what I taught him because I lost my temper. I've been walking on egg shells afraid you'd find out what a terrible job I've been doing. It's completely out of control."

"What is, Private?"

"My relationship with him. He obviously thinks it's personal."

"And you don't."

She threw up her hands. "I do, too. But it wasn't supposed to be. I tried to keep him out, but I couldn't because I had to show progress or you'd…" She sighed. "You'd follow through on your threat, sir."

"I don't make threats, Private. And, I'll admit that I expected you to fail."

And she had. Her shoulders rounded and her throat began a familiar burn.

"But my wife was right. She told me to choose someone who couldn't quit and you didn't."

A tiny pearl of hope bubbled up inside her.

"Let me lay this out for you, Touma. Johnny needs to learn sign, but that's not your job. Never has been. Your job is to give him hope and make damned sure that he is occupied, engaged and interested. I don't give a fart if you sleep over and get breakfast in bed. I don't care if he knows how to swear in sign."

She winced, realizing that the captain had known all along what Johnny had said that first day.

"Johnny is happier than I've seen him since he was attacked. So you must be doing something right."

"I'm not sure what I'm doing at all, sir. Sometimes I feel like I'm drowning and I don't want to hurt him."

"We are close to a treatment, Touma. I am telling you. We nearly got this nailed. We've isolated the protein Johnny needs to be human again. So let me be very clear. You have my permission to eat Cheerios on his porch and learn how to cliff dive if you want to. Just stay with him. That's your job. Johnny's big and burly. He might look solid as a rock, but there are cracks, Touma. Serious cracks. So don't break him."

Knowing what the captain expected momentarily filled her with relief until the weight of his expectations pressed down on her. This was worse than being his teacher. She was responsible for so much more than teaching him sign language. She lifted her hand to salute. "Yes, sir."

"We've got another series of tests this week. So don't hug anyone else until then."

Her face went hot at his words but she nodded her understanding.

He rose. "And now, Private, you and I are going to see Johnny because he won't use the white board with me and I can't understand a thing he is signing." He rummaged in his drawer and retrieved a flip phone. He tossed it to her. "My number is in there with some others. My wife has asked that her number be included on your phone. Brianna wants you to call her. Seems you've made an impression all around."

The mention of his vampire wife's name made her skin tingle. Suddenly all she wanted to do was to get Johnny and get back up the hill.

"Yes, sir."

"Follow me."

They walked in silence down corridors and through automatic doors, each of which had a bright red button the size of a grapefruit that was used to open them. Panic did funny things to a person. It made her brain stop working. She'd been sweating and it was hard to breathe. Right now she had a cramp in her belly just thinking of Johnny. Was he still upset?

The captain stopped at a door that was clearly an exterior exit judging from the solid steel and the panic bar. He peered down at her.

"Upbeat, Touma. Upbeat and optimistic," said Mac-Connelly. "We nearly have this."

She nodded and he opened the door and held it. She passed through first and out into a central grassy courtyard that ringed a Koi pond. Wooden benches sat nestled before sprays of palm fronds and blooming tropical plants. A place of serenity in the center of the medical research lab. It seemed as out of place as an orchid in the middle of a gravel quarry.

"This was created at my wife's insistence. She said Johnny should have somewhere peaceful to wait before tests and lab work. You know when we draw blood we have to take it from his mouth because it's impossible to puncture his skin?"

She didn't, but the information just made the entire testing process more horrific. They'd been at this for six months? No wonder he was depressed. She began scanning for him. The door clicked shut behind them and Johnny emerged on the opposite bank, straightening from where he seemed to have been feeding the fish, judging from the number of the bright yellow, orange-and-white Koi swimming practically up onto the bank.

Why weren't they afraid of him?

Probably because they didn't know how much fish he ate. She smiled and started toward him, taking the fastest route over the high-arching foot bridge that spanned the narrowest part of the pool.

He was signing already. *Sorry. So sorry. Not try scare you.*

The captain's shoes rapped smartly on the wooden planking behind her. "What's he saying?"

She signed to Johnny. *It's okay now.*

She started signing and speaking in unison. "I was afraid. I thought I was locked in that exam room and you weren't there. I just panicked."

"And Webb is an idiot," added MacConnelly.

Johnny signed to his captain and Sonia spoke nearly in time.

"He says, 'I just lost it. It was stupid. I know how strong we are. No excuses.'"

"You did hold back," said the captain. "If you didn't

you would have killed him. It's easy to kill a man now. And you didn't bite him. I know that took restraint."

Johnny closed the distance to her and then paused looking uncertain. His hands moved with the grace of a dancer. *Forgive me, please. Don't want to lose you, too.*

He had lost so much already, his family, his squad, his old life and even his body.

"What did he say?"

"Apologies again."

"All right, Johnny. No more of that." He turned to the sergeant. "Touma isn't yours. She is a translator and a teacher. You need to check that territoriality. You got me?"

Johnny nodded.

The captain swiped both hands over his face and then drew a breath as if preparing to launch a missile strike.

"Johnny, is it true you can't remember the attack?"

Johnny stilled and then glanced at Sonia as he gave a slow nod. Her gaze dropped. Why did she feel like a traitor? He'd never shared any of her secrets, but she had shared his.

"What *do* you remember?"

Johnny began to sign and Sonia translated.

"He says it doesn't make sense because—" she paused waiting for more signs and then continued "—he saw the wolf jump but you stepped in front of him. He saw it bite you." She pointed to her shoulder a moment after Johnny. "Here."

Johnny kept signing and Sonia drew a startled breath at his words.

"Next he was on the helicopter. But, sir, he says he thinks he was still human. He saw you change, sir."

"Maybe he just hadn't changed yet."

Johnny's hands continued to move.

"He said he was uninjured, sir."

"That doesn't make any sense," said the captain. "We both changed. We're both werewolves. I bit him. I saw the report."

Sonia turned to watch Johnny and then began to speak. "He says his memory isn't clear. Maybe he's wrong, but that's what he remembers." She stared at one and then the other. "Haven't you ever talked about this?"

They both shook their heads. *Men,* she thought. They sucked at communication.

"I'm ordering an investigation," said her captain. "Anything else you want to tell me, Johnny, before I send you home?"

Johnny nodded and began to sign. Sonia found her words stuck as she tried to speak. "He says, 'I was prepared to die that day, Mac. But I wasn't prepared for this.'"

Johnny finished by sweeping a hand over his face and form.

Who could have ever been prepared for this?

"Give us a few more days. We are on to something now. The dogs aren't dying and they are still changing. Just hold on."

Sonia watched Johnny lift a fist.

"He says he's holding on."

The captain glanced from one to the other. "Dismissed, you two. Touma, call my wife." He rested a hand on Johnny's shoulder and Johnny pulled him in for a hug. The men clapped each other on the back. She heard the captain say, "I'll make it right for you. Swear to God."

Then the captain was retreating with a hasty step.

Sonia moved in to the place the captain had been.

She wrapped her arms around Johnny's middle. "Let's get you home."

They walked side by side up the narrow winding path. Sonia fell into step with him. Johnny could probably climb the hill in a matter of minutes but he slowed his pace to match hers and did not hurry her.

Once back at his quarters he stopped and grinned at her signing.

We are home.

She cast him a sad smile. "When I was a girl I imagined a house of our own with a swing in the yard. Now I just want a place I can heat without turning on the oven."

Johnny stared down at her. Had she said all that aloud? She'd never told anyone that before.

"I'm sorry. I didn't mean to be such a bummer."

He signed to her. *This home, my home is your home. Make it yours.*

She laughed at that. "Don't be silly."

Captain says you stay here or at base. You choose. Come. Go. Up to you. So, this your home now, too.

It was sweet of him to say. But it wasn't true. A home, well that wasn't just a place it was... Sonia stilled as she realized that a home was where you wanted to be. Where you felt safe and where you were with the ones you cared most about. By that definition she was indeed already home and that scared the crap out of her. She pulled back, staring, stunned, at Johnny.

What?

"It's not my home."

It could be.

"No. I'm not playing house, Wolf. I stay or go at someone else's whim. It's not up to me. So I'm not unpacking or settling in because I know what this is. It's a job."

He cocked his head. *Scared.*

"Hell, yes, I am most of the time."

That night Johnny cooked short ribs, the best she'd ever tasted. After supper he gave her the master bedroom with that enormous bed he never used. She stayed the night and the next morning she woke to an empty house. Johnny left a note that he was training with his assigned friends, the wounded warriors. Beside the note he'd left three things: a glass of juice, a bagel and a magazine with a scrap of paper set between the pages on an article about the decorative touches that make a house a home.

She pushed the magazine aside in favor of the bagel. Damned if she was going to be his interior decorator, too.

Over the course of the next three weeks their lives fell into a pattern. She had the mornings to herself. Sometimes Brianna came for a visit, always keeping a distance and never touching Sonia. The more time she spent with Brianna, the more she liked her. She wasn't frightening or distant, just cautious. She knew the harm she could do to humans by simple contact. Being a vampire that drew energy from other beings made her a prisoner of sorts. She was isolated just like Johnny, but unlike him she had no hope of recovery. Sonia felt terrible as she realized Brianna would spend her life in a self-imposed isolation to protect others from her powers. It would make for a lonely life. Thank goodness that werewolves were immune. That meant she had at least one friend in Johnny and a husband who could hold her in his arms. Better than many. Better than herself, she realized.

Johnny seemed distracted and she knew there was a shadow hanging over them both. He was still in werewolf form. Each day of waiting, the unspoken hung between them. Could they fix him? Because if they couldn't she would rather have him as he was than lose him in a failed attempt to make him human.

Sonia went still as she realized how much she feared the end might come at anytime. What if she lost him, too?

The call came the next morning just as they sat down to breakfast on the patio. The messenger surprised her. It was Brianna who appeared from nowhere on the lawn below the porch.

"They want Johnny at the facility at fourteen hundred to run a trial. And they want you there, as well, to act as his translator." Brianna smiled at Johnny. "This could be it, Johnny. They believe this will change you back."

Johnny signed and Sonia translated.

"He says, 'Will you come?'"

Brianna smiled, but shook her head no. "I'd have to be too close to the others. I'll wait here." She turned to Sonia. "Perhaps you can call me to let me know how it goes and if all is well, perhaps you two might have dinner with us soon?"

Johnny nodded his acceptance.

Brianna lifted a hand in farewell and vanished.

Sonia shivered. "I hate it when she does that." She faced Johnny who offered her a ginger-pineapple muffin grinning broadly.

For her, this news was like preparing to hear a jury verdict and she didn't know if Johnny would win his freedom or be sentenced to death. Either way she'd lose him.

His wide grin faded as he dropped his black jowls over his white teeth.

"What if something goes wrong?"

Already went wrong.

"But something might happen to you."

Worth the risk.

She disagreed but it was not her decision.

"I'd rather have you as you are than see you…" Her words trailed off. She couldn't bring herself to say what was in her mind as if keeping from speaking that word would somehow keep him safe.

Die, he supplied. Then he took her hand before releasing it to sign. *I would rather die than live like this.*

"Is it so bad?" she asked, tears welled in her eyes, making his image swim.

Yes.

Her little fantasy bubble burst. Had she really thought that she and Johnny could live together in this bungalow on the hill forever? That he would be content with her companionship and nothing more?

Chapter 9

Sonia watched as Dr. Zharov stroked his tie speaking to Johnny who lay on the surgical table. There were lead lines from his body to various machines taking his heart rate and reading brain function. The machines scared her silly. Zharov had six assistants. If it was safe, why did he need so many doctors and why was there a crash cart behind the table?

"I've isolated the absent protein from Captain Mac-Connelly's blood. My team inserted the protein into your own blood cells to prevent the kind of rejection you witnessed. The injection works on dogs and monkeys. We have had zero fatalities with this new procedure. I have advised that we wait another two months. That is twice the time that we saw any negative outcomes but unfortunately that is not my call."

Johnny shifted in a nervous gesture as if trying to get comfortable on the stainless-steel surface.

"Do you have any questions?" the doctor asked.

Johnny shook his head and retracted his gums, silently asking for the injection. He had already signed the releases holding the U.S. Marines blameless if anything happened.

Captain MacConnelly stepped forward. "I'm right here, Johnny. Don't worry."

Johnny nodded.

Zharov drew a long breath and lifted the needle. The fluid inside looked like blood. Sonia felt her entire body tense. Would it hurt him?

"Private, please step out," said Zharov.

Johnny grasped her hand and then signed.

"'My translator. She'll report what I feel,'" Sonia said.

Zharov grimaced. "This won't be pleasant, Lam. Just bringing this to your attention."

Johnny held his hand palm up and bent his fingers.

"He's ready," she said, finding her voice as harsh as coarse sandpaper on metal.

The doctor told Johnny to open his mouth and then he stuck the needle into the pink flesh between the upper and lower jaw as if Johnny were a dental patient being prepped for a root canal.

Sonia felt a hysterical bubble of laughter rising inside her. Johnny lifted his hand toward her and she took it gladly. She had the irrational thought that if she just held him tightly enough, it would keep him safe. He squeezed her hand and winked. She squeezed back looking at his familiar yellow eyes as her heart thumped in her throat so hard that it hurt to breathe.

She signed with one hand. *So afraid to lose you.*

I am right here.

What happens next? Do you feel anything?

Johnny's eyes fluttered closed. He drew a long sharp breath. His eyes popped open and Sonia stared. They were no longer yellow, but brown. Deep as dark chocolate, so dark that she could not see his irises.

"Johnny?"

His fingers went slack but she held on. Then his body slumped. His mouth gaped and he gasped as if suddenly struck in the stomach. His back arched.

"Step away." Zharov pushed her aside. Johnny's hand slipped from hers. "The transformation takes several minutes," the doctor said to her.

Sonia was breathing so fast she felt dizzy. But she refused to faint. Johnny's eyes rolled back so she could see only white and his muscles spasmed into one long rigor followed by a seizure.

"Normal," said the doctor staring at the monitor on the EKG. Johnny's heart rate was fast and the usual up and down of the heart monitor's moving line seemed to be flattening out. Sonia looked back to Johnny to see the fur on his arms dropping away in great hairy clumps leaving patches of perfect smooth skin.

"That doesn't happen when I change," said Mac-Connelly to the doctor.

"Normal," he repeated. "Just like the subjects we studied."

"Not normal," said MacConnelly. "I don't lose my coat. It just changes with the rest of me."

"You and Johnny are different. You make the necessary protein to allow you to change back and forth."

Johnny's teeth receded into his bleeding gums as his jaw bone retracted with a cracking sound that turned Sonia's stomach. Johnny arched and the leads attached to his head fell away with the ones on his chest. The straps were now too big as his entire body contracted. Muscles corded. She could see his muscles.

Johnny cried out once and she realized it was a sound she had never heard. A sound of agony but the sound made by a man with the vocal cords of a human being.

She couldn't watch him writhe, so she threw herself across his body, gripping him tight as he bucked beneath her.

"Oh, God, make it stop."

"Get her out of here," ordered Zharov.

Sonia was bustled from the room. The door clicked shut behind her. She stood gasping and panting as she stared through the small window. They surrounded him. Fur fell from the table in black clumps landing at their feet like hair on the floor of a beauty salon.

She could see only the men's backs and the jumping line of the EKG. It was spiking impossibly fast. Her knees gave way. Someone caught her.

"Hold on, Touma." That sounded like the captain's voice, but it was so far away. Why couldn't she see anything?

Dora Morton huddled in the filthy packing crate. Shouting did not bring help. Banging on the solid padded walls brought no rescue. Soundproof they had said and so it was. Dora shifted her weight and groaned. Even her remarkable ability to heal did not bring her full recovery from her capture by the male vampires.

She thought of their pitiless leader. He had malevolent cloudy eyes and freakish white skin that looked waxy as a beluga whale's. Her shoulders shook as she wept. They had taken her in Hawaii. The miles of ocean water had not protected her after all. Her mother had been wrong about that, but not wrong when she had told her daughter that vampires were ugly, but, oh, even her terrible descriptions had not done them justice.

Her poor mother had done nothing but try to protect her child and their terrible secret. And for that, they had attacked her. Had her mother survived?

Dora's clothing still stank of them. But that was better than what awaited her. She'd met a female years ago, one who had been through it. She had explained it to Dora's mother. The ones who hunted her were vampires. Her daughter was a vampire, too, with the power to self-heal and to inspire greatness in mortal men. And she was fast as the wind. But not, she now knew, faster than the males.

Dora shifted in the foam padding and tried again to claw through the steel beneath. The metal burned her skin, forcing her to retreat again to the protection of the foam. Even through the padding, the metal made her head pound and her stomach heave. It was like being buried alive in a crypt. The long rectangular box was large from the outside. She had seen it. But inside it was a steel coffin. They shipped her as a dead body. She wasn't dead. No vampire was. Just other than human. If they went underground, it was only to hide from mortal eyes. That's what the woman had told them. A different species. A parasite. A predator. The bile rose in her throat and she went still.

"Please don't be sick." There was no telling how long she would be in this box. Would the air last? If she survived this trip, when they took her out she knew what would be waiting. The vampire woman had told them.

Ten years in their underground hive. Ten years of indoctrination, bearing children and then, finally, if she learned her lessons well, she might be set out on mortal men as an elite assassin, able to kill merely by spending a night with a man. Ten years without the sun. She'd be twenty-five then.

God help her and God help any female they captured.

Sonia came around to find herself stretched out on an orange vinyl couch. The ceiling tiles and lights shone relentlessly down on her and she blinked as she glanced about. She seemed to be in a waiting room of some kind. What was she doing here?

The answer swept down on her with such a rush that she felt as if she were under attack.

"Johnny!"

Sonia pushed herself up to a seated position and her head swam again. Had she fainted? Heat flooded her face with the shame. She was a marine, for God sakes, but a poor one. Johnny asked her to stay with him and she had fainted like a little girl who was afraid of blood.

But she wasn't afraid of blood. She was afraid of that heart monitor and those electrodes. She scanned the room, surprised to find herself alone. Well, they had more important things to deal with than her. A moment later a marine stepped into the room chewing on a chocolate bar. His eyes snapped to hers as he froze and then glanced behind him. He definitely looked as if she had caught him doing something he wasn't supposed to be doing. Was he told to watch her?

"You're awake," he said, trying for a friendly smile, but the lump of candy bar in his cheek ruined the effect. He quickly choked it down and stowed the rest, torn wrapper and all, in his pants pocket. "I'm Corporal Gail. How are you feeling?"

She'd lost her hat, she realized and her neat bun had come loose. Where were her hair ties? Sonia pushed herself to a stand and then grasped the couch back for a moment as she swayed.

Gail came forward reaching. "Take it easy now."

She lifted a hand to stop him. "Where is Lam?"

"Moved to Recovery."

"Alive?" She held her breath.

He nodded. "Last I knew."

"Where?"

"They told me to send word to the captain when you were awake."

"You do that, Corporal. I'm going to Recovery." She walked past him and she saw his hand snake out. She glared at him. He changed his mind and motioned down the hall. "This way."

He stopped at the recovery room door before the large sign that read Authorized Personnel Only. Do Not Enter.

Sonia pushed the door open and stepped inside. There was activity at only one of the curtained cubbies. She headed for the sound of the beeping heart monitor. Her steady, hurried step slowed as she crossed the large white floor tiles. Her heartbeat pulsed in her ears as she saw Zharov standing at the foot of a bed beside the captain and Major Scofield. All three stood grave and silent. But the monitor beeped so Johnny's heart was beating. Wasn't it?

But what if he was on life support? She imagined the machines keeping him alive and listened for the hiss of a respirator. *Please, God, don't let him be brain-dead.*

Scofield saw her first and offered her a smile, looking both tired and worried. She came to stand beside the major forgetting to salute in her hurry to see Johnny.

Zharov spoke. "None of the test subjects lost consciousness."

She glanced at the bed, her eyes moving up the white sheets that covered him from his feet to his waist. His arms rested still beside his hips, as if placed there. Human arms, arms that were well muscled and had just a dusting of black hair on the forearms. There was a monitor on his index finger and an IV taped to the back of both hands. His broad, muscular chest looked like a circuit box with all the electrodes running every which way. The sight of him so still and helpless made her throat go tight and her breath catch.

They'd managed to put a needle into him, so his skin was normal again. That was good, wasn't it? And Johnny was very definitely a man. He wore no hospital gown and so she noted the clean line of his collar bones as it swept from his muscular shoulders to the V below his Adam's apple. She inhaled quick and sharp as her body reacted to the sight of him. His skin was smooth and slightly lighter than her own light brown Latina coloring. And then she looked at his face, first taking in the dark shock of straight chin length black hair that fell back to the snowy pillows. Her fingers itched to rake through that thick hair. Johnny no longer had a G.I. haircut. She next studied his face. He had a strong jawline, broad forehead and thick arched brows. His eyelashes were full and feathery against his cheeks. His face was square with a long nose and a wide generous mouth. It was a striking face. A stranger's face. Sonia frowned. She knew Johnny well, but she did not know this man.

"It worked," she whispered.

MacConnelly glanced at her and then back at his comrade. "They don't know why he won't wake up."

Zharov tapped the tip of his pen to his lower lip as he

stared at his patient as if he were some puzzle. "There's nothing wrong with him. He's perfect."

The captain motioned toward the bed. "He's out."

"Brain activity normal, everything normal."

"Except his eyes are closed," reminded the captain.

Sonia inched past the men.

Scofield rested a hand on her shoulder. "Why don't you speak to him, Touma. Let him know you're here."

She wanted to say that she didn't know this man. That she wanted Johnny back. But that notion was so completely ridiculous she merely nodded and leaned forward.

"Johnny? You in there? It's time for your lesson."

Johnny did not move but his heart rate increased. She lifted his slack hand and turned it palm up. Then she began to finger spell into his palm as she spoke.

"Come on now. Lesson then swimming."

His eyeballs moved beneath his closed lids and then he went slack again.

"Say something else," ordered Zharov, his body tense, his gaze alert.

Sonia gripped Johnny's hand and leaned forward whispering into his normal, well-shaped ear as she signed into his palm. "Johnny, wake up. You promised to take me dancing."

His fingers threaded with hers. She drew back enough to see his eyes snap open. Brown eyes, she realized, deep, dark, lovely eyes. Where were the yellow ones she had grown so accustomed to?

He seemed to be struggling to focus but at last he flicked from her to the men behind her and then back to rest on her face. The corner of his mouth twitched and her stomach fluttered. Her visceral reaction to him so startled her that she had to press a hand to her chest in a vain attempt to slow her racing heart. She reminded herself that this was Johnny.

Johnny's voice came as a hoarse whisper, his vocal cords likely weak from disuse. "Is it done? Am I human?"

"Yes. And as soon as you are up to it, you are taking me out on a date."

He lifted their clasped hands and stared at his own. "That's my hand." He pressed his free hand to his chest and then glanced up to see the three sentinels at his foot rail.

"Welcome back, son," said Major Scofield.

"I told you I could do it," said Zharov.

"Johnny." The captain's voice cracked as he moved up the opposite side of the bed. Sonia stepped back as the two men embraced. Johnny's finger monitor slipped off and the machine shrieked. The two drew apart and Zharov replaced the monitor and reset the machine.

Johnny turned to his doctor. "When can I get out of here?"

Sonia laughed and brushed the tears from her face. Her captain's Adam's apple bobbed.

"Tomorrow," said Zharov.

"Tonight," said Johnny.

"It's nearly midnight, son," said the major. "You need sleep and look at Touma. She's practically swaying on her feet."

Johnny looked at her, really looked. She pushed her hair back from her face and smiled.

"You all right?" His voice was rich and low and did funny things to her insides.

She nodded and dropped her gaze but her skin still tingled from that look.

"Tired?"

"We're all tired, Johnny." She signed, *Stay the night. I'll stay too.*

He pursed his lips and looked to Zharov. "I'm leaving tomorrow. I have a date."

Johnny grinned at Sonia and her stomach did a funny little quiver. She had been fond of the wolf. But what she was feeling for Sergeant John Lam was something else entirely. Something strong and exciting and scary stirred inside her. Funny to be more afraid of him now than when he was a werewolf.

She'd failed to keep her distance from him then. What chance did she have now? But a promise was a promise and he was taking her out tomorrow night.

She needed a dress.

Sonia startled awake at the alarm, confused by her surroundings and disoriented with fatigue. The barracks, she realized. Johnny insisted she find a bed and it didn't seem right to sleep at his place any longer. He wasn't there and when he returned, he'd be a man. That changed everything.

He was a man again, and one that made her insides curl up like a ribbon on a birthday gift. She'd seen his photo, of course. The captain had showed it to her, but that photo wasn't Johnny, or a least not this Johnny. The boy in the photo had been a young marine before he'd ever seen action. Then his face was more angular, his body more lithe. Now his mouth was pure sensuality. And his body had bulk, mass and a power that she suspected came from his werewolf side. And his hair, well instead of the short bristle of a man in uniform, he now had long sweeping straight black hair that reminded her of an Asian Antonio Banderas. It was long enough to draw back at the nape of his neck, a look that she found sexy as hell.

But there was something else, something dark. His eyes reflected a palpable danger. Time, experience and his injuries had changed him. He had transformed to human form but held on to that sharp edge of the wolf.

Sonia stretched and rose with the other women in her barracks. They went about their business casting her odd looks as if they'd found a toadstool growing in the center of the room. She had the fastest shower of her life and then reported to the medical facility, feeling oddly uncomfortable in her fatigues. But Johnny wasn't there. They said they had him running some physical tests and she was not going to see him until they released him at seventeen hundred hours. She couldn't believe they were releasing him at all. He'd left her a note that was written in a crisp, bold, unfamiliar hand. His transformation would change so many things between them. She felt lost and sick to her stomach as she read that he would pick her up for their date at eighteen hundred and to leave him a message as to where to find her. She scribbled her reply on the bottom of the page explaining that she would be at Brianna's home, then returned the note with the messenger. Then she checked to see if there was anything she was supposed to be doing. No one knew.

She was Johnny's translator, only he didn't need one any longer.

Sonia recognized that she was about as necessary as a fur coat on a weasel. John Lam no longer needed a teacher or a companion. He no longer needed his private entourage and he no longer needed her. How long until they sent her packing? Suddenly the nervous excitement of their date was replaced with a twisting anxiety. She knew how things worked. She had top secret clearance for a job that had just disappeared. What would they do with her now?

Sonia left the base and walked up the hill to the home of Brianna and Captain MacConnelly. Brianna greeted her warmly and asked for news of Johnny. Sonia told her what she could and right there in the middle of her description of Johnny's transformation she began to cry. She sat on Brianna's white couch beside the arrangement of birds of paradise as her shoulders jumped like a semiautomatic rifle, her breath coming in short uneven gasps. Brianna did not come to sit beside her or wrap a comforting arm around her shoulders.

Sonia's embarrassment grew as she continued until she glanced up and saw Brianna pale and wide-eyed, gripping her hands together so tightly that her knuckles had gone white. Then Sonia recalled that Brianna couldn't go to her, couldn't offer physical comfort without also causing Sonia physical harm. Brianna nudged a box of tissues in her direction and then fetched a glass of water.

Her hostess set the water on the black lacquer coffee table before Sonia. "Travis says Johnny is doing really well today. Strong as a bull, that's part of the condition. They retain that strength, acute hearing and enhanced sense of smell even when in human form. But no one is sure if Johnny has reversed back into human form permanently or if he will be able to change between forms. I know he still smells like a wolf."

Sonia lifted her face from the tissues and gave a questioning look.

"It is one of my powers, the sense of smell. I can also see in the dark."

Sonia knew her eyes must be the size of saucers but

she could think of nothing to say, so she reached for her water and took a sip.

"Did you see him?"

Brianna rubbed her palms together and stared absently at the floor and then met Sonia's eyes, forcing a smile. "Last night. No one saw me. He seemed human but there is that darkness clinging to him. I only feel that around werewolves. Travis says that it is because they are my natural enemy that I sense them. In any case, no one is sure if it is possible to make a werewolf truly human again."

Sonia's disquiet grew as the unease rippled over her like a hot breeze and she availed herself of a tissue to wipe her eyes.

"Travis is going to try to teach Johnny how to transform today. At first it takes a few minutes and it is not pleasant to watch.

Sonia remembered witnessing Johnny's change and shivered.

"Travis can change very fast now. I asked him once if it hurt and he said, 'Hell, yes.'"

"If Johnny learns to change at will then he won't need sign language anymore," said Sonia.

"That's right," she said brightly. "He won't." Brianna's smile faded as she regarded Sonia's glum expression. "Oh, I see. Has anyone spoken to you regarding your future?"

Sonia's breath hitched. "Do you know something?"

"No. But I understand your concern."

Sonia shifted uncomfortably on the pristine white sofa. With no visitors it might always look this sterile and new, she realized. There were no children here, no pets, no life other than the vampire and her werewolf husband.

"Johnny seems very comfortable with you and you seem fond of him. I don't think his new condition will change that."

"It will if I'm reassigned. I don't expect them to keep me here with no job to do."

There was an awkward pause and Sonia realized Brianna was glancing at the door. She hurried to get to the reason for her visit before this strange woman sent her away.

"We have a date tonight. I promised him that when he changed back he could take me dancing."

Brianna smiled brightly. "How romantic." Her smile flickered and faded. "But I didn't think marines were allowed to date one another."

And they weren't. Sonia groaned. Why hadn't she remembered that rule when she had promised Johnny that they would go dancing.

She cradled her head in her hands and exhaled. "He was so angry after the last lab failure. I was just trying to cheer him up." It wasn't exactly true. She was trying to give them both hope.

"Well, I suppose you could get permission. Does Travis know?"

"He must. I was talking about it when Johnny was unconscious." Sonia wondered how she was going to get out of this one and then felt a sharp tug in her heart. That's when she realized she didn't want to get out of it. She wanted to go out with Johnny so much it hurt. She lifted her gaze to Brianna issuing a silent plea.

"I'll call Travis. These are hardly ordinary circumstances. He'll have to understand."

When Sonia didn't return her smile Brianna cocked her head.

Sonia rose and took a step toward Brianna, thinking to throw her arms about her and the vampire lifted a hand again to stop her. Sonia halted.

"I'm sorry. I forgot again." Just thinking of going out with Johnny made her heart ache and her blood rush and she knew that marines weren't allowed to fraternize, but she was thinking of fraternizing him right out of the clothing that he now needed. Her original problem now rose in her mind. She rubbed her neck and said, "I have nothing to wear."

"I'll handle that. Is that the only reason for the long face?"

Sonia shook her head. "He's so different, like another person."

Brianna's brows swept lower. "Sonia, I never knew him before he was a werewolf. But I know he is the same inside."

"But not outside. You've seen him. He's gorgeous. And he doesn't need a translator and as for a date, he could have his pick."

"And he picked you."

"I don't know what will happen next."

"If you mean what will happen tonight, that will be up to you. He's been in wolf form a long time, but he is still a gentleman. You only need to say no."

If she *could* say no. Johnny was so appealing it frightened her more than the first time she'd seen him.

"Sonia?"

She glanced up and noticed that she had torn several tissues into tiny little pieces.

"Oh! I'm sorry. I'll clean that up."

"You *have* dated men before. Haven't you?"

She didn't really consider them dates. She'd met men in a variety of places. She'd even slept with a few. But she never went back for seconds and made sure that they couldn't, either.

"Not exactly a date."

"What exactly?"

Sonia held it in a while longer and then decided that Brianna was as good a sounding board as she'd likely find.

"I'm not a virgin. But I've never had a steady boyfriend by choice." She was careful and always very clear that she was not interested in a relationship. In that way she had satisfied her needs. "I don't like the idea of being trapped in a bad relationship and I don't like the idea of being vulnerable. I've got baggage. Bad home, yada, yada. Anyway, it feels safer to just keep to myself but sometimes…" She glanced up and saw the pain reflected in Brianna's eyes. If anyone understood the need to keep apart, it was this vampire. She chose her own company, as well, but for different reasons, selfless reasons.

Brianna nodded. "Funny, before I knew, I was just the opposite. I'd do just about anything to switch places with you, be able to have friends, go out in public. I'm lucky my husband is immune or I'd have no one. And here you are able to make connections and you don't."

"Maybe I just haven't found the right guy."

"Or you prefer to be safe and alone. But Johnny slipped under your radar because he wasn't really a man, more like a nine-foot Labrador Retriever right?"

"I never thought of him like that."

"Well you clearly didn't see him as a man or you would have kept him at arm's length."

"That wasn't possible with Johnny. He wouldn't… I didn't… Well, he was very stubborn. And he knows stuff about me that no one else does."

"You can trust him with those secrets, Sonia. He'll never betray them." She rubbed her hands together in anticipation. "So, what time is the date?"

Sonia glanced at her watch. "At six. I hope you don't mind, I told him to pick me up here."

"We have to get you ready!"

Brianna herded Sonia into the bedroom and had her try on a series of a half-dozen dresses. Demure midnight blue, sleek short black, shimmering silver sequins, elegant gold halter, regal purple, a crazy black and white shredded silk number and then a slim, high-waisted poppy-red cocktail dress.

"Why do you have so many dresses when you…" Sonia stopped herself too late.

"When I don't go out?" Brianna's smile never reached her eyes. "Travis does my shopping. He likes to see me in dresses. We have date night at home, order in."

Sonia thought her captain would also like to show off his beautiful wife. But he couldn't.

"That's the one," said Brianna pointing at the red. "It looks lovely with your skin tone and with a red lip you'll look like the kind of woman that every marine in the world wants to take out for dinner and dancing."

What kind of woman, Sonia wondered, did Johnny want her to be? As she stared at her reflection in the full-length mirror it suddenly hit home that Johnny had not been with a woman for many months. Did he hope that she and he… Sonia blanched, not because she could not imagine sleeping with Johnny but because she could imagine it in great detail and it made her skin flush and her body grow damp.

She wanted to sleep with him. What she didn't want was a relationship because a relationship meant trust and she didn't trust her heart to anyone. Besides, it couldn't last. He was a war hero and she was, well, the opposite of all that. Johnny didn't need her anymore and she'd be stupid to let herself need him. Sonia knew she was many things but stupid was not one of them. Realist, pessimist, whatever you called it, she knew it wouldn't work out between them. So she told herself to keep it light and casual. So why did her heart ache with the dread at their impending breakup? And how did she get out of here with her dignity? She didn't do relationships, but now, because of her work with Johnny, she already had one and it was about to get complicated. Johnny's condition had caused her to lose her secrets. He knew her deep down and now he was a man, an alluring man who wanted to take her out.

She closed her eyes and imagined Johnny's hand low at the center of her back.

Brianna's voice came from behind her. "Sonia, are you all right? You look a little flushed."

She met Brianna's gaze in the mirror. "What if he wants to…"

Brianna's eyebrows lifted. "It's up to you to decide if and when you and Johnny do more than dance." She turned toward the door and paused in the opening. "Feel free to use any of the makeup in that drawer."

"Yes, ma'am."

The flutter of excitement in her stomach told her she really wanted to have Johnny's arms about her and not just on the dance floor. But she'd never been with someone she really cared about.

Brianna returned with three perfumes. Sonia gave her a panicky look.

"It's only a date," said Brianna.

"Yeah. Just a date."

Chapter 10

Just a date, Sonia thought as she returned to Brianna's home hours later to prepare for her evening with Johnny.

But it was more, much, much more. Sonia felt the truth of that in her heart. He was tall, dangerous and his very presence threatened her nice, safe world. And now that he was human, Johnny stirred all her sexual fantasies.

He'd come through this nightmare. But his experiences must have scorched him. Had it been too much? Had they ruined him the way the drink had ruined her mother?

Some hurts are too big to heal, her mother had once said. *Your only chance is to drown them.*

Weren't Johnny's sorrows bigger than her mother's, bigger than her own? She knew Johnny and respected him. But now he was human and her confidence fled.

Whatever happened tonight, there would be consequences. She just didn't know what they would be.

Sonia went to work applying eyeliner and curling her eyelashes. Then she applied a red lip that made her mouth look lush. Brianna insisted she tuck the tube of lipstick in her borrowed clutch.

When her makeup was finished, Sonia began pacing in her silver high heels, borrowed from Brianna, as well. They shared a similar foot size, dress size and an affinity for werewolves.

But Brianna had sought and had achieved a lasting relationship with the captain. That took a kind of optimism Sonia had never had.

She paused to regard her reflection in a full length mirror. Their dress size might be the same but their body type was not. Sonia was sure that the dress that looked elegant on Brianna's willowy form but it looked like an invitation on her curves.

What would Johnny think? He'd seen her in a bathing suit, but not in makeup and red lipstick. He deserved a pretty, feminine date. Besides, Sonia wasn't a girl to be dressed in pink, but neither was she the confident sexy woman who stared back. She'd never wore red before in her life and now she knew why. Brianna's reflection appeared behind her in the mirror. Sonia met her gaze but did not return her encouraging smile.

"I feel like the cape that the matador waves before a bull," she said to Brianna.

Brianna chuckled. "Yes, I can see that. I reached Travis. He's given his permission." Brianna searched Sonia's expression and opened her mouth to say something before cocking her head. "They're here."

Sonia stopped as if suddenly frozen and her heart jolted along at a gallop.

"I don't hear them."

Brianna shrugged and tapped one ear. "Super hearing," she muttered and headed for the door but she paused close to Sonia and smiled. "Have a wonderful evening and please come and see me again soon. You're welcome anytime."

Sonia felt a welling of gratitude and a sense of how very few people Brianna would welcome into her home.

"I will. And thank you for the dress and, well, everything."

Brianna smiled, reached toward Sonia and then drew her hands back, folding them tightly before her. "I hope they play a slow dance." Then she opened the door to an empty driveway, but a few moments later a Jeep appeared. Brianna waved her inside. "Go into the bedroom. Make an entrance for goodness' sake."

Sonia did as she was told but watched from the window as the captain emerged from the driver's seat, wearing his beige cammies. Her gaze flipped to the passenger seat but the glare prevented her from seeing Johnny until he stepped out. His dark head appeared first, his hair pulled back at the nape of his neck. Her breath caught at the sight of him. Tiny sparks of electricity fired inside her belly as he straightened. He was still tall, over six feet, surely. The last time she'd seen him he was in a hospital bed attached to various machinery. Now he stood in a charcoal-gray suit and crisp white dress shirt that made his skin look dark by comparison. His tie was red and he stroked it once as he glanced toward the house. She held her breath and backed away from the window. Had he seen her? Sonia checked her lipstick and added more. Her lips and mouth felt so dry all of a sudden. Then she checked the contents of her borrowed bag and found everything in order, brush, lipstick, tissues, money, credit cards and— Her fingers brushed something cold and unfamiliar. She drew out a green foil packet and realized it was a condom. Several condoms that Brianna had added to the bag. Sonia pictured sliding the rubber sheath over Johnny's erection and felt dizzy all of a sudden. She sank to the bed and fanned her hot skin belatedly realizing she held the spread of three condoms like a fan. She tucked them deep into the purse and exhaled.

"Just a date."

There was a gentle tap on the door. Brianna stepped in and Sonia made an attempt to fiddle with the silver buckle on the high-heeled sandals.

"He brought flowers!" the vampire squealed in a hushed voice. "Red roses. Are you ready? Sonia, pinch your cheeks you've gone pale again."

"First time I've ever gone out with a man who knows my last name."

Brianna's brow wrinkled and she chuckled, then glanced at Sonia and stopped as she must have realized Sonia wasn't joking. "Well, not the only first tonight, I suppose." She worried one hand with the other until Sonia stood and made for the open door. She preceded Brianna out and found the men in the living room. Johnny spoke to the captain who spotted her first and frowned. Her commanding officer did not look happy as he shook his head and glanced to his wife who shrugged. Johnny stopped speaking and turned in her direction. He was so handsome in his new suit she felt her throat close. She stopped and Johnny came to her, hands extended and a smile growing on his generous mouth.

"Sonia, you look so beautiful."

She didn't need to pinch her cheeks because she felt

the heat flooding them now. "And you look very handsome." She reached for his tie, straightened the knot then slid her fingers down the silken fabric. When she lifted her gaze to his she found his eyes blazing and his stare intense. He leaned in and kissed her cheek, lingering as his warm mouth brushed her skin. She flushed right down to her toes. His rich spicy scent lingered after he drew away.

"Don't forget these," said Brianna handing the roses over to Johnny.

He presented them to her and she cradled them as if she was Miss America. The florist had arranged them in a spray intended for carrying and had mixed in just enough tropical greenery that she would not forget that she was now on an island paradise.

"They are lovely, Johnny. Thank you."

"Ready?" He offered his arm.

She clamped the tiny silver shoulder bag against her side and nodded, wondering why all she could think about was those damned green foil packets. Brianna handed her a brightly colored shawl at the door and kissed Johnny goodbye. The captain drew her aside and leaned in.

"Put this phone in your purse. Call me directly if you need me. I'll be close and get him back here safe." He straightened and gave her a forced smile.

Sonia swallowed back her anxiety, gripping the phone. He'd be close? What did that mean exactly?

Johnny helped her over the rough ground and guided her into the Jeep, shutting the door and then dashing about the front with such speed she could almost believe he was half vampire.

The captain stood stiff with disapproval as Brianna waved from the steps. Johnny helped Sonia into the passenger seat and then took the wheel, backing out and then left the captain and his vampire wife behind as they headed down the mountain. The silence between them was new and unfamiliar. Finally she asked about his day and discovered that he had failed at changing back to his werewolf form.

"What does that mean, exactly?"

"Mac thinks I don't want to change. Might be right, too."

Their conversation died away again. Sonia stared out the window and noticed they were not heading for the security checkpoint. When it became clear that they were heading across base she had a sudden flash of panic that they were aiming for the mess hall, a move that neither of them would ever live down, but Johnny drove them to the docks and carefully escorted her onto one of the boats where Sergeant Domingo Cavillo, one of Johnny's exercise companions, ferried them the ten miles to West Maui and the oceanfront resort where he had made reservations. She wondered if the sergeant would wait for them, but her stiletto heel no sooner hit the dock than the boat headed away.

"I can call him for a pick up."

Can? She lifted an eyebrow because she realized that he could just as easily not call him for a pick up and they were at a resort with palm trees, blooming jasmine, newlyweds and many, many vacant bedrooms. The possibilities stirred her blood and she stopped walking as she glanced up into Johnny's intent brown eyes. The captain wanted her to get John back safe while she wanted to wake to mimosas and a rumpled bed.

His mouth stretched into a wicked smile and she forgot how to breathe. He placed a hand on her lower back, ushering her along as she tried not to dwell on the warmth of his hand or the strength of his graceful stride, slowed now to match her smaller one.

They walked slowly along the dock in the early evening, past the snorkelers on the beach and the poolside restaurant.

"Lots of honeymooners here," he commented, his voice and his implication making her skin tingle.

His hand slid from her back and he offered his elbow. She clung to his arm more tightly as they left the dock for the brick walkway. Beneath the fine fabric of his jacket she could feel the steel of his muscles.

They strolled past the bar and families enjoying casual dining. Johnny was the only person in a suit and their appearance turned more than one head.

"We're overdressed," she whispered.

"We're not eating here."

Inside the hotel lobby Johnny strolled with the casualness of a confident man. He nodded at the concierge and continued on through the etched glass entrance of the Waterfront Steakhouse, pausing to open the door for her and then again at the hostess station. Johnny spoke to a young woman wearing a red hibiscus in her hair while Sonia admired the tropical fish in a large saltwater tank.

A hostess escorted them to the restaurant's interior and a table with a killer view of the sun setting over the Pacific Ocean. She even took Sonia's flowers and returned with them in a lovely arrangement for their table.

Johnny glanced at the wine list and then set it aside asking for sparkling water and two nonalcoholic frozen drinks. The drinks arrived a few moments later with huge glasses topped with orchids and a skewer of fresh fruit. She sipped a sweet icy strawberry drink and smiled up at Johnny.

"Perfect."

He nodded. They watched the sun dip toward the water, a huge orange ball that gradually melted into the sea. As it set, the sky blazed with streaks of orange fire that turned the clouds violet and gold.

"I've never seen anything so beautiful," she whispered.

"I have," he said and she glanced up to see he was staring at her.

The compliment pleased her and she beamed. "You've seen me before."

"Not at sunset. Not at my table in a dress like that."

"I liked the meals you cooked for us at your bungalow."

"I'll be glad to cook for you for as long as you like."

"That's good news because you've spoiled me for the mess hall forever."

The silence between them seemed more complicated now and she was relieved to see the appetizers arrive. She tried the potstickers which turned out to be delicious little dumplings with a salty brown sauce. She'd never had to struggle to find a topic of conversation with Johnny before, but as she crunched her way through her salad she stretched to think of something, anything to say. The tension between them made her stomach ache and she had trouble eating the special, a pecan-crusted tilapia fillet with a mango and pineapple chutney. Johnny's appetite was epic as he polished off his favorite, very rare steak and potatoes and the entire bread basket.

During the main course, the recorded music ceased as a band set up on the large balcony. The steel drums' ringing rhythms drifted in on the Pacific breeze, exotic and alluring. Still she wished they were back at Johnny's place. Alone, instead of here in the open with his goons across the room watching her as if she and Johnny were on pay-per-view.

"You seem nervous," he said.

She snapped her eyes back to him, wondering how it was possible that he hadn't seen his wounded warriors yet. "I suppose I am."

"Why?"

She watched Corporal Del Tabron give her a small nod before lifting his beer glass. They knew she was aware of them.

"Hmm? Oh, I never really go on dates. Just one-nighters mostly. I don't even tell them my real name." This was met with silence and she snapped her gaze to his to see his brow low over his dark eyes and a definite edge of danger in his expression. What the hell had she been thinking?

But she hadn't been. She'd been so busy looking at his wounded warriors, she hadn't censored her reply.

"Sonia, what does that mean?"

Her shoulders dropped with her spirits.

"Just that. I told you I don't like people. I don't trust them. They either want too much or I want too much. Relationships are complicated. I like to keep things simple."

"You mean sex."

She pursed her lips for one long intake and exhale. Then she answered. "Yeah. Sex. Sex with guys I don't know and never wanted to know. Scratch the itch. Move on."

She'd shocked him speechless.

"You think I'm bad."

"I think you're broken."

"Yeah. That's about right."

Right then, in the middle of his deciding she was as

dysfunctional as a car on blocks, the band played their first slow dance.

Perfect timing, she thought.

"Listen, John, you can take me home. I'll understand."

Instead, he set aside his napkin and offered his hand. Sonia sat poised between wanting to leave the room and wanting to be wrapped in John's strong arms.

"May I have this dance?"

"Are you sure?"

"Never more certain."

She accepted his hand, surprised at the thrill of excitement that rippled from the point of contact.

He walked her past the other tables to the dance floor surrounded by brightly burning torches. When they got there, they were by no means the only couple enjoying the trade winds and starry night.

Johnny laced his fingers with hers and splayed his other hand on her back before sweeping them into a slow circle.

Magic, she thought, as she moved in time with his steps on the most romantic of all dance floors. So why was her heart jackhammering so loudly that she could barely hear the music? He didn't draw her closer, just moved with a grace that rippled with sensuality. She was acutely aware of the sway of his hips. The second dance was slower and couples around them seemed to melt into their partner's embrace, moving in perfect synchronization, obviously relaxed and at ease in each other's company. Sonia felt awkward and uncertain as she edged closer resting her cheek on his shoulder. She was unwilling to press her body to his mainly because she wanted to so badly. This was a dangerous road, she realized. Her skin tingled and her breasts ached.

She knew the signs. Sonia sighed as his cheek brushed the top of her head and closed her eyes. Sonia let the music and John Lam take her deeper into the enchantment of the night.

She wanted Johnny's body, but in the morning there would be no escaping him because unlike the rest of the men she had slept with, Johnny knew where she lived. He knew other things, too, secret intimate things. Things she never expected another person in this world to know about her. She shivered in excitement as she rocked her hips from side to side, matching his lead, wanting to let him lead.

What was she doing and where would this end?

Johnny breathed in her fragrance. The tiny capillaries beneath her skin opened wide bringing a beguiling pink flush to her cheeks and the scent of the rose petals that she had carried all the way from the base. Johnny's sense of smell remained acute and despite his inability or unwillingness to change, he felt the wolf still inside him. It hadn't disappeared as the doctors feared. It had just gone deep.

How long had he dreamed of this night? How many nights had he imagined holding her in his arms and having her see the man that he had always been instead of that monster that still lurked within?

Now she was here with him but instead of the easy falling together he had dreamed it would be, Sonia revealed a new hesitancy in conversation and a reluctance that troubled him. Why had she never had a second date and what did that mean for them? He knew her name. He knew her secrets. He knew Sonia and he wanted more. Would she be willing to sleep with him knowing that she couldn't just disappear in the morning?

He scented her arousal but also her fear. Now that he was a man, she no longer trusted him. Or did she just not find him appealing. Didn't she like his looks?

Every time he moved closer, she stepped back. His hips were a tantalizing inch from hers, her breasts nearly brushed against his chest but she kept just out of reach. It was all he could do not to drag her against him. He didn't want to frighten her but he'd never wanted a woman more. Not just any woman. He wanted this woman.

Johnny had broken off with his high school steady when he joined up and had only had occasional companionship since then. Now all he could think about was kissing Sonia everywhere and of seeing her lying naked in his bed by candle light and then again in the morning, her long hair tangled in the rumbled bedding. His insides squeezed and the steady thrum of blood beat insistently within him. He wanted this woman.

He glanced down to see her eyes closed as her cheek rested on his chest. Even with her eyes closed, her expression looked pained as if she wanted to be anywhere but here. Well, that was exactly what he wanted, but now he worried that Sonia did not imagine this night ending as he did. He glanced around the room, seeing other couples, ladies clinging to their men, pressing hip-to-hip or gazing longingly into each other's eyes.

Honeymooners, he realized, now recognizing his mistake. He'd taken a woman who was terrified of commitment on their first date and dropped her into the center of a room full of committed couples. How stupid could he get?

She didn't press herself against him like the other women draped like boneless cats against their new husbands. Sonia wasn't a bride in the arms of the man she loved. She was a young marine on her first date with a werewolf. It was a wonder she didn't fly screaming from the room. And then it hit him. She couldn't. She couldn't say no to this date any more than she could quit teaching him. She was stuck because she'd robbed a house, so now if she didn't make him happy, they'd send her back where she came from. Back to jail, back to that damned dog cage.

No wonder she barely touched her dinner.

Suddenly Johnny felt sick. He didn't want her here against her will. He drew back.

The song ended and the band played a faster number, with steel drums and a Caribbean sound. Sonia looked up at him with eyes that asked for rescue. He felt the same aching need he always felt when she looked at him and then as now he wouldn't act on it because he'd never know if she wanted to or felt she must. He knew she'd do anything to keep from going back to jail, even, apparently, go out with him.

He hated the idea of taking her upstairs now. Would she look at him as she did on the dance floor as if he were some distasteful obligation to be discharged as quickly as possible? He'd bought her flowers, put on a suit and she'd dressed in red. But it was all a lie.

"Are you all right?" she asked as he held her chair back at their table.

"Yes." He said it a little too quickly.

"You look as if you are in pain." Her eyes went wide. "Johnny, you'd know if you were about to change. Wouldn't you? Because the captain said…"

God, he hadn't even thought of that. No wonder the captain and the major had been so against his coming out and why she was tense as a newbie at boot camp. Why had they let him go? He had another thought and glanced about the room, finding the bar and three familiar backs perched like crows on a wire. He met the eyes of Carver, Zeno and Kiang in the mirror. Apparently the major hadn't let him off the leash after all. They'd just made it a little longer. His mood darkened. Had they enjoyed his awkward little dance with Sonia?

Sonia noticed the direction of his gaze and he heard her groan.

His gaze narrowed on the men.

"Yeah. Maybe I'll just go say hello."

She clasped his arm and he stopped as suspicion grew.

"Why don't we just order our desert?"

He was in a fishbowl. Had anything really changed?

"Did you know?"

She lowered the menu. "They're here for your protection and to protect all the people here."

"Did you all think I'd go crazy?"

She lowered the menu. "They can't know what will happen next any more than you do."

He knew she was right but the situation now stuck in his throat like an overlarge piece of steak. "I wanted to be alone with you."

"Then we should have stayed at your place on Molokai." She reached across the table and rested her hand on his. "Johnny, we've had a lovely meal and you are an excellent dancer. Let's have desert."

"And then head back?"

"If you'd like."

Johnny glanced at his three escorts. His bodyguards and the realization that Sonia might not be here by choice made the evening about as romantic as a frontal assault. Johnny ordered an espresso and Sonia had a crème brûlée. She seemed relieved to be escorted back to the dock where the boat he hadn't called was waiting. Johnny wanted to kick someone's ass. Instead, he helped Sonia aboard and then handed her the vase of red roses. He felt stupid and betrayed all at once.

Sonia wrapped the shawl over her shoulders and huddled about her flowers protecting them from the wind.

Back on Molokai, he drove her to the barracks and walked her to the entrance.

"John, I know that the evening didn't go as you would have liked. But I had a lovely time and I want to thank you."

He stared down at her, his heart so full of hope and despair he could not even summon a single word.

"Please be patient with me. I just need a little time."

"Time," he parroted. How much time? Time to do what? He'd had too much damned time—time alone, time as a monster, time with her when she couldn't see how he felt. Now she wanted more of it. Finally, he nodded because he had no other choice. "All right."

"Will I see you tomorrow?"

"Sure. Come up in the afternoon. You can teach me some more signs." Like frustrated, sullen and pissed-off, he thought.

She lifted on her toes and tried to kiss him. He turned so her lips met his cheek accepting it for what it was, a mercy kiss.

"Thank you for the flowers."

He made a fast retreat and headed off base. Behind him he saw the lights of a Jeep which he had no trouble ditching. He ended up in one of the three places he'd heard his groupies mention and just as he'd expected there were single women at the bar, working girls who didn't care who you were and didn't expect you to be patient. He looked over the bunch and picked the one

who had dark hair and mocha skin. She was native but
she had Sonia's coloring. She smiled an invitation but
Johnny recognized the feral glint in her eye, the look
of a wolf hunting.

"Hi, handsome," she said. "You want some company?"

He stood his ground and she slid from the stool and
sidled over, swaying her hips as she approached. The
moment she brushed her hand over his cheek he knew
coming here was a mistake. He thought this was what
he needed, one of them beneath him. He'd just close his
eyes and pretend it was Sonia. Now instead of the flush
of heat and lust, he felt stone cold.

"Damn it," he muttered.

"You got a ride, soldier? We could take a ride." She
licked her sticky pink lips. "Or take a walk in the moonlight."

He could have her and be done. But somehow he
knew he'd never be done. Not since he'd first set eyes
on Sonia. The woman wrapped her arms around his
neck and pressed her small breasts against him. Ciga-
rette smoke clung to her hair and her soft body only reminded him of how Sonia held back. Johnny dragged
the woman's arms from his neck because he didn't want
her. He wanted the woman he'd been dreaming of and
lusting after for weeks and weeks. He'd spent too many
nights imagining Sonia to settle for this clinging woman
who smelled like stale beer and male sweat. He pulled
her off and moved to the other end of the bar.

He didn't want sex with this stranger. He wanted
Sonia.

She'd asked him to be patient. Damn her.

He ordered a whiskey and then threw it back. The

burn in his throat was familiar but there was no second kick.

The front door opened and in walked his captain, dressed in jeans, running shoes and a marine sweatshirt on inside out. Johnny just knew he'd gotten him out of bed, that nice warm bed he shared with his bride. Johnny snorted, not feeling one bit guilty. If he had to sleep alone, the captain could, too.

"Waste of money," said Mac, nodding toward the empty whiskey glass.

Johnny stared sullenly at him.

"You can finally talk and you got nothing to say?"

Oh, no. He had plenty. But he was pretty sure the captain didn't want to hear it.

"You remember when I found you and Brianna together in my bed?" asked Johnny.

Mac winced. Suddenly it was the captain who had nothing to say. He ordered two beers just to have something to do and pushed one at Johnny before taking a long pull of his own. Finally he banged the long-necked bottle on the bar and turned to him. "I remember."

"I was pissed she picked you. Hoped she had feelings for me but she couldn't see me so I never had a chance. Not with my…condition."

"Johnny…." Mac stopped there and had another swallow of his beer.

"Did you pick Sonia to be my companion? To keep me company while I waited for this?" he swept a hand over his form.

Mac's fingers tightened on the neck of his bottle and his jaw muscles twitched. "What if I did? She kept you from using that gun, didn't she?"

Johnny scowled.

"You think I didn't know about it? Well, I did."

Johnny released his beer and made several gestures.

Mac watched in silence and then said, "Say it to my face."

"I said you're a fucking asshole and Sonia is treating me as if I've got the clap."

Mac stared at Johnny's hands. "What's the sign for clap?" he asked.

"You have to finger spell it."

Mac exhaled through his nose and made a face as if he didn't have the time or energy. Johnny finished his beer in several long swallows. Mac signaled the bartender by raising two fingers then returned his attention to Johnny.

"She's treating you like someone she just met. John, look at you." Mac gestured toward the mirror. "She doesn't know you."

"The hell she doesn't."

"You look different. Give her time. She asked you to be patient, didn't she?"

Johnny slammed his empty bottle on the table. "How do you know that?" Had he bugged the restaurant? Was their date scripted?

"She said it right in front of me." He rubbed the back of his neck. "Did I have eyes in that room? Yes. I couldn't let you go out alone. There are too many variables. You don't know how to control the wolf yet. Strong emotion triggers the change. I couldn't have you going all furry in public."

"Strong emotion? Then I ought to be wearing a fur coat right now."

"Listen, John, I'll teach you how to control it. You'll get the hang of it and if Sonia is right for you, she'll come around."

"What if she doesn't?"

"Well, she won't if you keep acting like an asshole and chase her away. Do you know about her mom?"

Johnny nodded.

"Her sister?"

Another nod.

"Then you know she's cautious. So what is wrong with going slow? Her usual M.O. is a one-night stand. Would you rather have her only once. Slow might mean she's, I don't know, interested. So go slow."

"Do I have a choice?"

"Yeah, you do. Go slow or fuck it up. Now can we go home?"

Chapter 11

Johnny woke alone in his king-size bed to the ringing phone. The bedsheets still smelled of Sonia, who had slept here, just not with him. He checked the phone's screen and saw Mac's image. He groaned, almost wishing he was in wolf form just so he wouldn't have to pick up the damned phone.

He was at the medical center an hour later. Despite Johnny's best efforts, he was still unable to change to wolf form. The team of doctors revealed that some of the earlier canine test subjects faired the same. Most changed back, some didn't and they were at a loss to determine why. His sight and vision remained acute. He picked up an uneasy vibe from the group as if not changing was a bad thing. He couldn't say he was the least bit sorry about that until he looked into Mac's eyes and saw the worry there. Then he remembered the vampires stalking Mac's wife. Now his captain would have no help protecting her. Mac had lost his wing man and Brianna had lost one of the only two werewolves in the world who were willing to protect a vampire from her own kind. Most of the werewolves would have gladly turned her over or killed her on sight.

Johnny met his friend's troubled stare and knew he'd be worse than useless against vampires now, like a toddler with a butter knife going against a medieval knight.

"I'm sorry," he said.

Mac's brow furrowed in question.

"I can't help you protect Brianna," said Johnny.

Mac dropped his gaze but recovered quickly and pressed a hand to Johnny's shoulder. "I told you when we came here, that was never your job. She's not your responsibility. She's mine."

Easy to say, but Johnny knew that when the vamps came, they came together and one werewolf might not be enough. They'd need to get her to the lock-in facility.

"Johnny, if you're human again, mostly human, then you can live a normal life. See your sister and your mother. I'll keep my wife safe. We have the entire secure perimeter right here. I'll scent them in plenty of time to get her to safety."

Johnny gave him a long look and Mac nodded. The weight of that responsibility ebbed away. He smiled.

"I would have defended her."

"I know it. We're both happy for you. Eventually Sonia will be happy that you won't be going all furry on her, too. Give her time."

"I haven't seen her since last night."

Mac rubbed his neck. "You want me to have her report to your place?"

"For what, a lesson?" Then it hit him. Sonia must have realized it right away. Of course she would have.

"What's going to happen with her?"

Mac shrugged. "Not sure. She'll keep her clearance but…"

But he didn't need a translator. Holy shit, they'd be reassigning her. "No, I want her here."

Mac nodded. "I know you do, buddy. But it might not be up to you. And besides, if you stay human you can have your combat assignment. You'll be leaving anyway, just like you wanted."

Leaving Mac and Brianna behind. Leaving Sonia behind. He'd been badgering Mac to get him back to combat duty for months. Now he could go, but where did that leave Sonia? Uncertainty oscillated inside him like water sloshing in a bucket.

"Yeah, like I wanted," said Johnny and rubbed his jaw, not sure he wanted to leave the island and realizing it wasn't the island he didn't wish to leave, but Sonia.

"Well, not so fast. The doctors want to observe you awhile. You still have your sense of smell and you're too damn strong for a human. So some part of you is still wolf."

"What about Sonia?" asked Johnny. "Her assignment?"

"She can stay awhile."

But she was leaving or he was. Johnny felt sick. How long did they have?

Johnny left Mac and headed for his quarters. He was halfway up the hill when he scented something familiar and froze to the spot as if he had just realized he'd stepped on a land mine.

Vampire. Had to be. But not Brianna. This was sweet and cloying, like heavy perfume mixed with the tang of spilled blood.

Johnny changed direction, running to Mac's home.

As he went the scent grew fainter and fainter until he was not sure he had smelled it at all. He drew out his phone as he ran and called Mac. Johnny arrived in Brianna's yard to find her standing in her garden, where she had obviously been working. She would have heard his approach as he crashed from the undergrowth. Her welcoming smile faded as she looked at his wild expression and she clutched her other hand over the first.

"What is it?" she asked, but already her gaze was flitting about for any sign of the vampires and she was vibrating as she did before she vanished from his sight. Brianna could move so quickly that even he could not track her movements.

"I smelled something down the hill. I called Mac." He no sooner said the words then she was at his side, clinging to him. Then she gave a cry and pushed off and away staggering backward.

"I forgot. You're human again. I can't touch you."

He'd forgotten, too. What did he do now—stay with her, wait for Mac, take her to lockdown or send her down alone? She could be there in five seconds but if they were here that would not be fast enough. For the first time since the change, Johnny felt powerless. He motioned away from the house. It would be better not to be where they would expect to find her.

They did not have long to wait. Mac roared into the yard in his gray werewolf form a few minutes later. He huffed from his exertions. Johnny realized he must have fairly flown up that hill. And as an odd turn about now Johnny could speak and Mac could not.

Mac moved to stand beside Brianna who collapsed against her husband as naturally as if he were in human form. She did not cringe or show any sign at all that his fearsome appearance troubled her. In fact she looked damned relieved.

"Did you scent them?" Johnny asked.

Mac shook his head.

"It was down the hill before that second turn. Very faint. Do you want to bring her down?"

Mac gave another nod.

"Walk or drive?"

Mac lifted his hands as if on a steering wheel then pointed to Johnny. He wanted him to drive. Johnny motioned to the Jeep and Brianna climbed into the back seat leaving the larger passenger seat for her nine-foot werewolf husband. Johnny drove fast but not crazy fast. At the bottom they drove straight into the secure facility built to study one werewolf and protect one female vampire. The metal doors shut behind them.

Johnny now began to wonder if the vamps were inside the base or if his senses were screwy. The perimeter fence included their houses above the base and were rigged with special motion detectors sensitive enough to detect male vamps. The high-speed cameras recorded everything that moved. If intruders broke perimeter, they'd know it. That meant they weren't on base…yet.

Major Scofield waited inside the lockdown facility, meeting both Mac and Brianna.

"Where's Sonia?" Johnny asked.

Mac pointed up the hill and Johnny's heart shuttered as cold terror flashed through him like flood water.

"I've got to get her," he told his commanding officer and took off without waiting for approval. Ten minutes later he roared into his driveway. It bothered him that he could not run the distance, that it was now faster to drive. What if the vampires were at his house? Mac was down below with Brianna and Johnny would no longer be a match for them. He left the Jeep and raced into the yard, charging up the stairs. He threw open the door to his place so hard the knob crashed through the sheet rock. Sonia, in the kitchen, turned and screamed. She took one look at him and ran in his direction. He didn't explain, just grabbed her and turned, running with her in his arms, holding her like a tackle dummy as he tore across the yard and back to the Jeep. When she was seated and he had the Jeep in Reverse she asked him what was happening.

"One of them is here," he said, eyes on the road as he threw it into gear.

"Vampires?" she whispered.

"Yes. Down the hill."

"Brianna!" called Sonia as they flew past her driveway.

"Already at the base in lockdown."

Sonia clicked on her belt and held on as they sped down the road and into the fenced compound.

"Did they trip the perimeter alarms?"

They hadn't. So they'd beaten the perimeter or they were still outside the fence.

"No. I smelled one."

It wasn't until they reached lock-in and he stopped the Jeep that he allowed himself to believe Sonia was truly safe. He reached across the seat and dragged her into his lap.

She threw her arms about his neck and their lips met in a fierce kiss. His mouth slanted over hers and she held him tighter as she gave a cry deep in her throat and opened her mouth. His tongue slid along hers as they deepened the kiss. She was safe, he realized and pulled her closer, so thankful she was out of harm's way that his eyes drifted closed. Fear melted to relief and the kiss changed from frantic to fire. Pure liquid heat ignited in his core and his body hardened. Her fingers raked through his hair, those trimmed nails leaving a tingling path in their wake. She rubbed against him and he felt the aching pressure of her soft, round breasts pressed to him in a way that he'd imagined many times. But this was better. So good. She writhed against him and he angled her closer so that she sat between the wheel and his chest, with her bottom planted firmly on his erection. She sighed and shifted, rocking against him as he deepened the kiss. The horn blared and they both jumped. Sonia broke away staring at him in shock, her lips parted and pink. He tried to kiss her again but she slithered back to her seat.

He shook himself, trying to drive away the arousal and the aching need. Nothing in his imagining could ever compare to that kiss. She had a hand on her forehead as she breathed heavily through her open mouth.

"Wow," she said at last.

He blew out a breath and nodded.

"Should we report?" she asked, glancing toward the entrance and the surveillance cameras

He should, but not in his condition. If strong emotions triggered the change than he was definitely not changing to wolf form any time soon because he had never felt an emotional tsunami like that one. He swallowed.

"I need a minute."

She glanced at the long ridge of male flesh sheathed in his beige cammies. "Oh, sure." She straightened in her seat tugging at her shirt and her face flushed.

"What were you doing at my place?" he asked. Not really caring, but fighting hard against the urge to drag her back onto his lap.

"Oh, well, I thought we should talk." She sagged in her seat and then turned to face him, picking up with sign language, only this time she didn't accompany each word with speech.

I am so sorry I ruined the evening. I'm confused and afraid. What will happen to me now? Her eyebrows tented at the question. *You don't need a translator or any of the sign language I taught you. You don't need me.*

He made his response in slow careful movements. *I need you now more than ever.*

Her bottom lip trembled and she reached for him, throwing herself into his arms. "I knew this would happen," she said.

"What?"

"I didn't want to get attached. Then I wouldn't care about leaving. But now." She sniffed. "I knew something like this would happen the minute I did."

He felt a spark of hope that died as he took in her bereft expression. He stroked her hair. "Sonia, it's going to be all right."

Someone banged on the driver's-side window. Sonia sprang back to her seat, wiping her eyes. Johnny turned to the jerk who interrupted them and saw Major Scofield.

"Need you both inside, son," said the major.

Johnny nodded and opened the door, but hesitated as he looked back to Sonia.

"Johnny," urged Scofield.

He exited the vehicle as Sonia scrambled out the other side, her face now red as she saluted.

The major motioned with his head. "Touma, you're coming with me. Lam, you've got perimeter with Mac-Connelly."

She gave Johnny one long beseeching look before scrambling after the retreating major.

She signed, *Be careful.*

Johnny found Mac, still in werewolf form. They spent the rest of the afternoon sweeping the hillside and surrounding area but found no trace of the scent of vampires.

"False alarm?" asked Mac that evening.

"Might have been. It was faint. But I could swear I smelled them." Were his senses playing tricks on him, leaving him all together? "I was sure."

"But then why can't we track him? And why no perimeter alarms or surveillance footage?"

Johnny couldn't answer but the doubts crept in. He could no longer trust his senses.

Everyone stayed at the compound that evening. Johnny checked on Sonia, finding her eating alone in the mess hall. She said she was fine but she seemed nervous and upset. He wanted to linger, but he had a duty to Mac and the others here, so they swept the hillside again that evening and once more the following day. He and Mac remained on patrol, one or the other, circling the compound and scenting for vampires.

The base remained in lockdown one more night before calling an all clear. Scofield put extra security details on assignment and patrols on the hill. Johnny didn't like the company, but he could see that it relieved Brianna. *It shouldn't,* he thought. Marines were no match for vampires. The volcanic hillside was steep and impassible in places, even for a vampire. That was why they selected this spot. It allowed Brianna the distance from others, while affording them a defensible position. Despite their assurance that no vampires could attack from above them, they still had a perimeter fence, high speed cameras, infrared trip wires. All had been checked and all came up empty. Which made him wonder if he'd imagined the entire thing.

The only one here who stood a chance against them was Mac and he was all set to face however many they sent for Brianna. Once they found her, that might be a lot. If he were hunting her, he'd be damned sure he came with more vampires the next time.

Johnny heard the Jeep when he was in the shower and assumed it was Mac. He threw on jeans and a T-shirt before coming out onto the porch, then paused as her scent came to him on the breeze.

Sonia.

She'd come back to him at last. Over the days and nights of searching for some trace of the vampire his mind kept wandering back to that kiss in front of headquarters. Johnny closed the door and retreated into the house flicking off the overhead lights, leaving only the lamps on the end table illuminated and the lights beneath the cupboards in the kitchen. He didn't want to meet her in the driveway or the stairs or his porch. He wanted to meet her in his bedroom. He might not manage that, but he could at least greet her in his living room beside the couch that had always been too small for him—until now. Now, it was just the right size for two with one stretched out on top of the other. His skin tingled as the sound of her footfalls upon the stairs reached him.

She rapped on the door and he came to her. The breeze carried no hint of danger as he opened his arms. Thankfully she stepped into his embrace kissing him quickly on the cheek before stepping inside. Not what he'd been hoping for, he thought, but better than nothing.

He glanced past her to the hillside. His night vision

was still good and he scanned the yard in twilight wondering if he were still strong enough to kill a vampire if one appeared.

Johnny inhaled once more and, finding nothing unusual, he followed her inside. He managed to hold his smile, trying to pretend that he wasn't already burning for her. She'd asked him to wait and he had waited. Was the longing now too much for her, as well? Did she want him, but only for one night?

Sonia shifted restlessly before him, rocking from side to side as she stood in a pair of tight-fitting jeans and a pretty pink sleeveless top. The cut of the garment showed her toned arms and the pale brown perfection of her skin.

"How are you?" she asked, peeking at him from beneath thick lowered lashes.

He breathed deeply. She'd put on a light body spray at her throat and her stomach. He smiled and inclined his chin. "Better now that you're here. I've been missing you."

He watched her swallow as if nervous. She rubbed her hands together absently and glanced around the living room.

"Have you?" Her eyes met his in an expression that he thought was hopeful. Then she cast a look toward the door as she pressed her lips together. He grasped her elbow and guided her farther into the house, farther from the front door.

"Come sit down," he said, bringing her attention back to him.

"Oh, I can't stay."

He moved back, giving her space and hoping to bring her farther into the room. He'd never seen her so nervous before and it made him wonder if she was here for what he hoped or for what he feared.

"I'm making you some tea. Iced green oolong with ginseng."

He thumbed over his shoulder toward the kitchen and she nodded, following him. She perched on one of the stools that faced the counter and watched him work. He set the kettle on the gas burner. Tea was a ritual, a comfort and an art form. He set out a small ceramic teapot and threw the dried leaves in with the crushed ginseng powder. He had made her tea before, many times. Now he felt her eyes upon him as he worked. The silence buzzed between them louder than the peepers outside.

He waited for her to speak first.

She cleared her throat. "You'll be able to see your mother and sister again soon. Won't you?"

He smiled imagining that reunion and then thinking of bringing Sonia to meet his mother. What would these two women think of one another?

"I guess I can."

"And you can fly on an airplane and go out in public." Something about her tone drew his complete attention because it was flat, lacking the usual passion her words so often conveyed. Where was she going with this?

She stared at the teapot and blew out a long breath. "Talk on the telephone. Have dinner in the mess hall. All the normal things you've missed."

He missed seeing her sign as she spoke.

"Yes. Sonia what are you saying?"

"You can do all those things now and more. You can talk Johnny. You can date anyone you want. You can get that assignment you've wanted. Make that higher pay grade."

He met her gaze and saw the sorrow reflected in her light brown eyes. She was trying to say goodbye. Well, he'd be damned if he'd let her. He was keeping Sonia, one way or another. She was the one who took the time to get to know him, to cheer him and to understand him. Yes, he'd had to play hardball at first, but he wasn't letting her go before they finished this. He needed to know. She needed to know what it was like to be with someone you cared about, someone who knew you like nobody else.

His hands stilled on the bag of dried leaves. He set it carefully on the counter and continued his deliberate movements, lifting the boiling kettle and pouring water into the small ceramic teapot. He filled two tall glasses with ice as the tea steeped in the little pot. Then he brought the glasses and teapot to her, setting them on the counter between them.

"This isn't because of that kiss," he asked.

Her denial was quick. "Of course not."

He'd shaken her. And she'd shaken him. Only he wanted more and she was turning tail. Well, he wasn't going to let her run until she knew good and well what she was leaving behind. Then if she wanted to run, he'd let her.

"Maybe against your best efforts you've grown attached to me. Maybe that kiss scared you because it was so damn good. So now you want to go."

Her eyes widened and she pushed back from the counter so that her hands gripped the lip of the marble surface and her arms were stiff before her.

"I did my job but it's over, John."

He signed to her. *And you did it well.* "Are you afraid of me?" he asked.

"I wasn't before. Now I am."

He nodded. "Ah, I see. Then you're afraid of us."

"I liked it the way it was, when we could talk and just…" She shrugged one shoulder.

"So you came up here at night, alone to tell me that you wish I was still a werewolf."

She absently ran her index finger along the smooth edge of the counter. He watched the rhythmic stroking, tracking each tiny movement like a cat watching a water bug. Her finger stilled and he lifted his gaze to find her motionless as a paused image on his television, except for the widening of her eyes and the pulse that pounded at her throat.

"I don't want you to still be a werewolf. But I don't want this, either. I didn't want to come here. Now I don't want to leave."

"I don't want you to leave, either."

She made a fist and pounded it on the counter. "But I will be leaving. Any day now." She lowered her head. "I'm sorry. Is the tea ready?"

He opened the lid of the teapot to allow the steam to escape.

"Are you always this nervous around men?" he asked, trying to make the question casual as he reminded her that he was now a man.

"I never was before. But that was because they only touched me here." She pressed a hand over one breast cupping herself and he watched riveted as her fingers sank into soft flesh.

He gripped the handle of the ceramic teapot and he realized he was dangerously close to snapping the clay handle like a piece of chalk.

"I never let them in here." Her hand shifted so that it lay flat over her heart.

Did she know he could hear it beating in her chest, the throb of blood surging and the valves snapping shut?

"You're trying to shut me out again."

She nodded, not trying to deny it. "You're a marine trying for combat duty. I'm a marine trying for a nice safe spot on the sidelines until I'm discharged. I don't see a whole lot of options for us."

He poured the hot tea over the ice cubes in each glass. They cracked and hissed as they dissolved. He stirred the fluid in each container with a long necked spoon until the glasses and Sonia both began to sweat. Then he added more ice to each glass and handed one to her, being certain that their fingers brushed. Here they had no escorts, no prying eyes to watch them together. They were not parked before headquarters. She was right to be nervous because her words of caution did not mesh with the gleam in her eyes or the flush of her cheeks.

He watched her as he lifted his tea and downed the contents in three long gulps. Then he wiped the remaining moisture from his lips with the back of his hand. Her mouth dropped open as she clutched her own glass.

"Aren't you thirsty?" he asked.

She lifted the glass and took a sip. Her hand was shaking, but not from fear. Arousal, he realized, scenting her desire. His pulse jumped and his body hardened, ready for her.

"The way I see it, you have two choices. You can cast off and run, which I know you are damn good at doing, or..." He lifted a brow as he plucked the glass from her fingers with one hand and captured hers with the other. He gave her a lazy grin.

"Or?" she asked, leaning toward him.

"Or you can get the answers to all those questions."

She cocked her head and her brow knit. "What questions?"

"Would we be good together? What would it be like? Will he be gentle or rough, fast or slow? And then there is the kicker, if you don't will you live to regret it?"

The tip of her pink tongue peeked out to run the width of her lower lip. Witnessing that tiny action sent a lightning bolt of desire streaking to his groin. He thought he'd been hard before, but now he pulsed for her with each heartbeat. He felt the hunger and thirst for her in his gut as the need beating through him with his blood, hot, burning hot and so strong that his shoulders ached as he held himself back. He wanted her to come to him. No, he needed her to come.

He leaned toward her. "You can still run away in the morning, but at least you'll have your answers."

Her eyes gleamed. Her mouth glistened and her head inclined in a barely perceptible nod.

He blew out a breath at the mingling of relief and desire. He'd have her in his bed tonight. Now all he needed was a way to keep her there. But how could he? She was right. She was going or he was going.

But they still had tonight.

He lifted one hand over his head and grasped his cotton T-shirt at the spot just between his shoulder blades, dragged it off and tossed the shirt aside. The gauntlet had been dropped. Her gaze dipped, raking his chest. He felt his skin pucker and tighten. She reached with both hands as her eyes flashed hungry as a tigress. He opened his arms wide.

Chapter 12

Johnny lowered his mouth to Sonia's in a hard, demanding kiss. He dragged his fingers through the thick satin of her hair and then gripped her, controlling her head as his tongue glided against hers. Her yielding mouth and hot tongue drove him crazy. He needed to get her to that bed, needed a moment to regroup. The fragrance of her skin and the softness of her body pressed to his, filled his mind with crazy thoughts, Sonia on the counter, legs splayed. He planned to go slow, but she was rubbing against him and he wanted her so badly.

It was Sonia who broke the kiss, but not to reconsider. No, judging from what her nimble fingers were doing to his zipper, she wanted him naked. He worked the buttons free on her blouse and offered a prayer of thanks at the sight of the black lace bra that cupped her breasts in a way that made him jealous.

He drew her in, needing to feel her soft skin pressed

to his. He kissed her neck and the shell of her ear, taking the lobe into his mouth to suck the sweet morsel. She gasped and clung, lifting a leg and locking a heel behind his back. Sweet mercy, they'd never make it to his big empty bed.

"Bedroom?" he whispered.

She shook her head against him. "I can't wait. Here."

He reached behind her back and unfastened her bra, then pushed off the blouse. She rounded her shoulders and the lacy scrap of fabric fell away. He stopped to stare at the wonder of Sonia topless in his kitchen. He'd seen her in her cammies, a bathing suit and in that red dress. He'd imagined her this way, and now she stood still for his appraisal. Her breasts were larger than he'd realized. Everything she wore until this evening downplayed her lovely cleavage. Sports bras and cammies all flattened her glorious curves. Her nipples where budded tight and a dusty rose color. He reached. Her head dropped back and her eyes shut instantly before he touched her. She leaned forward, eager for him. He splayed his hands over her plump flesh and a moan rumbled deep and feral in her throat. He kissed and licked his way from one plump breast to the next as she arched against him. Johnny moved north, back along the lovely column of her neck, the enticing hollow of her throat and the secret recesses of her mouth.

He wanted to touch her everywhere. He knew that she wanted his body, but she wanted to keep him at arm's length. He wouldn't allow it. Just like all those days and weeks ago when she had tried and failed to shut him out of what really mattered, out of what made her who and what she was. Tonight he would allow no holding back. He would do whatever it took to make her open not just her body, but herself. He needed to be inside her. But he also needed to be inside her thoughts and her dreams and hopes. Sonia was the only woman he'd ever met who completely captivated him.

He lifted her up onto the breakfast bar. She gasped as her bottom hit the hard marble surface and her eyes popped open. They shared a wicked smile. Then she reached and dragged his trousers and boxers along his thighs. She glanced down, measuring him first with her eyes and then reaching, taking him in her hands, stroking the underside of his erection. He set his teeth together and inhaled through his nose, clenching his jaw to fight the need to take her, giving her a chance to explore his body as he explored hers.

She lifted one hand to her mouth and licked her palm, then used that moist surface to stroke him again. Slick fingers wrapped him tightly and he gasped and groaned at the pounding beat of desire. When the fire burned too hot he drew her hands away and tugged at the waistband of her blue jeans.

"Take them off," he ordered and she did.

A moment later she sat there on his breakfast counter like a bounty, creamy mocha flesh light against the black marble. He memorized the sight of her, treasuring the gift she gave him and vowing to be certain she never regretted one single minute of this night. Regret. It made that small still-functioning portion of his brain reengage. Something he needed.

He groaned. The condoms were all the way in his bedside table. They might as well be on the moon. She kissed his neck now, her hands traveling down his back and over his hips, then she used her nails to graze his skin on the return trip. He closed his eyes and groaned in pleasure and frustration.

"Bed," he said and scooped her up against him. She

clasped her arms around his neck and her legs around his waist, riding high on his hips as he carried her deeper into the house. The fragrance of her filled him like nectar. He breathed deep, drunk with the scent of her skin and the scent of her arousal. As he moved she pressed tight to his torso, giving him the unbelievably arousing pressure of her breasts hot, soft and heavy against his needy flesh. The light from the hall spilled across the floor of his bedroom in a bright rectangle. Johnny cradled her against him and he reached the bed and lowered her to his coverlet. She stretched out before him like a lithe cat. Reclining now, waiting. He took a good long look at Sonia naked and aroused. He found the sight the strongest of aphrodisiacs. And he hadn't even tasted her yet. But he could smell her need and see the slick pink flesh as she lifted her knees and splayed her legs.

He dropped to the carpet before her as her gaze wandered over him, pausing at his chest, his stomach and finally his engorged sex. A sensual smile broke across her face and he returned it. He'd been afraid to break the mood. But that was nonsense. The look in her eyes said she wanted this, longed for it, just like him. This ache great like a monsoon. Neither of them could turn back now.

He eased himself onto his outstretched arms and then lowered himself to kiss her sweet mouth. She arched to press her chest to his and he made his way south, taking his time, exploring every nook and hollow, every succulent bud of flesh and each long flat plain. At last he reached her core, savoring how she stilled when he took her in his mouth. Loving the soft panting and tiny quavering cries she made when his tongue dipped inside her. As he sucked and licked and petted her, she arched, pressing to his mouth. He slipped his hands to her bottom, splaying his fingers and he lifted her, rocked her, drove her mad.

She gasped and bucked, rubbing against the friction he lavished. Sonia seemed to stop breathing as he continued to kiss and suck and taste. She was the sweetest thing that had ever come into his life and he wanted so badly for this to be perfect for her. He wanted—no needed to give her this release. He would do anything for her. Did she know that?

Sonia's breathing told him she was close. She came in a rushing sound, a long extended moan that went on and on as her release rolled and her fingers curled into fists in his hair. Then, by slow degrees her fingers slackened and fell away as her body went limp in his hands. She stretched as she made a humming sound of female satisfaction. He rubbed his slick mouth on her thighs and then moved back up her body, dropping a hundred tiny kisses along the way. When he neared her head, she lifted an arm, moving with a clumsy lethargy he knew well, as she stroked her fingers through the tangle of his hair.

"I've never felt anything like this, oh, Johnny, it was so delicious."

"More where that came from." And he knew he wanted her coming back for more, needed her to come back. No more one-nighters with a stranger for her, he vowed, no, never again.

She groaned and closed her eyes. "So tired."

He kissed her neck and her ear. Slowly she rose to his gentle stroking. Reluctant, playful and then aggressive, reaching for what she wanted. Well, he was happy to give it to her. This time, when she came he planned to be looking at her lovely face.

He let her fondle him, even though he was approaching the point where need grew too raw, too mindless to be controlled. Then she slipped from his embrace and lowered her mouth to take him. It was too much. The pressure of her hand as it gripped him and her tongue moving over his wanting flesh drove him wild. He pulled her back to his arms and she smiled up at him with swollen pink lips, slick with moisture. And he could see it all with just the light from the hall. Bless his werewolf sight, he thought, wondering if she could see him at all.

"You're driving me crazy," he whispered.

She chuckled and straddled his hips. He stilled her by grasping her at the waist. She lifted her brows in a silent question. A moment later he had the silver foil packet out of the drawer. She plucked it from him and tore into the foil. Then she unrolled the sheath over his aroused flesh.

"I've imagined doing that," she said, smiling down in satisfaction. She rocked her hips over him, sliding her slick folds along the length of him.

He held her hips and pulled her down beneath him in a quick take down that would have made his high school wrestling coach proud. She smiled up at him, with her eyes hooded and her pupils large and black.

He rocked against her once and then drew back, slipping into position. She spread her legs, lifting her heels to his hips to encourage this last joining. He stared down into her eyes and dropped until their hips locked, sheathing himself within her body. He watched her as he began to move. The sight of her flushed face and parted lips made his stomach twitch. He wanted to bring her pleasure again, wanted them both to fall into that madness together. But she was so hot and so wet and it had been so long. He growled as the need gripped him, rocking harder, deeper into her body.

Sonia cried out in pitiful little moans that grew louder and more frenzied. She raked his back with her nails and tossed her head from side to side.

Go ahead, he wanted to say. *Go ahead. I'll follow.* But he could not say anything because he was so close. He gritted his teeth and held back, closing his eyes for a moment to try to retain the control that slipped away like water in his hands.

She arched and howled, crying out his name as the contractions beat inside her. He felt them grip him and cast him into mindlessness. He came in a mad rush of heat and power, the pleasure pulsing out from his core and burning along his nerves like fire.

Sonia went slack and her eyes dropped closed. Johnny fell to his hands, holding his weight off her before collapsing down at her side. He had just enough strength in his trembling arms to drag her against him. She nestled, one leg sprawling over him like a boneless cat.

"That...was...wonderful," she sighed.

He brushed the hair from her face, kissed her mouth and wondered what he had ever done to deserve a night with Sonia Touma.

When her skin grew chilled, he dragged the comforter over them before drifting to sleep. He woke as the moonlight stole across their bed, leaving her to walk to the window and stare up at the silver orb ringed in a yellow haze. When he returned it was to find her half awake and reaching for him again. They made love more slowly this time as he explored her body from toe to fingertip, becoming familiar with each curve and the arousing cocktail of her body spray mixed with her desire. Late in the night, long after the moon had set, she woke him again, pressing the third condom into his palm.

The woman was trying to kill him. But as they say, what a way to die. Werewolves had great stamina. He just never knew that included sexual stamina.

He dozed with Sonia tucked close to his side and dreamed of running in the woods after vampires. The scent of them was heavy in his nostrils. He growled and felt Sonia stir beside him.

"Johnny!"

The panic in her voice brought him instantly awake. One deep breath told him there were no vampires here. But she was shaking him and calling his name.

"Johnny!"

Why was she so little? He reached out to stroke her face and ask her what was wrong. But his voice failed him. He froze at the sight of his own hand covered with black hair and tipped with thick curling claws. He startled and fell out of bed then scrambled to his feet, staring down at himself. It was morning and he was once again a werewolf.

She was crying now, her voice bereft and full of pain. "Was it because of what we did? Strong emotions, they said. Johnny, did I do this to you?"

Sonia's heart thudded painfully against her ribs as she scrambled out of bed, taking the bedsheet along with her. She clutched it to her body as she stared at Johnny who was now covered in black fur and his face had distended into the elongated shape that was neither man nor wolf.

"What happened?" she cried, the tears already welling so his image swam before her. Guilt lashed through her stomach, tearing her apart inside. *Oh, God, was this my fault?*

His feet slapped the floor as he staggered back against the wall and patted his own hairy chest as his mouth gaped showing long, dangerous teeth. The strangled sound he made left no doubt that he attempted speech, but that ability was gone with his handsome face and form. He stared at her, his brow wrinkled in confusion. Then he started signing.

Don't know. Why didn't I feel it?

"Maybe you're learning to change. Maybe you just don't have control over it yet." But in her heart, she knew something was very wrong. This wasn't supposed to happen. The change had to be called. That was what the captain said. Deep inside herself the panic began creeping up into her body, clouding her mind. It threaded through her like the roots of some invasive plant. She had not felt this panic since her childhood, but she recognized the darkness growing stronger. Johnny stood before her, his nostrils flaring as he waited. For his sake, she reined herself in. He needed her. She couldn't fall apart. But she wanted to scream, "What is happening?"

I dreamed of vampires, he signed. *Could that cause the change?*

"I don't know. Maybe." Sonia reached for the phone. "I have to call the captain."

He lifted a hand and waved it.

Give me a minute.

Johnny sank to the bed and cradled his forehead in his hands. Sonia wound the sheet tight about her and rolled the top as she would with a bath towel and then she sat beside him. She wrapped one arm around his waist and rested her head on his shaggy side and whispered into his pointed ear.

"They'll figure it out."

He lifted his head slowly as if it were suddenly too heavy to bear. His yellow eyes were bloodshot and red rimmed. He moved his hands and she read his words.

Step back. Let me try to change.

She moved away and watched him as he closed his eyes but nothing happened. He glanced up at her and then cradled his head in his long, clawed hands. Finally his arms dropped to his sides and he looked up at her. The defeat was clear in the hunched shoulders and woeful expression.

I can't.

Sonia grabbed the phone and made the call. Thirty minutes later she was dressed and they were back in the underground medical facility. Doctor Zharov looked grim and the captain's bright pink complexion showed he was clearly livid.

Sonia listened carefully to the doctor speak to Johnny, who sat still and silent on the examining table.

"This happened with a small portion of the test subjects. Involuntary change."

Johnny signed his question. *It was a full moon last night. Does that matter?*

Sonia translated and the doctor answered. "No, the moon has no effect on your condition. Superstitious nonsense. Possibly people were more likely to see werewolves in the moonlight. But it doesn't bring a change."

Sonia asked the next question. "Johnny and I were together last night."

Zharov's brows shot up as he looked from one to the other.

"You said strong emotions can trigger change. Was it because…because…" Words failed her.

Zharov rubbed his chin and considered. "I'm not sure, but I doubt it. I have some tests to run. Then I'll know better how to answer your question."

Johnny was signing now. Sonia waited and then turned to the doctor. "He says there was no warning."

"No. Had you been awake there would have been. Dilation of the capillaries just prior to the change would make you feel flushed, perhaps light-headed."

Johnny signed again and Sonia spoke. "Why can't I change back?"

The silence in the room was deafening. Sonia felt brittle as glass as she looked from the doctor to the captain and her hope died. Zharov clasped his hands behind his back and rocked from heel to toe. The captain scrubbed his bristly jaw with his knuckles and winced.

"Answer his question," she said, her voice a feral growl. The news was bad, obviously, but he was entitled to hear it instead of being kept in the dark. She inched closer to Johnny's side.

The captain glanced at the door as if he wanted to be anywhere but here. Then he gestured with his head and Zharov backed away and out that same door. Sonia's chest felt tight as it did when her mother left them alone in the apartment to go out. The air seemed thinner as she tried to breathe.

"You better go," he said.

She shook her head. She was staying. The captain nodded his acceptance of her decision.

The captain's mouth went flat and grim. Johnny braced, gripping the edge of the table as he waited for his captain to speak.

"It's my fault. I wanted you human again, so I told

him to go ahead and give you the injection. Zharov said he couldn't guarantee it. He's working to make it right. But it looks like you are one of the fifteen percent that doesn't hold his shape. That means you can't change back without another injection."

Sonia's blood flashed hot. "Don't you think you should have told him this was a possibility before you gave him the treatment, instead of making the decision without him, sir." She spat that last word, turning it into an insult.

Johnny motioned for the captain to bring him another shot. Sonia's ears began to buzz as she recalled his reaction to the first one.

"No," she said and grasped Johnny's hand. "We have to wait until they get this right. Until they can be sure that you'll stay human."

"That might be a while," said the captain.

"We'll wait," she said, making the decision for both of them, as if she had any right.

Johnny shook his head. She met his yellow eyes and read his thoughts before he even signed to her. He was going through with this.

His fingers moved and his hands swooped. *Not waiting. Bring the shot.*

She repeated his order to her commanding officer.

"It isn't that simple," said MacConnelly. "Diminishing returns, they call it. You were human for four days. The next time will be less."

Johnny straightened and began signing.

"How much less?" she said, repeating his question but finding her voice a strangled thing.

"We aren't sure."

Johnny was signing again.

Sonia cleared her throat but her voice still cracked.

She was coming apart inside stitch by stitch. "He asks, 'Is there anything that will make me stay human?'"

The comrades exchanged a long look. Finally the captain said, "I'll arrange another shot but that's all I can do. But first they are going to need to run some tests on your blood the way it is now."

Johnny started signing and Sonia's eyes went wide. She felt her ears heat as the words poured out of him.

"Slow down," she said.

"What is he saying?" asked her captain.

"He's angry. I don't think—"

"Tell me what he said. You're his translator. Not his damned editor. So translate."

Johnny now had his arms folded over his chest and was glaring at MacConnelly.

"He said that you need him like this to defend Brianna. You don't want him human. That you're just like…" She glanced at Johnny and he spelled the name for her again. "Just like Colonel Lewis?"

The captain's face went red and his hands curled to fists. Sonia blinked as she noted that his blue eyes were changing color. The captain was fighting off the transformation. She knew it and instinctively stepped closer to Johnny. His arm went about her waist for a moment and then slid away as he began signing again.

"He says he's not your dog anymore and if he has to die to be human than he'll die. At least his mother can bury him in a casket instead of dumping him at the vets." Sonia clasped her arms across her chest as she waited for the captain to speak but he didn't. Instead he just spun in a half circle and marched out of the room.

She looked at Johnny. "Do you really believe that he would do that to you?"

Johnny didn't hesitate before shaking his head. He

began to sign. *He wouldn't. But I can't stay like this anymore, Sonia. I can't be a monster.*

Sonia felt her throat burning and knew she was about to cry. She threw herself against him and he gathered her in his arms.

"You're not a monster. Just wait. I'll wait with you. I'll be able to stay now. We can be together. I'll live with you. You can cook for me and…we can go home." Tears choked her as she realized what they'd both lost and threw herself into his arms. He held her for a little while and then set her aside so she could see him sign.

It's not our home.

"Please, Johnny."

I want the shot.

Sonia began to cry.

Chapter 13

Burne Farrell waited for his chaser to return. Chasers were those whose job it was to track and capture their females as soon as they became sexually mature. Most females tried to run. But up until Brianna Vittori, none had succeeded for long. It was a sore spot with him and with his best chaser.

Burne didn't like Hawaii. Since his arrival, the stars and the moon were too bright and the lack of cloud cover meant it never grew truly dark. The cities here were small and lacked the amenities to which he was accustomed. A creature who moved only in darkness needed a place with 24-hour services and plenty of people venturing out at night. New Orleans, now there was a city that understood the pleasures of the night. He hoped Hagan had finished his sweep of this wretched little volcanic disgorgement so they could continue to the next godforsaken upheaval of rock.

Burne stood on the balcony of the Palm Breeze Hotel inhaling the scent of roasting pig. It seemed they were always roasting something and banging those infernal drums. He saw Hagan Dowling race across the pool deck below, moving at a speed too fast for a human to perceive anything more than a slight breeze. But Burne could see him clearly. His legs pumping and his cadaver-like white arms flashing at his sides. A moment later Hagan knocked on the door of his eighth-floor suite. Farrell had to rent the room wearing the stretchy elastic beige face covering worn by burn victims, a tactic he disliked but was sometimes forced to employ in public.

"Enter," he commanded and his chaser let himself in, lifting his sensitive nose and then following it to his superior on the balcony.

Hagan's ghostly composition already showed the tell-tale road map of blue veins on his arms and face, the pulsing blood vessels engorgement indicating that his chaser had stopped for a meal.

Irritated, Burne scowled.

"Good evening, sir," said Hagan. "I have heard from Richard Gould. He reports strong signals of a female on the island of Molokai and also the presence of two male werewolves."

"It's her!" Burne could not resist pumping his fist in triumph.

"I agree, the signs are good. But he withdrew without visual confirmation, as you requested."

"Thank God one of my chasers follows orders." He paced the balcony as his mind raced. "We go in force. Every available man. How long until they are assembled?"

"I can have six chasers here within twenty-four

hours. If you are willing to wait forty-eight, I can call in our men in Europe and the Middle East."

Farrell rubbed one palm over the other. His greed for her urged him to hurry. And the more vampires that knew of her the more he would have to battle for her custody. Still she had evaded six before with the help of her two shaggy protectors. "Call them all. We go when we have a dozen. Two werewolves, even U.S. Marine–trained fighters, cannot possibly handle so many."

"True. But Gould says they have defenses. I suggest tunneling. The volcanic rock is riddled with existing channels. We could expand them to gain entry well past their perimeters."

"Fine."

"I will notify you when we are assembled. Would you like me to make a visual confirmation? I have seen her and would recognize her appearance."

"No. I don't want them tipped off. They would move her and we'll lose her again." Were all his men so reckless?

Hagan's mouth went thin and tight. Suspicion stirred in Farrell, rising like filth in a cesspool and he inhaled, finding the scent of a male who was sexually ready. Ready at just the mere mention of her. Was Hagan planning to steal her before he could assemble his team?

Farrell stared and Hagan swallowed. Did his chaser recognize that his master read him so easily? Hagan had best take care that his master didn't decide to open one of his chaser's arteries.

"Would you like to relocate to Molokai, master?"

"I'm going to lead the damned raid."

Hagan lowered his head and nodded. But not before Farrell saw the narrowing of his eyes and the threat burning in their depths. So he had another rival for

Brianna. He wondered if he should kill Hagan now or wait until after the capture.

"We will be honored to have you lead this chase, sir," said Hagan.

And I'll be honored to water my peonies with your blood, thought Farrell. He glanced at his chaser with speculation. It seemed doubtful that Hagan would live long enough to see his skin turn the color of a ripe plum.

In a fight, one should always put his money on the old dog.

Despite Johnny's insistence, Zharov refused to give him the shot until after all tests were completed on Johnny's wolf blood and the doctor had a chance to study the results. The following morning the tests were in.

Johnny and Sonia waited in silence in the medical facility for news of what was happening. Johnny knew Sonia didn't want him to take the shot and she'd done all she could to convince him. But damned if he'd stay like this. He only agreed to wait to could see if his blood work would reveal anything that could help maintain his human form.

It seemed hours before Dr. Zharov arrived in the examining room carrying a thick file folder. He was trailed by Mac, Brianna and Major Scofield. Johnny's skin prickled at the assemblage.

Brianna moved to the far corner of the room. Johnny knew with one glance at Brianna's face that the news was bad. Mac, more controlled, still showed a definite tell that Johnny recognized. Whenever he ground his jaw like that, Johnny knew he wouldn't like what came next.

"Well, it's not good," said the doctor without preamble. "Your body's immune system recognized the invading protein quickly and mounted an attack killing the agent you need to remain in human form."

Johnny signed a question and Sonia repeated it.

"He wants to know if he can have another dose."

Mac and Zharov exchanged looks. Brianna folded her hands and studied her white knuckles.

The major stepped forward and lay a fatherly hand on Johnny's hairy shoulder. "You can, son. But the result will likely be the same and faster this time, as your body has this particular protein on its hit list. It's a search and destroy with a known target. You understand?"

Johnny nodded and signed to Sonia. He tried not to notice the silver tear stains on her cheeks but they hit him in the gut like the butt end of a rifle.

"He says he still wants the shot."

Zharov looked to the major who nodded.

"Give it to him."

Sonia grabbed Johnny's forearm. "But he almost died the last time."

"Unlikely now. His body adapts quickly, too damned quickly, to new types of assaults."

Johnny patted her hand and peeled her away. Sonia shook her head, silently pleading with him not to go through with it. Didn't she understand, he'd do anything, anything, just to spend ten more minutes as a man. And to spend those minutes with her, it was all he wanted and he'd pay whatever price he must and when the shots no longer worked, well there was always the pistol.

"Do you have anything else, any other studies or something that won't do this to him?"

Zharov shook his head, fiddling with the tubing of his stethoscope. "I'm working on something but..." He glanced at Mac and Johnny saw the captain give a single shake of his head. What were they hiding? The doctor cleared his throat and continued. "We don't know why this protein is absent in Lam or how to encourage his body to produce it. We don't know why he's rejecting it when it is so prevalent in Captain MacConnelly's blood. In time we might...."

Johnny pounded his fists on the exam table, denting the metal. The doctor's words fell off. Johnny pantomimed a shot to his gums.

Zharov nodded and turned toward the door. Twenty minutes later Johnny lay stretched on a surgical table, Sonia standing beside him. Her skin was pale and her eyes round as a doll's.

"How long will he have this time?" she asked.

Zharov shrugged. "Less than the last time. Two days? I'm not sure."

Johnny opened his mouth and the serum was injected. Sonia gasped when his eyes fluttered. Zharov watched the machinery but Johnny did not lose consciousness this time. His heart raced and he felt a rush of electric energy shuttering through him, as if he'd touched a live wire. He watched the hair cascading from his hands and gave a little shake, sending more falling. His claws retracted and he saw his trimmed nails and neat, pink cuticles. The pain hit him then and he stiffened like an electroshock patient as his vision blurred. He could hear them, but his sight was gone. The ripping agony became the center of his existence as every muscle seized, then convulsed. The straps broke away and he tumbled to the tile floor. On hands and knees he panted and then retched, finally collapsing to his side.

This was better than the last time? Johnny was suddenly glad he'd passed out during the first shot. Gradually the pain ebbed and his muscles responded to his tentative efforts to control them. He sat up and Sonia draped a sheet around his shoulders, then helped him rise.

"Am I human?" he said, grinning at the sound of his own voice.

"Back on the gurney, Lam. We have to get you to a room. I want to examine you. Find the location of the initial attack," said Zharov.

"No offense, Doc, but I'm not spending my time in this stinking hospital playing doctor with you." He grasped Sonia's hand and headed for the door.

He met Mac just outside and for one minute worried he might order him back. But he didn't. Instead, he extended his hand and they shook.

"Thanks for the blood," said Johnny.

"Thanks for not dying on me." He released Johnny's hand. "John? I have some information about the night we were attacked in Afghanistan. I had them pull your medical records. Reports from the field hospital show your blood had traces of an agent used to cause memory loss. That's why you can't remember."

"Why would they do that?" he asked.

"Don't know. But we'll find out. We have to find the physician who treated us. Some of your files were destroyed. I'm looking into that, too."

A corporal appeared carrying a freshly pressed set of cammies and Johnny slipped into them. They left the captain and he and Sonia headed up the hill on foot to the home they might share for a day or perhaps two.

They stopped at the falls before Johnny's swimming pool watching the pulse of water cascading to the rocks before settling into the slow and gentle journey through the deep natural pond. Sonia gripped his hand.

"Maybe you should have stayed. Let the doctor check you. Maybe…"

"Sonia, please. I want to be with you."

"Do you think they might be wrong?" she asked.

"That I only have a day or two? No, Sonia. I think that's all we have. Maybe all we'll ever have."

Her lower lip trembled and she caught it between strong white teeth as she struggled with her erratic breathing. When she spoke, her voice was strained. "I wasted all those days."

"We were searching for a vampire most of it." He used his knuckles to lift her chin until their eyes met. "You didn't know."

"But they did. That's why they were concerned when you couldn't change. But they didn't tell us. Why didn't they tell us?"

Johnny gave her a sad smile. "I don't know."

"They're hiding something else. I feel it."

"Sonia, I've never met anyone like you. And if I only have two days I can't think of anyone else I'd rather spend them with."

She threw herself into his arms and he wrapped her up in a strong embrace. The sweetness of his body pressed to hers was punctuated by the knowledge that this would not last. She would not have him next week or next month. He'd be there, but beyond her reach.

"I should have been here. I just…I was afraid." She met his gaze, no longer hiding, no longer running. "Now I'm terrified."

He dipped his chin and she raised hers so that their mouths met with a sweet blending of texture and taste. But the need burned too hot in them both. Soon his kisses turned fierce. His tongue delved, mingling with hers in a dance of urgency. He caressed her throat, moving down to release each button of her shirt before casting the garment aside. She tugged his shirttails from his trousers and they separated for the time it took for him to pull his shirt over his head and for her to strip out of her bra. She fumbled with his zipper, the desperation making her clumsy. He dragged her to the soft grass and they tugged and pulled until their clothing lay strewn all about them.

Johnny gave her a wicked smile that heated her body more thoroughly than the humid jungle air. She stroked his cheek and then threaded her fingers in his hair and tugged. He kissed her lips and then moved steadily downward, each kiss bringing her a dart of pleasure. At last his arousing mouth covered her breasts. His tongue grazed across her nipple fanning the steady pulse of need into a blazing fire. The aching want beat low and deep inside her. She pressed against him and he laid her back upon the sweet, fragrant grass. The damp smell of earth mingled with the scent of this man. She breathed deep, hoping to remember each moment, each detail. How long did they have this time?

His knee pushed between her parting legs and she rose to rub against him, sending a shock of pleasure ripping through her body.

Her fingers delved into his hair. Frantic, she tried to touch him everywhere at once, exploring his back and arms, stroking her palms over his skin as she rubbed her cleft against his erection.

His fingers slipped into her hair, tangling in the long waves that fell about her and across the damp earth. His hips lowered to hers, pinning her to the ground. She felt his hard shaft against her trembling body, gliding against the moist folds of her genitalia but it was no longer enough. She needed to feel the thrust and grind of him inside her body.

He extended his arms, staring down as his dark hair fell about his face. Intent dark eyes stared and the moisture of her kisses still clung to his lips. She tried to memorize every line and plane of his face. This was how she wanted to remember him, young and naked and desperate for what she would give him.

How long until fate stole him once again? How long until his body finished destroying the protein that made him human and she lost him once more?

"Oh, Johnny," she whispered as the grief seized her again.

"Don't think about that now," he said. "Think about us and what I'm going to do to you. Give me this day to remember."

"I wish it were more."

"It's enough."

But it wasn't enough. It would never be enough.

He smiled and then lowered his chest to hers as he kissed her neck and ear and finally back down over her throat to find one plump breast and hard nipple.

There was only now.

This time when their mouths met there was none of the playful exploration or lustful heat of their earlier meetings. Now, he sensed a wildness, a frenzy that approached panic. Each second that ticked by was a second lost. Johnny gripped her tight and she wrapped her legs about his hips, her body slick and ready. He hesitated.

"I don't have protection."

"I do," she whispered. She drew a foil packet from the front pocket of her discarded clothing and tore it open before rolling the condom over the long length of him.

Another moment and he had slipped inside her in one long, delicious slide. She dug her heels against his thighs, driving still deeper as her tongue delved in frantic, greedy thrusts. They fell into that magic complimentary rhythm, the perfect blending of friction and slick liquid heat. Each moved in opposition and each thrust, each withdrawal brought them closer to madness.

This time the pleasure was so sweet, so piercing that her eyes rolled back in her head as the tension built and built.

She threw back her head and arched against him as she came, her rippling contractions gripping him and casting him over the edge with her. Her eyes opened wide to see him staring back at her with the same ecstatic amazement. Could anything ever be that perfect again?

Johnny felt the shattering orgasm go on and on as he forgot how to breathe. In that moment of supreme surrender, he knew that it was worth any price to have Sonia in his arms. He lay her back on the sweet-smelling grass falling beside her, rolling to his back. He stared up at the blue sky, there in little flashes through the green canopy. White and yellow butterflies flew in crazy patterns from one cascading group of flowers to the next. He pulled Sonia close. She nestled against his side, her hand resting familiar on his chest.

If only he could stay with her like this forever. How long did they have? A day? A night? He didn't know.

They stretched out on a soft cushion of moss in the warm humid air and her breathing changed as she dozed. He turned to watch her sleeping, memorizing the shape of her face.

He felt it coming this time. His skin tingled and then burned. His joints ached like the worst fever he'd ever had. Then his muscles pulled as if they were about to tear. He lifted a hand and saw the hair sprouting and his nails turning yellow, then black as they grew in a moment to claws. He glanced to Sonia, but she lay languid and still, with eyes still closed.

He called her name but the sound strangled in his throat.

"Johnny! Oh, no, Johnny, no."

He saw the horror in her eyes as the change gripped him. *No,* his mind screamed. It was too soon. He rolled in agony as if his skin were on fire.

The change back lasted only a few moments. He was a werewolf again and it had been less than half a day.

Sonia scrambled into her clothing. He stopped her when she had her shirt and pants on by grasping both shoulders in his big, thick hands. She kept her head down and he made a sound in his throat, a huffing sound. The sound of an animal.

She lifted her chin and met his gaze. Tears cascaded from her eyes and raced in silver ribbons down her cheeks.

"Oh, Johnny. It was too quick. What are we going to do?" She fell against him and he gathered her up in his arms.

He didn't know but together they headed back to the medical facility.

The next shot changed him back, but he knew it was the last time. He had time to kiss Sonia and tell her he was sorry. Then he changed back. Johnny tore the exam room to pieces. Even Mac in werewolf form couldn't stop him. But Sonia did by telling him that he was scaring her. He finally came to rest to see the metal table shredded like aluminum foil and the machinery shattered into a million tiny pieces. He slumped against the wall and Sonia fell into his arms, curling against him with her head on his shaggy chest.

"They'll find a way. And I'll stay with you. You won't be alone this time."

Johnny hung his head and covered his eyes with his gnarled hand. He couldn't have her. She deserved better than an animal for her guy. He realized one terrible truth. He did not want to live as a werewolf, even if Sonia was willing to stay with him.

Johnny just wanted to crawl under a rock, but there was blood to draw and tests to run and results to consider. He spent the night in the facility. Sonia refused to leave him so they brought in another bed. The next morning Scofield, Zharov and MacConnelly came with the news that Johnny already knew. The shots would no longer work.

But they did have another option. Johnny pushed himself up and stared from one grim face to the next. Whatever it was, not one of them liked it.

Sonia must have sensed doom, as well, for she inched closer to his side and curled her cold hands around his furry bicep.

It was his captain who broke the silence.

"Zharov has been working on an avenue that shows some promise. This is entirely different than what you had. It's not a treatment. More like a weapon. Instead of enabling you to change forms, it changes you back to human. All the way back. You'll lose your special vision, enhanced sense of smell and you'll lose your strength, too. We didn't want that for you. We were hoping to keep you as a shifter, like me."

So he could fight vampire assassins overseas?

The major took over here, seamlessly picking up where the captain left off and confirming her suspicions.

"This formula is being developed for enemy combatant werewolves to give our men a chance."

A chance that her captain and Johnny never had, Sonia realized.

The captain went on. "It works—100 percent in lab tests. It changes the dogs back to canine form."

Johnny's sign was obvious as he thumped his chest. The captain shook his head.

"Zharov has gone as far as he can with animal tests. We were hoping to field test it on an enemy werewolf before offering it to you. That opportunity has not been forthcoming."

Johnny signed his answer and listened as Sonia spoke his words.

"We're hard to catch."

Mac's smile seemed forced. "Yeah, we sure the hell are."

Sonia watched Johnny's words and then shook her head. He motioned to Mac. Sonia gritted her teeth as she spoke. "He says he'll be the first human subject."

Zharov stepped forward, hands clasped behind his back, seeming at ease, but Johnny smelled the stress pheromones pouring from him like mist from a lake.

"There is a seventy percent mortality rate, Lam. It's consistent and I haven't been able to increase the survival rate."

Johnny reached for the doctor gripping the front of his pristine white lab coat. Sonia saw murder in his eyes. The captain started towards Johnny, but Sonia was closer and she grabbed his thick wrist with both hands and tugged. She wasn't strong enough to stop him, but she was strong enough to distract him.

"Senior officer," she said, appealing to his training.

Johnny's eyes flicked to her and then back to the doctor. He leaned in and growled, showing his powerful canines. Then he let go. Zharov staggered back, holding his chest.

Johnny started signing.

"He says he should have been given the choice."

"It was decided that the best option was to keep you safe and…"

His words fell off and now Sonia was angry. They wanted Johnny to remain a werewolf. Sonia lunged at the doctor and Johnny swept her off her feet, holding her for the few seconds it took for her brain to reengage. She'd gotten into more trouble on impulse than anyone she knew.

"Thanks," she whispered.

He released her and patted her shoulder.

He signed his answer and Sonia threw up her hands angry at Johnny now. He didn't care. This was his life and his decision.

"What did he say?" asked Mac.

"He said better odds than he got on his last mission." She turned back to him.

Mac took over here. "This wasn't even an option until recently. This treatment, wasn't intended for your situation. This is a weapon developed to neutralize the enemy. They plan to use it to kill werewolves. It's lethal."

Johnny signed that they said they'd modified it so it wasn't as lethal.

Sonia spoke quickly, her voice sharp. "Not as lethal? Are you crazy? Didn't you hear them? Seventy percent, they said. I'm not going to stand here and watch you die."

Well, he wasn't staying like this and he told her so.

"Why not? Why do you have to do this stupid dangerous thing instead of being patient for a little while longer? Wait until they catch a wolf and try it on someone other than you."

He signed and she translated.

"Do you have anything else in the works?" Her eyes pleaded with the doctor, but Zharov shook his head.

"This is our best option to date. We are predicting that if he survives, he would be human and all traces of the werewolf protein would be eliminated. He would not be able to shift again."

Johnny looked to Mac as he signed. Sonia spoke in cadence with his signs.

He says, "What about Bri?"

Mac met Johnny's stare in silence for a moment. "Not your objective, soldier. You're relieved of duty."

Johnny turned to Zharov.

Do it, he signed.

She didn't translate. Instead she turned on him and clasped his hand in both of hers. "Johnny, don't. I'll wait if you will."

No.

She didn't give up. Just changed tactics like any good marine. "You have a family that needs you. Without you, they will lose their home. Remember? You're mom doesn't make enough to support them. Your sister won't go to college. Don't do this."

If I live, I can support them.

She rested a hand on her hip. "What if you don't?"

He drew a deep breath and met her angry eyes. *Death benefit.*

Sonia punched him hard in the chest with the backs of both her fists. He barely felt it.

If I do this, then I can have you.

"You have me. Johnny, you already have me, if you'll only wait."

Mac stepped to the opposite side of the bed. "I think she's right," he said. "It's too dangerous."

Johnny shook his head and began to sign. This time Sonia translated.

"He is asking you to look after his family, Captain." She pursed her lips and glared fire at him. "Don't you do it."

The captain flicked his gaze back to Johnny and nodded. "I'll see to them."

Johnny lay his head back on the examining table and closed his eyes, releasing his breath. *Just like dying,* he thought.

Sonia fell across his chest, warm and small and fragrant as summer flowers. "Johnny, I'll wait for as long as it takes. Do you hear me? I love you. I'll wait."

She stared up at him and he knew it was true. She did love him. He knew she had never said those words to anyone and never felt that way about anyone. Now she said it to him and he couldn't say it back because he was a goddamned werewolf again. No longer fit for her, no longer able to offer himself to her.

Johnny felt the sweet ache of longing for what he wanted most while knowing that he might never have it. He had her love. But it wasn't enough to keep him from trying for the brass ring. Because he loved her, too. But he wasn't going to sign those words. He was going to whisper them in her ear as they made love or he was going to die trying to be human.

She must have seen something in his expression because the hope drained from her eyes with the color from her face. He could not stand to see her hurting so he stroked her hair and held her until she pulled away.

"Look at me," she demanded, her words lashing angry and quick.

He did. She was flushed and her eyes flashed fire.

"You're still going through with this?" Her words were crisp, staccato, like gunfire.

Johnny released a breath, suddenly weary with all this. He met her troubled stare and nodded, knowing it was not what she wanted to hear.

"I love you, John Lam. Doesn't that mean anything to you?"

His heart twisted and throbbed in his chest because it meant everything to him. But her confession only made him more determined to go through with it.

She must have known she was losing the battle for she added a threat. "I won't stay to watch you die." Then her voice went liquid with promise. She whispered to him. "Be patient. It can be like before. We can go home together."

It could never be like that again. Maybe she believed they could go back to being roommates. He knew better. They had moved far past that. Sonia looked away. So she knew it, as well, but she was desperate enough to say anything to stop him. But he couldn't wait. Not if there was a chance for them. But he couldn't say all that to her. Couldn't say anything at all. So, instead he signed just one word.

Goodbye.

She stiffened and shrank back, huddling beside his bed.

"Johnny?"

He was a brave man, but not brave enough to see the grief on her face and the anguish glimmering in her tear-filled eyes. So he looked away.

Sonia turned and fled the room.

Chapter 14

Sonia waited for the captain outside Johnny's room. When he appeared he looked tired and unhappy. His gaze flicked to her and his jaw bunched as he returned her salute.

"Dismissed, Touma." He tried to stride past her but she took up beside him, matching his pace.

"I want a transfer."

The captain stopped walking. "You really going to run?"

"I'm not running." She flapped her arms like a flight-less bird. "Can't you see what's happening here? It's the gun in the medicine cabinet all over again. That treatment is the bullet only this time I can't stop him."

"You could stay with him."

"No, Captain. All due respect, sir, I can't." She cupped her hands over her eyes. "All right. Yes. I'm running. I'm not strong enough to see this through."

"Yes, you are."

Sonia swallowed back a sob. She'd seen her mother's self-destruction. But she wasn't riding along for Johnny's.

Her throat burned like fire, but she held it in refusing to fall to pieces, not until she got clear of the last security point.

"He gets to choose, Touma. His choice. Not ours."

She dropped her hands from her eyes and glared up at him. "But what choice is he making? Is he trying to be human again or is he just giving up?"

"Maybe he'd rather die than live like that." There was a haunted quality in the captain's tone, the truth that comes only from experience. "Who are you to judge him?"

Sonia stared in horror. The captain was giving up, too.

"Are you trying to bury him? Say a few prayers and move on? Better than having to look at him everyday and know what you did."

"You're out of line, Touma," growled the captain, his eyes changing color on their way from blue to icy blue, husky blue—wolf blue.

She didn't care. He was going to listen to her.

"Well, I don't want him to die. Especially when I know why he's so eager to be human again." She beat a hand on her chest in rapid succession. "Me. That's why. He's thinking crazy."

"He's a big boy. He knows what he wants."

"Yeah," Sonia said. "And either way he gets it. He's either human or he's dead." Her arms went slack as all the fight drained from her. "So do I get my transfer?"

He fixed her with wolf-blue eyes. "The sooner the better." He snorted his disapproval. "I knew you'd quit."

She leaned in, refusing to back down. "You told me to distract him, keep him occupied and you didn't care how. I did my job."

"Now I'm doing mine. You'll ship out tomorrow. Get packed. Dismissed, Touma."

She made it to the elevator on a hot rush of anger that erupted into tears before she reached the barracks. She was moving again. Running again. At least she wasn't going back to jail. She'd gotten what she wanted, hadn't she? She was still free.

It didn't take long to pack a footlocker.

Sonia headed up the hill in the late afternoon to retrieve the few personal items she had left in Johnny's place. She tried not to think too hard, tried not to look about the empty house or to recall how happy she had been here with him. Tried not to remember that for the first time in her life she had felt at home. It was all gone, vanished with her silly dreams of tomorrows. All anyone ever had was now. Johnny understood it. It was why he took that second shot.

But it was done and she had to move again because she knew very well how this would all end. She had held out her heart to him, had offered to wait and he had cast her aside. The pain of his rejection was so great that she just felt numb as if her spine wasn't really connected to her body. Just sort of moving through the motions as her mind was hidden safely away behind a hard armored shell.

Why had she ever let him get past that armor? She'd just never thought that a werewolf could possibly be someone she'd be attracted to and he had sneaked up on her. She'd made a mistake and now it was going to cost her.

Funny. This time it wasn't just her closing doors; he'd shut her out, too.

Sonia's throat was raw from crying and her eyes were puffy. She allowed herself one more look out the porch but instead of seeing the glorious vista of the Pacific Ocean, her eyes were drawn to the path that led to the natural grotto where Johnny had made love to her that last time. Sonia glanced to the path and then back to the stairs, feeling pulled in two directions. She didn't know if staying was right or leaving was right. She only knew that Johnny didn't love her enough to stay alive.

She wasn't enough. Had never been enough. Not for her mom and not for Sergeant John Loc Lam. Johnny was going to do this. Either way he would be going someplace she could not follow. She pressed the pads of her fingers to her chest over her heart and rubbed as if the pressure could ease the ache that went to her very core. Not good enough. Not good enough to keep, not good enough for him to stay. For just a moment in time she thought that Johnny shared her feelings. But just like every man, beginning with the father she never knew, he was leaving her behind.

Sonia spun away and marched double-time out the front door. She tossed the plastic bag of her belongings into the passenger side of the Jeep and headed down the mountain. When she neared Brianna's home, she found herself turning into the drive. She needed to say goodbye.

Brianna greeted her with a warm smile that flickered and died at the first look at her. "What happened?"

Sonia opened her mouth and the tears started again. Brianna ushered her in and then brought her some water before sitting across from her on the far side of the dining room table.

Through tears and some choking, Sonia managed to get it all out. Brianna shook her head.

"Men and their codes of honor. Of course Travis wouldn't see that accepting the duty of looking after his family would make it possible for Johnny to do this. Wait until I get a hold of him."

Sonia didn't want to cause trouble between newlyweds. "I told Johnny I loved him and he said goodbye. I want to make a home with him but…"

"Sonia," Brianna's tone sounded chiding. "No matter where Travis is he is with me. My home is in his heart and his home is in mine."

Sonia squinted at the cryptic comment. What did that even mean?

Brianna gave her a gentle smile and said, "If you love Johnny than nothing can separate you. Certainly not this."

Sonia squinted as she shook her head thinking of all the things that separated them. His condition separated them physically. And even if that wasn't the case, Johnny wanted a combat assignment and Sonia wanted to serve out her term of service in some safe little backwater. Johnny wanted to travel. She wanted a backyard. And there was that little problem of her transfer and the bigger problem of the rule prohibiting fraternizing. Brianna and her husband might not ever be apart, but she and Johnny most certainly would be. Often. Always.

"You don't understand, he's already said he doesn't want me."

"I don't believe that. I've seen you two together. Maybe Johnny just can't stand that you'd be stuck with him the way he is."

"I don't care," said Sonia, her voice rising.

"But he cares. The man has his pride, Sonia. We

don't always understand it, but we have to acknowl-edge it."

"I've been reassigned."

"I see. Then you'll have to go, won't you?"

Sonia noted Brianna's enigmatic smile. Why did Brianna make it sound as if Sonia had some choice, as if she were missing something? Brianna almost sounded ironic. As Sonia puzzled at her true meaning Brianna's expression went blank. Her hostess was on her feet an instant later and with such haste she sent the chair, upon which she sat, tumbling to the floor. Sonia stood, suddenly on alert.

"Do you smell that?" she whispered, glancing furtively about the empty room.

Sonia inhaled and found nothing but the sweet tropical air laced with the hint of jasmine. "What?"

Brianna's body began to vibrate and then, right before her very eyes, Brianna vanished.

Sonia stumbled back and nearly fell. Someone bounded up the porch stairs with a heavy footfall and Sonia turned to see something zip to the screen door in the kitchen at the same instant the front door crashed open. It was a man dressed all in black. Who wore a turtleneck in this heat? she wondered as he charged right for her. There was something wrong with his head. It was misshapen, as if he had some terrible allergic reaction or a dreadful skin condition. Purple welts covered the lumpy mass of his face. But it was the glowing white eyes that triggered understanding. The man opened his mouth and she saw the glint of his long white fangs and Sonia cried out.

How had they gotten past the perimeter?

She threw the chair at him and retreated, only to find herself captured by the one coming through the screen.

"That's not her," said the first.

Sonia struggled against the unbreakable grip, her skin chilling at the strange cool touch of her attacker.

The first one slapped her. The blow sent an explosion of pain blasting through her jaw and made her so dizzy she nearly threw up. The creature leaned forward and inhaled.

"Human," it said. "Kill her."

Instantly a hand gripped her forehead forcing her chin up, exposing her neck. The sweet, cloying scent of gardenias surrounded her, so strong she thought she might be ill. His mouth descended and she became unnaturally aware of the pounding of her heart and the thrum of blood in the great vessels at her throat. This thing was going to kill her right there in the captain's living room. She turned her head farther to the side and then dropped, as she had been taught in basic training, performing a quick half turn and elbowing him in the groin. Sonia had the satisfaction of hearing the wind leave his lungs before she dove away. But she didn't get far.

The other one moved with a speed that made him only a blur and she found herself in his arms, staring up at his hideous mottled face, slitted nose and the bone-white fangs pressing deep against his thick, liver-colored lips. She shrank back in horror and he smiled, showing the three-inch fangs all the way to his crimson gums. *Hideous,* she thought, trembling.

This one smelled like blood. Her skin dimpled as the chill took her. Sonia tried for his thumbs, intending to break them in her bid for freedom, but he struck her so fast she went dizzy. He had her in the crook of his arm, squeezing her like a boa constrictor. She fought fiercely at first but, as the dizziness increased, her movements became clumsy. He was suffocating her.

"Give her back to me," said the lavender one, his image blurring before her watering eyes.

This would be the last thing she ever saw.

"Johnny," she choked.

The second vampire released her and pushed her into the arms of the first. The fangs grazed her neck. Sonia inhaled, trying to clear the fog from her brain and mount another defense.

"No!" The voice was female.

Brianna appeared before her and threw a punch at the one who had already cut into Sonia's neck with his razor-sharp teeth.

"Get her," howled the mottled vampire and Sonia was discarded like an old banana peel as the two vampires shot after Brianna who had disappeared. She could barely see the males. But Brianna had vanished once more. The males chased her out the front door. Sonia reached for her phone and flipped it open hitting the favorites button as she staggered out into the yard. She had to help Brianna.

Before she could press the captain's number, Brianna appeared. "Get in the Jeep. Hurry!"

Brianna grabbed her arm and hustled her along. They were ten steps from the vehicle when the vampires reappeared, one, two, three…nine. Brianna's hands slipped from Sonia's arm.

"Let her go," Brianna ordered. "She's nothing to you."

Several of the males eyed Sonia and licked their lips.

"Take them both. Don't kill the human—yet," said the one with the purple bruises on his face.

Sonia took one step before they grasped her but she

still managed to hit the captain's number as the phone fell from her hand. A glance told her that they'd captured Brianna, as well. The vampires used thick plastic zip ties to secure Sonia's wrists and ankles and she remembered they hated metal, iron especially. What did she have that was metal? Her brass belt buckle. That was all.

Two of the males lifted Sonia carrying her so quickly that the landscape about her blurred. She shut her eyes to contain the dizziness. From then on, she felt the jarring gate of their run and the uneven ground over which they charged at superhuman speeds. Now and again she looked about and saw they were taking her over the opposite side of the volcanic peak, through dense cover and then open, rocky terrain.

Had the captain gotten her call?

Johnny waited, mouth open as the IV was inserted into an artery beneath his gums. It hurt of course, but there was no helping it since they couldn't get a needle through his skin. They'd placed a block between his teeth to keep him from moving and disrupting the IV. Also, he supposed, in case he went into seizures.

But if he didn't die, if he were human again, he could go after Sonia and explain, apologize and ask her to stay. If he didn't survive she was better off gone.

This treatment also involved a shot of some other damned poison that killed something in his blood. He didn't understand it, but he didn't have to. His job was to survive it. He thought he'd already survived worse.

Dr. Zharov put his hand on the white plastic switch on the IV line, his thumb poised to introduce the new treatment. "Here goes. You'll feel uncomfortable. Try to lie still."

This weapon was being developed in a gaseous form to spray any werewolves they found. But it would kill them. Turn them human and then stop their breathing. Now the chemicals were in liquid form. The good doctor aimed to avoid burning his lungs beyond repair. Some of the test animals had survived. A few pigs, half the dogs, zero rabbits, zero chimps. He was a Lam. Had they tested any lambs? He blinked his eyes. The sedative made his thinking fuzzy.

Mac stepped into view.

"You okay?"

Johnny lifted a thumb. He wished Sonia were here. Instead of staring at him with anxious eyes, she'd hold his hand.

He knew the instant the stuff hit his bloodstream. Uncomfortable? Was that what the doctor said? His body tensed and he could not keep from arching, his back rising from the table as the treatment burned like molten lead. He wheezed as the pain took the air from his lungs. His vision blurred.

"Johnny? You still with us?" Mac's voice, he knew, but he couldn't respond as he curled his fingers into the padding on the table, feeling the stuffing wad beneath his claws. "Doc, what's happening?"

"Attacking his red blood cells. I told you it would be rough," Zharov said.

"Do they all do this?" asked Mac.

"Yes."

The poison scalded down his arms and an instant later the muscles of his chest burned. A second after that his diaphragm stopped working. It was just like having the wind knocked from him. He could not breathe in or out. He stared up at Mac and saw the fear in his captain's eyes. Johnny's chest ached so badly he lifted a hand to press down on the spot and felt his heart go still. His fingers went numb. The pain ebbed. His vision darkened and his body went slack.

He felt the cold metal paddles on his chest and heard Zharov shout, "Clear."

The electricity jolted his body into involuntary movement. But he didn't feel it. In fact, he had a whole different view. Instead of looking up at the doctor and Mac, he was looking down on them from above. They were all leaning over something, hairy and black. He recognized himself but felt no attachment to that pain-wracked body. It was so much nicer here, above all the sorrow and pain.

He wanted to drift away like a cloud. The doctor shoved something that looked like a hard piece of white plastic down Johnny's throat. He watched himself and realized his old body was slack and still. A moment later a breathing tube was inserted. Monitors screamed and Johnny saw Mac cover his eyes with a forearm as he gripped Johnny's slack hand.

"No," Mac whispered. "Not Johnny, too."

Johnny felt sorry for his friend, but not sorry enough to come back. Maybe he would go to Sonia.

Sonia.

Johnny looked down at his body on the table and saw he was now human. It worked. He was human again, but he was also dead—or dying. He wasn't sure.

Zharov inserted an IV into his slack arm and red blood began to flow from the sack on the stand.

He thought about his mother and sister. Then he thought of losing Sonia forever. No. He wouldn't. He loved her and he wanted to be with her. In that instant, he dropped back into his body like a stone heaved into a lake. The reconnection jarred him and the pain seared his insides. Surely he wouldn't survive this much pain.

The monitor's stopped screaming. They beeped and blipped in an erratic rhythm, a cacophony chorus. Was that his heart beating? Johnny drew air into his oxygen-starved lungs.

"He's back," said Zharov. "Get an IV into his other arm."

Johnny smiled. He was human again.

"Mac," he whispered, still too tired to open his eyes.

"Here I am, buddy. You gave us a scare." His captain leaned close as Johnny whispered to him.

"Sonia. Don't let her leave."

"You got it. Just rest. She's not going anywhere."

Johnny came to in the recovery room and then drifted out again. He asked for Sonia and Mac and Sonia again. Mac was there, but where was Sonia? They fed him juice and Jello. He marveled at his hands, bare and smooth.

He inhaled and could not scent who was in the room when Mac sat right beside his bed.

"I can't smell you," he whispered.

"You're human, Johnny. No more super sight. No more super hearing. No more super strength."

That was right. He'd never been like Mac, changing at will, keeping his powers in human form. Now he was just human.

"You know what that means?" asked Mac.

"Less time trying to wear shredded clothing," Johnny said and grinned. His gums ached.

"It means I can kick your ass again."

Johnny's eyes drifted closed. "You wish."

When he came to again, he was in a private room

with the television playing a ball game. Playoffs. Angels were winning. Mac was speaking to Dr. Zharov.

"What time is it?" asked Johnny.

Mac startled and moved to flank the bed as Zharov took the opposite side. He was surrounded.

"Welcome back," said Zharov.

"It's sixteen hundred. How are you feeling? Hungry?"

"As a wolf."

Mac finally smiled. Then he reached for the buzzer corded around the bed rail. A woman's voice came through the speaker behind him.

"Yes, Sergeant Lam?"

"Bring some food, please," said Mac.

"Yes, sir."

Mac smiled down at Johnny. "Forgot how ugly you are."

"You're just jealous."

Mac's smile faltered a moment. "A little. But if I were human, I couldn't be near Brianna."

Johnny knew the truth of that. And now Johnny couldn't be around her any more. That realization made him sad. What else had he lost by losing his wolf half?

As if on queue, the doctor began speaking. "You're body's reaction to the treatment was worse than expected. We lost you for several minutes. Do you understand what I'm saying, Sergeant?"

"Yes. I died."

"Just so. But we brought you back."

"I remember leaving my body." He turned to Mac. "You said, 'Not Johnny, too.'"

The color left Mac's face at that and he glanced to the doctor who shrugged one shoulder. "Sometimes you can still hear when you're heart has stopped. It's been known to happen."

"I saw you. I was up on the ceiling."

That made the doctor give him a long hard stare. "Regardless of where you went, you're back now and I have to say that it is well you survived because you would never survive such a treatment again."

"How do you know?" asked Johnny.

"We've tried with test subjects. Turned some of the successful transitions back to their were-form. Zero survival rates on any of the initial survivors when attempts were made to return them to their natural forms. Congratulations, Lam. You're human and you'll be staying human so don't forget your flak jacket, because you're not bulletproof any longer."

If it meant he could hold Sonia, he didn't care.

"How long until I can get out of here?" he asked.

"I'm keeping you overnight. No arguments. Mac-Connelly said you don't remember the initial attack."

Johnny nodded.

"Still there should be evidence."

Johnny had bigger concerns. He turned to Mac. "What about Sonia. Is she still here?"

"Until tomorrow."

"Does she know I made it?"

"Not yet. I'll call her shortly."

"Why not now?"

"Because, even though you didn't die, you look like you did. You'd scare the shit out of her. I'll have her report here tomorrow. See if you two can patch things up."

"She doesn't want me to take a combat assignment."

"That's between the two of you."

"But you'll cancel the transfer?"

Mac sighed. "Looks like you got it bad."

"It's not bad."

Zharov patted Johnny on the shoulder. "I'll check in with you this evening."

"Thanks for everything, Doc."

Zharov gave a rare and brief smile, and strode from the room saluting as Major Scofield marched in.

"There's my boy," he said, smiling at Johnny. "You gave us all a scare, Lam. But I knew you'd make it. You've got the heart of a warrior."

The major shook his hand and then folded his hands behind his back glancing from John to Mac and back again.

"I've got some news. If you're well enough, Lam, I'd like to tell you what we turned up about your initial attack in Afghanistan."

Mac blanched but remained on his feet, his body tense as if he expected the major to punch him in the face. Johnny gripped the bed rail.

"Yes, sir," he said, still getting accustomed to the sound of his own voice.

"I'll cut to the chase. I got ahold of the missing video footage." He met Mac's gaze as he continued. "The ones from the helmets of your rifleman, Robert Towsen, and your grenadier, John Lam. We didn't get much from Towsen. But you sure could see what attacked him."

Johnny glanced to Mac noticing he looked positively ill. Was he recalling Bobby being swept off his feet by something they couldn't even see? All this time he'd carried the guilt of attacking his own man, of turning him into a monster. Now he was going to hear what really happened. Johnny knew it would be the truth because the major was a straight shooter. His grip on the bed rail tightened.

"Captain, Lam's camera footage is very clear. You

can see it for yourself, though I'd understand if you preferred not to. The camera captured you knocking Lam out of harm's way and the werewolf attacking you then leaving you for dead."

"But that doesn't make any sense," said Mac.

"I had Zharov check Johnny over. He doesn't have a scar anywhere on his body. No bite, Captain."

Johnny knew it was true. He and Mac stared at each other. Mac reached up to rub his shoulder. Beneath his shirt, Johnny knew there was a massive scar that covered his shoulder, back and chest from the jaws of their attacker. Still his friend couldn't understand what the major was telling him. He clung to his guilt like some lost child with his stuffed bear, afraid to set it aside and walk away.

Johnny lifted his hand from the bed rail and clasped Mac's forearm as the major explained.

"You didn't bite him, Captain. You saved him. And he saved you. Carried you out, called for medevac." The major turned to Johnny. "A fine job on your first time under fire, son. You make an old Devil Dog proud."

Mac looked to Johnny who nodded. His captain, his first sergeant and the man who had lead him into combat covered his face with his hands and wept. Johnny dragged him into a fast embrace, dropping a kiss on his head.

"Is it true?" whispered Mac.

"You didn't do it," said Johnny.

Mac drew back and stared at him in confusion then turned to Major Scofield.

"So how did he end up a werewolf?"

The major made a face. "Records have been destroyed. But I know he was human when you left that building and a werewolf when he left the field hospital.

Zharov thinks Colonel Lewis used your blood, Mac, to inject Johnny. Not sure if he did it or if he ordered someone else to do it. But you bet your ass, I'm going to find out."

Mac shook his head as if he had an earache.

"Might be that not being bitten was why you couldn't change. Zharov is looking at that possibility now. Back to his research. He really doesn't like treating patients. Prefers white rats, I think." The major chuckled and gave them each a final look. "Well, I have reports to file and asses to kick." He left the room muttering. "I'm going to cause holy hell over this. They'll wish their mommas never met their poppas when I'm through with them. Gonna be some court-martials."

The captain's phone rang and he drew it out. "It's Touma." He sounded surprised as he frowned down at the screen, jabbing the connect button and lifting the phone to his ear. "Touma?"

His frown deepened. Johnny pushed himself up as the first wisp of worry curled inside him like tobacco smoke. "What's wrong?"

Mac stared at the phone and then lifted it back to his ear. "Touma?" His eyes flicked to Johnny. "Dropped. We're three floors deep here. Spotty service." He disconnected and headed to the wall phone. A moment later he was calling her. "No answer."

"Where is she?"

"Barracks, I suppose. Maybe calling to check on you." They stared at each other. Both had seen enough action not to ignore that trickle of uncertainty.

"You'll check on her?" asked Johnny.

"Done," said Mac, lifting his phone again as he strode from the room.

Johnny ate his meal in record time and removed

his IVs under the nurse's protests, then he wouldn't let her put them back in. Mac came back and ordered the nurses out. He'd had the grounds swept for Corporal Touma and did not find her. She'd checked out a Jeep but had not left the base. Johnny got dressed and switched off the ball game.

"She might be at your place," said the captain. "She have things there?"

"Yes. She also might be at yours."

They both thought of the phone call, the open line with no one on the other end. Realization brought the captain to stillness.

"I have to go."

"I'm coming, too."

"No, you're not. You can barely walk."

The captain headed out the door with Johnny on his heels. The captain didn't protest further. "Do you think it's them?"

Johnny didn't have to ask who he meant.

Vampires.

Chapter 15

Somehow Johnny kept up with Mac as they leaped into the Jeep. He was faster now than Johnny remembered, but that was the werewolf in him. Johnny glanced down at his watch and noticed the numbers were a bit blurred and suddenly he recalled the glasses he used for reading and now obviously needed again, though his distance sight had been twenty-twenty.

"Brianna's not answering," said Mac gunning the engine.

The radio on his hip clicked on as he accelerated up the road leading to their two homes. The voice on the other end sounded tinny.

"No perimeter alarms, sir. Your wife is not visible on any outdoor cameras, but everything looks quiet."

Mac lifted the radio. "Check the last twenty minutes. Use the super slow-mo."

"Roger. Out."

"She might just be indoors concentrating on her work," said Johnny.

"No, she would have answered. Doesn't feel right. Touma's not answering her phone, either."

Johnny set his teeth together as worry ate away at the lining of his stomach. A few endless moments later they roared into the driveway. Mac threw the Jeep in Park and leaped out.

"Bri!" he shouted and charged toward the open front door.

Johnny stepped to the drive and saw something hot pink on the ground. He stooped and lifted Sonia's mobile phone, neatly cased in the brightly colored rubber sheath. His fingers curled around the phone and he knew something terrible had happened. He searched the ground for blood.

Mac charged out of the house. "Not here. Can you smell them? The vampires are everywhere."

Johnny lifted his nose but the air smelled as it used to, giving him no useful information.

"Sonia?" he asked.

"Some of her blood is inside," said Mac.

Johnny charged past him, finding a small red puddle on the tile in the living room. Not much, just enough to stop his heart. He spun to face Mac. "They took them?"

Mac nodded. "Both. And headed up the mountain. I'm going after them."

"I'm coming, too."

Mac shook his head. "You can't keep up. Even if you could you can't beat a vampire anymore. Johnny, you're food to them now."

He stared at Mac as the truth of his words tore through him. He'd lost his tough skin and his claws and everything else that might keep Sonia alive.

"I'll change back."

"You can't. You heard Zharov. You barely survived the transition. He told you to your face you'd never survive it again."

Johnny didn't care. He had to save Sonia.

"You could bite me."

"Are you crazy? No! Get back to base. Tell them what happened and bring help."

Johnny hesitated under the direct order. "Why did they take Sonia?"

Mac didn't answer because they both knew. They were going to drain her blood and leave her behind as a warning to not follow. Johnny swayed.

"Take the Jeep and bring a squad with full body armor. Seal off all ports and close down the airfields. The bastards can't swim and they are not getting off this island."

"How'd they break perimeter without us knowing?"

He shook his head in bafflement.

"How many do you detect?" asked Johnny.

Mac lowered his head. "Nine." They both knew the captain would never best that many. Not alone, he wouldn't.

"They'll kill you," said Johnny.

"They have my wife."

Mac tossed Johnny his radio and phone. The captain lay his personal sidearm on the hood of the Jeep before dragging off his shirt, boots and trousers. His transformation was so fast Johnny barely had time to retrieve his weapon and climb back into the Jeep before Mac was charging up the mountain after the scent of the vampires. Johnny barked orders into the radio, closing the ports and grounding all aircraft. He also ordered Zharov to the medical facility, issuing orders that Mac had never given him. He didn't care.

Without him, Mac was dead, Sonia was dead and Brianna was worse than dead. He knew what they'd do to Mac's wife. She'd be a living breeder for the next decade, bearing as many vampires as possible in that time. All the while the indoctrination would take place. A year, a decade, it didn't matter so long as they turned her into a puppet and all the time her soul-killing powers would be growing until just one night in her arms would mean death to any human unfortunate enough to be her target. The perfect assassin.

Johnny floored it. Was Sonia still alive? He knew that the moment they recognized Mac was on their trail, they'd kill Sonia. Johnny skidded to a halt before the medical facility and raced inside to find Dr. Zharov in his lab.

Zharov was none too pleased that Johnny had checked himself out of the hospital and was now issuing orders.

"Mac ordered that you release one vile of his blood to me."

Zharov's eyes narrowed.

"Direct order. He needs it to fight the vampires," said Johnny, but he could see his lie didn't work.

"His blood won't do him any good. It's not toxic unless injected...." His words trickled to a halt as he stiffened. "No. He can't ask you to do that."

"He didn't ask."

"Lam, are you crazy? I explained it to you. You do this and you never come back."

"Give me the shot, Doc."

"I will not."

"They took Sonia."

The doctor remained where he was. Johnny knew where he kept the blood and made for the refrigerator. Zharov tried to stop him. Johnny disengaged himself as gently as he could. Still, he thought the doctor would have one hell of a shiner. He retrieved Mac's blood, neatly labeled, and found a syringe. He'd been around this place long enough to know how to fill one and how to get the air bubbles out.

Zharov rose from the floor, rubbing the place where his head had cracked the wall.

"Lam. Don't. There has to be another way."

"There isn't."

Sonia's capture had made everything so clear. Johnny didn't hesitate. He had to rescue Sonia even if it meant he'd be a werewolf forever because he couldn't live knowing he might have saved her and didn't. She was his family, too. Not the kind you were born into but the kind you choose. He pushed the plunger into his arm. Mac's blood mingled with his. Either way, he'd have no regrets because he was doing all he could do to save her life.

The rush of power flooded his nervous system. He threw his head back and roared as his body shifted, stretched and transformed into his wolf form. His senses buzzed to life. He headed out the back, charging up the mountain, following the scent trail that was now as clear as an open highway.

Nine vampires and two were familiar to him. He recognized their odor. These were the ones who had escaped the first attack, back in California. This time, none of the vampires would escape because he planned to kill every last one.

I'm coming, Sonia. Please don't die.

* * *

Johnny tore over the open ground, leaping like a lion over the rocky pinnacles and dangerous chasms. How did those vampires beat their perimeter alarms?

Sonia's image floated before him, urging him on. He knew he would catch the vampires and he knew he would kill them. But he did not know if he would be in time to rescue Sonia and help Mac or if he would be there only to exact revenge.

The promise of her recovery and the pain caused by the possibility of her impending death stabbed at his heart, peaks and valleys of hope and despair. He loved her. That truth he could no longer deny. He would rescue her if he could or he would die in the attempt.

The scent of the vampires grew stronger with each powerful stride. He followed Mac's trail, straight at those purple-faced monsters. He could find Brianna's sweet fragrance there, as well. He scented Mac's fear and Sonia's terror. He knew Mac's upset came from the same place as his own. He did not fear death, except the death of the one he loved.

Close. He was close now. As he tore into the cover of the jungle he heard the helicopters thumping blades as they sought a visual on the escaping vampires. But Johnny knew, even burdened with two women, the vampires moved too fast for even a werewolf to see. It was one of many advantages to the bloodsuckers. They were fast and they could only be killed by opening a vein and keeping it open until they bled out. Impossible for a human to accomplish because the vampires healed so damned fast. But they couldn't heal a wound inflicted by a werewolf. Advantage, werewolf.

Vampires had teeth strong enough to puncture a werewolf's hide and, once open, they could inject their deadly poison. They used a little to stun their prey, but they could inject enough even to stop the heart of a werewolf, if they got a good hold. Advantage, vampire.

He pictured Mac facing nine of them. Seeing them only when they slowed to take a bite. Brianna could see them, too. She could also move as fast as they could. But only if she were free.

He heard Mac's roar an instant before he broke from cover and took in the scene. Two vampires were down, bleeding out, one decapitated and the other torn nearly in half. Four surrounded Mac, circling like hyenas as another two held Brianna and Sonia. He didn't think. Just acted on instinct, leaping at the closest vamp and using his front claws to puncture its lungs as he tore a bite out of the side of its neck. He dropped the dying carcass and bounded toward Sonia's captor who released her, pushing her at him like a weapon as he ran. In an eye's blink he had vanished.

Johnny changed direction and swiped at Brianna's captor, tearing away the side of his face. Screaming, the vampire released her instantly, baring his teeth and lunging. His movements were lightning fast. Johnny could not see them, but he blocked and got in a lucky blow, sending the bloodsucker reeling. It took only one more slashing cut of all four of his claws to tear through flesh until he contacted the thing's spine. It writhed and screeched, not recognizing it was already dead. Even its ability to heal would not save it because the blood poured in a river from the artery that supplied the lower half of its body.

"Look out," shouted Sonia.

Johnny ducked and rolled, coming to his feet as another vampire sailed past him in a vain attempt to land on Johnny's back. He saw Brianna chew at her bonds and Sonia grab a rough bit of volcanic slag to saw through the bonds at her legs. Then she stood and removed her belt.

Johnny turned to help Mac, seeing he had killed another and now faced two more. One disappeared. A moment later Brianna screamed. The thing had her and was vibrating as he prepared to vanish with her. Sonia stood only a foot away. She had wound her belt around her hand, the buckle on top like brass knuckles. She smashed her fist into the creature's cheek. Flesh seared as it screamed and released Brianna who vanished instantly. The vampire reached for Sonia who had time for one backward stride before it had her.

Johnny leaped and got hold of its leg cutting the calf muscles to the bone. The vampire screamed and crumbled to the earth. That would teach him to touch Sonia. *Let's see it run with no Achilles tendon,* Johnny thought. He used his claws like a mountain climber's crampons to climb the bloodsucker's downed body as if it were K2. When he reached the thick thigh, he twisted its leg to expose its inner thigh and he sliced with his right and his left, opening deep gashes, shredding the femoral artery that spouted in a red fountain like a dying sperm whale. The thing made a last lunge at Johnny's throat and Johnny cuffed him with an open hand. He died in a pool of his own warm blood.

The remaining vampire rushed Mac and got so close to biting him, Johnny saw the poison squirting from his distended fangs. Johnny flipped, grabbing his enemy's head and twisting until he heard a snap. He knew that wouldn't kill him, but it gave Mac time to bite its neck, tearing away a massive amount of muscle and bone. Mac then dropped the body to step onto the center of his enemy's lower back gaining better leverage. He twisted until he severed the head, tossing it away. It came to rest in a tree, the eyes still blinking and its lips still moving.

Johnny looked to Mac who held up two fingers. Johnny scanned the ground finding seven bodies. Mac had told him he scented nine. Johnny had scented nine, as well. He knew the scent of the vampire he remembered calling the shots in California. None of these scents matched.

One had run. One had been long gone when Johnny arrived.

Now they faced a dilemma. Track the two remaining vampires or get Brianna and Sonia to safety.

Chapter 16

"Brianna?" Johnny heard Sonia call for her friend.

The female vampire reappeared before her husband who was still a blood-covered gray werewolf and threw herself sobbing into his arms.

Johnny gathered Sonia up in an embrace. She held tight, clutching the fur at his chest, the bloody belt dangling from her trembling fingers. He wanted to tell her how brave she had been, but that could wait. There were still two vampires loose and if they didn't kill them, they'd be back.

He stroked her head and relished the feel of her tucked close to him. He'd done it: he'd gotten to her in time and she was alive. That was all he wanted in the world.

Johnny lifted his head to see Mac and Brianna locked in a similar embrace. The two marines caught each other's gazes and Johnny motioned in the direction

the retreating vampire had taken with a slight gesture of his head and then lifted his brows. Mac shook his head, glanced at his wife and then back toward the base. Johnny understood. He wanted to take them to safety. He drew back and Sonia met his gaze. He started to sign.

Sonia watched him, speaking as he gestured. "He says, 'We need to go after them now or they'll come back with more.'"

Mac could not si... ...he vessel. Bou... ...ing again. ...that the vampires might have set an ambushe taki... ...e quick attack, one bite and the vampires won. But if Johnny and Mac could get a hold of them, they would finish them.

It was hard for a nine-foot werewolf to go unnoticed and as they had feared, the vampires had human sentries who sounded the alarm with a cry and gunfire before Mac got on deck and threw the shooter overboard. Johnny took out the other two humans, heaving one into the water after his comrade. He could sense the vampires stirring below decks and Johnny and Mac separated, blocking the two exits.

The first ran right into Johnny's arms. He tried for Johnny's neck as Johnny opened his and left him to bleed out on the steps. He met Mac before the main cabin. One vampire left and he was behind that door.

"I know you're out there," said a male voice. "I also know my associate is dead. I have a deal to propose."

Mac made a snorting sound, dismissing any deal. Johnny kicked down the door.

The vampire stood with his back to the window, his white eyes seeming sightless and his mottled skin a mask of scarlet and purple blotches. God, he'd seen snapping turtles who were better looking.

Mac and Johnny followed their scent trail over ground and through a short mostly natural volcanic tunnel that undermined the fence system and broke ground beyond the reach of cameras and sensors. The trail lead overland from there and continued all the way to the docks, ending at a sixty-eight-foot yacht.

Mac and Johnny surveyed the vessel. Close quarters gave them a large advantage because their quarry could not outrun them here. But the vamps had speed and knew the layout of that ne~~~~~ recognized ~~~~~~~~~~ ~~~~~~ Mac and Johnny One ~ ~Brianna to safety. Johnny started si~~~~~ b~~~sh.

Sonia shook her head, not liking his idea but translated word for word. "He says, 'They can't fly. Get the women to the helicopter and then we can track the bloodsuckers.'"

Mac nodded and started off in the direction of open ground. The journey seemed to take forever with Mac and Johnny scenting the air and listening for signs of attack. He knew he wouldn't see them. They moved too fast. Brianna could, however, and she kept her head swiveling as if she were center court at Wimbledon. Once on the rocky ground above the cover of the jungle it didn't take long for one of the pilots to spot them. Johnny loaded Sonia onto the helo and Brianna kissed Mac's furry cheek.

Once they were away, Mac and Johnny communicated wordlessly. They found the trail of the vampires and pursued. Both were determined to finish this and them. Surprisingly, the two vampires did not separate, which would have been a better tactical move. Perhaps the vamps didn't feel pursuit was likely because they had the advantage of speed. True, they were faster than werewolves for short stretches but they lacked the endurance of the wolf.

"Others of my kind know our position. If you kill me, more will come."

Mac pulled up extending his hand to Johnny.

The vampire spoke very fast now. "I have to report in. If I don't, they'll know. But I could lead them away from here. Keep her safe while you escape." He let his words die.

Mac looked to Johnny who drew a finger across his throat. He didn't trust this vampire. Better to kill him than leave him knowing their position.

Mac stepped back behind Johnny and transformed. Johnny kept his eyes on the vampire, waiting for an opportunity to kill him.

"Why should I trust you?" asked Mac.

"Because you are a marine. We work much the same as you. What would happen if a squad did not check in?"

Johnny and Mac exchanged looks.

"What are you offering for your miserable life?" asked Mac.

"I will depart for our next location. I won't report any trouble until I am in, let's say Japan. That gives you time to move to one of the locations we have searched, Europe, Africa, North America. We haven't finished the Middle East or South America. They are all looking for her there, too."

Johnny knew why the vampires would go to such trouble for one of their own. Mac had told him how rare Brianna was.

"This female we hunt is special, you know," said the vamp. "First generation. Her mother was an actual Leanan Sidhe, a true fairy muse. So this halfling can bear children from vampire or humans. But I don't know if she can bear your young. To my knowledge there has never been such a liaison between natural enemies."

"Maybe if you didn't keep your women captive, they'd be more likely to stick around."

The vampire laughed. "Look at me, Captain. What woman would willingly choose this?" He motioned to his deformed face. "The rest of me is just as pretty. My kind does what it must to survive."

"What's your name?" asked Mac.

"Burne Farrell. We met briefly in California."

When he and Mac had killed all but two of his men, Johnny thought.

The vampire glanced at Johnny. "Your friend was in werewolf form then, too. Brianna said that this one can't change back. Is it true?"

Johnny growled. Why would Brianna tell them this?

"Why should you care?" asked Mac.

"Just curiosity. We've never seen that before. Did you know that you cannot sire werewolves? Unlike Vampires, werewolves are made, not born."

Johnny saw Mac's shoulders sag with relief before he stiffened again. His captain had never mentioned children to him. Now he knew why. Mac didn't want to pass his wolf trait to his babies. Johnny realized it was a problem he had not even anticipated, Sonia having his children, the children being werewolves. He narrowed his eyes on Farrell, feeling a renewed sense of hate. The vamp might have killed her.

"Why should I believe you?" asked Mac.

"I have no interest in helping you create more werewolves. Why would I lie?" He flicked his gaze back to Mac. "So, do we have a deal?"

"You might just as easily call in more men."

"I might. Or I might value my life more than you do."

"All right." Mac extended his hand.

Burne drew his closer to his chest and stared at the offered hand then glanced at Mac. He was wise to be cautious. Mac could kill him just as easily while in human form. Finally Burne accepted. Mac clasped his hand and pulled him in so that their noses nearly touched.

"She's my wife, Burne. If you visit us again nothing will stop me from killing you."

Burne cowered and Mac released him.

"Understood."

"You've got ten minutes to be off this island," said Mac. "We'll be tracking you. If you turn back, I'll have your ship blown out of the water."

"As you wish. Until we meet again, Captain," said Farrell.

"We better not."

"Oh, I don't know. We often work with your government agencies. Our paths might cross after they let you off your leash."

"Ten minutes," said Mac and left the vampire and his dead comrade on their floating morgue.

Sonia sat next to Brianna as their helo circled far above the island. The view would have been incredible if she was not sick with worry over Johnny and the captain. Finally the pilot received the call that the marines were both safely back at base. She was so relieved that Johnny had not gone through with the treatment. That, even more than their rescue from the vampires, filled her with hope and joy that lifted her like a bubble in sparkling wine.

When they touched down, Major Scofield waited and hustled them into a secure facility. The major seemed more harried than usual to Sonia, though still thoroughly in command.

"Lam and MacConnelly are waiting inside."

The marines guarding each entrance snapped to attention at their passing.

Scofield continued speaking as he returned their salutes without breaking stride. "You gave us a scare, Brianna. I thought you could outrun them. That was the only reason I gave you permission to live off base."

Brianna glanced away.

"It was my fault, sir," Sonia said. "She came back for me and they caught her. She saved my life."

The major stopped and turned to look from one to the other. "That was very brave, Brianna. But if it ever happens again, you run. Touma is a marine. She knows how to fight."

"I hate to contradict, Major, but no human can best a vampire unless the vampire is lying on a bed of iron and even then I'd advise extreme caution." She looked at Sonia and her eyes twinkled. "Though Corporal Touma did manage to use her belt buckle to burn the face of the one holding me. Kept him from making off with me and gave Mac and Johnny an important edge."

The major stared at Sonia and smiled. "I'm not surprised. She's a Devil Dog, after all."

Sonia felt a painful bubble in her chest. It took a moment to recognize the unfamiliar emotion as pride. She smiled at the major and he returned it with one of his own. Then he motioned for them to precede him.

"Let's get you two secured. Lam and Mac are waiting. Lam, however, is in some very deep shit." The major followed them into a bunker of a room, located two floors down and surrounded by volcanic rock. "Oh, apologies for the language."

Why was Lam in trouble, Sonia wondered. Before she could ask, the major left them. Brianna drew a chair from the conference table and dragged it to the far corner of the room. Sonia sat at the opposite side, restlessly jiggling her leg as they waited.

A few minutes later Mac entered the room, tall and handsome in a uniform that showed fold marks on the trousers. Brianna rushed to meet him, kissing her husband with an enthusiasm and vigor that made Sonia's cheeks go hot. Johnny was not right behind him and Sonia grew worried. The major stepped into the room and cleared his throat. Mac pulled away from his wife, seeming to only just notice them.

"Where's Johnny?" Sonia asked.

"I ordered him to the medical unit," said the major, "So they can check him out. Damn stupid thing, he did. Brave, though. Very brave."

Sonia's skin tingled in dread as she wondered what Johnny had done. She was happy Brianna intervened because she found her voice had suddenly abandoned her.

"What did he do?"

Mac stared from Sonia to his wife and then back again. He left his wife and came to stand beside Sonia.

"Sit down, Touma."

She sank to a chair, her heart now racing in her chest. She waited tense and still, one hand cupped around the other which was bunched in a tight fist.

"He took the treatment," said her superior without preamble.

"But it didn't work?"

Mac shook his head. "It worked. Johnny was human again. Then we got your call and we searched and found you both gone. I knew from the scent what had happened and I took off after you both. Johnny saw your blood, Sonia. I ordered him to the base to get help, which he did. But then he disobeyed orders. He…" The captain cupped his hands over his eyes.

Brianna came to stand beside him, resting a hand on his shoulder. Her eyes were wide and glimmering with the tears that already filled her lower lids to near flood stage.

Sonia's back went rigid as her jaw clenched. "No. He didn't take the treatment. He's still a wolf."

Her captain dragged his hand down his face and cast the major a beseeching look and Scofield took over the tale.

"Johnny survived the transition to human and when he discovered your abduction, he came back here and, long story short, he injected Mac's blood into his vein without permission. He did it to help Mac and to save the both of you."

"I was losing when he showed up. There were too many," said Mac.

Sonia, bewildered glanced from one man to the next. "What does this mean?"

The major lowered his head. Sonia thought he looked as if he stood beside an open grave.

"Zharov warned him that he'd never survive the treatment again. None of the test subjects have. He barely made it the first time. He didn't, actually. He died and Zharov managed to revive him. But he was dead for several minutes. Despite that, he injected himself with werewolf blood. He's a werewolf, Touma, and he's not changing back ever again."

Sonia was on her feet. "I need to see him."

Johnny heard them coming. He heard everything again, private conversations from the nurses' station twenty yards away. The ding of the elevator past the double doors and the familiar footfall of Private Sonia Touma.

She didn't stop at the door but rushed at him and threw herself across his chest, weeping. He supposed she knew the truth now. She was alive and she was leaving. It was hard, but he pushed her gently away and looked to Mac who stared back with that screwed-up face that he'd seen only once before, after they lost all three fire teams in the Sandbox.

He signed to Sonia to stop crying, but she didn't. Even though she couldn't seem to speak, she managed to sign.

They told me. Oh, Johnny, why?

To save you, he thought. But he signed back that Mac needed him.

Sonia signed, *That's not true. You did it to save me.*

Mac is my captain. Couldn't leave him to fight alone.

He could see from her expression that she wasn't buying it. It was the truth, but only part of the truth. He might have done it anyway, but it was the image of Sonia in trouble that made it easy to push that plunger.

"Maybe in time they'll think of something they can do to change you back," she said, her words raw as her anguish.

He shrugged. *No going back.*

She grasped his hand in a fierce grip and sat at his bedside. "It doesn't matter, Johnny. I love you and I'll wait. I'll wait forever if I have to. I just want to stay with you."

No, she wouldn't because he was not letting her throw her life away on a man who would never be a man. She was going to serve her time and get out, like she planned. She was going to get herself that house she always wanted, the one with the rope swing and a yard. And she was going to fill it up with children. Sonia was going to be a mother, and have a family who loved her because she deserved that.

You have transfer orders, he reminded her.

Her grip faltered. "But I'll ask to stay. I don't want to transfer. I want to stay here with you." Sonia looked to her captain. "He needs a translator again."

Johnny met Mac's eyes and shook his head. Mac understood. He wanted her out of here.

"We'll talk about it at another time," said Mac.

Sonia turned back to Johnny. "This is because of you. You tell them the truth, John Lam. You tell them that you love me and that I love you. We were meant to be together."

He made the sign for *finish,* shaking both hands. The signal was clear. It was over between them. Only this time she did not look devastated. She looked pissed.

"You're hurting. I understand that, but I'm staying. It will be all right."

Mac took Sonia's arm and tried to bring her to her feet. "Come on, Touma. Another time. He needs rest."

"No." She jerked her arm free and fell back across him, clinging now. "You fought for me. Now I'm fighting for you. You love me. Tell them, Johnny. Tell them you love me, too."

She was breaking his heart. Johnny looked away to gather his nerve. In a moment she'd be sorry she ever taught him to sign. He turned to face her and formed his words with care.

Love you? You are the reason I am a wolf again. If not for you, B-R-I-A-N-N-A could have escaped and I wouldn't have had to come after you both. This is your fault. I want you gone.

Sonia gasped, releasing him as she staggered back from his bedside as his words slashed like a straight razor across her heart.

"Johnny?" she gasped.

"What did he say?" asked Brianna.

Johnny pointed to the door.

"He said it's my fault. The whole thing," Sonia whispered. "And he's right."

Johnny watched in relief as Sonia darted toward the door. Brianna reached to stop Sonia and then let her pass.

Zharov entered the room studying a chart and then belatedly noticed the crowd circling his patient's bed. He saluted the major. "He's as he was. Same exactly, except he has less of the human proteins than he had before this second injection." He looked at Johnny. "It was too much. The count was half your levels after Afghanistan."

Johnny shrugged. What did it matter? He knew the price. He would pay it. But what he wouldn't do was let Sonia throw away her future waiting around for his shaggy ass. He didn't have much left but his pride and that was still dear to him.

Brianna stepped to the end of the bed. "I had a talk with one of the chasers. A vampire named Hagan Dowling. He told me that werewolves are made, not born."

Johnny knew that very well because Burne Farrell has said the same thing to Mac.

"He also told me that all werewolves can change form at will."

"Clearly not," said Zharov, pointing at Johnny.

"Why were you speaking to them about this or anything else?" asked Mac.

She smiled at her husband. "Because they thought carrying Sonia was slowing them down and they wanted to kill her. My questions kept them from doing that."

Johnny's stomach dropped as he recognized how close he'd been to losing Sonia forever.

"Hagan also said that werewolves are made only by a bite and only in the very rare circumstance when the inflicted wounds are not fatal. Most werewolves attack to kill," said Brianna. She stroked her husband's chest and Johnny knew that was the place that Mac bore the scars of his attack. Somehow he had survived, but he was the only one. "I don't think you were bitten, Johnny."

He had arrived at the same conclusion.

Zharov interjected here. "I've searched his body and found no scars. All evidence points to the same conclusion to which you have arrived, Mrs. MacConnelly. Johnny was made intentionally by the U.S. Marine Corp."

"No, sir," said Mac. "He was made by an embarrassment to the uniform, former Colonel Lewis, may he rot in hell."

The major chimed in. "He will, son. No doubt about that."

Zharov pressed the tip of his pen to his lower lip. "I've already opened this avenue. I've been using infected rats to bite normal rats. The delivery method is more effective and all rats can transform."

Johnny had a moment's flare of hope. Could that work—a bite?

"I'll be exploring this method on rabbits, canines and monkeys over the next three months."

The hope winked out and he groaned.

Zharov ignored him and continued. "But for now, everyone out. Lam needs rest. It's very late and we have more tests tomorrow."

Tests and tests and tests, thought Johnny. He was tired of waiting and of Zharov's methodical, tedious research.

The major motioned to the door and Brianna swept out, followed by his doctor. Mac tried to follow but Johnny made a sound in his throat and motioned him back. Mac told his wife he'd be right along. Brianna hesitated and then nodded and withdrew.

"Be careful," she said.

Johnny stared at Mac wondering if he'd do it.

"You want me to bite you, don't you?" asked Mac.

Johnny nodded.

"Damn if this doesn't work we are both fucked."

Johnny waited as Mac disrobed down to his boxers.

"Where?" asked Mac.

Johnny threw back the sheets and pointed to the thick musculature of his thigh.

"You sure about this?"

He nodded. Johnny didn't have to remind him that he'd just saved his ass and helped rescue Mac's wife. Mac knew he owed him. He was ready to pay up.

"You believe that I never bit you?" asked Mac, his voice a tight whisper.

Johnny knew the burden the captain has born, thinking all this time that he'd attacked his own man.

Johnny nodded. Then he bared his teeth and made a pantomime of a vicious bite.

"Okay, deep. I get it. Grab the call button and press it before I bite you."

Johnny nodded, lifted the button and pressed down.

Chapter 17

Sonia got almost to the door when she realized she had done it again. She had let Johnny decide whether she came or went. She'd allowed him to sever the ties between them. Running again, she realized.

Sonia stopped and lowered her head as a certainty filled her. She didn't want to wait out her service with the easiest, least challenging assignment possible and she certainly didn't want a home if Johnny wasn't in it. Suddenly she understood the meaning of what Brianna had said back there before the vampires attacked. Her cryptic words rolled through Sonia like a perfect breath of fresh air.

No matter where Travis is he is with me. My home is in his heart and his home is in mine. If you love Johnny than nothing can separate you. Certainly not this.

Now Sonia understood. Brianna was right. Johnny wasn't tossing her aside. He was trying to protect her.

But she wasn't going, because now she knew exactly what was missing from her life. It wasn't a house and a yard. Not a wall she could paint or a garden to plant. It wasn't a place at all. All this time what she wanted had been right here. She had been searching for Johnny. What was missing was the one person who made a place a home. That's why she was so comfortable in Johnny's bungalow. Not because of the view or the flowers, but because Johnny was there. *He* was her home.

And she *wasn't* getting evicted because he was trying to protect her from living with the big bad wolf.

She spun in place and marched back the way she had come, her determination growing with each stride. The buzz of activity in the corridor outside Johnny's room slowed her progress and brought a leaden lump of dread to her throat. She stared at a cart covered with blood soaked pads and bandages. Now her heart pounded in her throat as she saw Zharov exiting Johnny's room, his head down as he removed the bloody blue rubber gloves and tossed them in the red biohazard container in the hall.

He lifted his gaze and spotted her. She did not recall setting in motion but she was suddenly there before him unable even to form the question.

"He's a crazy man. You know that? They both are," Zharov said. "Who else but a crazy man would do something so reckless. I could have MacConnelly arrested for attacking him and that's just a start."

"What? What happened?"

But Zharov merely thumbed over his shoulder and continued on his way muttering, "Should get disciplinary action at the very least. They have to follow orders with the rest of us."

Sonia glanced toward the door, feeling her feet heavy

as she crossed the threshold. She saw Mac buttoning his shirt as he glanced at her. Was that blood on his mouth?

"What's happening?" she said, surprised to hear her voice coming from such a long way away.

Mac stepped aside giving her a view of Johnny's hospital bed, which was empty save for the bare mattress and rumpled, bloody sheets. Her gaze flashed about and came to rest on the man standing just beyond. All the air whooshed from her lungs and she swayed, grasping the bed rail for support. She recognized him, even though his head was still sheathed inside a fresh white T-shirt. She'd know that abdomen anywhere. His muscles flexed and knotted under his healthy copper skin as he drew on the undershirt, covering his taut stomach. His head emerged a moment later from the neck hole, leaving his long hair mussed. She rounded the bed and hesitated as her gaze dropped to the bandage visible beneath his boxers. The thick gauze covered him from hip to knee and he carried all his weight on his uninjured leg.

Johnny was human again. He spotted her now and his eyes sparkled. "You're here! I thought I'd have to run after you."

She stood blinking at him in astonishment. "But they said… They said."

Johnny waved a hand. "Doctors. They think they know everything."

The confusion and relief battered Sonia like a stick to a piñata and she felt her bottom lip begin to tremble. Johnny limped over to her, gathering her up in his arms.

"I'm not leaving, Johnny. Don't ask me to."

"I won't. Not ever again. I'm sorry for what I put you through." He held her tight, his strong arms making everything seem all right. *Home,* she thought. *I'm finally home.*

Johnny shifted and did a funny hop, recalling his bandaged leg to her mind. She pulled back and looked at the enormous wrapping. "What happened?"

"Werewolf bite." He grinned, seemingly delighted. "First time."

Sonia gasped and her gaze flashed to Mac. Johnny drew Sonia under his arm and leaned heavily upon her as he held her tight to his side. "Seems you need a bite to be able to change shape."

Her fingers gently grazed the bandage. "Does it hurt?"

"Like a son of a bitch, but I've never been happier. Besides, I'm a fast healer."

"Might leave a scar," said Mac. "Mine did." He rubbed his shoulder.

"Small price," said Johnny. "See you around."

"Not sure you can go yet."

Johnny and Mac shared a silent exchange.

"Dismissed then," said Mac. "I know where to find you. Call if you need anything."

"Driver," said Johnny.

Mac made the call and Del met them out front. A few minutes later, Del had Johnny settled in his own bedroom.

Sonia walked Del out and then returned to Johnny.

Johnny sat on his bed and she stood in the gap between his legs, careful not to touch his bandage.

"I saw the blood at the hospital. Your blood," she said. "Scared me to death."

Johnny smiled. "It bled. Mac got the femoral artery. We had to be sure his spit got into my blood."

Sonia scowled up at him. "You might have bled to death."

Johnny shrugged. "Doc stitched it up. I'll be healed by morning."

"It's already morning," she said.

He wrapped his arms low behind her back and dragged her slowly forward. "So it is."

"Johnny, I understand if you need time to recover. But I don't want a transfer. I want to be with you."

"Well that's very good news because I'm in love with you."

Her heart gave a funny little shudder and her eyes closed for just a moment as she felt the joy of those words rising like mist from a deep lake. Then she opened one eye and narrowed it at him.

"You said you *didn't* love me," her tone was accusatory.

"Tactics to encourage a retreat."

She lowered her chin and gave him a smug smile. "Backfired, didn't it?"

"Should have known."

"Why's that?"

"Because you are a marine. Marines run into trouble, not away from it."

"Well this marine is done running. From now on I stay put. So what does that do to your tactics, Sergeant?"

"Ground conditions have changed. I have a new objective."

"And what might that be?" She trailed a finger down his cheek and the strong column of his throat, becoming familiar again with his smooth skin.

"Getting you to spend the rest of your life with me."

She tapped a finger to her lower lip as if thinking.

"I might be willing to sign up for that tour of duty. Is there a signing bonus?"

He lifted his brow in speculation. "Might be."

"Super. You know there are regulations against this."

"And did you know I can get you honorably discharged?"

"What!"

"If you want to be discharged."

She shook her head in bewilderment.

He tugged her closer and then stroked her cheek. "You don't mind that I'm still half monster."

She smiled. "No more monster than most men, less than some. And I like your wolf side."

His shoulders sagged with relief. "And your home? You'd be willing to wait until I finish my tour of duty? It might be six years or more."

Sonia used her hands to speak to him. *I love you. So I'll follow you if I can and I'll wait for you if I must because you are my home.*

Johnny threaded his fingers in her hair and his mouth descended to brush hers. She relaxed into his kiss, feeling the rush of sweet desire and the rising ache of need. He eased her down beside him on the bed, kissing her in a hot rush of passion, taking and giving. He stroked her, as he trailed kisses over her most sensitive places. Sonia stretched back and let him touch her with greedy hands and a hungry mouth until her emotions blended with pulsing sensation. He knew her, this man who was part wolf; his instincts were as perfect as his timing. Her need quickly grew impossible to bear and he finished her with a bright burst of bliss that drove through her like a conquering army. This marine certainly knew how to capture and hold territory, she mused as her thoughts reengaged.

"That was wonderful," she whispered, her body settling languid and replete.

He tucked her close beside him, her body half sprawled over his. Johnny flicked the sheet over their glistening bodies and she shut her eyes.

"When you first arrived," he said. "I tried everything I could think of to get you to quit."

"I almost did," she murmured.

"Now, each day for the rest of my life I'm going to do everything I can think of to make you stay."

"Everything?"

He nodded, his face suddenly serious. She stilled at his solemn expression losing her playful grin.

"What is it, John?"

"I love you. And I want to wake up beside you every damn day."

She managed a smile as her eyes welled up. "I want that, too."

John drew her down for another long, languid kiss. When she came up for air, his eyes were blazing with heat and her body hummed with need. She draped a leg over his waist and then straddled him.

Thirty minutes later she lay panting at his side and he lay motionless with one hand draped over his eyes. "I didn't know you could ride like that," he whispered.

"Save a horse, ride a marine," she muttered, her words slurring as she drifted toward slumber.

"We need to get you a ring."

"We need to get me some sleep."

Johnny chuckled and closed his eyes.

Johnny did, indeed, heal quickly. The following day, Mac and Sonia watched as the bandages were changed. Sonia saw the wound had already closed and the scar tissue was raised and pink. The ghastly horseshoe shaped marks marred the otherwise perfect skin of his thigh on both the front and back of his leg.

"Does it hurt?" she asked.

Johnny grinned and she couldn't help smiling back, he seemed so happy.

"Never felt better."

Sonia left him so she could shower. When she returned it was to find he had shifted into his wolf form. Her initial panic was quickly allayed by his hurried signs. He'd changed intentionally, his first time and after reassuring her, he lifted her off the ground to spin her in a circle.

Mac insisted she leave the room while he shifted back which she did with reluctance. Ten minutes later she was readmitted to find John sweating and pale, but still in high spirits.

"You did it!" she said, elated.

Sonia rushed to his side arms open wide. She didn't know who was more pleased that he now had control of his transformation, her, her captain or Johnny.

"He'll get better at it," said Captain MacConnelly, the relief evident on his tired face. "Just takes practice."

She flanked Johnny's bed and he scooped her up beside him for a celebratory kiss. The captain cleared his throat and Sonia tried to scramble off the bed, but Johnny refused to let her go.

"Touma, my office in thirty to discuss your reassignment."

She went cold and then hot as she recalled her transfer orders. Suddenly the room did not seem to have enough air. Was he shipping her back to the mainland? Johnny lifted her chin so she looked back at him instead of at her captain's retreating back.

He was signing, reassuring her. Still she wouldn't be at ease until she heard what the captain had to say.

He told her that Johnny needed a translator once more and he needed to learn sign so that the two of them could better communicate in the field. The discovery by the vampires made it imperative that he quickly get his wife out of the Pacific. He and Johnny were shipping out to Germany in just one day and her orders were to accompany them.

The captain and Johnny would train for combat assignments while she acted as translator and taught them sign. When they were in the field she would accompany them as far as possible and in some circumstances she would watch by remote camera, translating their words to headquarters.

Sonia liked the assignment. The work was important. She would be near Johnny and she would be useful. The only concern she had was teaching Captain Travis MacConnelly because he still made her nervous.

What didn't make her nervous was leaving the country and all that was familiar to her. She didn't care where she was as long as Johnny was there, too. There would be separations, of course, but she would bear them because it was important to Johnny to "get back in the game" as he called it. She no longer wanted to serve out her time in a quiet backwater. She wanted to be with John Loc Lam.

The rest of the day was a hectic frenzy of preparations for departure. Her second ever flight was much more relaxing than her first as she no longer feared her future. Instead she anticipated it. She began speaking to the captain both verbally and with sign, just as she had done with Johnny.

Her quarters in Panzer Kaserne unfortunately looked

nearly identical to her old ones. And Johnny no longer had his pretty little cottage on the mountain. He didn't need one. But they both missed the privacy. Johnny missed it so much that he proposed after only a week in Germany. Sonia accepted both the proposal and the lovely white-gold engagement ring set with a single half-carat diamond.

Three months later, Johnny and Mac, as she now called him, had finished their training and received orders to return to the Sandbox. Sonia would be joining them as far as Kabul, Afghanistan. But before deployment there was one final bit of business to finish. And to accomplish it, Sonia left her uniform behind in favor of a lovely mermaid style lace wedding gown. Paperwork had been signed, exemptions made and approval received in triplicate. Sonia was cleared to marry Sergeant John Loc Lam.

Johnny stood beside her in his dress blues looking so handsome he took her breath away. She was even getting used to his new haircut, though she did miss all that thick long hair. Johnny had promised to grow it back when he was discharged. Sonia suspected she would have a long wait.

Behind them, their guests filled the first three rows of the nondenominational chapel on Marine base as the chaplin, Father Tejada preformed the ceremony. Beside him, a female translator kept up with his words. To John's left, Captain MacConnelly stood, ramrod stiff, clutching their two rings in his fist as if their protection was vital to national security. Marianna, Sonia's sister stood to Sonia's left. As maid of honor, she held both bouquets in a gentle hand, rendering her momentarily speechless. Her sister shifted her attention between the translator and the chaplin, reading the signs and his lips as she waited for the moment when she would return her sister's cascading arrangement of white orchids and rosebuds. Beside Marianna stood Johnny's sister, Joon, as her only bridesmaid.

The chaplin called for the rings. Her captain dropped them from his hand onto the open bible as one might release dice and stepped back, his duty done. The rings came to rest and where exchanged.

Sonia stared down at the twinkling diamonds that studded the white-gold band and felt herself well up. It was real and really happening. Johnny's mom and sister had flown all the way from San Francisco to Germany to see them wed. And somewhere back a few rows, as far from the others as possible was Brianna, Mac's wife, intentionally leaving space between her and the humans she so affected.

Father Tejada raised a hand to God as he spoke about the power vested in him and gave his permission for John to kiss his bride. Johnny turned to her and lifted the short, modest veil.

Sonia beamed up at her new husband who looked proud enough to bust a polished brass button. He held her lightly by each shoulder and leaned forward from the waist to kiss her lips, sealing his promise. The cheers reached her and Johnny drew back to present his bride to the assemblage, raising their joined hands as if they had just completed a race.

Sonia looked out at the happy faces, some cheering, some whistling and others dabbing their eyes. Marianna kissed her sister and returned her bouquet. Johnny drew Sonia's hand into the warm crook of his arm and covered it with his opposite hand. Then they marched in unison down the aisle and toward the new life they would make together.

In that moment she felt the promise of a future bright with love and hope. He said she had given him a reason to live again but he'd given her much more than that. Johnny had made her a part of his family, his brotherhood and his life. He had given her his love and her first real home, right there in his heart.

* * * * *

Doranna Durgin spent her childhood filling notebooks first with stories and art, and then with novels. She now has over fifteen novels spanning an array of eclectic genres, including paranormal romance, on the shelves. When she's not writing, Doranna builds web pages, enjoys photography and works with horses and dogs. You can find a complete list of her titles at doranna.net.

SENTINELS: ALPHA RISING

Doranna Durgin

Dedicated to tree huggers everywhere! And with thanks to the Hitchin Post, where they not only help me take care of my own horse, they answer silly questions with a grin. The same could be said of my wondrous agent, come to think of it.

Chapter 1

Lannie Stewart fell back against the brick wall with a startled grunt of pain and a rare flash of temper. *Son of a bitch has a knife.*

His hand closed around the grip of the small blade now caught between his lower ribs; he twisted it slightly, releasing it...sending the white-hot scrape of sensation back at his attackers in the form of a snarl.

All five of them.

One of them cursed. The others didn't have a chance. Lannie plowed into them, throwing the knife aside and drawing on the wolf within.

Alpha. No-holds-barred.

That made him faster than they were, and stronger, and riding the awareness of every pack he'd ever built. Not to mention infuriated by their assault of someone older and weaker and not looking for trouble.

A quick flurry of blows—fierce, efficient, effective—and they fell back, stunned not just by the impact but also by Lannie's unexpected participation in a fight that had started out as five men kicking around what seemed to be easy prey. The men hesitated—suddenly wary, not willing to come back at him and not quite able to run.

Human submission. Or as close as they could be in this moment.

Fury still gripped Lannie, swelling against every breath. He eased back one step, then another—and there he held his ground, breathing hard but still perfectly ready.

The men got the message. They assessed themselves and their injuries, spat a few frustrated curses and bent to haul up their faltering friends. Lannie stood silent, letting them limp away—even if they did so with many a backward glance, not trusting Lannie to stand down when he'd gained such advantage.

But that was what a true alpha did.

Later, he'd find out who these men were and why they'd thought themselves safe not just to trespass, but to claim this space as their own. Most likely they'd come for a bro party involving six-packs and fisticuffs, but Lannie wouldn't assume. Not with the recent threats— and losses—the Sentinels had taken lately.

For now he watched until they were truly away, loaded up on their four-wheelers and bouncing away through the dusk as if they belonged on this remote and rutted dirt road. But this was Lannie's own property on the outskirts of the tiny high-country town of Descanso, New Mexico, even if the road itself defined the easement to the old community well house behind him.

Behind that hid the old man who had once again come out here to smoke his occasional joint—this time, apparently, also looking like tempting prey. Or maybe his whimsical coyote nature had once again gotten the better of him, and he'd approached and aggravated the men in some way.

Not that it made any difference, with five against one, youth against age. But the old man knew better.

"Aldo," Lannie said, warning in his voice. He pressed a hand against his side, feeling the hot blood of a wound still fresh enough that it hadn't quite pulsed up to pain.

The injury didn't worry him. Not when he was Sentinel, and belonged to an ancient line of people whose connection to the earth gave them more than just strength and healing and a variety of power-fueled skills. His heritage meant he carried within him the shape of his other—his wolf. His exceptionally strong blood meant that unlike most of his ilk, he could also take the shape of that other.

Alpha wolf.

So no, the injuries and the pain didn't worry him— but they damn well annoyed the hell out of him.

The thick scent of pot stung the air. Lannie said, *"Aldo."*

The old man came out from behind the well house, carefully pinching off his joint. "They made me anxious," he said, and kept his gaze averted.

Aldo had never been alpha of anything. But until lately, he'd been irrepressible, with a cackle of laughter and a strong side of levity. Now he bore his own bruises, and a vague expression of guilt. "I didn't do anything, Lannie. This has always been an okay place for me."

A safe place, on feed-store land. Lannie's cell rang, a no-nonsense tone cutting through the falling darkness—a rare connection up on this mountainside. Lannie didn't even look as he silenced the call and shoved the phone back into his pocket. "It *is* an okay place for you."

Or it should have been, and now Lannie's temper rode high on a flare of hot pain and swelling bruises. If Aldo's recent alarm hadn't slapped through the pack connection and drawn him out here into the fading heat of dusk, the old man would have gone down under that knife. Aldo was a strong sixty, but he was still sixty.

"We'll sort it out," Lannie said, lifting his hand to assess the bleeding. Dammit, this was one of his favorite shirts.

"Let me help," Aldo said. "You know I have some healing."

"So do we all," Lannie told him, already feeling the burn of his blood as the Sentinel in him took hold; the bleeding would stop and the wound would seal. And then it would leave him to grouch and ouch, wisely not spending resources on a wound that no longer posed a threat.

Aldo ran a hand over thick, grizzled hair cut short, tucking his stubby joint into the pocket of a shirt that had seen better days even before its recent misadventure. "You know what I mean."

"It's fine," Lannie said. A vibration against his butt cheek signaled cell phone voice mail. "Let's get back to the store. Faith is worried."

Aldo squinted at him, cautiously pleased. "She tell you that, or you just picked up on it…?"

Lannie made an amused sound in his throat. "Do you think she had to *tell* me?" Not when he was enough of an alpha to take a stand when necessary, to back down when appropriate, to remain in the background unless needed. And to have a singular skill for building teams and pack connections, even among the mundane humans who had no sense or knowledge of his *other*.

It was a skill so deeply ingrained that he'd learned to factor it into every part of his life—the depth of his friendships, the instant flare of his attractions, the strength of his anger.

"Yeah, you just picked up on it with your pack mojo," Aldo concluded, and rightly so. Faith's rising concern had come through in an undertone, the taste of anxiety with the faint whisper of identity that belonged to the young woman named Faith.

They struck out across the land of transitional high prairie, where ponderosa pine mingled with cedar and oaks and the land came studded with cactus and every other kind of prickly little scrub plant. The undulating slopes took them down to the feed-store lot with its storage barn, back corrals and low, no-nonsense storefront building.

An unfamiliar car sat in the lot out front of the otherwise bare lot, and Lannie thought again about that unexpected phone call, his annoyance rising. *Sabbatical from Brevis duty means* leave me alone.

Faith bolted out the store's back door, all goth eyes and piercings. "It's Brevis," she said in unwitting confirmation, a little walleyed along the way—and so thin of Sentinel blood that no one knew just what her *other* might have been. A little bit rebellious, a little bit damaged, a whole lot of runaway just barely now of age.

She had no idea that Brevis—the regional Sentinel headquarters—had once quietly nudged her in Lannie's direction. She was one of his now. *Home pack.*

"What are *they* doing here?" she demanded. "I'm not going back in there. Do you think they can tell I'm—

that I *was*—oh, for butt's sake. *Look* at you. What did you get him into, Aldo?"

"Nothing!" Aldo protested, trying to sound righteously indignant and not quite pulling it off. Hard to, with the scent of pot still following him around. "It wasn't my fault."

"It wasn't his fault," Lannie told her, and she closed her mouth on a response sure to have been stinging, regarding him uncertainly. "I'm fine," he said. "Why don't you help Aldo clean up in the barn. The Brevis folks can cool their heels a moment." Because Brevis or not, this was *his* turf. They didn't get to upset his people.

Especially when they hadn't warned him of their arrival in the first place.

Especially when they shouldn't have even been here. Not after how things had gone down with the last group he'd pulled into pack status. Too little time, too many challenges…and one damaged individual who had fooled them all.

He headed for the barn, where the stairs along the outside led up to a section of finished loft. Before he reached the top step, he'd peeled off the shirt and wiped himself down with it, heading straight to the bathroom to slap an adhesive strip over the now-barely-oozing wound.

The bruises were what they were; he didn't so much as glance in the distorted old medicine-cabinet mirror before heading out to the half-walled bedroom area to hunt up a fresh shirt, tugging it on with care.

The phone rang again. He let the ringtones cut the air while he stood quietly in the rugged old barn loft… eyes closed, recent encounter pushed away…muting the underlying home pack song in favor of the Sentinel whole. Shutting himself away from his own people, in spite of their upset, to prepare himself for whatever Brevis had come to ask of him.

For a strange, brief moment, the home song resisted his touch. It spun around him in a dizzying whirl, closing in like a warder's web and throbbing with an ugly, unfamiliar dissonance.

He took it as a rebuke. It was bad timing to interrupt pack song in the wake of such disturbance, and he knew it. He swallowed away the unease of it, settling into his own skin. Felt the aches of being there, and settled into that, too, accepting and dismissing them.

The dissonance slowly faded.

Finally, then, he reached for his larger pack sense, the one that made him ready for the outside world and whatever Brevis might ask from him. The bigger picture—the one that would ride him hard.

More so, in the wake of Jody. In the wake of her death. *In the wake of all their deaths.*

One more breath, deep and quiet, and then…he was no longer just plain Lannie. He no longer hummed to the tune of his own small pack but had set them—temporarily—aside, so existing pack song wouldn't interfere with the formation of whatever was to come.

He was the unentangled alpha that Brevis had come to see.

Babysitters.

Holly Faulkes wanted to spit the words at them— the man and the woman who'd brought her to this tiny New Mexico town of Descanso. They'd driven an hour through the desert mountains, pulling her away from her family during a still-heated discussion about her past, her present and her future—and all so she could wait in this cool, shadowed feed store with its cluttered shelves and dry dust, its thick scent of hay and oats and molasses and leather.

Sentinel babysitters.

As if she hadn't even been part of the recent Cloudview conversation, sitting beside her parents in silence—all of them tense, all of them terse. As good as prisoners in the old town hotel.

And as if she hadn't just missed meeting her brother Kai for the very first time since childhood, hearing of his feral beauty and of the lynx that peered out from under his skin at every turn, but being whisked away from both Cloudview and her parents before the Sentinels could call Kai in from the mountains.

Sentinels. If not exactly the enemy, also not her friends. Not considering she'd hidden from them since she'd been born, sheltered first by her family and then by deliberate, active choice. God, she didn't want to be here. And at twenty-four years old, it should have *stayed* her choice.

"Are you all right?" The woman eyed her. Her name was Mariska, and she was far too knowing for Holly's taste. Far closer to *bodyguard* than *escort*, with a short sturdy form both rounded and strong—not to mention a sharp gaze that gave away more than Holly was probably supposed to see. So did her complexion, a distinctly beautiful brown shade that might have come from south India but instead came from the bear within her.

"You're kidding, eh?" Holly said. "*No*, I'm not all right. Why can't you people just leave us alone? Leave *me* alone?"

Mariska transferred her gaze to Holly's hands, where they chafed against her arms in spite of the distinct heat still overlaying the fading summer day.

"Being here makes my skin crawl," Holly told the

woman, which was only the blunt truth. She'd felt it before, this sensation…on her Upper Michigan home turf, when she first started a restoration on an old clogged water feature. *But nothing like this.* One final squeeze of her upper arms and she let her hands fall. "You have no right to do this to me."

But she'd always known they would. Just as she'd known that her parents would pay the price for hiding their family to protect Kai.

"Maybe we don't," Mariska said. "But we hope you'll come to understand." She lifted her chin at Jason, the tall man who served as her partner; they exchanged commentary in a silent but very real conversation, the likes of which Holly had previously seen only between her parents. Jason raised his phone, hitting the redial button. *Again.* Trying to reach the man they'd called *Lannie* with a strange mix of familiarity and deference.

"If you're trying to reach him, why don't you just *talk* to him?" Holly gestured between them in reference to the silent exchange they'd just had, only peripherally aware that the crawling sensation in her blood had eased.

"Lannie prefers that we don't." The woman gave her a wry look, one that said she had chosen her words diplomatically. "Besides, not all of us do that."

"*I* don't," Holly muttered. Because she didn't need it and she didn't want it. She had no intention of letting someone else in her head—

It's not real.

No way.

"What did you say?" Holly asked, a wary tone that drew Mariska's surprised glance. Her glance would have turned into a question, had not a ringing phone pealed from the back of the store.

Jason made an exasperated face. "You might have picked up instead of just coming in," he muttered, slipping his phone away—but he sounded more relieved than he might have.

Holly looked at him in surprise, understanding. "You weren't sure he'd come."

"Oh," Jason said drily, "we were pretty sure he'd come. We just aren't sure—"

"Shut up," Mariska said, sharp and hasty, her gaze probing the back of the store.

It's not real.

Holly spotted the new arrival against a backdrop of hanging bridle work and lead ropes, and understood immediately that this man owned this place.

That he owned any place in which he chanced to stand.

It wasn't his strength, and it wasn't the quiet but inexorable gaze he turned on her companions. It wasn't even the first shock of his striking appearance—clean features with even lines, strong brows and nose and jaw, a sensual curve of lower lip and eyes blue enough to show from across the store. His hair was longer than stylish these days, layered and curling with damp around the edges.

No, it was more than all that.

"Oh, turn it *off*," Mariska said.

Something changed—Holly didn't even quite know what. Only that he was suddenly just a man in a casual blue plaid shirt yoked over the shoulder, half-buttoned and hanging out over jeans and boots, a heavy oval belt buckle evident beneath.

Cowboy, Holly thought, and found herself surprised by that. For the first time, she noticed not only bruises, but fresh bruises. A little smear of blood on a freshly washed cheek, a stain coming through the side of the shirt. An odd look on his face as he watched her, something both startled and somehow just as wary as she was—and then that, too, faded.

"That's better," Mariska grumbled, but the words held grudging respect. She exchanged a glance with Holly that was nothing to do with their individual reasons for being here and everything to do with a dry, shared appreciation for what they'd seen—a recognition that Holly had seen it, too.

The man rolled one sleeve and then the other, joining them with a loose walk that also somehow spoke of strength. "A little warning might have been nice," he said, a quiet voice with steel behind it.

Jason held up the phone. "We called."

"Did you?" the man said flatly. He eyed Holly with enough intent to startle her—as if he assessed her on a level deeper than she could even perceive.

She suddenly wished she wasn't still wearing well-worn work gear—tough slim-fit khakis over work boots and a long-tailed berry-colored shirt. Her hair was still yanked back into the same ponytail high at the back of her head, and it was a wonder her gloves weren't jammed into her back pocket instead of in her overnighter.

She released a breath when the man turned away from her.

Jason scowled, eyes narrowing, and Mariska stepped on whatever he was about to say. "Look, Lannie, this all happened fast, and we're making it up as we go. There's no cell reception between here and Cloudview—and we did call as soon as we could get through. If we'd been able to *talk* to you—"

Silently, she meant. Even Holly understood that

much. But Mariska had said it. *Lannie prefers that we don't.*

Lannie didn't raise his voice...somehow he didn't need to. "You aren't supposed to be reaching out to me at all."

"No, sir," Jason said, just a little bit miserable. "The Jody thing. I know. But that wasn't your fault, and we—" And then he stopped, apparently thinking better of the whole thing—and who wouldn't, from the quick, hard pale-eyed look Lannie gave him?

Holly found herself smiling a little. After hours in the care of these two, unable to so much as use a toilet without an escort, it was gratifying to see the tables turned. Even if she did wonder about the *Jody thing.*

But Lannie didn't linger on the moment. He ran a hand through his damp hair, carelessly raking it back into some semblance of order. "You want coffee?"

"Holly drinks tea, if you have it," Mariska said, apparently well-briefed on all things Holly. "So do I."

Jason looked as though he'd drink whatever Lannie put before him.

They joined Lannie in a tiny nook in the back hallway, which had a coffeemaker and electric teakettle, a diminutive refrigerator, a sink and half a box of donuts sitting on an upended fifty-gallon drum. Lannie reached for the teakettle plug...and hesitated there, leaning heavily on the counter.

As if for that moment, the counter was the only thing holding him up.

Holly shot a startled look at Mariska and Jason, finding them involved in some sort of mostly silent but definitely emphatic disagreement. By the time she looked again at Lannie, the teakettle was firing up and Lannie had pulled a bowl stuffed with tea bags from the nar-

row, open-faced cabinet above the sink—right next to
the big green tin of Bag Balm, some half-used horse
wormer and an open bag of castration bands.

"So," Holly said. "*Lannie.* My name is Holly
Faulkes, and I don't want to be here."

He pulled four mugs from the half-sized drainer
hanging in the sink, and she realized she hadn't told
him anything he didn't already know—but that unlike
everyone else in this mess, he wasn't impatient or annoyed by it.

"Phelan," he told her, swirling the coffee in its carafe.
"Phelan Stewart. But yes. You can call me Lannie." He
filled one of the mugs with coffee and handed it out to
Jason without looking; the teakettle activity built to a
fever pitch. "What's your story, Holly Faulkes?"

"What's yours, eh?" she countered. "Why are they
dumping me on you?"

Lannie held out the tea bags without any visible reaction, and Holly plucked out a random blend and passed
the bowl to Mariska. Lannie put his hip against the
counter and sipped coffee—only to immediately dump
it down the sink, exposing a gleam of torso through
the gaping shirt and annoying Holly simply because
she'd noticed.

"*Faith,*" he said, as if that explained it all. And then,
"Holly Faulkes, if you'd come with a group, I'd say you
all needed to become a team. Since you're here alone,
you're probably not playing well with others in some
way." He lifted one shoulder in a shrug, patently ignoring Jason's dilemma over whether to try the coffee.
"You must be important to them."

She found herself amused. "Because Brevis only
bothers you with the important things, eh?"

"Something like that. And the fact that I'm on sabbatical." He held out his hand. After a hesitation, Holly offered him her tea bag. He took Mariska's, plunked them both into mugs, poured hot water on top and handed the mugs over. "Your turn. Or would you rather have *them* tell your story?"

Holly relaxed, curling her hands around the mug. He might be Sentinel, but he wasn't pushing her. He'd given her options.

Even if they were both bad ones.

So she told him the truth. "I'm not a Sentinel, I don't want to be a Sentinel, and I'm not going to drink your Sentinel Kool-Aid no matter how you dress it up in obligation and heroics."

She heard Mariska's intake of breath, but Lannie's quick blue glance quelled her. "*Sentinel* isn't something you get to choose."

"And yet it's a choice I made a long time ago," she told him, not an instant's hesitation. "It's a choice my family made—that we were *forced* to make. That's not something you can change, eh? But it's obvious you'll have to work that out for yourself."

"You'll stay long enough for me to do that?"

"As if *that's* a choice." But she felt the briefest flash of hope, felt herself halfway out the door.

"Brevis pulled Mariska in from Tucson. So either you're in a great deal of danger or they think you'll run—and if you do, that you'll be good at it."

"Run?" Holly shot Mariska a baleful look. "How stupid do you think I am? You people already found me once. My best chance of getting on with life is to let you figure out what a waste of time this is. If you don't, then we'll see about *running.*"

"Fair enough," he murmured. "Give me your word

on that and these two will leave, and we can get you settled."

Holly's temper flared hot and strong. She set the mug on the counter with a thump. "Pay attention, why don't you? I'll be *settled* when I'm back home in the Upper Peninsula, rebuilding the business you've just destroyed!"

She transferred her glare to Jason and Mariska. "And meanwhile, who's feeding my feral cats? Who's holding my best friend's hand when she has her first baby? Do you people even *think* about what you've done, or do you just ride through on the strength of your astonishing arrogance?"

Jason summoned up a bright smile, only a hint of panic behind it. "Ohh-kay, then," he said. "My job is done. I'll just wait in the car."

"Jason," Mariska said, annoyance in her voice.

"Thanks for the coffee." Jason inched behind Holly to put the mug on the barrel. "Such as it was."

"Faith," Lannie said again—but his voice didn't have the same quiet strength, and Holly shot a look at him, finding his knuckles white at the edge of the counter and his tanned face gone pale, his shoulders tight…his expression faintly surprised.

But only until he saw her watching. Then the weakness disappeared; he returned her gaze with an even expression.

Holly, it seemed, wasn't the only one hiding the truth of herself from the Sentinels.

Chapter 2

For all her resentment, Holly found herself regretting Mariska and Jason's departure, as they unloaded her single, quickly packed suitcase, handed Lannie a thin file folder and drove away.

They were, if nothing else, familiar.

Not like Lannie Stewart—not only unfamiliar, but just a little more Sentinel than she wanted to deal with on her own.

But she'd known all her life that this day might come. If she blamed the Sentinels for anything, it was for being the kind of organization that sent her family into hiding in the first place.

Lannie locked the door behind them, made sure the open sign was flipped to Closed and went behind the cash register counter to do...

To do cash register things, probably. She didn't care.

Although she had the impression that he was, somehow, actually assessing her. That his attention never left her.

Screw that. She glanced pointedly at the full darkness that had fallen since her arrival. "I haven't eaten yet." Of course, she hadn't wanted to. Until he'd come into the store, her stomach had been unsettled by that funky discomfiting feeling under her skin, the faintest bitter taste in her mouth. How he'd buffered that, she didn't know. But now her stomach growled.

He made a sound that must have been acknowledgment. "In, out, or fast?"

"It's your game. You choose."

He stopped what he was doing, a bank bag in hand, and she drew breath at the blue flint in his gaze. "Nothing about this is a game."

"Lannie!" A young woman's voice rang out from the back of the store. A waifish young woman emerged from between the shelving, her hair dyed black, her makeup dramatic and her piercings generous; she dragged in her wake a wiry older man with mussed hair and a bruised face—eye puffy, lip split and swollen. "Lannie, did you see what those men did to him? What business did they have back there, anyway?"

"None," Lannie dropped the cash bag on the scratched counter over a glass-front display of fancy show spurs and silver conchas, and lifted his brow at her. It had been her task, apparently.

"That's not my fault," she protested, confirming it. "First you lit out after Aldo, and then those strongbloods came when they should be leaving you *alone*—" She stopped, scowling, her attention riveted on him. "They got you, too. I *knew* it."

"Faith." It was a single word, but it had quelling impact. Holly fiddled with her suitcase handle, and it occurred to her that she *could* run. She'd never promised. And they weren't paying any particular attention.

Lannie looked down at the splotch of blood at his side, briefly pressing a hand to it.

"Five to one," the old man said helpfully. "Our boy took care of it."

Lannie grunted. "No one's *boy*," he said, but Holly heard affection for the old man behind his words. "And it's not bleeding anymore."

"You'll need food," the girl said, as if she'd somehow taken over. She closed the distance to the counter with decisive steps, picking up the bag. "You go. I'll take care of this."

"Faith," he said, and it sounded like an old conversation. Finally he shook his head, a capitulation of some sort. "Learn to make the coffee, would you?"

Faith tossed her head in a way that made Holly think the coffee wouldn't change. "See you tomorrow, Lannie." And then, on her way out the back again, she offered Holly an arch glance. "Don't you cause him trouble, whoever you are."

Startled—*offended*—Holly made a sound that came out less of a sputter and more of a warning. But the young woman was already moving out through the same aisle that had brought her.

The elderly man held out his hand, a spark of interest in his eye. "I'm Aldo. And this is Lannie."

There was nothing to do but take that dry and callous grip for a quick shake, contact that brought a whiff of something potent. *Pot?* She startled, looking to Lannie for confirmation without thinking about it, and found a resigned expression there.

Lannie came out from behind the counter. "She

knows who I am, Aldo. And don't you go charming her."

"No," Aldo said, looking more closely at Holly. "Not this one. She's all yours, Lannie. I'm sleeping in the barn tonight, good with you? Good. You'll be right as rain tomorrow, see if you're not."

Holly took a deep breath in the wake of his abrupt departure. Then another. Trying to find her bearings, and to refocus on the resentful fury that had gotten her through these past twenty-four hours so far. "Let's get one thing straight," she said. "I'm not *all yours*. Not in any sense of the word."

"Not yet," he said mildly, and caught her elbow as if she would have stalked by, luggage and all, to batter her way through that locked door and out into the world. "The truck's out back. Let's eat."

Lannie tossed the suitcase into the truck bed and climbed into the pickup with a stiffness that made him very much rue that *five against one*.

He let her open her own door simply because she needed the chance to slam it closed again. And she did, too—not once, but twice, then reached for the seat belt with a brusque efficiency that spoke as much for her familiarity with this model truck as for her simmering anger.

He inserted the key and waited. It didn't take long.

"Not yet?" Holly made a noise in her throat. Lannie took it for warning—and he wondered how strong her Sentinel blood ran, and if anyone else in her family took the cat.

He turned to look at her, unhurried, hand resting on the gear shift between them. "That's why you're here."

She snorted, a wholly human sound. "So, what—so I can *submit* to you?"

He shook his head. "So you can figure out that's not what this is about." And he kept his voice matter-of-fact but couldn't help the impact of her words. *Too independent.* Not just struggling to form pack bonds, but resisting them with everything she had. What was Brevis thinking?

She lifted a lip of derision at his words and crossed her arms over her chest. The feed-store front light hit the end of its timer cycle, plunging them into darkness.

But Lannie had a Sentinel's blue-tinged night vision, and he saw her perfectly. Knew her hair to be brown unto black, and drawn into a shiny fall of a ponytail. Saw her upswept eyes to be equally brown unto black, and snapping mad beneath brows that might ordinarily be softly angled, but now just frowned. A thick ruffle of bangs scattered over her forehead, offsetting features that could have looked at home under a high-society do...if it weren't for her rugged work clothes and the matter-of-fact prowl beneath her movements, an innately graceful glimpse of her *other.*

She tipped her head at him in annoyed impatience, quite possibly not aware of his scrutiny or how well he could see her. But he felt nothing except what he'd perceived in this woman before he'd even quite seen her: a throb of hurt and anger and fear, somehow striking deeply into his own soul and spiking a very personal, protective response. In spite of knowing better.

It's not real. It never was. *It's not personal.*

It was just who he was. That quick connection, that ability to spin it into something more permanent.

Even when it wasn't right for either of them.

She gave him a wary glance. "Did you say something?"

He turned the key. "Not yet."

He drove her on winding roads to the other side of the small town, where the ElkNAntlers Bar & Grill scented the area with barbecue and sizzling steak. He waited for Holly at the front of the truck, and then waited again inside the entrance, giving her time to absorb the ambience—families scattered around tables, a bar off to the side, and antlers...

Everywhere. Mulies, elk and pronghorn—antlers high, antlers low, and the occasional full cape head mount. And, naturally, a few token jackalopes scattered over the bar.

The owners, Jack and Barbara, had been aiming for quirky humor. Lannie thought of it more as Dr. Seuss.

Barbara waved at them from where she unloaded a tray of glasses at the bar, raising her voice over the mixed early-evening crowd. "Hi, Lannie. Find yourself a spot."

Holly gave the interior one final skeptical look and chose a table from afar. He wasn't surprised when she led him to a corner, and he wasn't surprised when her limber, graceful movement only reinforced his initial impression of her *other*. Her clothes might have been rugged, but the bright thermal top hugged a lean, curvy figure, and khaki pants followed the roll of her hips to perfection. Sturdy ankle-high boots should have looked clunky, but instead only reinforced the confident precision with which she placed her feet.

Something inside him tightened.

But his response to her wasn't real. However intensely he felt her presence as the pack bond formed between them, the effect would fade when she moved on to her true place in the Sentinels. It always did.

But that didn't mean it wouldn't complicate things along the way. Or that he didn't still need time to deal with how it so recently had.

She slipped into her chair and picked up the plastic-coated menu, glancing at Lannie only long enough to reassure herself that he had, in fact, followed.

Barbara appeared at their table to slap down a complimentary basket of jerky chips. "Welcome to the ElkNAntlers," she said. "Need a rundown of the menu, or are you good here?"

"I'm fine," Holly said. Her smile changed her face, bringing stern lines into beauty; it quite suddenly caught Lannie's breath. *Dammit.* "And I'll take whatever you suggest from the barbecue side of the menu."

"Smart woman," Barbara said, collecting the menu and glancing at Lannie. "You?"

"Whatever you bring her." Lannie lifted a wry shoulder. "It's not like I haven't had it all."

Barbara grinned, tucked her pencil behind her ear, and took Lannie's menu, too. "I'll surprise you, then." She nodded to someone behind Lannie as she left, and a young man appeared to pour them each a generous glass of ice water.

"Drink it," Lannie advised as Holly simply eyed hers. "The desert and the altitude will get you if you don't stay wet." He drank half of his in one go, knowing he'd done himself no good turns out by the well pump house, and waited until she'd done the same. "Exactly why are you here, Holly Faulkes?"

She looked at him as though he might just be a little bit insane. "Because I didn't hide well enough or run fast enough, youbetcha." When he didn't rise to that, she asked, "Who's Jody? And why is she a problem now?"

He stiffened. He hadn't thought she'd catch it through the undertone so quickly when she had so much adjustment to do on her own account. He certainly hadn't expected her to parry with it. Or to recognize just how it affected him.

Too little time, too much resistance. Both Holly and Jody were without the concept of teamwork that made Sentinel field operations viable—and if Holly had both Jody's arrogant certainty that *her* way was the right way, and Jody's willingness to make such choices outside the team framework, then Holly also lacked the most basic foundation of what it meant to be Sentinel in the first place. And Holly had spent her life in extreme independence.

Not teamwork. Not the faintest suggestion of it.

So he didn't answer her. He *couldn't* answer her. Not with the voices of Jody's team still riding him, the memories of their deaths ripping through his lingering pack link.

He tried to ease the strain in his voice and only half succeeded. "Talk to me. They brought you here for a reason. A good one."

"That's right. Because Brevis only bothers you with the important things." She shrugged. "Didn't Mariska give you my file?"

"This is the story the way you'd tell it, not them."

She sat back in the chair to regard him. "It's not much of a story. My brother needed to hide from you and the Core. When he was fifteen, we left him stashed up near Cloudview and we went to hide in other places so we couldn't be used against him."

"How old were you?"

"Not very old. Eight? Nine, maybe?" She shrugged. "What's it matter? Old enough to know that if you people had been willing to leave him alone, our lives would have been so much different. I wouldn't have a brother I don't even know...my mother wouldn't have cried so much...and I wouldn't be here now, when my life is somewhere else entirely."

Another challenge that he didn't take.

After a narrow-eyed interlude, she shrugged and filled the silence. "Things changed. This spring, he came out of hiding to save his turf from the Core—and to save the rest of you from what the Core had planned. He's a good man, my brother. Maybe I'll get the chance to know him now." Another dark look, aimed his way. "Supposing the rest of you let me."

Lannie could figure out the remainder of the story. "Once your brother was out in the open, Brevis realized you existed, too." And the Sentinels didn't allow strongbloods to roam unconnected. Such individuals had too much potential to create havoc...and Brevis had too much need of them.

He gave her a sharp glance, suddenly understanding. *"Kai Faulkes,"* he said. "Your brother." The long-hidden, barely tamed Sentinel who took the Lynx as his other and who had almost single-handedly undermined the Core's infiltration of his high mountain paradise.

"Kai Faulkes," she said, her pride coming through in the lift of her chin.

And then the Sentinels had found her, sent a strike team and extracted her from her life. For her own protection, but not without self-interest.

Right now she probably saw only the self-interest.

"Look," she said, spearing him with a direct gaze. "This isn't my world. Your fights aren't my fights. I

have no training. My folks could never take the forms
of their others, and I never even tried. I don't know what
I'd turn out to be and I don't *care*."

He wondered if she saw the irony of it. Kai Faulkes
was a Sentinel's Sentinel. He lived his other to the full-
est in the absence of Brevis; he lived their mission of
protection as naturally as breathing.

Holly didn't even know what her other *was*.

"Don't you get it?" She gestured impatiently at his
failure to react. "*You* made me this way. Now it is what
it is, and you can't change that. I'm not one of you and
I never will be."

He straightened, frozen in the act of unwrapping
his silverware, suddenly understanding the unspoken
piece. *Should have read that file.* "You haven't been
initiated, have you?"

She made that small, catlike noise of offense in her
throat again. "That's none of your business!"

Of course she hadn't. She'd been so young when her
family separated, going from inconspicuous to deeply
underground.

But initiation changed everything. She wouldn't truly
know who she was, or what she was, until she had that
first adult connection with another Sentinel—careful,
skilled intimacy, bringing her powers to fruition.

No wonder she'd never truly felt the itch to reach out
to her other in spite of its expression in her movement,
her mannerisms and even her expressions.

"Stop staring," she told him, mouth flattening in
annoyance. *Ears flattening, head tipped just so.* "And
stop doing that thing."

"That thing," he repeated without inflection.

"Yes, *that thing*." She leaned over the table, creating
such privacy as was possible in the tavern. "What you

were doing in the store, and Mariska told you to turn
it off. *That*. Stop it."

Ah. The alpha. When he'd put his unexpected visitors on notice.

But he couldn't turn it off because he hadn't turned it
on. Whatever she saw came from her own perceptions
of his basic Sentinel nature as much as his presentation.
No doubt she had other perceptions she wasn't used to
managing outside her normal life, and she'd probably
adjusted to a certain element of heightened sight and
scent, but this...

This would be new. And different. And she'd been
thrust in the middle of it.

He found himself reaching for her pack song.
Through pack song, he could understand her, assess
her, support her—

But an unexpected, unprecedented crackle of mental
static snapped through his mind. *What the hell?* Surely
she wasn't resisting him; she didn't know enough to do
it. Surely he could get at least a hint of her—a single
note, a thread of inner melody...

An orchestra.

Her music flooded him, waking the alpha after all.
His pack sense rose to absorb and receive and, just
maybe, drown in the rich complexity she offered. He
watched her eyes widen and then narrow, and a thread
of anger gained clarity in her song.

She half rose from her chair, elbows on the table as
she closed some of the distance between them. "Stop it,"
she said, but there was no force behind those breathless
words. She took a visible breath, a flush bringing out
the color on her cheeks, dark eyes and dark hair con-
trasting against otherwise fair skin.

Not that *stopping it* was an option, even if he tried.

Not with the glory of all she was coming at him, unfiltered and unfettered.

Her voice gained hard strength. "Fine," she said. "Be an asshole. Your friend can bring my dinner over to the bar, because that's where I'll be sitting. *Without you.*"

She didn't storm away. She didn't have to. She made her point with the rolling precision of her stride, the hard line of her jaw…the straightness of her back.

Whoa.

Lannie could do nothing but stare after her, only beginning to understand that she'd done to him as much as he'd done to her—and she had no idea.

Maybe because it wasn't her fault. Maybe it was the pack mojo gone wild. Maybe—

Barbara slid between tables to deposit his meal in front of him, whisking Holly's abandoned napkin out of the way to do the same for her. "Now, when she gets back from the ladies', you be sure to tell her I'll swap this out if it's not to her liking."

Lannie wasn't quite ready to trust his voice; he nodded at the bar, where Holly had taken a spot apart from the rest and hitched her hip up over the bar stool, already reaching for the nearby dish of pistachios.

Her back was still stiff enough to tell the tale.

Barbara's brow rose in surprise. "Never thought I'd see *that* day," she told him, and reclaimed Holly's deep-dish plate of shredded elk over crisped sweet potato medallions. She slipped in to place the plate beside Holly, her words clear enough to Lannie's wolf. "Here you go, honey. You want a beer to go with that?"

Holly nodded, and Lannie jerked his attention to the casual approach of the slender man who took a seat in Holly's empty chair.

This time when Lannie drew on his alpha, he did

it deliberately. He eyed the man without welcome and without apology.

The man met his gaze without rising to that challenge. Faint concern lived in the lines gathering at his brow. "I know I'm intruding," he said. "Hear me out. We have a common interest."

Lannie gave the man a sharper look. He'd dressed out of Cabela's outfitter catalog for the evening—high country fisherman casual, all fresh from the package— and while he hadn't quite shaved down his balding head, he'd come close enough for dignity. His watch was high quality without being ostentatious; his single ring was black onyx in a masculine setting and his ears went unadorned.

No particular threat there. But on this night when Lannie had taken responsibility for Kai Faulkes's vulnerable, wayward sister, he didn't much like coincidences. "How many of your conversations start out this way and still end well?"

"I'm interrupting," the man said, a touch of car salesman in his demeanor. "I understand that. But I need to talk to you about what happened earlier this evening."

Lannie kept his stare flat. "Earlier this evening I closed down my store, met a friend for dinner and came here. You're sitting in her seat."

Earlier this evening, he'd taken a knife between the ribs and still put five men down...and then walked away from it.

But this man couldn't know that unless he'd been part of it somehow.

"I'm not doing this well," the man said. "I'm more than aware that under other circumstances, we not only wouldn't be companionable, we wouldn't even speak—"

And then a cluster of casually raucous men moved to the bar, and Lannie saw their faces.

Familiar faces. Battered faces. Only four of them, because the fifth apparently hadn't recovered from the consequences of sticking a knife into Lannie.

And there was Holly, sitting alone and upset, and completely unaware.

Lannie didn't much like coincidences.

"You should have talked faster." He rose from his chair with the wolf coming out strong, already silent in movement. "Your friends tipped your hand." He hesitated, briefly, to loom over the smaller man. "Whatever you want...this was a mistake."

"You misunderstand," the man said, drawing back—but at Lannie's expression, his protests died back into annoyance. After a final hesitation, he rose from his seat and strode for the exit. Lannie might have grabbed his arm—might have demanded an explanation—but Holly came first. He headed for the bar.

Barbara crossed his path with empty serving tray in hand and caught sight of his expression, freezing there a moment. "Lannie?" But then she saw the men, and muttered a curse. "I see them. But this is a family place, Lannie." He passed her by, snagging the tray from her unsuspecting grip along the way. She let him have it but still followed him. "Lannie!"

Lannie moved in beside Holly. She made a startled sound and sent a glare his way.

"Right," he said. "You're pissed at me. I get it. Let's go."

"I'm eating." She turned away from him and forked up some sauce-smeared sweet potato.

"Lannie," Barbara said from behind, "what—"

"These guys are not our friends." Lannie caught

Holly's gaze, nodding at the little gang. They hadn't spotted him yet, but they'd be looking. They were just having fun along the way.

"I see them." She took a swig of her own bottled beer, and her Upper Peninsula accent came out strong. "They're rude. Big *wha.* I run my own crews, Mr. Stewart—you think I haven't handled rude before?"

"Holly." Lannie took the beer from her, set it on the bar, and ignored her fully justified glare of astonishment. "These guys are *not our friends.*" It didn't matter that Lannie got no sense of Core from them; he wasn't sensitive to that particular stench in the first place. They'd already attacked his pack, and they'd attacked him. They were the enemy, and he needed to get Holly out of here, and he told her so with his expression and with his eyes and with every bit of the alpha within.

Holly's eyes widened; she closed her mouth on whatever she'd been about to say and cast a more thoughtful glance at the men, three of whom were giving the bartender grief while the fourth caught sight of Lannie and stiffened, his expression darkening.

"Uh-oh," said Barbara from behind him, and hastened away.

"I'm hungry," Lannie told Holly. "Grab your meal and your beer and we'll eat somewhere else."

By then the gang was headed their way. Lannie took the step in front of Holly and felt more than saw as she slid off the stool to stand at his shoulder.

"Look who we found." The lead guy came to a stop, his expression just a little too bright, his bruises from earlier in the day blooming puffy and dramatic. "The idiot who showed up in the middle of nowhere to mess with our business."

Lannie kept his voice even and his hands low. "*Out*

in the middle of nowhere happens to have been my property. And the old man you beat up happens to be my friend."

The man offered him a nasty smile. "You should have thought of this moment before you butted in."

"There were five of you and one of me, and I'm still standing. This time there are only four of you. Is this really something you want everyone to see?" He didn't, at the moment, feel the aches. He didn't feel the wound on his side. And he didn't hold the alpha inside.

"Let's just go." Holly's low voice held disgust rather than fear. "You were right. We can eat somewhere else."

A camera flashed from behind Lannie, highlighting the man—tall, muscle-bound and graced with a graying blond beard that crawled unmanaged down his throat to his chest. His friends started as the flash went off again, and Barbara made a satisfied noise in her throat. "Got 'em. Now you scoot, Lannie. If they wanted to take a poke at you in *my* place, they should've been faster about it."

"Yes'm," Lannie said, easing a step aside without taking his eyes off the men. This would be the moment, if they—

The big guy in front went for it, dropping his shoulder for driving punch that would have caught Lannie pretty much where the knife had.

Lannie whipped the serving tray up between them, bracing it against the sharp impact; hot pain tore at his side. As the man cried out and grabbed his injured hand, Lannie yanked the tray up and cracked it in half over his head.

The man dropped like a rock. Lannie held the other three with his eye, waiting that extra beat. When they exchanged an uncertain glance, he dropped the tray halves on top of their fallen friend.

Barbara had more than a camera; she had a short bat, and she tapped it meaningfully against her palm. "We done here, boys?"

That could have been it. That *should* have been it. But the fallen man surged upward with offended fury and Lannie snarled it back at him, grabbing the bat from Barbara—

Heavy glass thudded dully against a hard head. The man collapsed in a moaning heap.

Holly looked ruefully at her beer bottle—upended and now empty. She placed the bottle carefully upright on the bar. "Maybe we can get those dinners to go?"

Chapter 3

Awesome. A bar fight.

Holly sat on her suitcase in the bed of Lannie's pickup, a take-out container balanced on her knees, a new beer at her feet and anger tempered only by the weight of fatigue. She'd done no more than catnap since the Sentinels had snatched her from her home, and right now it didn't seem to matter that the food was good, the incredible expanse of night sky was filled with diamond-sharp stars and the companionship was currently undemanding.

Because it didn't change anything. She'd lost a life she'd fought hard to have, and one she loved. She could be furious or she could grieve, but right now this dull, exhausted anger suited her just fine.

"You suck," she told Lannie, who sat on a hay bale beside her.

"Yeah," he said, and took a pull on his own beer. "Maybe."

"Will you ever let me go?" she asked him, making no attempt to hide her frustration.

"Me?" He tipped his head back to watch the stars as if considering—but flinched at the stretch, his hand going to his side where blood had dried earlier in the evening. "Yes."

"But not *them*," Holly said, hearing his unspoken words.

Lannie put aside his empty takeout container and rested his elbows on his knees. "Never entirely. It doesn't mean you won't end up back where you were, or where you want to be."

She made a derisive sound in her throat. "Sure. As long as I'm not too valuable so you people aren't willing to let me go. And supposing that the Atrum Core stays hands-off."

Lannie pushed a thumb at the knot of discomfort between his brows, a gesture her unusually sensitive eyes saw just fine. Maybe he had a headache. Good.

He said, "You're Sentinel, Holly. Having a connection to the whole is part of that, and that's all you're here to find. Where you *fit* in the whole is up to you. But until things settle out, you're not safe at home."

She laughed outright. "*Safe?* Are you even listening to yourself? How *safe* is your friend Aldo? How *safe* was it to be in that tavern with you this evening?" She set her beer down with a clunk of heavy glass against the truck bed lining. "If you weren't what you are, we wouldn't be eating dinner out here in the bed of a *truck*."

He didn't reply right away; she chose to believe it was because he had no defense. When he did speak, it was only to say, "Well. It's an awfully pretty night."

She made a derisive sound.

"Don't get stars this clear from the ground in Michigan," he said. "Don't get them without mosquitoes, either."

"Maybe I like mosquitoes!" she snapped at him, which was so patently ridiculous that she was glad when he didn't respond. After a round of silence, the breeze rustling through piñons behind them, she sighed. "God, I need a shower. I don't even know where I'm sleeping tonight."

"My place," Lannie said—and offered the faintest of smiles in the darkness in response to her scowl. "I'll sleep somewhere else, and tomorrow we'll sort things out. I didn't have much notice."

"Yeah," Holly said. "I gathered that. I feel so welcome, eh?"

He straightened. "No," he said, his hand pressed back to his side but his voice taking on that note of command she'd heard there before. "Don't."

"Don't what?" she meant to demand, but he stepped on the words.

"Don't think of yourself that way. Don't think of me that way. Unprepared isn't the same as unwilling or unwelcoming."

She didn't even have to see him to know. Or to feel. He was doing it again. If she looked, she'd find him *more than*. She'd find herself drawn to him in spite of the fact that she didn't want to be here in the first place. Just as he'd done to her in the tavern, right there in front of everyone—looking at her so steadily from those dark-rimmed pale eyes, somehow drawing her in and waking the impulse to go to him—to smooth the lines from his brow and kiss the faint lingering bruises on his face, and even to trace her tongue over the luxury of his mouth.

She found her voice, strained as it was. "Stop. Doing. *That*."

But he didn't stop. He even looked as though he might reach out to her. She tensed in anticipation of that touch, wanting it, already responding to it—

Holly reached for all the strength she'd ever had—all the personal sense of self she'd developed young and hard in a life of hiding who she really was, her family split beyond repair. *Independent. Capable. Without need for any Sentinel identity.* Somehow, she made her voice cutting. "Really? This is your plan? To use Sentinel mojo to seduce me until I can't think straight? You want to tell me how that's any different than slipping me some drug?"

He drew in a sharp breath, and for that moment she wished she couldn't see so well at night after all. Not his startled expression, and not the way her words had hit him like a cruel blow.

It was almost enough to make her wonder if she'd gotten it wrong.

But not quite.

Lannie faced the morning without enthusiasm, standing not so much behind the farm store counter as draped over it, his head resting on his forearm and buzzing like the inside of a sonic toothbrush.

He wanted to blame Holly.

Pack song was a touchy thing. To be so abruptly disengaged from his home pack, to encounter such resistance from his new pack…

He wanted to blame her but couldn't. No more than he could blame her for the residual stiffness in his ribs and shoulders, or the half-healed wound on his side.

He wasn't so certain about the suddenly uncontrollable nature of his mojo. She'd called him on that the night before, but…

He would have said he wasn't tapping into his alpha at all.

He would have said she'd somehow done it *to* him.

Except it didn't work that way, and the situation left him uneasy and half-aroused and extra wary about doing the right thing for her—about whether he even *could, given the circumstances*. It left him without much sleep, a buzzing head, and a semitruckload of hay on the way in.

"Hey, boss!" Faith said cheerfully, buckling her work chaps around her waist with the legs still swinging free as she strode from the back to slap her gloves against the counter. Her piercings glimmered, an incongruous counterpoint to the cap crammed over her black hair. "I should have another go at that coffee before the hay gets here, right?"

"God, no," he said, working hard to inject just the right matter-of-fact note into his voice, just the right alacrity into his movement as he raised his head, turning a deliberately discerning eye her way. "The overflow area ready for unloading?"

He knew it wasn't. So did she. "Javi's not here yet," she said, which started off sounding like an excuse and ended with a quick shift to determination. "I'll go get started while I'm waiting."

You do that. He waited until she headed out the front door, setting the bells to jingling and trailing one of the several store cats in her wake.

Hay delivery meant shifting old stock, sweeping out corners…disturbing mice. The cats always knew.

So did the wolf. The wolf also knew when Holly entered the store from the back—and it rose to greet her, humming with a possessive intensity.

Lannie didn't ever remember pushing the wolf away. Hadn't ever needed to.

He did it now.

Holly stood beside the closest shelving endcap, her expression faintly wary and definitely uncertain. She made no attempt to hide her scrutiny of him; her gaze traveled from his features to his shoulder and quickly checked out his side, where no stain would show simply because he'd grown impatient and slapped on gauze with Bag Balm and far too much duct tape.

He eyed her back, easily able to see the tension riding in her shoulders. She wore no makeup to hide the lingering bruises of fatigue under her eyes, and glossy hair spilled from a high ponytail, a style that highlighted the clarity of her features and her large, impossibly rich brown eyes. She wore the same khaki pants from the day before and a no-nonsense polo shirt quite clearly tailored for a lean feminine form. The embroidery on her left shoulder read *Holly Springs* in a bold but elegant font interwoven with leaves, and beneath that in plainer text, a simple *Holly Faulkes*.

It told him a lot. It told him the kind of life she led— hardworking and active, and tied to the natural world. *More Sentinel than she thought.* It told him she truly hadn't had much time to pack. And it told him that whatever life of hiding her family had chosen, they hadn't considered their names to have been a risk. They'd somehow never been in official Sentinel roles.

It meant that her parents had never had the confidence and familiarity to turn to Brevis in the first place. And there was no telling what misinformation they'd given Holly along the way.

Or failed to give her.

She said, "I ate your sausage and oatmeal. I hope you expected that."

His stomach grumbled. But he knew better than to start the day with the pastry treats Faith left around—not with the wolf prowling so close to the surface, itching for a hunt.

The wolf grew surly on carbs.

Holly gave him an uncertain look; only then did he realize he hadn't said so much as *good morning*. Too lost in the static of his thoughts…and in his wolf's response to her. *It's not real,* he reminded himself, and said, "I hope you found everything you needed."

"Actually, I need a number of things," she said, her eye wandering to and clearly catching on Horace, the full-size fiberglass horse model at the front of the store. She visibly shook off the sight of Horace's current dress mode—makeup applied to mirror Faith's—and returned to her thoughts with determination. "Depends on how long I'm going to be here—*here*, at your place, and *here*, in New Mexico."

He lifted one shoulder. "Couldn't tell you."

She rolled her eyes. "Oh, come on. Surely you don't want to continue sleeping wherever you clearly didn't actually *sleep* last night."

So much for any impression of invincibility. He said only, "I was perfectly comfortable." Probably she wasn't ready to hear that the wolf slept where he would, and that last night's barn had been a luxury.

"Well, I'm not comfortable *here*, so if you can manage to give me some idea of how long this whole thing will take, I'd appreciate that."

The answer was only the same. Lannie didn't repeat himself.

She looked like a woman hanging on to her temper by a very thin margin. She spoke with a snappy precision he knew to remember. "Fine. I need clothes. I need more than the three ounces of shampoo that were in my travel kit. I need feminine products. And I want a bike. Do you want details, or do you just want to hand over your credit card?"

Lannie said, "A bike?"

"Yes. I bike. Therefore I need a bike."

"There's a bike shop in Cloudview," he said. A bike shop, good hunting territory, and…Holly's brother. Seeing him—realizing that she *could* see him—might go a long way toward settling her resentment.

And seeing him immersed in his Sentinel nature might go a long way to helping her accept her own.

"Cloudview?" Holly crossed her arms under her breasts, emphasizing both toned arms and modest but perfectly formed curves; Lannie found himself standing straighter. "What's the catch?"

Faith opened the front entry just long enough to sing out over the bells. "Hay's here early! Javi's late!"

Lannie allowed a faint grimace. "That," he said, "is the catch. Twenty tons of hay to unload first."

Holly didn't hesitate. "Then I'll go get my gloves and help."

Lannie *did* hesitate. She hadn't come here to heave two-string orchard grass.

"Look," she said. "I *work* for a living. I'll go insane all that much faster if you don't give me something to do while I'm waiting for whatever magical things you people want to see happen."

Magical. Yeah, something like that.

He reached under the counter for the stack of mismatched work gloves and dropped them on the glass. "See if anything here fits."

Holly quickly selected snug gloves of leather and stretchy backing—one an alarming pink, one blue— and tugged them on, flexing her fingers to settle them.

Lannie led the way to the barn overflow, filling his lungs with a deep, surreptitious breath and letting it out slowly—letting the restless wolf fill his skin, trying to appease the other in him until he had that time to hunt.

Holly wasn't far off his shoulder. She muttered a faintly singsong *"Stop that..."* and startled the wolf away.

Lannie barely stopped himself startling, too.

You weren't supposed to see it.

All in all, Holly Faulkes was far more Sentinel than she knew.

Javi arrived only a few moments into the unloading, allowing Lannie to step back and inspect the bales, approve the load and meet up with the trucker to handle paperwork.

"New hand, eh?" The man moved efficiently to wind and stash the webbing straps that had secured the semi-truck's load, and then came to stand beside Lannie as he scrawled his signature without bothering to prop the clipboard against the truck. "Have to say I approve."

Lannie gave him a hard glance. The man was twice Holly's age, his admiration frank but at a distance. Lannie's initial irrational irritation faded; he glanced up to where she worked the truck—strong and confident and more graceful than thou while she was at it, braced in perfect balance over the hay bales. She'd already figured out the rhythm of the work, the perfect combination of leverage and muscle to make the bales sail down in quiet arcs to a thumping impact. Her face had flushed pleasantly with the exertion, and from the looks of it, she was only just getting warmed up.

In the end, Lannie said only, "She'd eat you alive."

"You, too, buddy," the man said, affably enough. "Best watch yourself, if it's like that."

It wasn't like that. She was his job, and his response to her was no more real than ever in the opening stages of creating pack. But that wouldn't keep him from responding, and it wouldn't keep him from watching her. Appreciating her.

Beautiful, he thought—and then drew a hard breath when she jerked to a stop, turning to stare down at him.

Best watch yourself, Lannie Stewart.

He handed over the paperwork and put himself back to work. The familiar rhythm of it warmed stiff muscles and tugged as much against the duct tape as it did against his healing side. For long moments, he let go of his thoughts, giving over to the muted conversation of familiar teamwork, the occasional grunt of effort, Faith's giggles in the background when she lost her grip on a bale and it went pinwheeling off into the yard. When the truck sat empty and swept, the driver pulled away to leave them to the stacking…and eventually that was done, too, and Holly stood beside Lannie looking flushed but relaxed, mismatched gloves tucked away in a back pocket.

Her song trickled through to him, complex and self-confident and, at the moment, devoid of the resentful edge.

"Three hours," Faith said. "Not our best time, but decent."

"Thanks to Holly," said Javi, his eye already gone worshipful when it turned to Holly.

"Yeah," Faith said, older and wiser by not very many years, her back propped against the towering stack of hay and out of the sun. "You don't wanna go there. Just say thanks again."

"Right," Javi said, blushing beneath the olive tones of his skin. "Thanks, Miss Holly."

Holly seemed bemused to find herself back in a conversation—and a normal one, at that. "I was glad for it," she said. "I needed to get the travel kinks out." She brushed hay from her shirt and reaching for the neckerchief Javi had given her shortly after his arrival—a hesitant offering, gratefully received, and now full of enough hay to have proven its worth.

"Oh, no," Javi said, backing away a step just in case. "You keep it. You'll need one of those around here."

Holly's smile made Lannie straighten. Once again he found himself pushing back the wolf, the little growl in his mind that said *mine*.

Maybe so. But too strong or too fast with this one, and he'd lose her altogether. If it had been easier than this, Brevis wouldn't have brought her so precipitously to his doorstep.

"Drink something," he told Faith and Javi—and Holly, for that matter. "Bottled water in the fridge."

"Cool," said Faith. "Hey, Javi, I got some power powder to try in it. It'll turn your mouth blue."

"No, no," Javi said, following her anyway. "*Mi madre* would whip my behind if I come home with a blue mouth."

"She would not." Faith's words floated back over her shoulder as she rounded the corner of the barn overflow, and Lannie knew that Javi's mouth didn't stand a chance. So did Holly, to judge by the amusement lighting her expression—though that faded when she looked his way.

"You, too," he said. "Especially you."

She dusted at the hay on her legs. "And then?" When he only looked at her, she said, "Then what? We're going to Cloudview, I know. But I'm here for a reason. Do we have team-building games to play, or do I have homework, or are you going to put me on a shelf while you do other things?" Before he'd had time to truly consider that, she added, "One thing they should have warned you—I like to keep busy."

"I can arrange for another load of hay," Lannie said, deceptively mild.

"Sure," she said, just as evenly.

"What's next specifically," he told her, "is that we dust the hay out of our hair and get something to drink. Then I'd like to take a few moments to sniff around the well house—you can come or not, as you please."

He wasn't sure if sniffing around qualified as busy or boring, and in truth he wasn't sure he wanted her along. He'd just as soon take the wolf for this particular task, and he didn't think she was ready for that yet. When it came to that, he didn't think he was ready for it. Not to ride the edge of the most primal part of himself while she was nearby.

"And then Cloudview," she said. "I *know*. But after that. I don't get the sense that you have any sort of plan when it comes to me."

Lannie stood taller in a stretch, rotating one shoulder slightly. "I tend to play it by ear."

"Awesome," Holly said flatly. She pushed away from the hay bales. "Since we have such a good plan, we might as well get to it." She headed for the front of the overflow area—a tall, three-sided pole structure—and turned in the direction of the store, striding across the ground like she owned it.

Lannie watched the languid roll of her hips and wanted to follow. The wolf watched the casual strength in her and growled, chafing, wanting to follow.

Lannie made them both wait, and settle, and swallow back the *wanting*. Only then did he allow his feet to move, strangely distant from the earth and from the new pack song he already ached to call his own.

Holly avoided a flat, shrunken prickly pear, her thighs aching from the distinctly uphill hike. Lannie Stewart moved with assurance, familiar with the terrain and taking his own strength for granted. When he stopped and checked back for her, she knew for certain it was only for her sake, and not because he found himself winded.

But Holly was glad to suck in air. She was fit— she was damned fit—but she'd already helped unload twenty tons of hay and she was fit at *sea level*.

He nodded up ahead, and she belatedly saw the upper half and roof of a wood structure that looked more like a community pit toilet than any official well house, clearly placed just beyond the crest of this slope. "I'd like to take a look around before we add more footprints to the area."

"You want me to stay here." She realized it with surprise. Some part of her had enjoyed these silent moments of climbing the hillside together, no matter the effort, or the fact that she hadn't wanted to be here in the first place. *Still didn't want to be here.*

But that didn't mean her best option wasn't to wait this situation out, going through Sentinel hoops until she could walk away.

Lannie eyed her as if he was trying to read her thoughts from her face, and nodded. "Only a few moments. Catch your breath, look around. There's more going on in this forest than you think."

She wouldn't have called it a *forest* at all. But she only nodded, plucking a final stray piece of hay from her shirt, and he hiked on without her.

She watched until he moved out of sight, hidden by a trick of terrain and brush, and then sat herself down to look around. Low, flat cactus here…bushy treelike things dotted along the hill and set on gravelly, sandy soil. Sparse clumps of bunchgrass offered barely a hint of green, and the occasional long-needled pine towered over all.

"Forest," she snorted. But she wrapped her arms around her knees and tipped her face to the sun, realizing for the first time the true impact of its heat. A quick relocation to the shade of a spicy cedar brought out goose bumps, and she finally put herself half in, half out, and rested her forehead on her knees.

Maybe she shouldn't have. Maybe she should have kept moving. The quiet gave her space to recognize a strange, small edge of unease running through the center of her—a ripple of vertigo, and an escalation of what she'd experienced on arrival. She put her hand to the ground, eyes still closed, absorbing the textured feel of the cedar sheddings—tiny dry twigs, gritty soil, the angular hump of an exposed root. The connection steadied her in some way, but her sense of unease failed to fade.

Lannie had been right. She needed more water. Something to trail her fingers in, something to fiddle with.

Then again, it was nothing that going home wouldn't fix. A reasonable altitude, a reasonable humidity and a sun that didn't feel so close. *Anyone* would feel disoriented.

Song intruded, humming into her thoughts with such an insidious ease that she startled when she finally recognized it there, jerking her head up to scan the hill where Lannie had disappeared. She caught the glimpse of flickering light, a coruscation of energy; the song swelled and then faded. *What the—?*

Holly clambered to her feet to squint up the hill, swiping her hands off against the tough material of her work pants, hesitating on the verge of hiking on up. Lannie had had plenty of time to look around, and what if he—

He came into sight at the crest of the hill, appearing from between two junipers to wave her onward, and she suddenly understood. Lannie had gone uphill to take his other—whatever his *other* was. The light, the energy, even the humming song—those had all been the edges of his return to human. And now he stood there waiting for her, all matter-of-fact confidence and underlying strength.

She hiked the last hundred feet more quickly than she'd thought she had left in her, and greeted him with demand. "Was that you?"

She didn't truly expect his frown. "Maybe," he said, and thought about it until he shook his head. "Did it bother you?"

"Bother?" She found her hand was still gritty, the thin soil pressed into the lines of her palm, where she'd grabbed at the ground in her reaction to that song. She realized, too, what she really, really didn't want to admit—that her body had responded, humming along in its own way, and that now it had warmed to him in a clear defiance of how she felt about Sentinels, being here and being anywhere near him in the first place.

Good God, she *wanted* him.

Except she didn't. She didn't want any part of being here, Lannie Stewart included. So she, too, finally shook her head. "It didn't bother me," she said. "It *surprised* me. It was *rude*."

He pondered that, watching her with an awareness she wasn't sure she liked. "Probably so," he allowed, and left it at that, switching his attention to the well house now completely within view. "There's nothing much up here. They didn't waste much time trying to chase Aldo off." He shook his head. "Just an old man taking a smoke."

Holly took a few more steps in that direction, eyeing the faint track of an unofficial lane. The well house itself didn't do anything to offset her initial impression, and its security consisted of a simple aged hasp and lock. "Why would they even come down this road?"

Lannie walked past her to the lane, scuffing his way across it. At her inquisitive look, he pointed downward. "This ground holds a track a whole lot better than you might think. I'll know it when someone comes through this way again."

Tracks. She looked down at that weird mix of silty, gritty soil overlaying hard ground, and discovered herself in the midst of them.

Not all of them human.

She crouched, running a forefinger around the outside of the nearest track. The nearest *huge* track, doglike in shape if not in size. Lannie's? Or had it been here all along? "You're right," she said. "This ground holds a significant track." She glanced up at him. "You should have brought a broom."

."Maybe I will." He paced down the road, looking along its length as if the guy gang and their truck might come barreling back down it any moment now. Holly pressed her hand over the track, obliterating it, and stood up. A few steps took her to the only snatch of color in the pale ground, and it took her some moments to recognize the splatter of dried blood. Her gaze flickered to the faded bruising on his face, and he shook his head. "Not mine."

"Nice," she said. "They probably never knew what hit them."

Because he was Sentinel. He was stronger. He was supposed to pull his punches.

"There were five of them," he reminded her.

"Sentinel," she reminded him, out loud this time.

To her surprise, he lifted the front tail of his shirt. At first she saw nothing but the gleam of skin over surprisingly hard muscle, the light scatter of hair toward the center of a torso leaner than she'd expected. She stuttered on a response—and then realized the steep shadow between two of his lowest ribs wasn't a shadow, but the angry and slightly gaping lips of a knife wound.

"Sentinel," he said. "Not Superman. You should know. Your blood is strong enough."

"I never thought so," she said, more faintly than pleased her. "I'm not truly different from anyone else. Not like—"

You. With the way the wild strength sometimes gleamed straight from his eyes, or how the very way he stood broadcast the dangerous nature lurking behind a laconic exterior.

"Look in a mirror sometime." He let the shirttail fall.

"I don't understand." She tore her gaze away from his side to search his expression, finding little she could read there at all. "I don't heal much faster than anyone else." She made a face, and admitted, "Yes, a little. But I thought Sentinels healed *really* fast."

His grin was wry; it changed his face, made her want to reach out to him and take his hand and bump a companionable shoulder. She took a step back instead, startled at herself. He said, "If we're badly injured, the early healing comes quick. Hurts like hell, too. But it keeps us alive when we might otherwise die." He shrugged. "After that? You already know. We heal a little more quickly than normal. That's all."

"Then that must have been a whole lot worse yesterday." Realization struck. "Right after I got here." And then she leaped forward to a whole new understanding, and she speared a glance at him. "You were loading hay with that?"

He frowned down at the injury, resting his hand lightly over top. "There was hay to unload."

She exhaled a sharp and impatient breath. "For everything you say, I swear there are two things you're keeping to yourself."

"Maybe," he said. "But never things about you, *from* you. Just ask."

She made a noncommittal noise in her throat that sounded no more convinced that she felt; he looked sharply at her. "Altitude catching up with you?"

"Maybe." She looked down the slope—the unfamiliarity of the terrain, the unfamiliarity of the scents and even the sound of the bird flashing bright blue from the brush as it scolded them. The unfamiliarity, yes... and deeper, beneath it all, the sense that something else was missing, was *wrong*. Something she'd been leaning on so long she hadn't even known it was there and now couldn't begin to define.

"Still want to go to Cloudview?"

She jerked her head back to narrow her eyes at him. "Don't you dare go back on that."

Was that amusement on his features, lurking at the corners of his eyes, in the slight lift on one side of his mouth? She took a step toward him, a light growl vibrating somewhere in her chest. "Are you *laughing* at me?"

At the same time, she heard it again—the hint of song, beguiling cello tones weaving beneath faint strains of barely whispered complexity. The intrusion stunned her—the affront of it, the fact that she could hear it at all—but she'd barely drawn breath to protest when he grinned outright. Also unexpected, and also stunning—in its own way, striking deep into the heart of her.

By then he'd taken the few steps between them and wrapped an unexpected arm around her shoulder in a gesture of startling affection.

She wanted to sputter at him. She wanted to say *I didn't invite you to do that* and *You have no right*— but her body was already melting into him. Just long enough to feel the upright strength in him, and to understand how clearly his gentleness was a choice.

Then he stepped back, framing her head between both big hands to look directly into her gaze, piercing eyes gone somehow softer. "It gets easier," he told her. "Let's go see your brother."

And then he took her hand and led her down the hill.

Chapter 4

The familiar terrain gentled as Lannie led the way back to the feed-store cluster, revealing a barely sloping spread that held not just the feed-store grounds but a faint scatter of buildings along the curving country road. Lannie's two mules engaged in some sort of conversational disagreement, gamboling without grace but with power to spare.

Holly might have hesitated, taking it all in, but Lannie kept them moving. The noon sun had brought out the heat of the day—and as much as Holly seemed to need activity, allowing her to help with the entire load of hay hadn't been the smartest choice of his day.

Too damned bad he'd been so distracted by watching her.

"We'll grab something to eat on the way out of town," he said. "I just need a moment to square away—"

Pain shot through his side; the faint music underlying

his soul burst into brief static. He blinked, and found himself looking up into bright blue sky. The uneven ground pressed into his back, sharp with myriad little stones and prickery bunchgrass, and his legs were ungainly, bent and sprawling as if they'd simply forgotten how to be legs. "What," he said quite clearly, "the hell?"

"You tell *me*," Holly said, and couldn't hide worry with her scowl. She had one hand pressed on his shoulder as if she knew the first thing he'd do was try to get up, and the other at his pulse—pounding hard and fast, but perfectly regular.

"Hey!" Faith shouted from the bottom of the slope, her accusing voice getting closer with each word. "What did you *do* to him?"

"*To* him?" Holly said, rising to that bait even as she kept Lannie's shoulder to the ground. But she only had leverage as long as he didn't roll aside—and that he did, rising as smoothly as he ever did. Holly made that disgusted little feline noise in her throat and came to her feet beside him.

By then Faith had reached them, heavy work boots amazingly spry along the way. "Yes!" she snapped at Holly. "You! To him!"

"Whoa," Lannie said as the static struck again, his alarm having less to do with going down and everything to do with the potential collision of Faith and Holly. When he could see clearly again he found himself on hands and knees, blinking at the ground.

"Why did you even get up?" Faith asked in exasperation, though it was Holly's hand at the back of his neck, quiet and firm.

Because that shouldn't have happened at all. Never mind a second time. Or, if he counted the odd moments of the previous evening, a third or fourth or a...

"Faith," he said, with as much authority as any man in his situation could muster, "this is not Holly's doing."

"Right," Holly said. "Blame me. Awesome. I am *so* glad to be here."

"You showed up and *this* happened," Faith said, bending to peer at Lannie.

"*This* was happening when I got here," Holly said, sounding so certain that Lannie lifted his head to look at her in surprise. "Oh, yes," she said, seeing it. "Last night. Right in front of me."

"You were watching me." It warmed something inside him, which shouldn't have mattered but did.

Holly made an exasperated sound. "Of course I was watching you. Under the circumstances, I'd have been an idiot if I'd done anything else, eh?"

He remembered to feel his own exasperation. He thought he'd hidden those moments of disorientation. Mariska wouldn't have hesitated to call him out if she'd noticed anything wrong.

"Lannie!" Aldo's whiskery voice carried uphill far too well. "No, no—this isn't supposed to happen!"

Lannie rubbed his hands over his face. His legs were his own again; his mind was clear, and his soul carried his own faint inner song. "Awesome," he muttered, deliberately echoing Holly's flat tone.

"Yeah, now I know you're not right," Faith told him.

Aldo reached them and knelt down to put a hand on Lannie's knee. "You okay, son? Ah, this is all my fault—"

"Aldo." Lannie said it firmly. "Yesterday was not your fault. I don't care *what* you said to them. There's no reason good enough for five guys to beat up on a sixty-year-old man."

"Seemed funny at the time," Aldo said, looking somewhat bereft.

No doubt it had.

Lannie sighed and regained his feet. He took a brief but ruthless check of himself and found nothing amiss—except for the dent in his pride.

Alpha wasn't bully, or overbearing. But alpha did mean strength.

His strength was smarting.

Holly kept pace with him as they headed downhill. "Look," she said, brushing off the seat of her pants as they walked. "I'd really like to grab some things from the closest big-box store."

"Ruidoso," Faith told her, slipping it in between Holly's words.

"And I'd really like to have time to rest this afternoon. *And*," she said, giving Lannie a sharp eye, "I don't really want to be in a car with you behind the wheel right now."

He squelched that little bit of sting. "Cloudview will be there tomorrow."

"Good." She nodded, more or less to herself; her ponytail swung to land gently over her shoulder. Lannie should have been prepared at the spark of amusement showing in her eye, but as they reached the back of the store, she managed to take him by surprise. Again.

"Keys," she said, and held out her hand—adding, when he only stared at her, "Ruidoso. *Truck*."

And then she smiled.

Holly made off with more than the truck keys; she pulled a local map off the Internet, acquired Lannie's credit card and his cell phone and escaped the feed store without an escort.

Not that she needed one. Lannie could no doubt find her anywhere now that he'd taken her in. He kept track of his people, that was obvious enough.

And like it or not, she was one of his people now. At least in *his* mind.

On the way out to Ruidoso—forty minutes of curving, challenging roads with the faint background buzz of disorientation in her head—she spent no little time wondering how she would have reacted to the man if he'd simply walked into her office looking for a consultation on a water feature. If there'd been no preestablished baggage between them.

The thought woke things in her that she would rather have left sleeping. Hot-and-bothered things that left her shifting uncomfortably in the truck's otherwise comfortable seat. Because never mind his muscled build and strong shoulders and perfectly lean cowboy hips. Or even his eyes—*Good God, those eyes.*

There was that something more about him. The charisma. The way he stood even when he wasn't pouring on the attitude. The way his other showed, even when he didn't know it—and even when she didn't yet know what other form he took.

The way he cared about his people.

He's still your jailer.

He was still a complicit part of the team that now kept her away from her own life.

Remembering that should have cooled her blood somewhat. *Should have.* Holly distracted herself by pulling off the road long enough to call her brother— not at a phone that would reach him directly, because no phone ever did. But she dialed the number for Regan Adler, her brother's love—and soon enough, his spouse.

"Hey," she said into the machine that resided in a

small but personable cabin home deep at the edge of Kai's woods. "This is Holly. Hello to Kai, but this message is for Regan. We might be coming your way tomorrow. If you have time, I'd like to meet up." Regan might be self-employed, providing lush and slyly quirky illustrations for nature guides of all sorts along with her own painting, but Holly knew better than to take her time for granted. Had been there, and had that done to her. "I know we don't know each other, but I'm hoping you can give me some perspective on this situation."

This situation. What a plethora of Sentinel sins that phrase encompassed.

"Anyway," Holly added hastily, "I hope you'll call. PS—this is Lannie Stewart's phone."

The rest of the drive went quickly, and once she reached the store she pulled her hastily scribbled list from her pocket and went to work with the focused intensity that had made her business successful, happy to hand over Lannie's card to buy a few reusable shopping totes with her goods, and toss the whole kit and caboodle into the bed of the truck behind the straw bale.

On the way back, the phone warbled a basic faux phone ring. Holly thought only of her message to Regan, and pulled the phone from the seat divider to accept the call.

"Holly?"

Holly's breath caught on the decision to hang up. "Just listen," Faith said, and her words were low and hasty—in the end, intriguing Holly just enough to stay on the call.

She found a wide spot by the side of the road to pull over. "I'm here."

"Look," Faith said. "I don't really know what's going on with you being here. I know what Lannie does for

Brevis, so we do get people here sometimes, or he goes somewhere else, but there's something different about this. About *him*."

"You still trying to blame it on me?" Holly said. "Because as far as I'm concerned, you can take your Sentinels and—"

Faith's heartfelt and indelicate noise in response did more to get Holly's attention than anything else could have. "Look, I'm such a light blood that only someone like Lannie can even tell I'm Sentinel. They're not *my* people—I ran from them a long time ago."

"They let you go?" Holly asked, a flicker of hope in her voice.

After a hesitation and a number of muffled sounds, Faith replied. *"Light blood,"* she reminded Holly. "But listen. This is about Lannie. Something's not right. And since he had to pull out of his home pack in order to deal with you—"

"He what?"

"God, don't you know anything?"

Anger made its way to Holly's throat, tightening it. "No more than I've been told."

"Then ask Lannie. He'll tell you as much as he can. But look, what I'm doing is asking you to keep an eye on him, okay? Because we can't. Not the way we're used to."

Responses jumbled through her mind—the bitter awareness that she couldn't ask for information when she didn't even know enough to frame the right questions. The rising curiosity about Lannie and his home pack and his Sentinel other and what he did with it—or what had happened with the *Jody thing*. The cold hard fear of realizing anew that her life was totally out of her own control.

For now.

"Look, I get it." Faith's words came with the white noise of something brushing across the phone, and Holly suddenly realized that she was crouched somewhere in the feed store, trying to hide the call from Lannie. "You don't owe us anything and I was a bitch to you. But this is about Lannie, okay?"

And Holly found herself saying, "Okay."

She hung up the phone in a bemused state, taking the remainder of the drive home with a slower speed than the car behind her probably would have preferred. At the farm store, she pulled around back to park as if she'd always been here, always been driving Lannie's truck…always been the one to co-opt his pack. When she disembarked and grabbed her bags from the back, the midafternoon heat bore down on her in a sizzle of sun—one the shade of the barn quickly quenched into a chill.

She began to understand why people here dressed in so many layers.

She took the exterior steps up to Lannie's barn apartment two at a time, and realized how much better she felt for the chance to collect her thoughts.

Or maybe it was just her Sentinel constitution after all—adjusting to the altitude more quickly than expected after her morning's difficulty.

Maybe.

She let herself into the apartment and stopped short at the sight.

Lannie.

To be more precise, Lannie's back. He stood at his kitchen sink, shirtless, muscles flexing as he reached overhead to put away a set of mugs. Enough spicy humidity filled the air so even if she hadn't seen the gleam of dampness across his skin and in the slight curl of his hair, she would have known he'd just stepped out of the shower.

He barely turned his head to greet her and she realized that of course he'd known she was coming. If he hadn't heard the truck, if he hadn't heard her steps on the stairs...

She had the feeling he still would have known.

"Get what you needed?" he asked, as if this would be some plain old conversation about simple things.

"More or less," she said, playing the same game. "Should I unpack them?"

He grabbed a basin from the sink, handling it carefully enough so she knew it still held water. "Is that your way of asking if you're staying here?"

Without waiting for a response, he took the basin to the other side of the loft—to the giant hexagonal window she'd admired so much that morning, however briefly. Iron scrollwork crawled around the edges and the supporting grids, intimating leaves and twining vines, and light flooded through to fill the loft. Before it sat a motley collection of plants, each of which now received a careful portion of what must have been his rinse water.

Not that she cared. She was too caught up in watching him move, handling the awkward chore with a masculine grace.

When he glanced over his shoulder, she realized just how hypnotized she'd become.

Maybe she should have blushed and stammered at being caught, but she didn't care to. He was worth watching. So she smiled.

After a moment, his mouth quirked in what might have been amusement, and might have been response.

"Yes," he said. "You're welcome to stay here while we figure out the most obvious solution to the situation."

Reality intruded. "But what about—"

He shook his head, returning the basin to the sink, and then propped himself against it to regard her. "I shower and eat here. Where I sleep isn't an issue." At the disbelieving look on her face, he laughed, a quiet huff of humor. "Trust me, Holly. It's fine."

"Trust you?" She let the shopping totes slide gently to the floor, refusing to be distracted by the flat planes of his sparsely furred chest or the window light skipping across his abs. Absolutely refusing. Even when the knife wound he'd so readily dismissed caught that same light, raw and inflamed and hardly healing. "Is this is a test of some sort?"

He cocked his head, barely enough to see it. "If you like."

"Fine," she said. "I have a test for you, too."

He planted the heels of his hands against the counter and waited. Holly took it for invitation. "What did Faith mean, you've had to disconnect from your home pack for me? What does that mean to *you*? Why, *exactly*, am I here? It's not just to keep me safe while things settle down. And also, you need to let me do something with that." She nodded at his side. "Like take you to the local urgent care."

Lannie snorted. "I can take myself anywhere I need to go."

"Really?" Holly smiled at him, so beatific. "Because as I recall, just this morning you were a little unpredictable about staying on your feet."

"I'm fine," he said, and this time the words had a little growl behind them, one that showed in his eyes.

Holly found herself delighted to have gotten under

his skin at all. Lannie Stewart, she thought, was used to being the one with the answers.

She lifted his truck keys. "I bet you keep the spares down behind the store counter. Want to bet your little friend Faith has already hidden them?"

This time the growl was unmistakable. It reverberated against something inside Holly, something she hadn't even known was there. She hid the shiver of it from him by flipping the keys back into her hand and tucking them away in her front cargo pocket. "You might have thought this was about protecting the resistant younger sister of your latest Sentinel hero, but it's much, much more—and so am I. No urgent care? Fine. Get your first-aid supplies. Then we'll talk."

Lannie had little in the way of Band-Aids and gauze, and little patience for any of it. He was Sentinel; he would heal. He didn't often take serious injury in his work, but he'd been there enough to know.

Holly found the employee kit in the store's break room, grabbed self-sticking horse bandages from the shelf, and returned to the loft no less determined than she'd left it.

Lannie had spent the time basking in the window sunlight as wolf, pretending the occasional peak of underlying static didn't break through his thoughts. He heard her coming at the bottom step and almost didn't make it into human—and into his pants—before she opened the door.

He'd forgotten how she took those steps two at a time.

"Here," Holly said, even as she came through the door with her bounty, a tube of hydrogel included. "Faith said you would use this stuff."

"You told Faith?" He couldn't quite keep the alarm from his voice.

She made an amused sound. "Did you think she didn't already know?" At his silence, she added, "And you shouldn't have left that mess of a man-bandage in the counter trash if you wanted it to be some big hairy secret. What was that, half a roll of duct tape?"

"It didn't stay on anyway," he grumbled with generalized disgruntlement.

"While we were doing that hay? No kidding." Holly seemed more cheerful now that she'd outmaneuvered him regarding the truck keys. If it made her feel as though she'd gained some control over her life, she would have it.

For the moment.

Holly busied herself pulling butterfly bandages from the box and lining them up on the tiny breakfast bar jutting out from the wall between the kitchen and the window area. Aside from the plants, the window space held exactly one couch—it was as close to a social space as the loft got, with the bed tucked in behind the half wall across from the window and the bathroom taking up just as much room across from the kitchen. He'd roughed in an unheated closet, but he doubted she'd discovered that particular feature yet.

It wasn't a bachelor pad so much as the space of an alpha wolf still alone at heart.

"There." Satisfaction tinged Holly's voice. "Come on over and lean against the bar."

Lannie released a silent sigh and complied, leaning to expose the injury to the light and grunting at the painful stretch of it.

Holly made a dismayed sound in her throat. "Have you looked—"

"It's *fine*," Lannie said. "If it was a problem, the fast healing would kick in—and I'd know if that was happening. It hurts."

"And that doesn't?"

"It hurts *more*," he said pointedly.

Holly rested hesitant fingers on his side; he twitched against it, swearing inwardly as the wolf reared up and took interest. Warm fingers, gentle touch...for an instant, it was the only thing he could feel. At least, until the rest of his body figured it out and responded.

Well, the wolf was alive. And so was the man. And Holly's touch reached them both.

"It's ugly," Holly said, her fingertips pressing lightly around his ribs as she assessed the cut. "Really irritated. Until it does heal, you ought to quit taking yourself for granted."

He frowned at the countertop. "Ow!"

"Like I said." She dabbed ointment along the edges of the wound.

His hands bore down on the counter, as much irritation as bullet biting. "It shouldn't be that—*ow!*" He jerked away, turning a glare of impatience on her.

"Uh-huh. Whatever. Stop growling."

By dint of will, he did, and he held himself still while she pinched the edges of the wound and placed a generous row of butterfly bandages. By the time she finished—by the time she stretched her arms around him to wind the self-sticking elastic around his torso— that pain was a thing of the past, and her touch was again the only thing of the present—light, skimming his flesh with authority, patting the whole arrangement into place. Lingering, while her scent permeated the air around him—his shampoo and her own personal perfume, mingled into something that felt so very much like possession.

She stood, fumbling the bandage onto the counter—hesitating, when she might have been stepping away, her face flushed. She visibly hunted for words, her teeth lingering on her lower lip before she found them. "I don't know how long that'll last, but…try to take it easy?"

He barely heard her. From behind the static, a sweet melody flowed, winding through Lannie like the vines winding along his window. He leaned into it, breathing it deeply into his body, his eyes closing as he absorbed that brief purity.

When he opened them again and found her so very close, so visibly trembling, he had nothing to say—nothing he *could* say. Not when enthralled in such a deep thrum of underlying need. *Mine.* A singular thought, threading through sensation. *Mine.* Not as alpha, not as Sentinel. Just as man.

Mine.

Holly's eyes opened wide; she stood taller and straighter, and her nostrils flared. "I am *not yours*." She looked right back up at him, her pupils grown big within a narrow ring of darkening brown. She might even have stood on her toes, leaning into him physically just as he'd breathed in the song of her. "I am not *Sentinel* and I am not *yours*, and nothing you can do *will change that.*"

The song stuttered back to static, staggering him as much as the connection had done. Holly slapped the remainder of the elastic bandage on the tiny breakfast bar and turned on her heel, going down the steps with the same authority with which she'd come up.

And Lannie stood there with his side aching from her touch and aching *for* it, and knew she was exactly right.

Chapter 5

Lannie snagged Holly's file from the cupboard nook where he'd stashed it and went to his thinking spot—or at least the thinking spot he used while in human form.

He sat beside the mule paddock, leaning against the join of two metal corral panels and propping his knees up to serve as a desk for Holly's file. He'd pulled on a worn chambray shirt, rolled up the sleeves and left the tails hanging out. Not customer-worthy and not concerned about it even if the store had another hour to go before closing. Everyone knew better than to bother him when he went to sit with the mules.

Everyone except Aldo.

The old man approached with a sideways sort of step, not quite looking at Lannie, a giant plastic travel mug in hand.

"Hey, Lannie," he said.

Lannie blew out a sigh. "Hey, Aldo."

"Brought you iced tea."

"Did you, now."

Another few steps and Aldo held the mug out. He looked his usual borderline disreputable, his thinning gray hair drawn back in a braid, his red-checkered shirt only half buttoned, and his jeans a size too large and hunting for a place to settle on skinny hips.

Lannie took the mug—although when he lifted it for a gulp, he stopped long enough to ask, "You didn't put peyote in this, right?"

Aldo affected an offended expression. "Wouldn't do that to you, Lannie-boy." Although when Lannie raised a skeptical brow, the old man added, "Least, not without telling you. And this time I'm telling you *not*."

The tea went down cold and crisp, and Lannie set the offering aside. "What's on your mind, old man?"

Aldo looked around, not half as surreptitiously as he likely thought. "That Holly girl gone?"

"Up the hill," Lannie told him, perfectly aware of the thin thread of Holly's presence. "Using your spot, I believe. Let her be."

Aldo only nodded, somewhat more sagely than often. But he was coyote; he had a nose for knots and implications, and he knew as well as any that Lannie wouldn't leave Holly completely off leash. Not yet. "Already bringing her into yourself, then?"

Firm if not unkind, Lannie said, "It's not your business."

Maybe a little more firmly than usual.

Aldo only smiled, a thing often not to be trusted. "You're okay, then."

Lannie looked the old man straight in the eye—only the faintest hint of threat in his eye, at the edge of his lip. Gone alpha, because with Aldo there was no giving ground. Not when questioned about pack matters.

Aldo offered instant sulk, which was also as it should be. "Just asking, just asking."

Lannie waited another moment and said, "Good tea, Aldo. Thanks."

Aldo straightened some. "Sure," he said. And then, very carefully, "It's just that if...well, if you weren't...I mean, I would want to know. Just in case."

Lannie didn't even know what to do with that, so he did nothing—his thoughts already tugging back to Holly, and the very thin file at his disposal—the first pages of which had been all about her brother Kai and his extreme sensitivity to the land, and to all traces of Core magic. Unlike any other known Sentinel, Kai could instantly, reliably, perceive the presence of the new silent Atrum Core workings.

Lannie wasn't certain that Lily and Aeron Faulkes had chosen the best course by bringing their small family to this area. The Core princes and posses preferred their comforts and amenities; they preferred hiding within clusters of humanity. And unlike Sentinels, so many of whom gravitated toward the land, those in the Atrum Core were related by blood line and activity but not by nature. They had no *others*; they had no sense of the Earth and no ability to navigate its unseen ways.

They never heard Lannie's song.

He looked up, realized Aldo was still waiting, and said, "Something else?"

Aldo fished in one baggy jeans pocket and pulled out Lannie's phone—last seen in Holly's possession as she headed out for her errands. "This was ringing in the truck."

Lannie scowled at it. This was not a place he brought the phone. "And it couldn't have waited?"

Aldo shrugged, radiating inoffensiveness—which only meant that he'd done something he likely shouldn't have. "She called Regan Adler. Regan Adler called back."

"Give me that," Lannie growled, holding out his hand. "Go help Faith prep the store for closing, and I'll put you on the clock for a couple hours."

Aldo brightened, handing the phone over with a new energy. Brevis covered Aldo's basic needs, but picking up sporadic hours at the feed store added a tiny bit of luxury to his spare life. Sporadic because that was all Aldo had ever been, and because in these past weeks he'd only become more so. "Appreciate that, Lannie."

"So will I, if you keep Faith's mind on her work. Brevis spooks her, you know that." Not so much as it used to be, but Aldo would take it to heart. "Git, then."

Aldo hustled back to the barn, though not without turning back to offer, "Want me to put hay by the door for those mules?"

Lannie lifted his head in thanks, already absorbed again by the contents of the folder, by the phone in his hand...by the deep tug from his wolf. *Find her.* He pushed against the bridge of his nose, hunting focus, and reached for the folder. But the next page turned out to be a scant recitation of Holly's circumstances—her tidy little cottage house in Upper Michigan, the sketchy notes of an upbringing that emphasized her independent nature, her steadfastly non-Sentinel lifestyle

He thought of Jody. He couldn't help but think of Jody. The woman had been raised Sentinel, but without humility. She'd never been exposed to the consequences of her reckless ways, but had been protected from them.

Her full-blooded nature and brilliance with stealth had put her in the field; her inability to mesh with her team had put the team in his hands...with only a few short days to integrate them before they'd gone south to deal with an exotics smuggling ring.

He'd done his best. He'd connected instantly with her—he'd felt her brilliance, her bright spark of life. And maybe she'd understood at that...

But she hadn't had time to live it. To practice it. And she'd gone out in the field and gotten them all killed.

He'd felt that, too.

And now here was Holly. Yanked from her home, from her life, from her very way of being. There was no telling how enmeshed she'd been in her surrounding territory, if she was anything like her brother—whether she knew it or not.

Her occasionally palpable resentment...

He deserved it. They all did. And if she had any idea she was working with an alpha still reeling from failure and its resulting disaster...

He picked up the phone.

Holly found herself back up at the well house for the second time that day, only this time she turned around to glare down at the amazing vista and think at it with loud, angry clarity. *I am not yours!*

That wasn't quite enough, so she did it out loud, too. "I am not yours!"

Her words rang loudly in the evergreen-studded landscape, and she should have felt just a little bit silly.

She didn't. And she hoped someone was listening.

Even if no one answered.

"Bother," she grumbled, and sat on the crest of that final hill to look down on it all. A massive canine paw print was pressed into the dirt at her side, and she stared at it for a good long while.

Wolf? Boy, wouldn't that explain a lot.

If her family had stayed within a brevis, would she know what her other was? Would she have tried to take it? Would she be initiated, and secure in her Sentinel abilities?

"The big question is, do I care?" She slapped her hand over the paw print, obliterating it, and propped her chin in her hand, looking out over Lannie Stewart's land. Maybe it wasn't the thick green woods in which she felt so at home…but if she quit trying to see it through Michigan-colored glasses, the undulating land did have its own beauty. This morning the sky had been crystal clear, bluer than blue and bigger than big. This early evening it was still big enough, but giant, towering clouds shifted across the sky, brilliant white above and glowering bruised blues below and scudding distinct shadows across the ground.

Holly lifted her face not to the sun, but to those clouds—drawn to the majestic purity of them. Without thinking, she stood again—stretching herself tall, arms reaching high and fingers spread wide, every bit of her body yearning to touch those stormy clouds.

She didn't. She couldn't. She came off her toes in a huff of disgust, not even sure what she'd been thinking.

Nothing. She hadn't been thinking anything. She'd just been *doing*, one woman alone on the hillside and completely out of her own place in the world.

She sat again, this time more slowly. Rather than reach for the sky, she pressed her hands flat to the ground and closed her eyes—looking for something, *anything*, that might be familiar. She pushed her own awareness, seeking…

Home.

Or some sense of it.

Instead she felt an ugly, distinct sense of rejection. The barrier wasn't a slap so much as an inexorable refusal to allow her to become part of where she was. It left her sitting perched on the earth, her eyes closed and her teeth biting her lip on the sudden certainty that she might just come flying free of the ground altogether.

She withdrew back inside herself, wrapping her arms around her torso and suddenly shivered—glancing up to find herself in the deep shadow of one of those clouds.

Her breathing slowed; her pounding heart eased. She sat, one woman alone on the hillside, yearning for something she couldn't define, and listening, listening for even the faintest hint of inexplicable song.

"Lannie who?"

The woman's voice at Lannie's ear sounded puzzled, and he didn't blame her. No one seemed quite to know what was going on around here.

"Lannie Stewart," he said, eyeing the sky and pondering the potential for monsoon rain. "I'm in Descanso. Kai's sister Holly is staying with me for integration work."

"Ah," Regan Adler said, wisdom replacing confusion. "The enforced indoctrination."

He didn't quite know what to say to that, so he didn't.

"Sorry," she said. "Maybe that wasn't fair. But Holly didn't even have a chance to see her brother before your people whisked her away. And does she even know her parents have been taken to Brevis?"

Careful, careful. "Her parents made their choices," Lannie said. "Not that I don't understand them. But choices have consequences."

"None of that was Holly's fault," Regan said. "But she's the one paying the price, don't you think?"

"More than she should," Lannie agreed. One of the mules came up behind him, reaching through the corral pipe to inspect Lannie's hair; he reached up to tug on the creature's chin, and mulish contentment rolled over him. "We're coming to Cloudview tomorrow to get Holly a bike."

Silence greeted that pronouncement, if only for a moment. "I thought it wasn't safe."

"It's not safe for Holly to be on her own," Lannie said. "She isn't."

Regan bristled audibly. "You know, we've done fine without you so far."

"Right," Lannie said, failing to rise to her anger one little bit. "And now you don't have to." He let the words settle. "More importantly, Holly doesn't have to. She has a lot to learn, Regan. I think it would help if she could see you and Kai. If you're not up for that, I'll handle it."

"I have no problem with Holly," Regan said instantly. "Damn you."

Lannie laughed. "We'll call once we have the bike."

"Fine," Regan said. "You tell her I'll be glad to give her perspective. Use those words."

"Yes, ma'am," Lannie said, without any sign of meekness. He grinned as he ended the call, struck by Regan's assertively defensive response to Holly's needs—struck by the similar strengths in the two women.

He reached over his head to give the hovering mule another chin tug. "I think I just might live to regret this."

When the mule snorted on him, he took it as agreement.

Lannie was waiting for her when she came down the hill—the folder tucked away, the mules happy with a flake or two of hay to carry them into the evening and the night growing cool around them all. The clouds had stalled, lurking up high with no indication of releasing any rain.

Holly returned in the twilight, moving easily downhill in that rolling walk. Lannie watched her progress with a semihypnotized gaze, instinctively reaching out to share pack song—

She doesn't want that. He stopped himself short, shifted subtle intent and let himself listen instead— waiting for the ongoing static to make way for the light and airy sense of her, and then breathing it in.

She stopped several corral panels away from him. "Mules, eh?" she said in that Upper Peninsula way of hers, as if it was a question.

"Spike," he told her. "And Grit." Big, solid sealbrown animals with wise eyes and mobile ears. "Do you ride?"

"Do *they*?"

"Better'n most."

"Well," she said. "Maybe, then. Sometime." And then she looked directly at him and said, "Faith says I should just ask you the things no one's told me."

Lannie thought of the thin folder he'd been given. "I have some things to ask you, too."

She drew back a little. "So what's this, then? Starting over? Because I'm not giving anyone a clean slate. Not after how things went."

Lannie scruffed a hand through his hair. "Fair enough. But Holly...you're here so I can help."

"I wouldn't need help if your people hadn't—" She started hotly enough, but broke off the words. "Okay. I'm sorry. I'm trying. I'm just so *angry*. And nothing seems *right* around here."

Lannie closed the distance between them. "*Ask* me."

She favored him with a narrow-eyed look. Her hand on the top corral pipe gripped more tightly than she probably realized.

He kept himself from touching her, because then he'd simply stop thinking and start doing. "Wherever you want to start."

"Fine," she said. "*Why* is it so dangerous for me to just be at home right now? *Why* is it so important to bring me into the Sentinels? Why couldn't I stay with the rest of my family in Cloudview?"

Lannie ran a hand over his face and regarded her in silence. "What," he said finally, "did your folks tell you about the Core?"

"Atrum Core," she said promptly. "Bad guys. Yada yada yada."

About what he'd expected. They'd sheltered her, and in no way prepared her to live in a world populated by both Sentinels and Core.

"Short version," he said. "The Sentinels and the Atrum Core come from the same roots."

She frowned. "You mean the story about the Roman and the Druid who fathered a child with the same woman?"

"Not a story," he told her, and had to stop himself from brushing juniper sheddings off her shoulder. "The Druid's line reached out to the earth and learned to take the forms of their others. The Roman's line reached out to darker places, and justified it by saying the Druid line needed to be kept in check."

"An arms race, Bronze Age style." The thought gave her a hint of a smile. "But I don't understand how that—"

He lifted a brow; she subsided to let him finish. "It

was a dark time, Holly. Things probably got out of hand on both sides. But when the dust settled, the Sentinels were still deeply dedicated to the earth—just as you are, in your own way."

"Waterscaping. Landscaping." She considered it. "And the Core…"

"The Core," Lannie said darkly, "cares more about stopping us so we won't stop *them*. They steal, they corrupt, and to their precinct princes—their *drozhars*—every Sentinel alive is a Sentinel who should be dead."

"Well, they suck," Holly said. "What's that got to do with me? Because *I'm not one of you.*"

"Even if that was true, they won't take chances."

She scowled for a long moment, fiddling with the ends of her glossy ponytail. "My folks told me they would never do anything overt. That in order for us each to live in this world without detection, we have a sort of détente."

"If the Core reliably honored that détente, your parents wouldn't have felt the need to protect Kai in the first place."

Her eyes sparked sudden anger, clearly visible to him even in the growing darkness. Sentinel vision, not always a blessing. "They hid him from *you* as much as from the Core!"

"It makes the Core no less dangerous. Until the local posses come to terms with the fact that Kai exists and is one of us now—that *you're* one of us, and fully protected by us—you're a temptation to them."

"So this is temporary." She said it with wary hope… with something of a dare.

Oh, God, I hope not. He closed his eyes, flinching from reactive thought. Hell, the wolf had fallen hard. Not in any way his human could truly understand, because the human saw her anger and her rejection. The wolf saw deeper. The alpha in him saw most deeply of all, to the heart of her—the independence and loyalty, the strength…

Out loud, he forced himself to say, "That depends on you. Because the other reason you're here is for us to decide whether *you're* the danger."

She made that noise in her throat—offended, angry. He didn't have to open his eyes to see her expression, but he did it anyway, finding in her that instant of wild glory, a feral willingness to fight her way free.

And she thought she wasn't Sentinel.

He made his voice inexorable. "You're of unknown skills. You're untrained. And while I doubt the same family that instilled Kai's values would raise a daughter who would abuse her nature, there's the very real chance that you could do just that without knowing it."

She'd drawn herself up, that anger churning; it came at him in discordant song. "Don't you even talk about my family! My father risked everything to warn Kai when he heard about those silent Core workings!"

That he had. Lannie took a sharp breath, knowing he couldn't keep the rest of the truth from her—and knowing how it would likely shatter her trust. She saw it—and this time she closed the space between them, grasping his rolled-up shirtsleeve in a demanding grip. "What about my family, Lannie?"

Nothing left but to say it. "Your parents aren't in Cloudview with Kai. They've been taken to Brevis, where Nick Carter—the Southwest Brevis Consul— will assess the situation. They might well be brought up on charges."

Her anger shattered into an equally fierce dismay; her grip on his shirt only tightened. "For *protecting* us?"

He didn't flinch from her. "We have rules, Holly. Even if they were always on the fringes of us, they knew those rules and they knew the reasons behind them."

She gaped at him in stunned disbelief, and he barely saw it coming—a lightning-swift strike, a slap with enough force to spark stars and rock him off his feet. Before he could do so much as reach for her, she whirled away, stalking for the loft's external stairs, taking them her standard two at a time—slamming the door with enough force so he knew better than to invade his own home again this night.

So he knew how much damage had been done.

He stood quietly, breathing of the night, calming the wolf. Just being, for those moments, and so aware of the static underlying the discord, so aware of the wolf's distress at being separated from one pack and denied by the other.

So aware of the impact on every part of him.

It was all he could do to keep from turning on Faith when her quiet voice spoke from within the barn doorway—knowing damned well to keep her distance.

"Lannie," she whispered. "I am so sorry. But I can't find Aldo."

Chapter 6

Holly faced the cool of the morning from the loft door, looking out at this foreign world that had so suddenly become hers.

The mules were in their big turn-out corral, industriously working hay from big, closely woven nets. The early sun splashed over the rising slope, a strong angle of stroking shadows alongside reflection so bright she had to squint.

The truck sat in the shade behind the store building next to a battered old hatchback and a dirt bike, the sunshade placed haphazardly across the dash from the night before.

Holly touched her pocket. *Keys.* How easy would it be to grab her suitcase, throw herself into the truck and wheel on out of here? A couple of hours north she'd find the Albuquerque airport, and the first flight out of this place was just fine with her. Wherever it landed, she could head not for home, but for the entirely separate stash her family maintained—one that came complete with identification, cash and a list of connections.

She could run.

Maybe it was worth the risk. And maybe this was her chance. Maybe it would be her *only* chance…

The back door of the store flung open, emitting Javier, the young man who'd helped with the hay. He grinned when he saw her.

There would be other chances. And just maybe she'd take them.

Or maybe you should stay here and deal with this, and take Lannie for what he is.

A good man. A man trying to do right by her in spite of the circumstances.

A man she'd slapped for telling the truth.

"Good news," Javi said. "We found Aldo!"

Found…?

"Awesome!" she said, generating a lame enthusiasm he somehow didn't see through.

"Also, Faith brought donuts." He gestured her inside, and if he noticed her infinitesimal hesitation, he gave no indication of it. "Gotta do a trash patrol. Back in a mo'."

"Have fun," she told him, and he grinned at her dry tone and moved on. She entered the back of the store, pausing as her eyes adjusted. These back shelves were a mystery of horse blankets and water tubs, looming dark and stacked tall. She passed the manure forks, the wormer and supplement, and stopped before she emerged into the more random area by the cash register—a rack of cowboy-themed greeting cards, another of gloves, a bin of sale dog treats.

And Lannie and Faith, talking, their tone low but not so low Holly couldn't hear them. Lannie wore the same clothes from the night before, except now the shirt held just a smudge of a stain along his side. "Just give me the spares, Faith."

"I'll run Aldo home myself." Faith cocked her head with a stubborn angle that spoke of a mind made up.

"Faith." There was warning in that tone, and weariness.

Faith didn't blink. *"Lannie."*

To Holly's surprise, Lannie didn't turn on the pack-leader thing. He didn't stand taller, didn't seem suddenly bigger. He didn't look down on Faith with that excessively piercing gaze.

He took a breath. A muscle in his jaw twitched. "I'll talk to him," he said. "He's embarrassed. He doesn't remember climbing into the loft and he doesn't remember falling asleep."

"In the farthest, darkest corner," Faith said with some annoyance. "If you hadn't gone wolf, we'd still be looking."

Understanding tickled in Holly's thoughts. *Wolf.* She'd been right, when she'd seen those paw prints on the mountain. And if he'd taken his wolf to find Aldo—that explained the newly stained shirt—the bandaging had been left behind. Only items made of natural materials, unless specially protected, made the change with a Sentinel. Holly knew that much, at least—if only because it had been the subject of many an amusing memory from her early life with Kai.

Not that she, as younger sister, ever would have altered his clothing to provide unexpected results when he took his lynx.

An unexpected smile took over her mouth; she put her fingers to it, squelching it. She wasn't in the mood for a trip down memory lane.

Whatever Lannie had said to Faith in the interim, Holly had missed it. But now he did straighten, and now he did put on the mantle of pack leader. *Alpha wolf.* Now he did seem *taller than, stronger than*—and now he did turn that blue and piercing gaze—*on Holly.*

He'd known she was there all along. And he was using that intensity of his as a warning—she was far from home free after the previous evening. "Make yourself at home," he said. "We'll leave for Cloudview as soon as I get this squared away."

Holly took a step forward, making herself fully visible. "Is Aldo all right?"

"Don't you worry about it," Faith said, and the piercing through her lower lip emphasized the hard set of her mouth. "We take care of our own."

Holly swallowed hard on ire, closing her mouth on the snap of a response. She liked the old man. She'd worry about him if she wanted to.

"Faith," Lannie murmured, but without any particular censure. "Get the register set up and I'll talk to Aldo. If he doesn't want to go with you, I'll need those keys. I won't have him walking this morning." He spared Holly a glance she couldn't read, and pulled the front door open with a sharp jingle of the overhead bells, turning back only to say to Faith, "And dig up Pete's number, see if he can take some extra hours this week."

"Yeah, yeah," Faith said. "And don't forget it's the second week of the month and Mrs. Allende will be in for a big haul of dog food. Got it covered, boss."

The first hint of a smile tugged at Lannie's mouth. "Yes, you do," he said, and left the store.

Faith didn't dig up Pete's number, and she didn't pull dog food off the nearby shelf. She turned on Holly. "What the hell is your problem? I told you to keep an eye on him, not make yourself his own personal goathead!"

For that instant, Holly had no reaction, caught as she was between restraint, anger and complete bafflement. Faith saw the latter well enough to snap, "It's a horrible plant with a horrible sticker!"

A goathead. How awesome. Holly found herself stalking up to meet the young woman, assessing the years between them—no more than four or five—and stopping more closely than she meant to. "Listen, little brat," she said, as Faith's eyes widened. "You don't know me. You don't know my family or my life. You don't know Lannie Stewart's part in my life. So unless you want to take me on, right here, right now, I suggest you think twice before you talk to me that way."

Oh my God, what were the Sentinels turning her into? When had she ever threatened someone with violence?

And still she felt it. She felt her own strength, her own speed—always there, lurking in ways that served her in her very physical life. She felt her own willingness to draw the line on what she would and wouldn't endure—and standing still to be Faith's punching bag was no part of it.

Faith shrank back slightly, Nordic complexion gone pale and stark beneath dyed black and crimson hair, her shorter stature never more evident. "I said *keep an eye on him*," she repeated with deliberate care. "Can't you see he's not right?"

"You told me to talk to him, too." Holly kept her own voice hard. "That didn't turn out so well, eh?"

Faith took another half a step back and ran into the display counter. "He did talk to you. I saw him. And I saw you run off in a snit, too." She lifted her chin in defiance at those words, but Holly saw well enough that the chin trembled, and so did Faith's hands.

Still. She took a crowding step forward. "I think you want to rephrase that."

Faith hesitated, glancing for the front door as if for help. Holly knew it, too—Lannie stood on the other side of that door. Watching, but not coming in.

Leaving them to work it out.

Faith whirled away to put space between them. "He *talked to you*," she said, leaving it at that. "Did he threaten you? Lie to you? Because if you say so, I don't believe it."

No. He'd done none of that.

He'd told the truth.

A good man in a hard situation.

Faith saw it in her, and her chin came back up. "So you asked him stuff and he answered. And you didn't like the answers. How is that his fault?"

Holly was the one to hesitate this time—torn between the truth of those words and the incomplete nature of that truth. She looked out the full glass door where Lannie stood, meeting his gaze head-on. "Why don't you ask him?"

Because she'd argued with Lannie. She'd stomped out on him not once, but twice. She'd slapped him. She'd found herself alone, struggling with inexplicable sensations on a rugged, isolated, *lonely* mountain crest.

And now she'd threatened another person. A *smaller* person.

If this was being Sentinel, she wanted none of it.

Lannie held the storefront door open for two women who quite clearly needed no such help but accepted it with a smile, and who promptly headed off to the pegboard display of bits, already arguing the merits of various mouthpieces.

Faith had, finally, gone behind the counter. She greeted him in a low voice. "What have you said to her, Lannie? What have you *done* to her?"

Lannie raised a brow, and it should have stopped her in her tracks.

But nothing was *should have* this morning.

"I hate that she's here," Faith said, busying herself with the register routine. "I think there's something going on with you and has been since she got here. But I think she's honest. Aldo likes her, too. She wouldn't be that mad if she didn't have a reason."

Damn Brevis, anyway. Yes, they'd been up against it; they'd done the best they could in an unusual situation. But bringing Holly here without warning meant leaving Faith, Aldo and his more peripheral home pack—the Ruidoso twins and the light-blood park ranger, the altogether human Pete and the loose scattering of others in this area. And now Faith was unsettled and pushing her limits, and Aldo was...

He wasn't sure what Aldo was.

So he gave Faith a steady look, giving no ground but not demanding any, either. "It's not about what I've done to her, Faith. It's more about what's *been* done to her."

Faith broke open a new roll of quarters with a brisk and practiced hand, not quite responding.

"Aldo's already hiking home," Lannie told her, without telling her how he knew. When the wolf tracked people down, it wasn't something they talked about in the store. "I need you to head out that way and make sure he made it."

"It's only a mile or so," she said. "He's a tough old guy. He's fine, Lannie."

She wasn't arguing so much as looking for casual ways to reassure him and he knew it, but he gave her a strong eye nonetheless. "Don't dawdle. Holly and I will leave for Cloudview as soon as you get back."

She arched a pierced eyebrow at him. "Does she know that?"

Know it? He'd be lucky if she hadn't gone without him.

He said, "*Now*, Faith."

She pushed the register drawer closed and reached under the counter to grab her car keys, straightening her sleeveless summer top with exaggerated dignity, and her eyes widening slightly along the way.

But the faintest humming had already warned Lannie, an earthy contralto song with angry, jagged edges and a confident beauty. Holly had returned, bringing every bit of herself back into his awareness. He realized only in retrospect that he'd closed his eyes to listen, his head lifting slightly and his body tensing with awareness and yearning.

It's not real.

"What did you say?" Holly said, sounding surprised with it.

It's not real. Because it never was, and because believing it now would lead to nothing but trouble. Lannie wrapped himself in a sterner control.

"Fine," Faith said, ignoring Holly to respond to Lannie's earlier command. "But before I go, I want to see your side."

"Faith's right," Holly said. "Let's see."

Oh, for—

But Lannie looked at Faith's stubborn expression, and he looked at Holly's implacable expression, and he knew when to save his energy—even if he did send

Faith a glance to warn her off pushing any more limits this day. With his mouth clamped on annoyance, he
lifted his shirttails.

"Oh!" said one of the women shoppers. "Good morning!" And together they clapped politely before returning to their perusal of the horse gear.

"Very nice," Holly said drily, coming closer in that
rolling stride that currently felt more like a stalk. She
crouched beside him, her hand resting lightly at the
edge of the wound. He flinched, and she looked briefly
up at him.

"Didn't mean to hurt you."

"I'll let you know if it hurts," he said, which was as
close as he'd come to telling her what that touch had
done to him.

*Wolf, reaching out...toes, curling. Knees, locked in
desperation.*

"This doesn't look any different," she said.

He let out a breath. "It's fine."

"It's not *any different*," she said, repeating herself as
if he'd totally missed the point the first time.

Maybe he had. It was hard enough to think at all.

"I see what she means," Faith said, peering at him
from a safe distance. "I know why you're not worried
about it, Lannie, but even with normal healing, there
ought to be some change."

He dropped his shirt, somehow forcing himself to
step away from Holly, no longer hiding the wolf within.

Her eyes widened. She froze, looking back at him.

"Get a room," Faith said, far too matter-of-factly.
"And Lannie, you better figure out what's going on
with your side." She hefted her keys and headed for the
back. "I'll be back in ten minutes."

In fact, she returned in eight with the report that

the spry old man was already back home. Lannie gave
the store over to Faith, reminded her to get Javi to help
cover the afternoon as he grabbed the previous day's
receipts, and ran up to the loft long enough to clean
up and change into another shirt, not much different
from the first.

He rolled up his sleeves and headed back to find
Holly waiting for him in the truck, the keys in the ig-
nition and two sport bottles of ice water stuck in the
seat console.

"Stop at the bank on the way out," he told her, taking
up the passenger seat with a passing awareness at the
unfamiliar experience of sitting on this side of the truck,
and with extreme awareness at her presence there. She
gave him an uncertain look, as if she felt it, too—taking a breath to say something and ultimately leaving
it alone...but leaving it hanging between them all the
same. *A tension, a promise, a wistfulness...*a potency
that he'd never expected to encounter in the wake of the
damage Jody had done.

With a determined exhalation, she started the truck,
flipped on the AC, and backed them out of the parking
niche with a familiarity that came from more than one
day's drive. "I'm going to guess there's only the one bank,
and it's the one I saw on the way through to the main
T-intersection yesterday."

"That's the one." He would have offered directions if
she'd seemed uncertain, but she pulled out onto the narrow two-lane that ran in front of the farm store, past the
garage down the road and the faint scattering of tucked
away homes between here and town. Ten minutes later
they passed the first formal edge of town—the upgraded
well house—and within moments she'd parked them behind another truck loaded for construction bear.

"Just be a minute," he told her, and headed in to drop off the receipts. When he came out, he found Holly sitting on the hood in the sun, giving the other truck a pensive look. She nodded at it. "You familiar with them?"

Denton Construction. Elephant Butte.

She didn't wait for a response. "Because I'm pretty sure one of those guys from the tavern was wearing a shirt with this logo."

"Could be," he said. "People do build things here."

She made that noise in her throat and pushed off the hood, for that instant more graceful than any woman ought to be. Then she quite prosaically brushed off the seat of her pants and headed for the driver's door.

He joined her from the passenger side. "Know where we're going?"

She held up a map that had been folded over to show Cloudview, its edges grimy from his glove box.

"Nothing left for me to do, then," he said.

"Take a nap," she suggested. "You look like you could use it, eh?"

"Aldo," he said under his breath.

But it hadn't been Aldo keeping him up the previous night.

And he was glad for the distance of the console between them.

He didn't think he'd sleep, not on this winding connection road between the two small mountain towns. Besides, he had questions for Kai Faulkes. He had questions for Regan Adler, too, and they endlessly kicked around in his mind. But he was barely aware when Holly reached over to tuck something soft and Holly-scented behind his head, and he drifted away anyway, his thoughts sinking behind a discordant static.

Halfway through the drive he heard Holly sigh in

some deep and honest relief, and he released the last
little bit of vigil, faintly aware that he'd slumped awkwardly against the truck door. Song hummed through
his body and into his dreams. Quiet, self-confident,
navigating its way right through all that alpha awareness to sink into his bones. It stroked him, making the
wolf blink and rouse and lift a nose to a quiet song in
return. Turning, twisting, tangling…dancing.

And then snarling.

Static. Static with claws, static with disruptive insidious intent, growing through him like cold, crack-
ling frost. The song grew distant, still whole and still
with him, but harder to hear under the assault. His side
flashed hot in fiery pain, his connection to his world
suddenly gaping, a chasm of disconnected sanity. He
jerked with sudden hunger for air, breathing suddenly
forgotten.

The wolf rose in a different way, surging forth to
do battle.

Surging forth to *kill*—

Lannie started awake, a snarl in his throat—*trapped,
trapped and fighting it, the space small and tight and
bands across his chest, striking out*—

"Lannie!"

He didn't recognize that voice at first, only that it was
sharp and strong and without fear—strong enough to
absorb the wolf's fury without bouncing it back at him.

Strong enough so he could think, grasping quite suddenly the details of where he was, when he was…who
he was.

Holly's hand closed around his arm just behind his
wrist, cool and firm. He discovered his hands clenched
around the confining seat belt and forced them to relax;

he discovered his body tense and trembling, and he made himself breathe.

He found himself in her touch, and pushed the wolf away.

"Bad dream?" she said, her voice dryer than he'd expected.

He let out a gusting breath. "Yeah," he said, and finally opened his eyes. He recognized their location immediately—one of the rare pull-offs on this narrow steep and winding road, the last approach to Cloudview. "Bad dream. But I'm—"

"—*fine,*" she finished for him.

He jerked his gaze from the dark pines lining the road and to her face, where the all-too-knowing richness of her eyes slipped right back through wavering defenses to grab the wolf's attention.

For the first time, she grew uncertain. "Lannie…"

He answered with the hint of a growl, with the intensity of attention he so rarely allowed himself. Not squelching the alpha and not squelching his response to her.

"That…that's not fair," she said, her voice fainter than it had been. She pulled her hand away from his arm and he caught it again, a lightning-swift snag of strength and speed without an ounce of *gone too far.* He stroked his thumb over the back of her knuckles, along the precise bones of strong fingers and then across her palm. An unmistakably gently, possessive touch. *Invitation.*

"*No,*" she said, and snatched her hand away. "*No.*"

He settled back, still turned to face her; with effort, he kept his hands quiet along his thighs. "Because you don't want it?" he asked. "Or because you *do*?"

"Maybe both," she snapped. "Maybe there's just too much going on right now. Maybe I want—" Her breath caught. Brown eyes narrowed at him over flushed cheeks. "I don't have to explain myself to you."

No. If anything, it was the other way around.

Just as soon as he finished figuring himself out.

Holly's heart pounded hard and strong all the way into Cloudview; she felt Lannie's touch on her hand every winding mile along the way, her skin supersensitized to the brush of her clothing, the lift of her hair in the truck's vent breezes. She made herself breathe evenly, steadily.

Even though he was right *there*.

Only after she became immersed in choosing her bike—a sweet 29er mountain bike—did she start to settle, no longer aware of her flushed face or her tingling skin.

She was still pretty much flushed in other places.

But she hadn't yet decided if she was more flustered over what had happened to Lannie, or over what he had done afterward. To see a man of his presence startling himself out of a sleep with such vehemence… it disturbed her deeply enough to tell her how much she cared.

She'd seen it coming. She'd pulled over. But she didn't want to think about what might have happened if he hadn't been restrained by that seat belt—or if he hadn't stopped fighting it before it gave way.

She'd seen the wolf in his eye.

She'd seen the want in his eye, too.

"Because you don't want it? Or because you do*?"*

"Good?" Lannie said, back to his single-word ways—back to his natural wolf ways, coming up behind her so silently that she'd felt his presence more than heard it.

"Excellent," she told him, and meant it. The bike would handle the trails in the national forest that surrounded Descanso, and it would handle the gravel and asphalt—and it would do it all with ease. Once she had it, she would no longer be trapped—dependent on his truck, his keys, his ways.

She would be free.

And if she really wanted, this bike would take her away from that place altogether.

If.

Lannie offered his credit card to the sun-weathered proprietor and put a hand on the bike seat, aiming it at the door. "You need gear for this thing? Best get it now."

She turned away to pluck the necessary extras from the wall displays—pump and bottle cage, the breakdown kit that would snug in under the seat. By the time she came out of the store with purchases in hand, Lannie's credit card extended to him, he was just about done tucking the bike down in the truck bed.

"Keep it," he told her.

"What?"

"The card. Keep it. Until Brevis gets you squared away." She frowned, and he laughed, a low sound. "It's not a trap, Holly. Keep the card. It's a business account—you won't have any trouble using it."

Maybe it wasn't a trap. But it felt like one.

Still, she slipped the card into her back pocket, where she would have been carrying her own slim collection of cards and photo ID if she'd still had it.

The Sentinels had taken that, too. Ostensibly to clean her of her past, making her a dead-end trail for anyone who looked during this vulnerable period—but at the same time hobbling her to them until they returned it or provided new documentation as they'd promised.

They had no idea how little she needed it, or how prepared she and her family had always been.

"Thanks," she said, leaning over the high truck bed to stroke the frame of the bike beneath the battered old horse blanket, tugging the tie-down straps to make sure the bike wouldn't shift along the way. "This means a lot to me."

He stopped, shifting to look at her, his gaze steadier than she'd been prepared for. "You're—"

Beautiful, her mind heard. Even knowing he hadn't said it, but hearing it in his voice all the same, just as she'd heard it in the store and out by the mules and—

"—welcome." He headed to the passenger seat without any further discussion about that arrangement. Maybe he, too, had been shaken by the incident in the truck, even if he showed no sign of it now. "Ready to see your brother?"

"More than," Holly told him with an undeniable fervency. She climbed in behind the wheel, flipped her ponytail away from the seat belt, and started the engine. "Just point me in the right direction."

The *right direction* turned out to be an abrupt turn just past the cluster of old storefronts lining the town's main street. Almost immediately, the road became rural and winding, taking them higher and deeper into the woods.

Only then did she allow herself to think about what she was doing, or how she felt about it. The farther she'd come up into the Sacramentos, the clearer her mind had become, the more grounded she felt. The more *alive.*

The more *herself.*

She couldn't figure it out, and she tucked it away for bigger things.

Kai.

She'd nearly met him, so briefly, when she and her parents had first been escorted to this tiny town only days earlier. Cloudview now bustled with summer people fleeing the hot lowlands, a tiny place tucked away in a narrow mountain gap. It was a barely remembered world so starkly different, so endlessly unfamiliar…*sun-warmed evergreen scents and dry air and huge, close sky.* Even now the afternoon storm clouds built above them, blinding white above and gathering bruised darkness below, scudding so close she felt she might reach out the window and touch one.

This was Kai's home. This was his *life*—so different from hers. She'd discarded her Sentinel self to hide; he'd immersed himself in his, all but leaving civilization behind. He'd turned out more Sentinel than any of them, working only on instinct and a drive to protect.

And Holly, the civilized one, still wanted nothing to do with any of it. Looked only to play along until she could figure out how to untangle herself.

What would he think of her, this older brother for whom she and her parents had sacrificed so much?

What did Lannie think of her, for all of that? She stole a glance at him, driving along the broad downhill swoop of a curve.

Lannie Stewart wasn't her brother—wasn't the overtly primal man Kai had grown to be. But he wasn't anywhere close to tame, either. Not beneath the surface. She'd seen those glimpses too many times to pretend.

She'd felt what they'd done to her.

Awesome. She was drawn to the part of him that she'd so resoundingly rejected in herself.

"It'll be fine," Lannie said, and nodded at the apex of the next sharp curve. "Take that dirt road."

"Easy for you to say," she said, slowing the truck for the turn. "You have your world all figured out, eh?"

He made a disgruntled noise. "Not so much as you think."

But it was a mutter, and she doubted he meant for her to respond. She concentrated on the rugged, lightly graveled road and followed it past one obscured driveway and on to the next, where the road itself ended. She took the driveway without direction, and the truck rumbled along in a low gear as they went up...up...

And there it was. Regan's cabin. The place the Core had been so keen to get their hands on, feeling they could operate entirely off the grid from this place, knowing that the area had only remote monitoring from the Sentinels.

Or believing it, anyway.

The weathered logs of the cabin looked comfortable and cozy in the flat dip of land between cradling ridges; local wildflowers lined the front porch in tended strips. Holly parked beside a diminutive bright yellow SUV, catching a glimpse of a barn and paddock behind the cabin, the swish of a dark equine tail. A huge mottled black dog stood on the porch, neither barking nor friendly.

Holly regarded it. "Huh," she said, thinking she would just wait right here.

Lannie did no such thing. He flipped his seat belt away and stuck long legs out the door, emerging to stretch and make himself at home. The dog sat, but didn't look a whole lot smaller that way.

Lannie tipped his head to some noise inside the cabin, and a few moments later a woman came barreling through the door, covered with an oversize paint-smeared shirt and smudged jeans, a bright splotch of blue on her cheek. But her strikingly bright hair was more or less captured in a braid and her smile couldn't have been more genuine.

Regan.

"Sorry!" she said. "I should have heard you coming. I got all caught up in—" She looked down at herself. "Well. I guess that's obvious. Come on in. Bob won't mess with you." She glanced up to the ridge, an unerring focus. "Kai'll be along shortly."

As Lannie strode forward to introduce himself, Holly climbed down from the truck into the contrast of pleasantly cool air and direct hot sun, coming no closer than to lean against the hood. Not wary of the dog, or of Regan, or even of Lannie. Just…wary.

After all, Regan hadn't returned her call. And everyone here, even her brother, had a common frame of reference…certain assumptions about their world.

Holly didn't. And she suddenly wasn't sure how she could move forward with her brother unless she lost that solid grip on her past.

Especially when it was a past she didn't yet consider *past*.

Regan unbuttoned the smock shirt and left it draped over the porch rail, coming out to meet Holly. "I'm glad you're here," she said. "When I talked to Lannie—"

Holly shot a glance Lannie's way, at first startled and then accusing.

"Ah," Regan said, looking over her shoulder to where Lannie rubbed the big dog's ears. "He didn't tell you I called back."

Lannie looked less than perturbed at his transgression. "Never had a chance."

Only the entire drive up here. But as much as Holly wanted to blame him, she couldn't. Not entirely.

"Things have been chaotic," she agreed. "But it would have been easier if I'd known."

Regan lifted her stained hand in a *what're you gonna do* gesture. "They think differently than we do."

"Sentinels?"

"No," Regan said, laughing. *"Men."*

Lannie left the porch, stopping at the edge of the cleared yard to gaze up into the looming peak beyond. "Does Kai still consider this area cleared?"

"Kai," Regan said primly, "is still recovering from what he's been through."

The look he shot her held apology but no retreat. "Could be I'm still on edge," he said. "But something down our way just doesn't feel right."

Regan made a face. "There's nothing active with the Core, I can tell you that much. But Kai's been out a lot lately. I'm not sure... He could just be restless. You'll have to ask him yourself."

"This is my visit," Holly said, turning to glare at Lannie's back. "Don't you dare use it up. I need to know... *everything*. How it's been for Kai all these years. How he made the decision to come out in the open again." She looked at Regan. "How *you* made your decisions."

Regan put a hand on her arm, squeezing slightly. "You won't find Kai to be a big talker," she said. "But I'll be happy to help. I'm really sorry I didn't keep calling until I reached you directly so I could tell you that."

Holly crossed her arms and looked at Lannie. "If I still had my own phone with my own phone number, it would have been a lot easier."

Regan lowered her voice. "I know," she said. "But they're trying to protect you."

"And my parents?" Holly said bitterly. Off somewhere in Arizona's Southwest Brevis facility for an extended debriefing, as close as they could be to imprisoned.

"Did what they had to and are accepting the consequences," Regan said. "Kai did the same. So did I, for that matter."

Something in her voice made Holly look twice at her—but Regan had turned away, looking into the woods. Bob did the same, lumbering down from the porch with old dog joints and a slowly wagging tail. Lannie returned to stand on the steps. Waiting, with just a little bit of the alpha showing.

Holly froze as her brother emerged from the woods. "Kai," she breathed, seeing him for the first time in too many years—for the first time as a grown man. "Oh, God… He's so—"

"—wild," Regan said, as hushed as Holly had been. "Yes."

Holly would never be that wild. *Could* never be that wild. Kai strode from the woods barefoot and shirtless, the sun gleaming off inky-black hair much like Holly's own. He wore only buckskin leggings and a breechclout, and he looked *right* in those clothes—he looked *right* in the woods. Even from here, Holly saw her father's eyes in those features, those shoulders; she saw her mother's beauty made masculine.

But none of those details truly caught her eye. It was the big picture—the way he moved, the way he held himself. The way he *knew* himself.

"Your Lannie is much the same," Regan said, deliberately quiet this time—a mere murmur in Holly's ear.

Holly shot her a look of *I don't think so.* "He's not *my* Lannie," she said, as the man in question stood tall and quiet on the steps. "And I'm sure as hell not anything of his."

"Easy there." Regan returned her ire with unexpected amusement. "Trust me, I know how hard this is."

Holly wasn't giving an inch. "Really? How long were *you* in hiding from your own people?"

"Years," Regan said easily. "In my own way."

Holly made a noncommittal noise in her throat, one that didn't hide her skepticism. Or her uneasiness, as Kai ignored Lannie to focus on Holly herself.

"Don't blame you," Regan said. "But we've got time to talk. The guys are going hunting."

"What? How—"

As if she'd get a chance to finish that question, with Kai's strides growing longer, closer—heading straight for Holly until she felt a brief burst of startling panic. *I don't really know you. I don't know what to do.* But he reached her and never hesitated, enclosing her in a brotherly hug that took her off her feet and swung her around.

"Holly," he said, as if he didn't have any other words. *"Holly."* He held her tightly, as if they could exchange, in one embrace, everything they'd missed about being *family* over the years. *Impossible.* And yet Holly found herself holding him just as tightly in return.

When she found her bearings again, feet solidly on the ground, hair mussed, expression stunned and completely out of her control, she realized that Regan had turned away to wipe at surreptitious happy tears, and Kai's eyes had a suspicious shine to them. Lannie stood behind her, solid and somehow intrusive.

Regan gave Lannie's arm a swat. "Chill, dude," she told him, and Holly felt more than saw him take a step back—though a quick glance showed a glimpse of his startled self-awareness.

"There," Kai said, looking down at her again, his

hands on her shoulders—and, she thought, only an impulse away from gathering her in again. "You should have had that when we first met."

"There was a lot going on," Holly managed to say. As there had been, all fraught with tension and raised voices—and that had been *before* Mariska and Jason swooped in to whisk her away over the curve and rise of the mountain range. "Kai, I—"

To her dismay, her own eyes filled with tears; her chin did the little quiver she hated. This was the big brother she'd once had and lost, and here he was looking perfectly comfortable in his world—*thriving, strong... completely himself*—and she suddenly didn't even know who she was any longer, never mind what her life would be.

"It isn't fair," he said, unexpectedly fierce. "It was *never* fair. Not to you." He did pull her close again, all but crushing her, and she couldn't help the little hiccup of a sob that escaped. He petted her hair, kissed the top of her head, and set her back. "We'll make it as right as we can. All of us."

"Then why am I in Descanso? Why am I not *here*?" Holly asked, trying to sound as demanding as she should be when her throat was still closed around the pain. *This, her brother...*

He was everything she'd kept herself from being. Everything she'd never *wanted* to be.

Everything she saw in Lannie, when he looked at her with that piercing gaze.

Kai shook his head. "My connection is with the land, little sister. I can't teach you what you need to know." He glanced at Lannie. "This man can."

"You don't have to teach me anything," Holly said, pulling on her own inner ferocity, the intensity she hid from her employees and subcontractors and friends. "Maybe I just need some time—"

Kai shook his head. "Neither of us grew up knowing exactly what we needed to know. But you…you don't even know *yourself*. That comes first."

Regan interposed herself into the conversation. "Descanso is little more than an hour away—you'll be able to spend time with Kai. My father lives in town here, did you know that? He and I are learning to be family again, too. I think we'll all do well together."

"No," Holly said, pressing her lips together when they threatened to quiver again. "I'm alone in Descanso, and you know it."

Lannie made a sound of protest—but Regan shook her head in a short, sharp gesture and he silenced. She said, most casually, "Lannie could probably use that hunt, and I'd like to show Holly around the place. Can you two be back here before the end of the afternoon?"

Kai glanced at Lannie, who—most uncharacteristically—hesitated. "Holly," he said, as if there was meant to be more to it.

"Go," Regan said, taking over the conversation. "I can reach Kai if there's any problem, which there won't be. Because, seriously—do you think the Core is going to poke around here again anytime soon?"

Kai grinned in response to that, an expression with an edge to it, and—quite unexpectedly—he gave Holly's ponytail a quick tug. He caught Lannie's eye and jerked his head at the woods, turning to lead the way.

Lannie bent to unlace his work boots, tugging his feet free and toeing off his socks, his fingers already at work on the buttons of his shirt. He pulled it off without so much as a glance at Holly or Regan, dropping it on top of his boots to stride after Kai, shoulders broad in the sun and just as barefoot, just as—

Holly sat in the gritty dirt right where she'd been standing.

Wild.

Everything he'd been keeping in, right out there for her to see. The sun gleamed off his shoulders, striking warm caramel tones in rich brown hair and highlighting a power of movement he'd been keeping to himself.

"No," Holly said, muttering the words as if a prayer. "No, no, no."

Lannie glanced over his shoulder as if he'd heard—certainly as if he knew she was watching—but his grin, she thought, was all about what lay ahead. It was about embracing the wild.

In another instant, visible energy gathered—first Kai and then Lannie, growing to engulf them both in shards of light that made Holly blink and squint and—

Lynx and wolf, still moving away—one padding on silent, powerful paws and one moving into a ground-eating lope.

"They're beautiful," Holly whispered.

Regan, too, stared after them. "I don't think I'll ever get used to that. I hope I *don't*." She grinned down at Holly. "Let's get you something to drink. I want to show you something."

Holly wasn't quite ready to get up. "Is that…in *me*?"

Regan shrugged. "If it is, Lannie will help you find it."

"Right," Holly said, and sighed. "Whether I want him to or not."

"Come on in." Regan headed for the porch, where the big dog was resettling and a scruffy yellow cat appeared from its invisible corner to meow his own demands. "I've got some things you should see."

Holly rested her forehead on her knees. Probably just as well that her wild brother had gone right off again. Probably just as well that he'd taken her suddenly also wild, always unwanted keeper off with him. Probably best that they wouldn't be back for a while.

She needed time to adjust. Not just to what she'd seen, but what she'd felt.

Had that been…*yearning*? And if so…was it for what she'd left behind in the life she'd made, or what she'd left behind in childhood?

Unless it was none of those things, or all of those things at once…including the yearning to taste that grin on Lannie's face. To taste *him*…embracing the wild.

She had a feeling she didn't really want to know.

Chapter 7

Kai as lynx moved with easy purpose, and Lannie made no effort to hold to his speed. He gave way to the need to move, loping forward along the ridge, snatching up a mouse along the way and flinging it up for a quick crunch and swallow, salty and warm, and running on. Not being alpha, not managing a pack, not humming any particular inner song.

Just being what he was, unapologetic in his raw strength.

By the time he curved back in on Kai, they'd gone high into the mountain, up beyond ponderosa and aspen to stunted, gnarly bristlecone pines edging the delicate tundra-like turf of the highest climes—and Kai waited for him in buckskins and breechclout, cross-legged on a massive flat outcrop that seemed to look out over the world. "Good?" Kai asked, after Lannie had dropped back into the human to join him.

The blazing high sun bit into the skin of his back;

the sharp air rose goose bumps beneath sweat already gone dry. He was thirsty, his side ached, and he found himself still recovering his breath in the thinning altitude. He grinned and sat down on the rock with plenty of space between them. "Good."

For the moment, they looked out over the rugged jut and fold of the rugged earth falling away before them.

Kai closed his hand over a cluster of pebbles, rolling them between palm and stone; his gaze was quick to focus on the flicker of a woodpecker in the trees below. But his attention was entirely on Lannie. "My sister."

As if Lannie hadn't known this was coming. "She's strong," he said, knowing that Holly hadn't ever had much choice. "She'll figure it out."

Kai made a sound in his throat, a familiar one at that. "Be careful."

And Lannie took that for what it was. Kai had seen. "Working on pack as alpha," he said, "isn't what you think."

It wasn't proving who was boss; it wasn't forcing loyalty. It wasn't propping himself up on the strength of others.

It was giving.

Sometimes, it was giving so much that he lost track of himself. Even knowing it could happen.

Sometimes, it was not knowing where *who he was* and *what he needed*—or *wanted*—stopped, and where the alpha began.

How to know where that line lay, when the one on the other side was Holly? Even now, when he thought he'd left such things behind, he could hear her song—the complexity of it, the strong undertones and the lighter phrases of vulnerability…the breathless, yearning note he heard only now and then. The fierce independence that put this pack bonding in such jeopardy…

The faint echoes of the notes that had made up Jody's song, and the bitter awareness of how they had led to her death.

Kai made some sound, and Lannie realized he'd closed his eyes, lifted his face to the breeze and the song…lost himself in both.

In Kai he found a shuttered amusement, if not one that lasted. "Be careful of her."

"This is none of her doing," Lannie said, dropping back into the awareness of a single man on a single rock at the top of the world. "As far as I can tell, it's been done *to* her. Right from the start."

Definitely a growl behind the glance Kai slanted his way. *Warning.*

These were Kai's mountains, and Kai's rock…and Kai's sister. Still, the feel of the wolf's hackles prickled along Lannie's neck. "Look," he said. "What was done was done. That's not the point, not anymore. But Holly needs to come to terms with what she might have been before she can decide who she is."

"The past," Kai said, more precisely than usual, "might be the point to *her.*"

Maybe. Maybe so. Lannie was so used to dealing with groups who needed to form in their present. Holly might well resent having so much of herself discarded in that way.

Without thinking, he reached for her song—not the easy perception of it that so often rode his awareness, but through his pack channels, tried and true and familiar. Maybe he could see—

Harsh static sliced through his mind, bringing a stab

of lightning-hot pain, a curse, a slip-sliding sense of reality.

Kai knelt beside him, a firm hand on his shoulder. Rock ground into his ribs; his temple ached from impact. Lannie cursed, heartfelt, and shoved himself back upright with such vehemence that Kai moved back, crouching there with ease.

"How long?" he asked, and then, when Lannie just scowled at him with incomprehension, the wolf pushing a snarl where it wasn't quite audible yet, Kai nodded at Lannie's fully exposed side. "How long have you been hurt?"

"I'm *not*—" Well, that was a damned lie, wasn't it? "It's not—"

And that, too.

Lannie gusted out a breath and went for the bald truth he was hiding—or trying to—from Faith and Holly and old Aldo. "Couple of days now. Just a dustup with some bullies. Shouldn't have been any problem."

Kai touched a round scar nestled beneath his collarbone, a thing remarkable simply because it existed; the scar, too, spoke of a difficult injury. *A bullet, laced with a silent Core working.* One of the reasons Kai had broken his silence, revealing himself to Sentinels and Core alike. "This was Core," he said. "But there is nothing of the Core about you."

"Doesn't make any sense that there would be." Then again, it didn't make any sense that the damned thing wouldn't heal. It didn't make any sense that he had static in his head. "Regan said you had concerns."

"Nothing here," Kai said, and looked back over the mountain—not down, but over it—a vista spanning a hundred miles and more. "And not Core." His gaze flicked back to Lannie. "I'm looking."

Lannie settled himself on the rock, kneeling with one knee up to look out over that same vista. "Hard to find it from here, maybe."

"Unless it *comes* here," Kai said simply, but there was nothing simple in his tone. "By then, maybe…too late."

The woods swallowed lynx and wolf, and Regan turned away from the sight to offer Holly a smile. "Come on inside. I've got ice water."

"I've never been offered so much water in my life," Holly said, so scattered by the circumstances that she didn't at first realize how rude she'd sounded. "I mean—"

"In this climate, no one takes water for granted." Regan stepped into the house and held the screen door open behind her, leaving Holly no choice but to grab it. Regan led the way through a small main room of comfortable old furniture and a small antique cubbyhole desk, bookshelves and a braided rug over a worn plank floor. A grizzled yellow cat squinted at Holly from the windowsill, flicking the end of his tail in a manner that wasn't precisely welcoming.

"Besides," Regan said, already opening the fridge door while Holly lingered in the narrow hallway, eyeing the cluster of doors and the tight stairway to the loft, "you need it more than most until you acclimate."

"So I'm told," Holly said, leaning in the kitchen entry. Indirect sunshine pushed into the room from the giant window over the sink; Regan's hair gleamed in it. "Repeatedly."

"Then you should probably listen." Regan offered an earthenware mug, a sturdy thing made delicate with its beauty—and smiled at Holly's reaction to it, a little sorrow around the edges. "My mother made it."

Holly held it in both hands, her fingers laced through the handle, and Regan laughed. "Trust me," she said. "She'd want it used. And it's my mother's...it's sturdier than it looks."

That, Holly thought, was supposed to mean something.

"Drink." Regan poured herself a mug. "And sit." She indicated the small table, a sturdy wooden thing worn with years of use—and then licked her thumb, rubbing it against a small, dark stain before giving up with some resignation.

Holly looked more closely at it. "Is that...?"

"Blood," Regan said. "Your brother's. He's a stubborn man."

Holly sat, staring at the stain. Trying to imagine what had happened here. She knew Kai had been hurt in his coming-out battle against the Core, but until now... it hadn't quite seemed real. She shuddered, feeling it sink in.

"He's fine now," Regan said. "Still busy turning my world upside down."

"And mine," Holly muttered, as other realities sank in, too. If Kai hadn't exposed himself so thoroughly...

She wouldn't be here. Missing her home, her life, her friends...her avocation. Her hands always in the water that ran so scarce here—shaping its flow, its sound, the ripple of light over movement. She closed her eyes, wishing herself back there—wishing with such a longing she could very nearly hear the clarity of trickled melody.

"It happened so suddenly," Regan mused. "I'm sorry

I wasn't there when you came through Cloudview. Kai said you were pretty confused by it all."

"Confused?" Holly pushed away from the table, no longer able to sit still. She settled for glaring out the kitchen window at a barn and paddock and dark roan horse, the mountain rising behind in a scene of stark beauty so jarring against her own inner turmoil. "Confused because an organization that once tore my family apart came swooping in to rip me out of my life? Because they took my parents off somewhere for a so-called *debriefing* and carted me off to some stranger who's supposed to brainwash me into seeing things their way? *Confused?*"

Regan cleared her throat. "Lannie mentioned you might be just a little angry."

Holly made a noise deep in her throat, not understanding or caring that Regan reacted to it with raised brows. "I don't want or need anything to do with this Sentinel life. I've gotten along just fine without them. Better than fine!" She turned the faucet to a trickle, letting the water run over her fingertips.

"Yes, and you can run again. I have no doubt that you're prepared, and that you'd be good at it. But you can't go if you want to know your brother or see your parents."

Holly said nothing. Regan wouldn't understand… she couldn't. She'd grown up in this place; she knew it and loved it, and every inch of the cabin spoke to that. And if Holly had come here hoping for insight to her brother and to an outsider's view of the Sentinel life, she suddenly realized she wouldn't get what she really needed. *Understanding.*

Regan didn't push. Maybe she knew better. Instead she nodded at the water trickle. "Something's going on with the well, I'm afraid. With luck it's just a little extra maintenance for the pressure tank."

Holly looked down at the water, only then realizing she'd turned it on. And here Regan had just reminded her of its value here in this place. She quickly turned it off, letting her fingers linger ruefully on the faucet. She thought of the clarity of the water in her own well, the sweet taste of it, the consistently free flow of it— and thought of it with such focus that for an instant her world tilted, and she wondered if she could wish herself back there after all.

"You okay?" Regan asked, making Holly realize the length of her silence.

"Fine," she said, a little too quickly. She returned to the table, to the mug, and gulped freely—flat, filtered water, not quite even there at all.

Regan said, somewhat abruptly, "You know, I never intended to stay here. My life has been in Colorado since I was old enough to do my own running."

Holly gave the homey kitchen a startled glance. "But—"

"This has been my father's home all this time." Regan looked at Holly with a direct gaze, a clear pale blue. "Not mine. Not even when I was living here, not once my mother died."

Holly frowned, not quite certain where this was going—or if she even wanted to go there.

"Let me show you something." Regan rose from the table, nodding at the mug. "Bring that. You'll see."

After a hesitation, Holly shrugged acquiescence. Regan took her down the hall and up the tight steps, and they emerged onto a second floor where the cabin opened up around them, a generous space of slanted ceiling and skylights. More shelves, a sprawling studio area and an unmade bed of rumpled covers. The scents of lavender and linseed oil mixed into something oddly pleasing.

In the corner, a cabinet held a variety of horsehair pieces, all simultaneously ethereal and solid, practical in design and yet as beautiful as the mug in her hand. *Art*.

All but for a single piece, inexplicably positioned in the center of it all. Holly frowned at it.

"You see it," Regan noted.

"What happened to it?"

Regan crossed to the cabinet, touching the piece with one reverent finger. "It's more about what happened to my mother."

Holly shook her head in mute failure to understand.

"My mother," Regan said, picking up the little bowl, "could hear this land."

What did *that* mean?

Regan didn't try to explain. "But no one believed that, and no one understood. So they 'cured' her. Sort of."

"Did they?" A meaningless response. It seemed the safest.

Regan nodded at the cabinet. "This is the work she did when she could hear." She replaced the bowl, just so, and indicated it. "This is what she did afterward."

Holly frowned. "I don't understand." Except she was afraid she just might.

Regan crossed to the bookshelves, pulling out a handful of titles with quick assurance—thin hardcovers with shiny, colorful dust jackets that she dropped onto the rumpled bedcovers, flipping them open to display.

Artwork splashed across the pages, bringing life to the room with deft clarity—insects and toads and camels, all embedded into their natural environments, the colors rich and natural. *"Things That Sting,"* Regan said, pointing to spread where a scorpion all but leaped out at them. "The latest. I kind of like it. *Bats Are All That* will be out next year."

She stepped back to tip her head at the display, a strange little smile at the corner of her mouth. Then she looked at Holly and said directly, "This is what I did when I was running. And no doubt about it—all the time I was in Colorado, I *was* running."

I still don't understand. But Holly didn't say it out loud this time.

With a few quick strides, Regan crossed to the studio area. When Holly didn't follow, Regan came back for her, catching her hand to tug her into the patently private zone beneath a skylight—into the redolence of linseed and the faint tang of turpentine, where the paintings became more than glimpses of color leaning against the wall or easel. No longer just pigment and canvas, brushstroke and layered paint. And although clearly done by the same hand that produced the rich clarity of the book illustrations, just as clearly done by a different *person*.

"These are…" Holly floundered for words and found them all inadequate. "These are…*amazing.*" The mountains, all vast, stark beauty and ponderous weight, scudding clouds and impending storms, birds where they should be, elk where they should be, the glimpse of a bear's shoulder…always the hint of a lynx, whether in track, in silvery shadow, in the wisdom of a blue eye. Never with the bold clarity of the illustrations, but as implication and whisper so effective that when Holly turned her eye away, she was convinced she'd seen every whisker.

"This," said Regan, "is what I paint now that I'm listening again."

Holly squeezed her eyes shut; her voice scraped against her throat. "I really, *really* don't understand."

And she really, *really* didn't want to.

Regan responded with gentle persistence. "Holly, the listening is what I was running *from*. And then it was exactly what made me whole."

Holly dredged up anger from somewhere, letting it flare. It was safer. "You aren't me!"

"I'm not," Regan said, readily enough. "My mother was so barely Sentinel that it didn't matter to anyone but her, and I'm even less so. And that makes what you're going through so much more powerful."

Holly dared another glimpse at the paintings, and wasn't so sure of that. Besides, she'd understood what she was doing when she'd put aside her Sentinel self all those years ago.

She thought she had.

"Think about it," Regan said, adjusting a canvas with a tip of her finger. "It's what you are. Even if you never find it truly fulfilling, it must take a lot of effort to deny it, day after day."

Maybe that was why Holly suddenly felt so tired, her angry resentment dulled but not quenched.

Or maybe she was just tired of fighting this battle—not only all her life, but now against people who knew nothing of her and thought they knew better than anyone.

But Regan had acted out of kindness, so Holly swallowed what was left of her anger, deliberately moving away from the painting to the window, looking in the direction the wolf and lynx had taken. "Seems like this is the sort of thing *he* ought to have been telling me."

Regan moved up beside her; her smile came through in her voice. "I get the feeling that Lannie Stewart is an unspoken kind of guy."

"Great." Holly hit the word with a heavy dryness.

"Watch what he does and how he does it as much as you look for his words," Regan advised, and laughed softly. "It's what I've learned to do!"

Her mind's eye flashed back to the car...the wolf in his eye...the *want* in his eye...the faint scrape of a rough thumb over her knuckles and the tingling chill of warning along her spine. *Seeing him.*

"Uh-huh," Regan said, and laughed again, while Holly's hand went to her suddenly flushed cheek and she swore. Regan had pity. "Come on," she said. "I'll take you out back and we can admire the horsie. He likes that, and I have chores to do."

Numbly, Holly followed her out of the loft and down to the kitchen, where Regan led her out through a back mudroom and into the beauty of the day. There, Bob the dog solemnly snuffled her hand and the roan mustang lipped her hair, and Holly unthinkingly dragged her hand through the water in the trough while Regan cleaned the paddock and hauled out fresh hay, scattering a handful of dark green pellets over the top of the slow feeder.

Then she took Holly on a quiet walk over nearby trails—just enough to stretch their legs. She entertained Holly with a description of the moments in which she'd first met Kai—out on the land and spooking the mustang into a bucking fit that had left Regan riding air. "I *bailed*," Regan insisted, a smile sneaking out as she glanced back at Holly. "Better than trying to stick it out on the side of a mountain."

"Sounds like luck that you even met Kai," Holly said. "If you'd stayed on the horse and headed back home…"

Holly smiled again as she ducked a branch on the barely-there trail, this time with something secretive about it. "Oh, I think it was just a matter of time." She held the branch for Regan, stopping to look out over the mountain. "Speaking of which. We'd better head back. It's not far from here, anyway."

Holly found herself reluctant to leave, recognizing nothing and yet knowing she had spent her first years not so far from here. She could so easily imagine this landscape after rain—where the water would gather and trickle, how it would sound…

"This way," Regan said, breaking off the trail to head straight downhill. They'd only just emerged onto the scrub of the rocky slope behind the barn when Regan stopped to point. "There," she said.

Only after Holly had squinted and waited and frowned did she see the men emerging from the woods, walking more comfortably in each other's presence than when they'd left.

Regan surprised her by breaking into a run when she reached the flat, past the horse and dog and house and straight at Kai—not even hesitating, but throwing herself at him. He caught her up as she wrapped legs around his hips and arms around his neck and laughed—and then Kai laughed, too, and Holly, for whatever inexplicable reason, quite suddenly felt like crying.

To hear her brother laugh, after all these years…

Lannie waited for her, letting Kai carry Regan off toward the porch, and Holly approached him with uncertainty, seeing him anew.

Seeing how he would have fit right into one of Regan's paintings, all the wild sparking through, the wolf apparent in every step he took. How had she ever looked at him and not seen it? How could *anyone* look at him and not see it?

"You okay?" he asked, his gaze direct, searching her face.

"Youbetcha," she told him, because what else was she going to say? *No. Maybe. I don't know.*

I don't think I'll ever know again.

Lannie understood quickly that Kai Faulkes was not a man to take for granted in any sense. Like Holly, he had become who he was with no direct input from the Sentinels. His honor was his own, his nature unfettered, with none of the casual, automatic assumptions of shared culture and shared secrets.

Just looking at the man made him think differently about Holly.

She sat across from him on the porch, which Regan had transformed into a picnic zone with the quick flip of a worn quilt and a scatter of cushions—not to mention the appearance of spicy, beef-crammed burritos. "Not mine," Regan had been quick to admit before they all settled into the silence of appreciative eating. "But homemade all the same. My dad, actually."

"Tell your dad thank you," Holly said with some fervency, looking nothing like Kai and everything like Kai at the same time. For even if her otherness didn't simmer and push at the surface, it nonetheless ran smoothly, quietly, beneath each shift of her weight, each step she took…even the grace of movement as she reached for a napkin.

Kai's nature, his history, was right out there on the

surface for anyone to see. *More Sentinel than thou.* So his family's past had made of him.

Of Holly, it had formed something completely different. Her exact nature ran so deep she could hardly find it herself. And all the assumptions underlying Sentinel existence—the cohesiveness, the common understandings and common goals, the overarching culture—had not only been missing from her life, they had been actively subsumed.

Lannie would have to meet her on *her* terms, not his.

Maybe Brevis had chosen the wrong alpha. The wrong *man*.

Because just maybe he couldn't separate his response to her from what was best for her. He'd proven that once already, when he'd believed in Jody instead of shutting her down—and far too recently.

The wrong timing, on top of it all.

Regan poured the last of the water from the pitcher she'd brought out and pushed to her feet. "Be right back."

"So what's up with your friend Aldo, eh?" Holly asked him, as if they'd been talking about it all along.

Aldo. The friend who needed help that Lannie couldn't give as long as he was disengaged from his home pack. "I'm not sure," he told her, not failing to notice Kai's keen interest. "He's as coyote as they come… hard to predict what he's up to at the best of times."

"Does he take the change?"

Lannie shook his head, leaning back against the porch rails with one knee up and his wrist propped there. "Maybe when he was younger." He thought of Aldo's history, or what he knew of it—never quite fitting in, if only because he never could quite help himself. Impulsive trickster, quick of wit and quicker to shoot himself in the foot. He'd finally ended up in Lannie's home pack, spending more time at the farm store than he did at his rickety old desert-rat trailer. There, finally, he'd settled—still erratic in nature but *trying.*

"But you're worried about him."

With Aldo's history, it was hard to identify his recent behavior as particularly troublesome—even managing to start a fight with five muscle-bound trespassers half his age. But even so. In the end all Lannie could say was "He's one of mine."

It earned him a sharp look from her. No doubt she heard the echoes of her own words from not so long ago: *I am not yours.*

No doubt she still felt that way, without ever understanding what it truly meant.

Regan reappeared at the screen, pushing it open with a freshly filled pitcher in hand. "Huh," she said. "That's…strange."

Kai didn't inquire so much as he focused his attention in a way Lannie well recognized. As relaxed as the man might seem, here on his home turf and his home porch, he and Regan took nothing for granted.

She saw it in him and nudged his knee with her foot before sitting, placing the pitcher in the center of their gathering. "I'm probably imagining it. It's just that the well has been acting funky, and now it's…well, it's not. It was probably sediment that got knocked loose. I should count our blessings."

Holly flinched. Just a little. And then shot a quick look Lannie's way, as if hoping he hadn't seen her reaction.

He pretended he hadn't.

Kai didn't. Not quite. But after a long, thoughtful look at her, he said, "I thought your eyes were blue."

Holly blinked those chocolate-colored eyes. "You what?"

"I remembered your eyes as dark," he told her. "I thought blue, like mine."

"No," she said, looking baffled—though she then gave him a considering look. "I didn't remember yours at all." Without warning, her eyes took on a watery gleam; her chin gave a single tremble. "There's nothing right about that."

"We make it right," Kai said. "From now on. As best we can." He glanced at Lannie, warning in the angle of his head, but understanding, as well. "We *learn*."

Chapter 8

"*We make it right*," Holly said, her tone somewhat dazed as she repeated her brother's recent words. She guided the truck smoothly around a sharp curve in the falling twilight. "You told him to say those things, didn't you? And Regan, with that business about her mother."

Lannie sat in the passenger seat where he didn't belong, all too aware that he wasn't healing correctly, that his pack sense had been wounded along with the rest of him…and that it all meant he couldn't quite do the already impossible job he'd been asked to do.

Such awareness made his words sharper than they might have been. "You really think I could tell your brother to do anything?"

She spared a quick glance from the road. "I don't know. He's as new to me as you are. Maybe that's the problem. You really know your job, Lannie, and I'm trying to find a good way through this, but if you think seeing Kai and Regan will magically bring me around to the Sentinel way of thinking, then you don't know *me*."

Except he did know her. And *that* was the problem.

Because it didn't matter that he wanted to help her, or what she'd already come to mean to him. He knew her resentment, and he understood it. He knew her independence, and he admired it—and he knew her strength of self, and it called to him. Had called to him this whole day, which should have been only about reintroducing her to her brother.

It called to him here and now, sitting beside her, aware *of her. Wanting her.*

But her safety was too critical to risk the bite of recent history.

Of recent failure.

"Lannie?" Her uncertainty pushed against him, right along with the song that called to him so deeply.

He rubbed a finger against an aching brow. "Okay. I hear you." If not in the way she thought he did. "Listen, I…" The words were hard to come by, even harder to say. "I'd better call Brevis. It might take a couple of days, but I think they'd better assign you to someone else."

The truck jerked from its smooth progress but straightened before he could so much as reach for the wheel. "You can do that?"

"You'll have to relocate." He found the words hard to say. "I know you'd probably rather be closer to your family, but—"

"You *would* do that?" Stiff shoulders, stiff neck, stiff jaw…

That was *outrage* in her voice. It was…

Hurt.

He found the words absurdly hard to say. "I don't think there's any choice."

"Choice?" She snorted, but her voice sounded wounded, and Lannie closed his eyes on a resounding echo of the pain in her song. "When has this ever been about *choice*? Not for me, that's for sure."

Not for Lannie, either. Not since the moment he'd seen her. *Heard* her.

He wanted her here. He wanted to make this right for her. He *ached* to do it, both as alpha and as the man who responded to her very presence beside him.

And he still couldn't risk it.

"It was never right," he managed to say, unable to find the words to tell her just why. *Death and failure,* and not enough time to heal. To find his center again. "But it's not about you. It's—"

"Not about me?" She jerked the truck over to the rare commodity of a waiting shoulder, braking to a stop with the crunch of gravel. "How can you even say that? Doesn't it even matter—" She paused, and didn't say it out loud. Lannie could guess well enough. *Doesn't it even matter how I feel about you?* Maybe she couldn't risk it—maybe his response to her somehow wasn't obvious enough. She glared at him, biting off the words. "It's so *easy* for you, isn't it? Whatever's convenient, no matter what it does to the life you people are jerking around!"

The frustration within him swelled, too big to hold—too big to be called frustration at all, but spilling over into a furious pain. Her eyes widened as he flung the truck door open and stalked around the front fender, getting just a glimpse of big eyes and pale face through the windshield, hands working the seat belt and reaching for the door. He yanked it open from her grasp, the wolf surging within—not so much the alpha, but the *wolf.*

And the *man.*

He hauled her out of the truck, pushing her up against it with nothing gentle in his manner. She shook him off and would have bounced back at him—she started to—but she gave him a second look and hesitated.

"Nothing," he said, leaning over her, *"nothing* about this is convenient for me. Nothing about it is *easy."*

She glared back with eyes narrowed and chin jutted, all but hiding her uncertainty.

"Every *time*," Lannie said. "Every single damned *time.* Do you have any idea what it feels like to build pack, only to have Brevis rip it away? To cut myself off from my own people for you? Do you even begin to understand why I have to be so careful about defining who is and isn't pack? Do you know what it's like when those people *die*?"

She didn't. He knew she couldn't. She hadn't ever tapped into the connections that lived between Sentinels. She hadn't ever *built* those connections.

She didn't even want them.

And she didn't want to know that her presence here had actually cost him—he could see that clearly enough. It wouldn't be quite so easy to assume why he made the choices he did if she knew.

The words grated in his throat, no longer shouting...but hitting just as hard. "In order to bring pack together," he said, and somehow his hand had found the tangle of her sleek ponytail, crushing it up against the back of her neck, "I have to *care.* I have to—"

She was the one to make that first move, grabbing his shirt to yank him forward in a way he'd never expected. He sprawled against her, instantly in contact from head to toe—his thigh pressed warmly between her legs, her hip pressing against a swiftly rising erection. Her hands went from his shirt to his neck, wrapping behind it to pull him in even closer—bringing their mouths together for a fierce kiss of instantly molded mouths and nipping teeth.

More than a kiss, as her hips moved against him and she made room for his thigh, two bodies in instant accord, barely room between them for her sound of surprise and his growl of response. Her fingers curled into his hair, clutching it with demand; his hands found her waist and jerked her away from the truck, supple as she willingly arched against him. It gave him room to cup the toned curve of her bottom, tugging her right up on her toes. Her gasp turned into a moan—

And suddenly he felt the heat of the sun-warmed truck radiating out at them both, the cooling evening air at his back, the shifting gravel under his feet.

Suddenly he realized what the hell he was doing.

She felt it in him, stilling enough so he pulled back an inch, then two.

What the hell. It's not real. Was there some point when he'd learn that?

"It *is* real," Holly said, just as fiercely as the kiss. "*I'm* real."

He tried to control his rasping breath, and failed. He tried to control the growl in his voice, and failed that, too. "I know you are," he said. "That's the *problem*."

But he knew she wouldn't understand. He didn't need her baffled expression, or the hurt behind it.

And the hurt behind it was the whole problem.

He pushed away from the truck to turn his back on her, breathing deeply of the cool evening air, his heart racing as it had never done on the run today. Out of pure desperation, he reached for pack song. Not to take part, but just to *listen*...

To steady himself.

But he'd cut himself off from the Descanso pack, and the song hesitated.

Her voice came low compared to his, husky around the edges. "I suppose now you'll tell me you have nothing to do with how I feel. Not just about you—that you're not doing this to me."

He was doing it to her, all right. He just wasn't *trying* to. And if the pack mojo was that far out of control...

He had to get her away from here. Away from *him*.

"I *suppose*," Holly said, come up behind him, "you're also going to tell me you have nothing to do with the way the world closes in around me now that we're getting closer to Descanso. You're going to tell that's not *you* with your Sentinel ways, tightening your grip."

The pack song filtered through only faintly, strained and unclear and scattered—and then it was gone again. Gone, somehow for good. Still, it gave him space to think. He heard her accusation more clearly, her underlying lack of trust. A weight settled over his chest. "That's exactly what I'm going to say. It's not me."

At least, it shouldn't be. He just didn't know anymore. But pack...

It was about making the world bigger, not smaller.

At least, it ought to be.

He breathed in the cool night air, fists clenched unto pain, nails biting into his palms. Floundering and hating it and looking for familiar balance. Looking for *himself*, here where the craggy twilight mountains tumbled away before them, a crystal clarity in blue-tinged sight. He could barely see the small gap beyond which Descanso was sheltered. Where his pack, from Faith and

Aldo and Javi to the twins to the ranger and beyond, now abided apart from him…no matter that they were still all in the same small town.

The wolf within him loosed a wild, mournful howl; Lannie tipped his head back and let it gust out as a sigh. And he indulged himself, one last time—hunting for Holly's own melody…the one that sometimes came to him all on its own. Complex, rich as her eyes, full of foundation and notes twining like burbling water over rock.

But now he heard it only distantly, and just when he thought he'd grasped it, the cymbal clash of static stiffened him; pain punched through his wounded side so sudden and sharp he jerked with it, losing air in a grunt and frozen there, stunned with it all.

Work shoes crunched gravel. She came up behind him, her hesitation in the catch of her own breath. "Lannie?"

He caught the movement from the corner of his eye—her hand, about to land lightly on his arm. It broke his stasis. He turned a snarl on her—everything of the wolf, set free.

She staggered back against the truck, taking it for the blow it was.

He straightened, settling into himself. Whole again, such as it was. A deep, steadying breath, and he turned to her again, his voice flat. "Brevis expected too much. From both of us."

And he ignored her quiet gasp, reaching past her to step up into the truck. *His* truck, his seat—quickly readjusted for his longer legs—and he'd damned well be the one behind the wheel.

Because he understood now. Amid the turmoil and the hot need and the yearning, he'd put the pieces of his floundering pack sense into focus. Because while he could—sometimes, somehow—hear her song, he could somehow no longer go looking for it. He couldn't blend it or guide it or be part of it. And as long as he didn't try, he was perfectly safe and perfectly fine.

Stop reaching for her.

Might as well ask him to stop breathing.

The morning found Holly tangled in those moments between sleep and wakefulness, her mind and body full of flavor from the previous evening—the explosive moments of temper between herself and Lannie, the distress of watching him falter—*again*—the complexity of her feelings when she realized how deeply he'd been affected by her presence...and that for him, it wasn't all good.

It wasn't even nearly good.

She opened her eyes to bright splashing sunlight and uncomfortably building warmth, the sheets twisted around her legs after a restless night of churning resentments and mixed guilt, her T-shirt twisted up to expose her midriff and very nearly more, snug satin sleep boxers drifting down to expose one hip bone.

It doesn't matter, she told herself. *You're alone here.*

And then the shower cut in, on and off again so quickly that it must have been only a fast, water-saving rinse.

She froze in stunned awareness and then rolled quickly out of bed, jerking her shirt down and her boxers up, and bending to search discarded clothing for pants to yank on and a second shirt to yank over. She hastened to stuff red satin down out of the way when Lannie emerged from the bathroom—shirtless, his own jeans not yet buttoned all the way to the top, and his manner...

Different.

No longer offering her a certain polite deference, but a man being himself in his own space.

To judge by the glance he gave her, he had not missed the glimpse of satin as she struggled to manage the zip and snap of her worn canvas work jeans.

He said, "Laundry day. If you haven't ordered clothes yet, feel free to use my card. I'll have them sent on to you if you've moved by the time they get here."

"I called the store yesterday," she said, somewhat dazed by the changes in the gestalt between them. She gathered up the sleek fall of her hair, twisting a hair band around it to create what was probably the world's messiest ponytail. "Have you already called?"

"Shortly." With quick, rough efficiency, he put together the makings for a small pot of coffee, sliding two mugs over the counter. "They'll need time to find another safe situation. Probably it'll be HQ in Tucson."

"In...the city?"

He shot her a look. "Not what you're used to, but according to the file, that's their second choice to Descanso."

"Tucson?" she said faintly, putting one hand on the wall to see if the world was not, in fact, whirling.

"Maybe with Mariska, who brought you here. She and Ruger are north of Tucson, in the Catalinas." He shrugged. "Newlyweds. Might not work out so well, but...better than a barn, I expect."

"Wait," she said. "You...you're really doing it?"

He speared her with a direct look, his eyes never sharper—all pale blue ringed with darkness—and left her words settling on his silence as he uncovered the loosely wrapped and visibly salted steak he'd been warming beside the refrigerator. He pulled a frying pan from beneath the stove, flicking on a burner. This, she realized, was closer to his usual routine than not.

Yes. Taking back his space.

And it came as the consequence of her own actions. Her own behavior. Striking out at him when none of this had been his fault. Blaming him when he was trying to help.

How was she to have known he had nothing to do with the way it felt to be here?

Ask him. Faith had given her that answer earlier the day before. But she'd been so angry...so willing to believe the worst of all of them...

And so deeply shaken by her visit with Regan and Kai—seeing things she didn't want to see. Their happiness—not in spite of being Sentinel, but because of it.

Lannie poured a dollop of oil into the pan and set the oil aside, putting a hand to his side—briefly covering the still-healing wound. It might have been her imagination, but she thought she also saw the faint shadows of bruising along his brow and cheek. Not new ones... but the ones he'd had the evening she'd arrived, somehow showing anew.

How did that make sense?

Then again, nothing of this situation made sense. And now she'd be moving again, her life still completely out of her own control.

"Fine," she said, a word laced with bitter acceptance. "What am I supposed to do in the meantime?"

He dropped the thick steak into the pan. "Ride the bike. Help at the store. Make yourself at home." Although it was clear he would no longer so thoroughly abandon his space for her.

She thought of Regan's cabin—the peace of it, and the acceptance Regan and Kai had given her. "Couldn't I stay with—"

Except then she imagined the expression on Kai's face when he realized how she'd treated this man, or Regan's disappointment at how quickly, how profoundly, Holly had rejected her heartfelt words.

"Never mind," she muttered.

Lannie dropped the steak into the smoking fry pan, creating the instant sizzle of cooking meat. For long moments, he said nothing—tending the steak, flipping it…finger-testing it and adding butter. Holly took in the combined scents and let out a breath on a groan, suddenly starving—and more than aware that he might not be cooking for more than one.

A final finger test and he put the meat aside under cover and turned to her, one brow raised. Only then did she realize how entranced she'd become—not just taking in his movement, his efficiency and unexpected if quiet expertise, but…staring.

Because he did still have his shirt off.

"Sorry," she said quickly. "Just…trying to absorb everything. I'll get out of the way."

"Wait," he said. His movements lacked their usual flow as he dumped cooking utensils in the sink and pulled out a couple of plates, and the tension bled through to his voice. "There's not going to be any better time for this."

She spotted a denim work shirt hanging over the back of the kitchen bar chair and tossed it at his chest. "For what?"

He snagged it out of the air before it reached him and shrugged it on—casual movement, but his voice sounded rough over his words. "I think you should look into initiation."

She snorted. "What? Seriously? You mean *Sentinel* initiation?"

He just looked at her, which she took to mean *yes*, and she laughed out loud. "Right," she said. "I'm going to have sex with an assigned stranger? I get what you're saying—what Regan was saying—but I'm completely comfortable with who I am now. So I don't think so."

"You want to figure out who you are? Then initiate."

She crossed her arms most firmly. "I know who I am. *What* I am."

Implacable, the wolf. "Not until you know all of it."

"Oh, wait." She straightened with sudden under-standing. "Don't tell me this is something that *you* would—"

Not that she hadn't wanted him. Didn't *still* want him. Didn't still feel his touch from the night before. But not like *this*.

His startlement was too real to be feigned—a stutter in his movement, a transitory widening of eyes gone dark. Not just startled.

Hurt.

But quickly shuttered, so quickly she suddenly wasn't certain she'd even seen it.

"Holly," he said, far too evenly, "You haven't been listening. I've already told you why that isn't going to happen."

Wolf, standing by the side of the road in fury, search-ing for control while she stood with the truck at her back. Wolf, his voice ragged, giving her the hard facts of pack life, his head tipping back on what sounded like a sigh to her ears but a sad howl to her mind.

And she knew. "You've already put me aside from the pack."

He huffed a breath of wry laughter. "It's not that easy." Something darker chased across his face, something inward.

"No? Then why *not* you? If I'm still in the pack—"

She hadn't seen it coming. She hadn't expected him to move at all, never mind that fast—that close. Just as with the evening before, suddenly standing right before her, close enough to again wrap his hand in her messy ponytail and capture it up against her nape, jerking her forward half a step to meet him.

There was nothing behind her. She could have taken a step back; she could have smacked his hand away and left him behind.

She stood her ground.

"*Because* you're in the pack," he said. "*Because* of what it would be between us."

She stared right back into his eyes, finding them dark and glowering and fierce, finding his nostrils flared— and knowing, with a sudden certainty, that he inhaled her scent in a way she'd never imagined anyone could.

"Step back," he said. "Or don't."

She didn't. She lifted her chin just that much, and if it gave the slightest quiver, she wasn't quite sure why.

His mouth came down on hers, no more gentle than the wolf in his eyes—hungry and wild and predatorial, taking what he wanted…and giving everything.

Everything.

And Holly took. Just like the evening before, she *took*. She wrapped her fingers around the open shirt plackets and pulled herself in close, taking it all and overwhelmed by it all—his presence, his touch, the strength of his body against hers…the way he instantly, obviously, roused to her. She loved the feel of hard muscle, the sensation of his strength…the tug of his hand in her hair, the pressure of his lips, the touch of his tongue.

She loved the wild surge of her own desire, rising to meet his.

He touched her with an assertion she hadn't expected, his hands firm and confident as they swept down her back, skimmed up the curve from hip to waist, and paused where his thumbs could trace her breasts. The faint pressure made her skin hum and tighten, and her nipples pebbled against him.

She slipped her hands inside his shirt, around his side and down the dent at the base of his spine, cupping tight muscle—clutching it. Shifting her hips against him, all but wrapping her leg up to climb aboard.

All from his kiss, so deep and full of beguiling power. All from the delicious touch of his hand on the back of her neck. All from his *presence*.

A gasp broke from her throat…a tiny little soprano purr. A demand.

He froze, drawing a sudden breath. A *shared* breath.

And then he moved away. Just as he had the night before.

Not far. Only an inch, maybe half. But it was enough, and in the next instant he'd gone even farther, until they suddenly stood apart, looking at one another— Holly with a dawning understanding slowly replacing her frustration, and Lannie with nothing more, nothing less, than pain lacing his desire.

She said hoarsely, "I'm not sure what's wrong with *that*."

"For you?" His voice came just as ragged, his shoulders stiff with new tension. "Probably nothing. For me…everything."

She swallowed hard, more hurt than she'd expected, not getting it. "Because you didn't feel…that wasn't…" *Didn't that mean anything? Didn't it rock your world like it did mine?*

He laughed, a short and hard sound. "More than you'll ever know," he said. "And losing that, when you leave…" He shook his head, taking a step back from her.

"That," he said, "would break me."

Chapter 9

"Lannie!"

The shout blasted up the exterior stairs, through the closed door and through the privacy of Lannie's loft.

Right through the moment he'd so stupidly started—and ended—with Holly.

Or tried to end. But his body wanted no part of *ending*, as if he'd sealed his very fate with a single kiss.

A hot, intense, extended *single* kiss.

He knew better. She might have rejected him; she might be on her way out. But he'd entangled himself in her, and entangled he'd stay—until she was gone, and until long after she'd found the new life she was looking for.

Now she only stared at him dumbfounded, probably not sure whether to be enraged by what he'd done or by what he'd stopped doing. Her nipples peeked through her T-shirt, exposed by the disarray of the long-sleeved work shirt she'd hastily pulled over top it.

But he'd seen her in his bed, sheets twisted around, long legs exposed, flat-toned midriff exposed...a posture of abandon.

In his bed.

Ah, hell.

"Lannie!"

Since when was Faith here so early? He glanced at his watch and decided the better question was *Since when do I run so late?* His fingers sought out shirt buttons, fastening them on the fly. "Enjoy the steak," he said, nodding in its direction even as his stomach growled.

He could have made Faith wait. But sharing breakfast with Holly? As if none of this had ever happened?

That he couldn't do.

He left the loft and headed down the exterior stairs into the bright, cool morning, clouds already building overhead and promising rain for sure.

"Yeah, yeah," he muttered at them. He detoured past the mules, making sure of their hay and water and silently promising them time under saddle—and then paused before he entered the store's back door.

Shaking it off. Hiding it away.

Faith, standing behind the counter, frowned at him anyway. "You okay? You get in another fight?"

She, too, saw the oddity of the reappearing bruises he'd found in the mirror that morning. She just didn't recognize them as old rather than new, as he had.

"I'm fine," he said, briskly enough to forestall further discussion. "What's all the bellowing?"

"No bank bag," she said. Today she wore a sleeveless shirt that hadn't started out that way, black and purple and tucked into black jeans cut so low they must have been hard-pressed to hang in there at all. He gave them the eye, she gave him the finger, and she went on. "You left us a starter bag when you went to the bank yesterday, didn't you?"

"Yes," Lannie said, already heading behind the counter to kick open the sticky old wooden cabinet door in front of their safe.

Faith moved well out of his way. "You're *checking* on me? Oh, come on."

Lannie hesitated. "Tell me you haven't given Aldo this combination."

She snorted, fiddling with the piercing at her brow. "Of course not. Doesn't mean he doesn't have it. But he was at home all yesterday, even after you left. And why would he…? He knows you'll help him if he needs it."

"If he *wants* it," Lannie muttered, thinking that the two weren't anywhere near the same thing. If he hadn't known it before, Holly was damned sure making it clear.

Faith gestured at the register drawer, popped open and forlornly empty. "He wouldn't do this, anyway. He's a pain in the ass, not nasty."

"There's a reason we both thought of him first." Lannie looked out the storefront window, confirming the emptiness of the lot—going straight to the heart of the solution. *The wolf's nose.*

Faith hastily boosted herself up on the counter, dusting the glass with her jeans as she swung her booted feet up and over to clomp down on the other side. "I know *that* look," she said. "Not with me right there…!"

Lannie gave her the rarest of grins, letting the wolf show in it—and then pulled his shirt off, letting the wolf out altogether and reaching to take fur and paw and long sharp tooth…

The wolf staggered into place, static in his head.

Lannie shook off most violently, almost losing his balance again in the process.

"Fierce," Faith said drily.

He curled a lip at her and stalked to the safe, confirming what he'd already truly known from the pool of scent behind the counter—Aldo had not only been here, he'd handled the safe.

A growl rumbled deep. Annoyance, yes, but…concern.

"Aldo?" Faith asked.

A flick of his ear said *yes*. But scent, as often, told him more than anything else, and Aldo's was subtly off.

Not only that, he also wasn't far away.

Lannie padded out from behind the counter and led Faith straight to end of the store, where Aldo slept soundly on a scattered stack of saddle blankets.

"Aldo!" Faith reached down to shake the old man's shoulder, then quickly backed away as Aldo startled awake, his eyes rheumy and his beard stubble past the point of masculine statement and into the territory of scruffy.

But he wasn't slow to understand the look on her face. "I didn't do it!"

Lannie sat in pointed expectation, haunches tucked and front paws precisely placed. Faith glanced at him and said, "We kind of think you did, Aldo. And we need that bank bag back."

He squinted up at her. "Bank bag? What's gotten into you? I would never mess with Lannie's store. Not like that!"

"Says he who swapped out all the supplements with the fly control stuff just last week."

"That's different!" Aldo protested, casting a pleading glance at Lannie. "You know it is!"

It was.

Lannie canted his ears back and returned to the counter, inhaling the scent there—identifying the age of it, and casting around for an older track. He circled out to avoid the big scent pool behind the counter and picked up a trail leading to the back of the store—which had been locked, but Aldo had a key the same way he knew the safe combination. Faith opened the door for him, and he sorted through his own human track, Aldo's entrance track, and the slightly more recent exit track.

Once he had it, he moved with swift confidence, easily managing the scent's whirls and eddies against the buildings, the changes from sun to shadow. He ignored a nearby mouse in the barn and, once he realized the scent went up the ladder, he left the track to bound up the step-stacked hay bales and scrambled up into the loft from the side.

Moments later, he returned to the store as human, the bank bag in hand, and followed muted conversation to the break room.

Aldo looked up from Faith's coffee as Lannie arrived, and his whiskery jaw dropped. "No!" he said. "I didn't!"

Lannie had no way to spare him. "I tracked it. I'm sorry, but you did."

"I'll stop smoking the weed," Aldo said fervently. "I swear, I won't be any more trouble."

"You're not *trouble* now," Lannie said. "And you won't stop smoking pot. We both know that." He handed the bag to Faith and jerked his head at the door; she scooted away.

Aldo couldn't meet his eyes. "No," he said. "I probably won't."

"Maybe," Lannie said drily, "you could cut back on

it a little. I can give you more hours here at the store if it would help."

Aldo dared a glancing sideways glance. "It's good to stay busy. I promise I won't swap any more product around."

Lannie sighed. "Yes, you will," he said, knowing better than that, too. "But when you do, you can swap it back again...*off* the clock."

Aldo straightened, tugging his worn brown vest into place. "Yes," he said. "I can do that."

Lannie clapped a hand on a thin shoulder. "Start with those saddle blankets."

Like Faith, Aldo responded with alacrity, easing past Lannie to trot away.

Lannie stood in the break room and tipped his head back, inhaling deeply of the coffee that would smell so much better than it would ever taste and reaching within himself to start the day anew. Calmer. Without the conflict in his loft or in his body.

Holly's pack song murmured beneath his thoughts, clear and quiet—and right *here*—and he abruptly straightened, caught out in a vulnerability he hadn't intended anyone to see.

Holly said, "I kind of expected you to come down on him."

He turned, a most deliberate movement, to find her standing out in the hallway. Watching, as she'd before no doubt listened.

Dammit, he should have stayed wolf. She'd never have come up behind him as wolf.

Except, he told himself, and knew it to be true, *she shouldn't have been able to come up on me as human, either.* He should have heard far more than a mere murmur of pack song approaching when she was that close.

For however long it lasted, she was still the only pack he had.

But he wasn't going to discuss any of that with her. "Why?" he said. "Because I'm the big bad alpha wolf? I thought we talked about this."

"You mean how truly being alpha means pulling out your teeth only when you need them?" She'd re-dressed herself and now wore only the bright long-tailed shirt over her jeans, her hair tidied and falling darkly sleek, her face pink from a good scrub. "He stole from you. I thought it might count."

"He's an old man who doesn't mean any harm," Lannie said. "This world wasn't truly made for him." He took a step closer to her, and another yet—but stopped far enough away so she'd know he wasn't going to back her up against the other side of the hall. He couldn't tell if that was relief or disappointment in her dark eyes. "The thing about an alpha, Holly Faulkes, is that we don't fight for things we don't truly care about, just to show what we are." One. Step. Closer. "But when there's something we want…really *want*…"

Her eyes widened.

Lannie stepped back, his smile short and dry. "And now, if you'll excuse me…I've got a shirt to put back on, a coyote to wrangle and a store to run. I'll let you know if I hear from Brevis."

"Right," Holly said faintly to his back. "Brevis." And then, more loudly, "I'm heading out on a bike ride. The steak was awesome, by the way."

By then he was far enough away so it felt safe to turn around, but not so far away that he couldn't see the defiance in her eyes.

Defiance and confusion.

"You're welcome," he said. "Let me know if I can do anything else for you before you leave us."

Distance. And confusion.

Most of it his own.

Holly wasted no time in the barn—easy enough to grab her new bike and the helmet. With the helmet snapped into place and her leg flung over the bike, she wasted no time getting the tires on asphalt, switching the gears into a rhythm that suited her.

For the first time since being snatched from her life, she felt a certain tension ebbing, her shoulders relaxing…her first truly deep breath.

Her first chance to stop thinking, and thinking, and *over*thinking—her past, her present, her future, her family…her temporary alpha.

All she wanted in her mind was silence. Silence and the same clarity she'd felt in Kai's higher mountain peaks.

She geared up just to feel the power of pushing against the pedals, the wind in her face as she swooped around a curve toward town…all she really wanted was open road. She passed an unexpected orchard undulating over the rolling hills of this moderate valley and foothills area, and pushed to gain speed as she conquered an unexpected rise.

There she stopped, propping herself on one extended leg—panting, and satisfied with that. Her mind, long used to the effectiveness of bike meditation, had cleared—leaving room for her to absorb the beauty of this place, to realize she hadn't used so much as a dollop of sunscreen, and to be grateful she'd filled her water bottle on the way out of the loft.

Ice crunched inside sturdy plastic as she pulled the

bottle from its cage and squeezed out a stream of water, gazing out on the high sere plains and predominant ponderosa of pronghorn and elk country. The low clouds scudding overhead were glaring white with bruising dark blue foundations, and even as a newcomer she knew enough to expect a thunderous storm before too long.

But she didn't have to go back. Not quite yet. She put her foot back to the pedal and pushed off into the day, replacing the water back into its cage along the way.

Clarity eluded her. A mile of more moderate progress and she'd found only the unpleasant taste in the back of her throat that had dogged her upon arriving here.

Feeling herself just a little bit crazy, she made herself open to that unpleasant taste—a thing acrid and sharp, biting at her tongue and her nose. A faint dizziness swooped through her head; she stopped the bike, planting her feet.

It came from the east.

Disbelieving herself, she waited for the world to steady and picked up the pedals again—and this time, when the main road curved around to the north, she took the chance to branch east.

The road turned to gravel; the taste grew sharper yet. *If I knew what I was doing...*

It was a fleeting thought, chased away by her first sight of activity along this road—a flat area where the natural vegetation had been scraped away and heavy machinery clustered. Bulldozer, backhoe, a scatter of little Bobcat vehicles, and towering over them all, a drilling rig. Off to the side sat piles of stone and gravel, and rows of piping and massive fittings.

She let the bike coast to a stop, thinking that the project looked large enough to be municipal but had none of the earmarks of official construction. And nothing that seemed the least bit untoward…just a handful of men, not particularly inspired, but not sitting around, either.

One of the Bobcat vehicles moved, revealing the truck behind it. *White pickup truck, familiar logo.*

Quite naturally, someone sat in the driver's seat of that truck, and now he slid out, clipboard in hand, to stare over at her. She had no doubt it was one of the guys from the bar, where they had not played nice and Lannie had not played nice right back at them.

"Move along, move along," she muttered to herself, and even as the guy tossed the clipboard in the truck to stalk toward her, she wheeled the bike in a tight U-turn and rode back the way she'd come.

She didn't quite make it. She hadn't thought him so close, or realized he would move so fast. He stood in her way as she straightened out the bike.

"Nosing around?" he asked, recognition on his face, his arms crossed in a Mr. Clean pose. Barely crossed at that, with so much beef to them that they couldn't quite make the wrap. Gym muscle, not life muscle.

Lannie had life muscle. *Using* muscle.

For that instant, she wished he was there.

"Not so much as I am following my nose," she said, spotting a second man heading her way. "Your friend needs to stay back, eh? Whoever you're doing this work for probably doesn't want an official incident."

He lifted his chin at his pal, stopping the man's progress. "Don't make this into something it's not."

"I could say the same to you," she advised him. "Seeing as you're the one who interfered with my ride on this very public road."

And looked as though he regretted it. "I just wanted to make sure you weren't lost."

I'm lost, all right. But not the way you think. Out loud, she said, "I'm just riding. How lost can I get?"

He hesitated, as if he truly wished he had reason to keep her there. But he didn't, and he stepped aside— just far enough for her to move past, foot pushing firmly down on the pedal to coast away and pretending she wasn't shivering slightly with relief.

Within moments, she reached the asphalt again, the shivers already burned away in the sun. There, she glanced in the direction of the farm store, knowing she'd probably already gone far enough for the day. *Done* enough.

But she still had water, and she still had the cool of the morning, and she definitely still had thinking to do—all the more so now—so she took the road away the store. Away from Lannie.

All the more because she wanted to ride right back to him—and that terrified her. After a lifetime of clutching tightly to independence from the Sentinels, it *more* than terrified her.

The breeze soothed her face; the sun beat against her back. She turned her collar up to protect the back of her neck and swooped along the curves, letting activity turn to meditation. Wondering how she'd have handled that man at the well construction site if she was as Sentinel as Lannie—and Regan, and her brother—seemed to think she was.

If she'd known herself the way that Kai knew himself, the way Lannie knew himself. If she *embraced* herself.

Maybe she would have understood what led her to the construction site. Or maybe she could have said what she'd felt to this man who'd beaten up Aldo and taken on Lannie. Maybe she could have prodded him into enough reaction so she could understand why he and his friends had done it in the first place—or at least offered Lannie some clues.

Maybe, if Holly had known more of her own nature, she wouldn't have been concerned about those men.

And she began to suspect that the answers she was looking for just might be found inside herself after all.

"Lannie?" Faith joined him at the sliding back door of the barn, looking out on the rise of ground behind the mules and fighting an unexpected yearning to lose himself in the woods.

He took a resigned breath. "What's Aldo done now?"

"Nothing," she said, with some evident surprise at the thought. "He's dusting the farrier supplies. And he's putting everything back where it belongs, too."

"Sounds serious." Lannie offered her a hint of a smile. "I know, Faith. He's not right. I'll call Brevis. We'll get someone out here to look at him."

"And you." Faith spoke firmly, her underlying trepidation evident but not stopping her.

He wanted to reach out through the pack link and reassure her...but he didn't have one. And he wouldn't be part of his home pack again until Holly was out of his system.

Excuses.

The hard truth was, he didn't know if he could have done it regardless. Even now he should have had some sense of Holly's location, an innate awareness. But when he even thought of it—

"And you," Faith repeated, more loudly this time. More firmly.

Lannie realized he was pushing fingers against his

brow, there where the static had settled. "Is Aldo alone in the store?"

She clamped her lips together, clearly biting back words. Finally she said, "You win. I'll go. *This* time. But maybe not next time."

Right she was.

Lannie patted his pockets, found the cell not there, and headed up to the loft through the building heat of the day, hoping Holly would read that cloud buildup for the promise it was.

The loft failed to yield the cell as well, though he found half a steak waiting for him and the dishes washed. He nabbed the landline phone—the store number, after a glance to make sure it wasn't already engaged—and dialed the toll-free Arizona number he knew by heart. Not just Brevis, but the Brevis field line for active operatives.

"Marlee Cerrosa."

"Lannie Stewart," he told her, knowing the caller ID would give her the farm store. "Descanso, New Mexico. Nick Carter is handling my op." As if Holly could be defined as a simple field op.

But she'd apparently been considered critical enough that the Brevis Consul himself was catching the calls on this one.

"Hold on," Marlee Cerrosa said. "Gotta forward you out to his place."

It took only a moment. "Carter."

"Nick. Lannie Stewart."

"Stewart. Hold on." Papers rustled; a keyboard offered up a brief tickety-tick. "Okay, go. I didn't expect to hear from you so soon after the hand off."

"Then you can guess that this isn't going to be good."

"She's not well positioned for this transition," Nick agreed, and left the rest of it unspoken.

Lannie didn't. "It's not about her."

Except that wasn't exactly true. It was entirely about her. It was just also about him. He growled under his breath, frustration pushing its way out—and just in time to hear a click on the phone line. "Faith. Get off the line."

"It's me," Aldo said.

"Then *you* get off the line." Another click, and Lannie almost apologized for the interruption—and then didn't. "The home pack," he said, "didn't have any chance to adjust to this one."

"No one did," Nick said. "What's the problem, specifically?"

"You know what the problem is. You knew what it would be when you set this up."

"Jody." Nick said the name with a sigh. "No one blames you for what happened to her."

"To *them*," Lannie said. "And I damned well blame me. I thought she was on board. I heard that song of hers so loudly, I didn't realize it wasn't truly part of that team. So I'll go right on blaming me until I can get some perspective. *Perspective*, Nick. If it's even out there to be found. I'm no good for Holly right now, and you know it."

Nick didn't hesitate. "You're exactly *good for her.*"

"Because I'm close to her brother? You can do better than that. It's too much, too soon—for both of us. She needs someone else to handle this." He gave Nick a moment to absorb that, and added, "Also, I need someone here to take a look at Aldo."

"There isn't anyone else to *handle this*. How urgent is the need for a healer?"

"Not critical, but the sooner the better. And if you send Ruger, he can take Holly with him. She respects Mariska—I saw it. They can give her what she needs. They can keep her safe and still give her space."

"So can you." Nick's words came without challenge, but without doubt. He, too, was alpha—if not as Lannie was.

Nick only *used* his nature in his work. Lannie was defined by it. Had never doubted it.

Until now.

"Not now, I can't." Lannie paced before his bedraggled collection of plants, along the edge of the sunshine, frowning at them. Were they...*greener*? "Maybe...not ever."

"What are you talking about?" Nick's tone changed, hearing the shift in Lannie. The reluctance.

"Something's off. Not Core—there's no official activity here, though there's a guy who smacks of Core you might want to check out—I'll send you some notes when I have a moment. Kai says no activity here, though." Lannie put a hand over his side, covering what had become an ever-present ache, a random snatch of striking pain. "It might just be..." Yeah, just say it. "Me."

Silence from Nick. A thoughtful noise. And, "You wouldn't mention it if it wasn't serious."

"No," Lannie said. "I don't want to be mentioning it now."

"Ruger, then." Nick tapped a few keys. "He's in the middle of something, but I'll tap him on the shoulder."

"And Holly?" Lannie couldn't help it, he swore. "None of this is her fault, Nick. She deserved better than this all along. What were you thinking, snatching her out of her life like that—and then splitting her from her family?"

"The first part was out of my hands," Nick said. Fair enough; consul for Southwest Brevis didn't mean consul for the world. "But she was in an area with an active Core posse—they didn't want to take any chances. As for the rest of it…do I really need to lecture you about how failing to disengage from existing pack interferes with the formation of the new?"

"You don't," Lannie said, the growl under his voice again, "need to lecture me. Period."

Amusement colored Nick's tone. "Sounds to me like your packing process is coming along just fine."

Because it showed. Of course it showed. Not that Nick didn't know Lannie's process by now, or how hard he could fall if he wasn't careful. "It's not in balance, Nick. And that's not the way it should be."

Nick made a low sound of assent. After a moment, he said, "I'll talk to Ruger about taking her. You're right about Mariska. She gave Holly a lot of respect in her report—even said she'd be glad to help further. But I have no idea how long it'll take to clear their schedules."

"Thanks," Lannie said, and meant it—even if he'd barely said it before he wanted to take the request back.

Maybe Nick heard it in his voice. "In the meantime," he said, "if it matters to you, then do what we alphas do best."

Lannie held his silence, too mixed up between head and heart to even know what that was.

Nick filled in the blanks with a certain unexpected ferocity. "Fight for what you want, Phelan Stewart. Fight for what matters."

One. Step. Closer. Holly's scent in his nose, in his

mind. *"But when there's something we want...really want..."*

Maybe it was time to learn what kind of alpha he really was.

Chapter 10

Holly dismounted the bike with a familiar stretch of muscle, swooping in on the barn while still balanced on the pedal and hopping lightly to the ground.

Aldo stood in the big black gap of the back door, looking out at the mules. "This time," he said, not looking at her—or at the mules, or even at the slope rising behind the barn. *"This time."*

"Aldo, you all right?"

He didn't answer. She frowned but left him, wheeling the bike to the store's back entrance and wrestling it inside with the efficiency of long experience, tucking it away to the side and hesitating in the hallway. The ride hadn't truly resolved anything, but it left her need for activity sated, her mind calmer.

Her body was fairly certain where it wanted to go from here. It hadn't forgotten being up in that loft, her leg wrapped around Lannie and her nerves gone golden with fire.

"You okay?" Faith stood in the hallway, cocking a quizzical head, her voice low enough to let Holly know she was, for whatever reason, lurking.

Holly recognized the same words she'd just posed to Aldo, and the same sort of tone. She laughed under her breath. "What do you think?" she said, giving Faith the benefit of the doubt by keeping her own voice low. "*Should* I be remotely okay under these circumstances?"

Faith offered an elaborate shrug, both far too young and far too wise for her actual years. "Dunno," she said. "This is the only place that's ever been okay for me." She peered out along the shelves, shifting to keep sight of whatever she looked at in the first place. "Poor Lannie. You've got him all inside out."

"I've got *him* inside out?"

Faith cast her a quick sideways glance, immediately returning her attention to the front of the store. "Do you know he took the *wolf* this morning? Right here in the store. I mean, only as long as it took to track where Aldo had put the bank bag, but…" She trailed off, shaking her head. "Right here in the *store*."

Holly had no good response to that. She bent to remove the twine from her pant leg. "What are you doing back here, anyway?"

"That guy," Faith said vaguely. "I'm watching that guy. He gives me the creeps." But then she smiled, more or less to herself, and not entirely pleasant. "Actually, any minute now I'm going to watch *Lannie* with that guy. He's off in the dog food section and here… he…comes."

Holly tried to imagine Faith hiding from *creepy* and couldn't quite do it. She eased up beside the young woman and found she had her own view of the man—a short figure of early middle age, his balding head shorn close and his chin somewhat inadequate for the rest of his face. His slacks and short-sleeved dress shirt were nothing out of the ordinary, nor was his expression or his demeanor.

And yet Holly understood why Faith had been bothered.

"Sorry about that," Lannie said, on his way from the dog food. "Just price checking…hold on…" He picked the phone up from the counter, his back to Holly and Faith. He spoke a few words to the waiting customer and then reached over the counter to drop the phone on its cradle with an ease that belied the awkward maneuver.

So it was easy enough to see how his shoulders stiffened when he finally looked at the man. And easy enough to hear his clear words. "I didn't want to talk to you over at the tavern," he said. "I sure don't want you in my store."

The man looked aggrieved. "Nor do I want to be here," he said, his words formed with the precision of a college professor. "Surely you don't still believe I had anything to do with the men who approached you that night."

"I think we don't look at things the same way and never will." Lannie strode to the door, pulling it open with an ironically cheerful jingle of bells. "Don't waste my time."

The man didn't move. "I'm doing anything but, and you are sorely trying my patience."

Lannie said, "Good." And waited by the open door.

Holly muttered to Faith, "I don't get it. Who *is* this man?"

"Dunno," Faith muttered back, an undertone of *shut up and listen* in her voice.

The man said, "You seem to have correctly surmised that I come from within the Atrum Core."

Core! Holly held her breath, scraping her gaze over the man—looking for the details that had alerted Lannie of his affiliation and finding nothing.

"But I'm not here for the organization. I'm here in spite of it, because I think—"

"There," Lannie said, abruptly interrupting, his patience quite suddenly evaporated and his stance shifting, ever so slightly but distinctly, in the way that now clearly spoke to Holly of the wolf. "That. The *thinking*. Stop doing it."

"I'm risking *everything*," the man said, a hint of desperation in his voice. He held out a scrap of paper. "Call me. Or have someone else call me. We need to work together. One of our East Coast labs was vandalized and—"

"Brevis will check it out." Lannie took the paper, moving a little closer to the man. "But we're done here."

"I knew it," the man said. "Too pumped with your own importance to—"

"—fall for your scheming?" Lannie jerked his head at the door. "Out. I'll let Brevis know you made contact. But I don't want you here. If I catch you bothering my people, I won't use words to get my meaning across."

"No fear," the man said, although in fact sweat dampened the back of his shirt, and Holly realized what it had taken for the man to walk onto Lannie's turf in the first place. "I won't likely have another opportunity to initiate contact. If you would only—"

"Out," Lannie said.

The man left, his movement stiff—with offense or

fear, Holly didn't know. Lannie released the door closed behind him, and Faith ran to the window to watch him go. "Shee-it," she breathed. "A Core minion, *here*!"

"Language," Lannie said, a rote reaction lacking the inflection to match his frown.

Holly emerged more slowly, stopping at the counter to give the man's car—now reversing from its parking slot to wheel around and spurt away—a puzzled frown.

"But why send him away?" She transferred her attention to Lannie, finding him grim. "What if he's for real?"

"Hoo boy, you really *don't* know anything, do you?" Faith sent an incredulous look Holly's way. "At least *I* know what I'm running from."

Holly recoiled from that derisive tone—and stood a little taller, felt a little stronger, took a step forward...

Lannie quite casually, and quite suddenly, stood between them. No taller, no more intense...just there. Alpha. Faith winced, and Holly took a breath, knowing she'd taken the intervention as the warning she'd needed.

"He might well be for real," Lannie said, as if none of that had happened. "But he's Core. He's working an angle."

Holly still didn't get it. Not really. "But...what if someone did break into one of their...*labs*...and now there's a threat from it?"

"We couldn't trust a Core minion," Faith said—a burst of words, as if she wasn't able to hold back. "And now Lannie will tell Brevis, and Brevis will find things out their own way."

"But...what could it *hurt*—"

Faith huffed impatiently, glancing at Lannie just to make sure she wasn't crossing the line he'd drawn. "You *really* don't get it, do you? Maybe you're here to learn to be one of them…*us*…but you're here to be safe, too. You think there's any way for Lannie to deal with this guy and do right by you at the same time?"

Holly's mouth opened in a little *oh* of understanding; she covered it with a hand, seeing the truth of Faith's words in her straightforward expression, and in the lift of Lannie's shoulder.

But Lannie didn't address it out loud. He said simply, "The man is here to manipulate us, one way or the other." He caught her gaze directly, all startling bright blue rimmed with black. "Besides, we already know something's up. So does Brevis. We'll be alert."

As if he'd dismissed it completely, he moved back around the counter, pulling out a clipboard with a neatly printed inventory list and tossing it on the glass toward Faith. "Aldo's been dusting. You know what that means. Find what he's done and fix it, before the Moores come in for those fifty bales of grass hay."

Faith groaned dramatically, scooping up the clipboard to head for the hardware section—clips and ties and hooks for stable gear.

"It hasn't ever been easy for her," Lannie said once she was engrossed. "Or for Aldo."

"Brevis knows exactly where they are, don't they?"

"Not because I told them," Lannie said. "But yes." He nodded at Faith. "Aldo isn't any secret, but Faith still thinks she's under the radar."

"I won't tell her any differently." She eyed him, taking in the underlying concern on his brow, some hint of…*something*…not quite hidden in his eyes. "You miss them, don't you? In your pack sense?"

"Yes," he said bluntly. "*All* of them." The very implacability of his expression told her just how much he hid with his matter-of-fact words—just how much of a price he paid for the work he did.

No wonder he didn't always answer his phone. No wonder he didn't accept silent communication—*in-trusions*—from those outside his pack. No wonder Mariska and Jason had deferred so thoroughly to him when they'd brought her here. It was about more than just his alpha nature.

It was pure and simple respect.

"I'm sorry," she said.

It surprised him. "It's not your fault."

"Still. It *is*." She took a deep breath. "I'm not about to make it any easier." She knew him well enough by now to know she wouldn't get a direct response to that—nothing so obvious as a question or demand.

And indeed, he only watched her, waiting.

"Can we talk?" She nodded at the back of the store—thinking of the land beyond it, and the privacy and clarity of being out in that space.

She didn't blame the flicker of wariness that crossed his face, but he only gestured for her to lead the way. "Faith," he said. "You have the register."

"Fourteen," she said loudly, plinking something heavy and metal into a box, and another. "Fifteen!"

Lannie grinned, unexpected and bright as the sun. "That's her way of saying she's on it." He led the way out the store and past the mule paddock.

Holly found she'd adjusted to the altitude, climbing the slope with less effort and more intent than before. The sun emerged from behind a fast-rising thunderhead, the heat stinging against her cheeks.

Lannie followed easily on her heels, making no demands of her until they passed through the first thick clusters of junipers and he made a *whuffing* sound—a grunt, a stumble, the scuff of a misplaced foot in dirt. By the time she turned, he was already on the way back up from that momentary fall, but staggering to a stop. Bent over his side, his hand pressed to that unnaturally lingering wound.

"Lannie!" Her cry of dismay surprised even herself as she reversed course to take his arm—not helping so much as being there *in case*.

He straightened, scanning the terrain as if to find an enemy lurking there. As if this had been an attack. A jackrabbit burst out of hiding from the nearest junipers and dashed away with great bounds of effort, skimming the top of the tall, clumpy bunchgrass.

Something about the bike ride had made her bold. She touched his face, there where the shadows of old bruises lay under the skin; she glanced at his side. "That's not right. It *can't* be right."

He made a disgruntled sound of agreement, still assessing the hillside; the sunlight stroked over the line of his cheek, the strength of his jaw.

Holly hesitated, and finally asked. "Do you think this healing thing is part of whatever that man was talking about?"

He turned to her, clarity of his eyes brighter than ever—the pupils like pinpoints, the rims dark and the overall effect more hypnotic than she wanted to admit. "There'd be more than just me if it was."

She managed to put an acerbic note in her voice. "What makes you think there aren't, eh?"

"Others?" He shook his head, glancing down at his hand with annoyance crossing his face.

"Right. Others. Don't look like that. How much have *you* told your vaunted Brevis about this kind of thing?"

From his brief grimace, no more than she suspected.

Still, he said, "I've told them enough." He patted his front jeans pocket, hunting and not finding, and let out an impatient breath.

"What...?"

He held out his hand, displaying a cluster of cactus spines. "Hemostats in the other pocket. Do me a favor and grab them."

"You want me to—?" She couldn't quite finish that sentence, her tongue too crowded with other words. "You *carry* hemostats? You fell on a—"

"—cactus," he said firmly, nodding at a disturbed prickly pear. "I run as wolf over this ground. I keep the hemostats on hand."

She eyed his jeans—comfortable, worn, and belted over hard hips and a strong curve of muscle—and then ostentatiously *didn't*, looking at the cactus instead. "I thought only natural materials traveled through the change. Cotton, linen, ivory..." Like the buttons of those jeans. Not that she'd been looking.

"There's always been a way to treat material so it can bring along small objects—knives, for instance."

"Or hemostats." The words came numbly. Strange how the small details were the things that got to her—reminding her how little she knew of this world that should have been hers.

"Brevis supplies the specialty clothes. Most of us mix and match."

"Your shirts," she realized. "They never go with you."

"Don't bother with 'em," he said. "Or shoes." He nodded at her. "When the time comes, we'll get you some basics."

Sudden panic flared. "I don't need your *basics*."

"You surely need something," Lannie said, matter-of-fact. "But you'd better decide just what it is, because at some point, *not deciding* will mean you get no choice at all."

She wanted to snap at him for that. Problem was, he was right. *And* he was reasonable. "Fine," she said. "Let's just deal with the cactus."

"Pocket," he reminded her.

"Fine," she said again. "Because that'll make what I wanted to talk to you about *so* much easier."

Well he should give her that wary look, and well he should stiffen slightly as she moved behind so she could slip her hand into his left front pocket.

"Initiation," she said, fingers sliding along hard, defined muscle, seeking thin metal.

"We talked about that already." His voice sounded pained. *Good.* Let him figure out that it meant something, this response between them.

It meant something to *her.* Along with the way she could feel the brush of his skin against hers even inches away, not even truly near touching.

She focused her thoughts. "We did talk about it. But I'm not done with the subject." She found and rejected a pocket knife sitting along the outside seam, spreading her fingers to invade more personal space. "You should be glad. Initiation was your suggestion in the first place."

"Not like this." His teeth were definitely gritted.

Fine. He'd put her in this position; the Sentinels had put her in this position. Forced to face choices and then forced to make them, even when the one thing she wanted was the one thing she wouldn't be allowed.

Let him deal with the consequences.

She curved her fingers slightly, scraping along sensitive skin through the thin material of the pocket. Wanting to touch him, practically able to feel herself being touched in return. Just his closeness grounded her, making the unfamiliar world more stable around her.

"Hemostats." He growled the word. The hand without the cactus spines clenched; his head turned just enough so she could see the flare of his nostril.

She found the business end of the things, fumbling in truth rather than as an excuse to touch him. "The thing is you're right. Without initiation, I'll never know who I really am. And doing it doesn't mean I can't choose to return to my life the way it was." *Or the way I can remake it, if I do run from here.* She extracted the small clamping pincers from his pocket and didn't imagine his sigh of relief, or her own regret at the loss of their brief intimacy.

She slipped around to face him, standing close again—taking note of how carefully he let his hands fall to his sides, how deliberately he prevented an even an accidental brush of skin. She told him, "But for all of that, if you think I'm going to let some stranger into my bed—"

His pupils had widened in defiance of the sun, darkening his eyes; his jaw had gone hard. "I told you—"

"You," she said. "It should be you."

"You don't even like what I *am*." He made the words hard, but she heard the note of desperation behind them.

"But I like the way you make me feel." There was more honesty in those words than she had intended. She touched his cheek again, tipping her face close to his—knowing he wouldn't retreat. "I'm not in your pack any longer, eh?"

He laughed, a dark humor she didn't understand. "It'll take a lot more than your say-so before you're out of my pack, even if I was never in yours."

She wanted to argue with him. She wanted to point out how much he obviously responded to her, that he obviously wanted her…whether he wanted *that* or not.

But it would have been no more appropriate than if he'd kept pressuring her. And he hadn't done that.

"Holly," he said, his voice scraping up from somewhere deep in his throat. Meant, she thought, to be a demand, but sounding more like a plea.

"I know," she said, and didn't quite step back. "Probably I should apologize. But you're part of this, no matter how little you had to do with getting me here. So if I'm trying to figure out the line between going after what I want and not pushing any harder than I want to be pushed myself…you're part of that, too."

"I know," he said, a deliberate echo of her words and sounding more certain of himself. Finally, he touched her—one hand coming up to finger the gleam of her hair before barely cupping the side of her head, his thumb brushing her cheek. "Trust me, I *know*. I wish—"

He stopped short; she opened her eyes to see that he'd lifted his head, looking over her shoulder. "Aldo. Go help Faith."

A muttered response came from the junipers. "Just… checking."

"*Now*, Aldo." And he waited, listening, as Aldo scurried off down the hill.

Holly hadn't moved. How could she, with his thumb brushing her cheek, his hand warm and a little rough and so very gentle…and with just the faintest sign of trembling. Alpha, not quite in control after all.

He kissed her temple, his lips pressing there a sweet moment longer than could possibly be called perfunctory. "We'll figure it out," he said, not so much taking a step back as setting her back with a mere shift of his weight. He held out his hand, cactus spines jabbing out from the base of his thumb—a request. "One way or the other, we'll figure it."

Right. But strangely, now that she'd so clearly separated herself from him, Holly wanted them to figure it out *together*.

Looking at the resolution in his face and the resignation in his shoulders, she didn't think there was much chance of that. She sighed, slipping her fingers through the hemostat handles. "Okay, then," she said. "Hold still. This is probably gonna hurt."

Lannie's hand still stung when he thought about it, but more than that, his body remembered Holly's touch. Responding to it, aching with it…wanting to turn on her and take her down right then and there.

Of course, he hadn't expected her to use her nails as she had. But it seemed that Holly, too, knew how to go after what she wanted. While Lannie…

Lannie wanted to know he was doing the right thing. For him. For her. And it was getting harder and harder to tell what that might be.

Their late afternoon outing wasn't distracting him nearly enough so far. It was an impulsive offering, one that meant leaving the store in Faith's hands—Aldo sweeping the aisles, Javi shifting hay around—and chivvying Holly into the truck.

He'd paid the conservatory attendant under an ever-glowering sky, and now they stood alone in the entry of the greenhouse—although Lannie hadn't quite expected Holly's awestruck response to the Desert Highlands Museum.

"I had no idea," she said, looking around the vast greenhouse, and through the glass to the grounds beyond where the native plants also lived outside in garden features. *"Here?"*

"It's a university thing," Lannie said, the warmth of her pleasure spreading to fill some of the empty pack space inside him. Not nearly all of it, but enough to matter.

Holly stopped to trail her fingers in the tiled entry fountain—a design of Spanish heritage and beauty, water trickling gently. She patted the water, watching the ripples…something in her expression relaxing in a way he hadn't yet seen. Although he hadn't reached for it—and now wouldn't presume to do so without good reason—the undertone of her mood came through in a simple, rich melody.

Her dossier said *water features*. He wasn't a hundred percent certain that he knew what a water feature was; he'd always just been glad enough to have *water*. "This is what you do?"

She laughed—that, too, came more lightly than expected. "Something like this. Smaller more than larger. But it's amazing what you can do with the corner of the yard, a little natural planting and a trickle of water." She looked out into the body of the greenhouse—a clearly sectioned structure with internal divisions. "It feels so strange not to know any of these plants. And for the water to taste so…*different*."

"Probably need to check our filter," Lannie said, with something of apology. He was used to the taste of things here—water hard enough to fight the softener. He'd installed reverse osmosis in the loft, but everywhere else it was just…water.

"Mmm, that's not it." She spoke absently, wandering to the first displays of the greenhouse and moving with that easy, rolling grace he'd first noted in her and from which he now found it hard to look away.

"Maybe," he said, "it's time to consider that you see your world with more than just a landscaper's eye. Maybe you see it with a Sentinel eye—and taste it, and feel it."

She hesitated, sharply enough so he knew she wanted to deny it.

And couldn't.

She looked away from him, off into the conservatory—a clear decision not to address his words. "I'll never absorb all this in one go."

Amusement colored Lannie's tone. "You don't have to."

"I probably do," she said, a bitter little note entering her voice. "Since I'm leaving."

"When Nick at Brevis can make it happen," he said. "Not today. Or tomorrow."

She paused before a display of the various native bunchgrasses of the desert, the scents of the place enhanced by the light morning watering. Realization lightened her expression. "I can reach this place on the bike!"

He couldn't help his reaction—a wince, a stiffening.

"Stop that," she said. "I'm perfectly capable—"

"Easy," he said. "I've seen your legs." Strong, lean and sweetly defined with long muscle. "I know you can do it."

She frowned, moving them along to a scattering of tightly furled primroses, each set in its preferred terrain and soil. "Then what's your problem?"

Blunt. Again. He didn't get enough of that. He found he liked it.

And he found himself unusually inclined to answer. "I couldn't find you."

She turned to him, walking backward in the otherwise abandoned greenhouse. Not a lot of traffic here on a stormy weekday afternoon. "Did you *look* for me?"

"Not like that," he said, not surprised by her misunderstanding. He loosely fisted his hand, touching it against his chest. *"Here."* He shook his head. "No one else has ever shut me out like that." No one else had ever been able.

Unless the truth of it was as he'd come to suspect— it wasn't about what Holly was doing.

It was about what Lannie somehow could no longer do.

And he'd started to believe that—he'd believed it when he'd told Nick that Ruger should come—except here they were, and here she was again. Right there, filling the center of him—brushing the edges of him where pleasure lived.

"Am *I*?" she said, stopping to look at him with what he thought held confusion. "Shutting you out?"

He wanted to touch her, and knew better. What he felt was merely an enhanced reflection of his packing process; what she wanted from him was something else entirely. Something transitory, and unclaimed.

He kept his hands to himself. "Not now. Now I can hear you loud and clear."

Give her that much; she knew he wasn't talking about her voice against his ears. "Hear me *how*?" she asked, reaching out to touch a brilliant penstemon and pulling her hand back at the last moment. Fire surrounded them, tall spires of scarlet and orange bordered with cool blues. "What's it like?"

What, indeed? He shook his head, helpless to convey the sense of it. "It's haunting," he said finally. "It's pack song. I've always heard it… I was heading for initiation before I realized that not everyone does. After that, it only got stronger. I had to limit myself."

"For your own sake," she said. "Pack song."

He never talked about this. *Never.* And yet he found himself closing his eyes to the desert blooms around them, pushing away the scents of damp soil, the sounds of the pending storm finally rumbling into thunder. "Pack song," he said, reaching deep...not filtering his words, as he always did. Not even thinking about them, but just thinking about the pack song. Being *in* the pack song. "It sounds like a river of music flowing through—" He flattened a hand over his sternum. "Here. It feels like the wolf's fur being stirred in the breeze. It's an endless whisper and it goes right through my heart."

"Oh my God," she said, her voice low. "You're a poet."

He jerked his inward gaze back outward, finding her eyes wide, the rich, radiating brown uninterrupted by so much as a speck of hazel, her pupils big in the shadow of low clouds glowering over the greenhouse. What had he even said? What had he revealed of himself, when he'd meant to protect himself from her? From *this*?

She must have seen that retreat. "Don't," she said. "Don't run away. This is important. I need to *know*. Is this what it means to you, being Sentinel? Is it what it means to Kai, and even to Regan?"

He hesitated. He tried hard not to run, not sure what he owed this woman. As far as his responsibility to Brevis was concerned, nothing. Not any longer.

But as Holly? As the woman who persistently touched him?

It's not real.

Except it was. It was real to *him*. "I can't say what

it means to them." God, he wanted to run. To close up and protect himself. He'd never felt more of a coward in his life, hearing the strain in his own voice. "But to me…yes. This is being Sentinel."

He didn't expect her heartfelt embrace as reply—her arms around his neck, her cheek pressed to his shoulder…her warm breath on his neck. No warning, and no way to stop his instant reaction, even as he held his arms out from his sides—half in helpless reaction, half in reflexive response. Eventually he allowed his hands to rest gently against the toned line of her back, fingers spread and barely even touching her—because if he'd allowed himself that, he'd have wanted more. *Taken* more, no matter how subtly.

She might have felt it in him. She drew back, looking up at him with a glimmer in her eyes. "Thank you for that," she said, her hands lingering on his arms. Thunder rumbled above them, louder than before.

He felt the touch of every finger. He felt her very presence, so close and yet again out of reach. "You're welcome," he said—barely managed to say, fighting a dozen impulses at once.

She reached up to brush knuckles across his cheek. "I'm sorry." Then she twined her fingers lightly with his in an unconscious, companionable way and looking ahead. "Oh, wha! Composites! And oh, look at the columbines—my favorite!"

"Composites," he repeated, allowing himself to be tugged along, oddly off balance by it all—the sweetness of her honestly effusive embrace, the tumble of feelings it brought out in him. Muted lightning sent a flash coruscating over glass, triggering the impulse to seek cover…except they were, of course, already there.

She glanced back, perfectly at home in the greenhouse environment and grinning with a true spark of humor. "Think of them as daisies and you'll be fine."

Indeed, the flowers in question were what he would have called daisies—all varieties of them, from tall, swaying coneflowers to tiny little white-petaled things hunkered in close to the ground. But he didn't watch the flowers so much as he did the pleasure on her face.

"My thing is the water features," she told him, again visibly resisting the urge to touch the blooms. "But I do love looking at flowers." She made a sudden sound of delight, breaking away to run to the niche ahead even as the first patter of rain hit the glass above them. "Oh, this is perfect!" She crouched beside the apparently natural flow of water over tumbled rock and the scattered plantings around it. "Just look at it!"

This time, she didn't stop herself from touching; she ran her fingers through the tiny pool at the base of the fountain and looked up at him. "Taste?" she asked as he halted beside her, not quite joining her on the bark path. "Do you taste your pack song?"

He couldn't help but smile at her unfettered pleasure in the fountain. "Not so far." *But I can hear you right now, more clearly than you can ever imagine.* A burbling, swelling song of relief and even a single clear note of joy.

She sighed, glancing up as the rain fell more steadily. "It's such a relief…" But she didn't finish, and just like that, her song fell away.

He should have thought twice—it wasn't his place any longer—but he didn't in fact think at all. Bereft of her presence, he reached out for her.

Static exploded inside his head, and—

"Shh," she said, and she was bending over him. *Over him.* Because he was face-planted on the fragrant chipped bark of the foot path. "There. Are you here again?"

Her hand soothed along his back, but noise thundered all around him and he had no instant sense of his surroundings, no sense of who might be where. He jerked upright, regretting it when dizziness clamped down— but not so much as he didn't rise as far as his knees, reorienting to the building.

"No one's here," she said, her voice a strange combination of matter-of-fact and concern. "With this rain, I think we're alone for the duration."

A flicker of light and the rumbling thunder to follow told him that the pounding din wasn't his, after all— merely the storm, bursting into maturity. But Holly's eyes were huge and worried, and he knew the matter-of-fact in her voice had been entirely for his benefit.

"What happened?" she asked. "This isn't because of *me*, is it? I haven't messed up your packing mojo?"

He sank back, sitting on his ankle with one knee upraised. "If you were that strong, you'd know it."

"Then what?" she demanded, frustration overhauling her worry. "Don't tell me this hasn't been happening since I got here!"

He didn't respond, because he couldn't tell her that. She'd been right earlier—whatever was affecting him had started the very evening she'd arrived.

Thunder crashed hard and close; Holly ducked, laughed at herself—and then glanced up. Awe replaced her amusement.

"Look at that," she said, lifting her face to watch the rain sheet across the roof glass. "Just *look* at that." She stood to it, stretching tall with every fiber of her being, head tipped back and eyes closed, shirt tight across her breasts and torso lean and reaching…as if she could touch the sky.

The song of her swelled right back into the empty spot inside Lannie.

"Holly." He couldn't help the strange note in his voice, the sudden impact of understanding.

He wasn't sure she'd heard him. "It's clean," she said, voice loud over the pound of rain, eyes still closed— completely unaware of his reaction to her. "It's beautiful. I was beginning to think there was something wrong with me, but that's not it, is it? It's this place, somehow…"

Not words that made any sense to him, but he tucked them away for later. "Sit," he said, putting a note of command in it. She looked away from the rain to regard him in surprise, a very clear expression of betrayal. *I'm happy,* it said. *Don't take that away from me.* He relented before it as her song faded. "Please," he said. "I…need a favor."

She sat, her expression a little wary. This time, when thunder crashed overhead, she did no more than flinch.

He said, "The way you felt just now, when you were…happy with the rain. Can you find that in yourself again?"

She sent him a cross look. "I'd still be there if you hadn't interrupted me." But he only looked at her, waiting, and she heaved a sigh and closed her eyes and—

Yes. There it was. Touching him. Reaching him. Rousing him. Making him want to reach back—with hands and mouth and legs entwined—

He drew a long, stealthy breath and made himself say, "Now…keep that feeling, but make it private."

Her eyes flew open. "Do what?"

He shook his head, running his fingers gently over

her eyes to close them again. "Don't think too hard about it. Just be in that place, but…privately. Close the door to that room."

She kept her eyes closed as his hand fell away, and shrugged. "If you say so…"

The song muted.

He moved closer, unwilling to shout over the rain. He leaned against the bench they'd eschewed and pulled her close so her back rested against his chest. "Now," he murmured in her ear, "open up again."

Pack song flooded him, taking him unaware—of course their touch would enhance it, of course it would take him so strongly, instantly rousing him to a yearning hardness.

And of course she couldn't begin to miss it.

She shifted away, and he caught her shoulders. "Never mind," he said, more harshly than he meant to. "Just…focus. Think about something else now. Think about quiet inside, and being totally closed in. A cave, a basement…whatever feels the most impregnable to you."

"Impregnable," she said, "is not a word you should be using right now."

He snorted, taken by surprise by that arch humor; his hands tightened briefly at her shoulders in appreciation. But… "Focus," he said, bending close to her ear. "See if you can—"

And then mourned the sudden internal silence, even as the rain beat the roof so hard it reverberated beyond thought.

"Good," he told her, not quite able to sound like he meant it. "Now just relax. Listen to the rain. Don't think, just…be."

"Why…?" she started, twisting to look at him.

He kept a firm grip on her shoulders, turning her to the front again. "In a moment. Just—"

She huffed out a breath and settled back against him, relaxing more quickly this time. He skimmed his hands down her arms to rest lightly at her elbows, and listened.

There she was. Not as loud, but just as clear. A deeper song, rolling within itself to take on a sensuous and twining rhythm. Her hands fell from their crossed position to rest along his thighs, sending an absurdly intense shot of pleasure straight to his groin. He swallowed what wanted to be a rumble of response, leaving her to explore her thoughts...her song.

Her breathing hitched slightly; her hair trembled against his face. Her fingers pressed more firmly against his flesh through the jeans, and her head tipped back ever so slightly, leaving her chest exposed, and her back faintly arched.

"I said," Lannie told her hoarsely, *"neutral."*

The rain faded to a steady patter, no longer a roar and no longer streaming rivers down the glass.

She came back to herself with a slight start, hesitating there—assessing. The pack song grew quieter.

But she didn't quite withdraw. And she emitted no sense of embarrassment, or regret. Her hands on his thighs felt more purposeful.

Lannie swore.

Holly made a sound of understanding. "Sitting like this isn't the choice I would have made, given what I'm asking and what you don't want to give."

But she wasn't unaffected. If he couldn't see her expression, he still got a glimpse of the high flush on her cheek, and scent the changes as she responded to him. She twisted, turning to face him, practically sitting in his damned lap.

"We want each other for different reasons," he managed to say. Barely. How had his hands fallen to her hips? Under what circumstances was it any kind of good that he'd tugged her a little closer? He already knew what would come of it—already *felt* what would come of it. "Not necessarily *good* reasons."

She narrowed her eyes at him, unaffected by a modest rumble of retreating thunder. The rain pattered more gently against glass, no longer coming down in flowing sheets. "See me unconvinced."

He found her ponytail, wrapped his hand in it... tugged it slightly. A censure, a warning...a touch he couldn't deny himself. The gesture did nothing more than light her eyes with defiance; he had a glimpse of a coppery tone in that brown before her mouth descended on his.

He thrust up against her hip without thinking and she bit down harder on her kiss, her fingers digging first into his arms and then into his back, twining through his arms so she could reach lower and pull herself more firmly against him, stroking them both with the motion and moaning into the delight of it, a sound that tingled along his skin and made him lose his breath in a short, startled huff. He broke free from her mouth so he could run his teeth along the side of her throat, finding a soft ear and the even softer hollow behind it.

The rain...the song...gripping fingers and nipping teeth...the enticing spiral of beckoning energy that came only from the lure of initiation—

Holly jerked back from him, her eyes bright, her lips moist and full. "What—"

"Initiation," Lannie said, or tried to say. He thought he'd put himself aside from her. At least that much.

At least enough to see it coming…and to head it off when it did.

He hadn't much counted on Holly. The woman who'd grown up in hiding, and who had the strength of spirit to know what she wanted—and to go after it.

Or him.

To have the strength of spirit to know what she didn't want, and to leave it behind.

The Sentinels.

And by default, Lannie. He who was so entangled in pack song that he would wither and die without it.

Lannie took a deep breath, finding his equilibrium again. Separating himself from her—only by a fraction of another inch, physically, but all the mental distance he needed. "Initiation," he said, with a voice that mostly maintained control, "is like that. It's why we're careful about the process. And why we train people to handle it."

"You're trained," she observed, still looking dazed—looking down at herself, looking at him—searching for something she evidently didn't quite see. "You said you'd done it before."

"I'm trained." He sat even straighter, regret for the distance it put between them. *Regret and relief.* "But sometimes it's not enough."

She touched her mouth, as if she expected it to feel different. She touched *his* mouth, and he somehow didn't nip gently at her fingers in a way that felt so entirely natural. Her brow furrowed slightly. "I didn't kiss because…because I *wanted* something from you."

"You're pretty clear about going after what you want," he said, keeping the censure out of it. "And you're pretty clear about *what* you want."

"I know." She acknowledged it with the twist of her

mouth, briefly biting at her lip. "But that's not what that was about. I didn't mean to…dammit…" She touched his mouth again, running a thumb along his cheek. "It just felt right, eh? It felt like something I should do. It felt like something you…wanted."

No doubt about that. "I did," he said. "That's the problem."

The problem wasn't having her. But what it would do to him if he lost her.

"And I'm still practically in your lap," she said ruefully, and tipped her head to look above. "The rain's slowing. Whatever privacy we had here—"

"I'll hear it if someone else comes in." He pushed his thumb between his brows, gathering his thoughts. Before she'd kissed him, before he'd lost so much control—

Ah. A deep breath. He met her eyes, finding them full of worry and an unfamiliar uncertainty. He wasn't about to make things any better. "I need to finish what I was doing."

She would have disentangled herself, pulling away entirely; he put a hand on her knee. "This is fine," he said. "I need you to be part of this."

She frowned. "Doing what?"

"Right now? Listening. Watching."

"I don't—"

Just do it. She didn't understand and she wouldn't understand. *Just do it.*

He reached for her. Not because he didn't suspect what would happen. But because he had to know. Not guess, in the wake of an incidental reach, but—

He didn't even have time for despair as the static erupted inside, the threat of internal lightning.

"—Lannie, come *on*—" and her hands groped his pockets. "Where's your *phone*—"

He didn't know how he'd come to be on his back, the scent of pungent bark chips again tickling his nose. He didn't care. He slapped his hand over hers as she tugged for access to his back pocket and the solid lump of the phone. "One more thing," he said. "I have to know—"

She barely had time for her horrified expression. "Lannie, *no*—"

He reached. Not for Holly, who had confounded him in so many ways already—opening herself to him of her own accord, demanding from him but not truly wanting—but for the pack he'd so recently left behind.

Lightning struck. Bigger than he was, searing through mind and soul. *Lightning...*

"Dammit—*let go*! You dumbass, I need *that phone*."

He made a sound in his throat and she stopped fighting him—sitting on him, she was, and somewhere along the way his hands had clamped around her wrists.

"Lannie!" Her words had a strange, tinny note to them, distant in their worry.

He made that sound again, the first and only response to come to hand. He didn't see her yet—more as if he wasn't bothering to see her. He hadn't yet figured out the rest of it yet. "What?" he managed, and his voice came out sandpaper.

She managed to tear away from him—if only to smack him a hard one on the shoulder. "Dammit! What did you think you were doing?"

Something tickled his upper lip, and trickled down the back of his throat. He rolled to his side, dislodging her, and spat, tasting coppery blood, and cleared his throat. "Being sure."

"Really? Because your *being sure* looked a whole lot like *being stupid* to me!" Her voice grew thick as she spoke. "God, you're a mess. It's like every bruise you had from that fight is right back where it was. And your side—!"

"It'll ease," he said, knowing no such thing. "I won't do it again." He got his elbow beneath him and pushed up, pulling up his shirt to dab at the nosebleed. Nothing more, just the same bloody nose he'd gotten from the fight that should have been long behind him instead of repeatedly coming back to haunt him.

"You'd better not!" She took the shirt from him, pulling it up farther to point. "Look!"

He made himself focus, not the least bit surprised to find the wound in his side—still short, still deep, still neat—again trickled blood. "It's okay," he said, and pulled himself back over to the bench, leaning against it. "I learned what I need to know."

"Right," she said, an acerbic bite back in her voice. "You're messed up. Surprise. You knew that. *We* knew that."

He shook his head, saying it before the impact of the words could stop him. "It means I've…" Who knew it would even be so hard to say. "I've gone pack deaf. What I've been hearing these past days is what you've been *offering*, not what I've been following."

She put a hand over his knee, her music gone so muted he could barely hear it—and suddenly it seemed so, so important that he could. That it should remain. He couldn't help a shudder, one that jarred every aching bone, every renewed bruise. He pressed a hand over the pain of his ribs.

"I don't understand—" she said, and then stopped to try again. "You mean…"

He made it easy for her. "Among other things—" *so many other things* "—it means the packing-up process isn't part of *this*." He simply snagged a hand behind her neck, pulling her in for a kiss—hard and possessive and unmistakable.

When he released her, she moved back only slowly, her tongue touching on her lower lip as if still tasting him. "You mean, the way you feel about me is…just the way you feel about me."

"Yes," he said harshly. "Just you. And me. As Lannie Stewart. Not as alpha."

She blinked, trying to absorb it. "But…that's good. That's simpler. That means—"

"Holly." He cut her off, his voice no less harsh, leaning forward to capture the back of her neck again—but this time to grab her attention. To make his point. "It means my pack song is *gone*. It means—"

I'm alone.

Chapter 11

It didn't matter that Lannie hadn't quite finished what he'd been about to say at the conservatory. Holly didn't need to hear it with her ears in order to know it in her heart.

I'm alone.

The bleak despair in his face, in his eyes…the way he'd turned from her to hide those things.

Or to try.

It hadn't worked. Holly had seen it then, and she'd seen it as he'd stood and held out his hand so they could put themselves back together and walk out into the breaking sunshine. She'd seen it back at the store where he'd taken over until closing, chasing Faith out when she would have questioned him—and she'd seen it in her mind's eye during the night's dreams.

Faith, it was clear, had seen it, too. And blamed Holly for it—her piercingly resentful look upon departure left no doubt.

It's not my fault!

It wasn't. She hadn't done anything except be here, and she hadn't even wanted that.

Except maybe if she'd handled *being here* with a little more grace, Lannie wouldn't have been so caught up in meeting her needs that he hadn't realized his own.

And boy, she'd expressed her needs. She wanted more than initiation; she wanted *Lannie*. She wanted the way he made her pulse pound in every nook and cranny of her body, and she wanted the way he evoked that sensation of unfamiliar emotional warmth—even as she feared it at the same time.

"Maybe it *is* my fault," she told the half-grown barn cat winding between her feet. Morning broke bright and early around her, not even a hint of a building thunderhead. She sat on an upended oval stock trough at the front of the store where the porch overhang just barely put her in the shade, working on the last of a yogurt cup with very little interest. "Maybe I could have seen it sooner, if I wasn't so hung up on my poor little self."

"Probably not."

She jumped; she hadn't expected that creaky voice. Aldo stood off to the side under the same overhang, when she would have sworn she'd been utterly alone out here.

He didn't apologize for her surprise; he more or less seemed to take it for granted. She reminded herself that this man, too, was Sentinel—no matter his age or his increasingly ragged nature. He said, "Lannie keeps to himself."

She gave him a sound of skepticism. "We're talking about the same Lannie? The one who holds so tightly to his packs?"

"Leading," said Aldo, "isn't the same as sharing." He

cocked his head, several days' of gray whiskers bristling around his mouth and chin. "Except with you, I think. So then, yes. Maybe so, after all."

She jabbed her spoon down in the yogurt container. "I don't follow that."

"I can't find my toenail clippers," Aldo said after a moment.

"I—" *Okay, what?* "I'm sorry, I haven't seen them." And all she did was look down at the cat in her arms, briefly rubbing her face against the top of its head. But when she looked up again, Aldo was gone just as quietly as he'd come.

"Holy wha! You are a strange man," she muttered under her breath. Inside the store Holly heard the sounds of the register drawer, the key in the door; a shadow lingered at that door, glancing out at her. *Lannie*, opening up for the day. She wasn't ready to talk to him, so she pretended not to notice.

And she kept her feelings, her mood, tightly to herself—winding them in as he'd so easily taught her the day before. A yellow SUV pulled in the lot and swooped around back with assurance, and the slam of the building's back door reverberated through to where Holly could hear it. Maybe they had a feed shipment coming in today.

Except that within moments, that same car swooped around front, parking sloppily before Holly. She recognized the gleam of Regan's golden hair just about the time she recalled seeing the little SUV in the cabin driveway, and came to her feet.

"Good morning," Regan said, emerging from the cheerful vehicle.

"Youbetcha," Holly said by way of greeting, otherwise pretty much at a loss for words.

"I beat the sunup today, and that's saying a lot at this time of year." Regan stretched, briefly exposing the sparkle of a naval piercing. She wasn't dressed for chores or painting this morning but in crop pants tied off just below the knee, a bright red bandana-print shirt and a pair of leather sandals that would serve on sidewalks but not on trails. "I'm heading into Ruidoso for some shopping, and I figured you could still use some stuff. Want to come?"

Holly came to her feet with an eagerness she hadn't suspected to be lurking—and stopped herself short. "Did Lannie put you up to this?"

"Pah," Regan said, wrinkling her nose. "It never occurred to him. He's a man and he has a pair of jeans. What else does one need, right?"

Holly laughed, relaxing. "I'd love to come. I have some clothes on the way, but I could use a thing or two besides."

"Something cute," Regan said, eyeing Holly's serviceable work clothes. "I know the best little consignment shop."

Holly nabbed the yogurt cup from the cat. "Let me tidy up a bit. I'll be right out."

"No rush on my account," Regan assured her. "I'll go back in and talk to your grouch."

"He's not mine," Holly said, halfway off the porch and pausing to give Regan a wary look. "But you'll end up talking about me, eh?"

"Probably. You confound him. That's not a bad thing." Regan grinned at her—a sunny expression from a woman who clearly assumed all would be well with the world in the end, and probably had no idea that Holly only waited for a transfer to Mariska and Ruger.

She certainly had no idea that in leaving, Holly would in fact leave Lannie alone. Truly, completely alone.

Nope. Because here came another smile, a knowing one this time. "Besides," Regan added, "it's only fair. You know you and I will talk about Lannie and Kai. We'll talk about them *lots*—and Lannie knows it."

Holly laughed. There was no doubt truth to that, too.

Though what had happened the day before—what Lannie had learned about himself, and what it meant to him—those things would stay secret. They weren't Holly's to share.

In the end, they talked mostly of clothes…and of Holly's work, to the point that Holly ended up blushing over expensive coffee and a warm apple-oatmeal cookie, surrounded by the charm of a rustic outdoor cafe. "I didn't expect to wax poetic over my work," she said. "Waterscaping isn't usually a hot topic."

"It's more interesting than you think," Regan said, glancing beyond their table's slanting umbrella to check the cloud status. "I think it's probably more important than you might think, too."

Holly stirred her coffee, a completely unnecessary gesture. "I don't follow."

"It took me a while, too." Regan rested her chin in her hand to regard Holly over the crumbs of her own cookie. "But the thing is, being Sentinel—even as little as I am—isn't something that changes what you are. But it *is* tied in to who you are."

"I *really* don't follow." Holly gave up on the coffee, leaning back in her chair to cross her arms—aware of the defensive posture and unable to defuse it.

Regan gestured at her. "Just think of what you do…

why you do it and how you do it. Those are your life choices, right? Now consider how *well* you do it."

And Holly thought about how she'd never had to advertise…about how she had more than enough clients, and how many of those clients came to her for modest jobs. People on careful budgets who had heard enough to make them choose a personalized waterscaping instead of new blinds or a newly topped driveway, not people who could choose one and still have the other. She thought of how often her clients remarked with surprise on the smooth progress of the job, especially when she was cleaning up after a previous installation. The thought about how the work energized her rather than sapping her.

And more, she thought about how she'd never been concerned to work as a lone woman bossing a crew of men—that she'd always felt strong and fast and capable, and they'd always treated her that way—even the rough ones. When they needed someone with sharp hearing to diagnose a pump issue, they came to her. When they needed someone with sharp eyesight in dim lighting, they came to her.

She'd taken those things for granted, just as she'd taken her ability to recover quickly after a few rugged days, or her ability to get through them in the first place. The perks of being young and healthy and inclined toward activity.

Regan watched her carefully, not bothering to hide it. "Being Sentinel doesn't *change* you," she said again. "It can enhance you, sure. But even without the Sentinel part of him, Lannie would still be a leader. Kai would still be a protector at heart. And I would still paint." Regan shrugged. "Of course, there's so little Sentinel in me that I didn't even feel any initiation effect when

I was first with Kai. I feel kinda cheated about that, if we're being honest."

"It seems to be a pretty big thing," Holly said, looking steadily at the wrought iron tabletop. "Initiation."

"Your folks arranged for Kai's initiation right before they took you into separate hiding. You were still too young for it, so…" Regan shrugged.

"Lannie thinks—" Holly stopped short on that sudden burst of words.

Regan didn't need to hear the rest. "What do *you* think?"

Holly spoke very carefully. "I think that Lannie's right in some ways. I can't make informed choices without it. And since there seems to be no going back…then I have to make those choices going forward."

"Uh-huh," Regan said. She leaned over the table, lowering her voice as a couple seated themselves nearby, and repeated herself. "And what do *you* think?"

Holly clamped her lips together, but in the end the words came out anyway. "I think I want to know just how well I can paint." She lifted her gaze to meet Regan's, knowing she'd gone fiercer than she meant to—and hoping Regan knew she wasn't talking about painting at all.

Just about *being*.

"Well, then," Regan said, and sat back, raising one eyebrow.

"It's not the same," Holly said, feeling a sudden flash of resentment. "It's not that easy. You had Kai. But Lannie…there's more going on…" She squashed a crumb with her thumb, quite emphatically. Just thinking about Lannie changed her body, making her intensely aware of the brush of clothing over her skin, the warm pounding of intimate pulse points. She shifted uncomfortably. "It's not that easy."

"It's never easy," Regan said, and something in her pale blue eyes kept Holly from asking what she meant by that—long enough for Regan to take a sip of her caramel-scented coffee and add, "First make the decision, Holly. Then figure out what to do about it."

Holly laughed out loud. "Is that all?"

Regan smiled, as if she was very much in on the joke. "That's all," she said. "And give me a call if you need anything."

"I need," Holly said, "someone to give Lannie Stewart a kick in the butt." It wasn't quite fair, and she knew it. But Regan laughed and Holly joined in, and it felt good to just be there in that space.

After that they spoke of more mundane things—making sure Holly had not just the basic shopping done, but a thing or two of luxury. Regan dropped her off at the feed store midday, promising to pass along a hug to Kai. Buoyed by the conversation and the company, Holly jogged up the loft stairs and fumbled around her shopping bags at the doorknob, remembering at the last moment that this wasn't simply her home, and that Lannie might well be there—

He wasn't.

She couldn't decide if she was disappointed or relieved. Mindful of her guest status, she didn't simply drop the bags on the bed—even if that, at least, was still hers to use. She quickly sorted through the purchases, pulling out the sunscreen and the black bike shorts, as well as a colorful short-sleeved bike shirt. The rest she tucked or folded away in a new overnight bag—Kai's treat, as it happened, because he'd pushed that cash into Regan's hand the day before.

Holly hadn't needed to ask why her brother had no credit card. After all, she'd been hiding only from the Core and the Sentinels, neither of whom had been aware of her in the first place. But all those years, Kai had been hiding from the *world*.

Except being found hadn't meant leaving his own world. It had, in so many ways, simply meant embracing more of it.

Holly shoved that thought away as unproductive, tugging on the new biking clothes and sighing happily at their familiar feel. She slathered on the sunscreen, finished tidying, freshened up and emerged into the main space of the loft.

There, she found the window area completely rearranged. The high sun lent only indirect light, leaving the newly reviving plants—a little watering, a little plucking, a little extra TLC—in perfect view in their more tightly clustered arrangement. And if at first she couldn't quite make out the unfamiliar jumble of shape and shadow off to the side, her other senses took over where her eyes failed.

The trickle of water, the clear, beguiling taste she'd perceived all along and simply not thought to investigate.

Because who, after all, tastes water from a distance?

"Me," she whispered, seeing then the artful arrangement of gleaming pottery, rounded river rock and copper foil. A fountain. Beautiful and unique and full of artistry. "I think…*me*."

Enough to know that this particular water had come from Regan's cabin, and that her new friend's visit here this morning hadn't been the least bit coincidental.

Sometime this morning, Lannie had gone out and

found this fountain for her—and he'd planned ahead to get just the right water for it.

Which meant that he, too, suspected that it mattered.

Holly crouched beside the fountain, taking in the details—recognizing the skill that had gone into creating the music of it. Almost without thinking, she tugged it closer to the center of the window area, shifting plants—tucking the fountain into the midst of them, and bringing fronds forth to fall over its edges of the fountain, a few bold leaves trickling into the water.

Then, quite matter-of-factly, she filled her water bottle at the RO faucet, scooped up the cell phone Lannie had once more left on the counter, and trotted down the stairs to retrieve her bike.

She had some thinking to do. Choices to make.

Because longing to go home wasn't a decision; it was a state of being. Worrying about her parents wasn't a decision. Aching for Lannie wasn't a decision.

Regan had been right. Before Holly could resolve any of those things, she had to decide what she wanted.

What she truly wanted.

Holly geared the bike up and pushed smoothly against the pedals, not sightseeing so much as immersing herself in the rhythm of the movement, the feel of the sun on her back.

She made it nearly all the way into town before the sight of a well house brought her up short. She pedaled slowly past it, straightening to prop on the center of the handlebars…cruising.

Nothing but a small building fenced off and tucked back into a cluster of squatty cedar and one towering piñon. And that taste…acrid and biting…maybe that was just the way the water ran in this aquifer. Maybe the particular rocks through which it had percolated, the particular piping that had been used…maybe the taint of old mine runoff.

She bent over the bike until she reached the nearby edge of town, where a visit to its little ice cream shop netted her a bathroom, a water refill and some excellent black cherry ice cream. She walked out of the place with a smile on her face, licking her fingers free of stickiness.

But as she approached the well house again, the pleasant aftertaste of the ice cream faded beneath newly familiar bitterness. This time, she coasted to a stop, putting her foot down for balance. Not just taking the taste in, but exploring it—reaching for it.

But only for a moment, during which she was almost instantly overwhelmed. She leaned aside, spitting the taste away and squirted water in her mouth for a quick rinse. The taste lingered, and she wondered, suddenly, if the privacy wall she'd so recently learned for Lannie would help…

Relief.

A car crunched gravel and came to a stop behind her. Even as she frowned at the faint familiarity of the vehicle, the driver emerged, making himself known.

The man Lannie called a Core minion.

Alarm spiked through her chest; she put a foot on the pedal, ready to push away—back to the safety of the ice cream shop, where she could call Lannie on his own phone.

"Please," he said, his voice holding its own urgency. "Don't go."

She glanced over her shoulder—he waited by the car, his hands spread wide and open. He said, "I need to speak to you."

"Step back, then," she told him, poised to go. "All the way to the trunk. And toss the keys out into those trees."

His mouth twisted wryly, but he did as she asked—smoothly, quickly…convincingly.

She regarded him with a critical eye, noting that his suit seemed less crisp, his demeanor less implacable. "I'm feeling just a little bit stalked."

"Pure chance," he told her. "I'm staying at the Descanso Hotel, such as it is." When she gave him a blank look, he said, "Across from the ice cream shop."

"So you saw me. It's still a little creepy. So talk fast."

"Twice I've tried to approach your friend," he said, taking her demand to heart. "It's true that our organizations haven't worked well together, historically speaking—"

"Historically speaking," she told him, "you suck. And your *organization* tore my family and my life into pieces. You sure you want to go there?"

He offered her a wry smile. "I simply wasn't certain how plainly I could speak."

"Plainly." She flipped a brake lever, letting it spring back into place. *Restless.* Wanting out of this place with its bitter taste. "Really plainly."

The man tugged at his suit, straightening it. "Excellent. Are you ready? Your friend Lannie Stewart is a hardheaded imbecile, but he's the only Sentinel I've been able to locate in this area. I presume that means he's the only active field Sentinel, which isn't unusual for the Southwest. I don't have time to find another. The materials stolen from our East Coast lab, in the wrong hands—"

"Blah, blah, blah." Holly put boredom into the words, hoping the man couldn't see how hard her heart was pounding. Not from fear of him, but from understanding that she played a game she had no business playing—one she truly knew nothing about. "No wonder Lannie didn't listen. Did you use this vague language of doom with him, too?"

"I hardly had the chance." The man eyed her with a sour twist to his mouth. "In an unfortunate circumstance, our mutual enemies showed up the first time I approached him."

"Wait, our what? When?"

"The tavern," the man said. "So charming. So many antlers."

"The ElkNAntlers," she said. "You were there. Right before the construction guys came swaggering through. But they weren't *looking* for you. Or for Lannie. They were just there, being drunk."

"Coincidence isn't so uncommon in a town of this size," he told her. "I see you from a hotel window. They see your friend Lannie at the bar. They didn't, I assure you, see *me* there—but then, they don't yet know that I have concerns about them."

She had the impulse to push off on that pedal and leave him behind. None of this made any sense, and talking to him...

It felt wrong. Like it might matter. And when it came to Sentinel business, she had no right to matter.

"They were just assholes," she said bluntly. At the bar, at the construction site. "Not East Coast thieves."

"Likely so." The man smoothed the front of his suit—*again*—and she came to realize that he was more than fussy. He was nervous. And not because of her. "Layers, my dear Sentinel. Layers."

"I'm *not*—" She stopped, rearranging her thoughts... changing what she'd been about to say altogether. "I'm not interested in this conversation. You still haven't told me what you want from me—what you want from any of us."

"Just for you to know. Our own private version of kryptonite is on the loose, and not nearly enough people *know*. If you and yours are smart, you'll do something about it. You should realize that none of my people are yet so inclined—they foolishly think this situation might play to their advantage. But they haven't seen the results in the field—" He shook his head. "There are many reasons I haven't invoked any of my significant number of personal workings since I got here. Being detected by *your* people is the least of it."

"So I'm supposed to convince Lannie that your threat is real."

The man offered her a faint sneer, his first true discourtesy. It ruffled her more than she expected. This man was, under any other circumstances—maybe under *these* circumstances—her enemy. A man who would readily do her profound harm, and who had the means to do it.

In contrast, what the Sentinels had done…what *Lannie* had done…

Suddenly felt entirely different.

The man said, "Convince him or not, the threat remains. So far they're just playing with the substance—testing their process of spreading it into the world. Don't tell me you haven't felt it."

Maybe she had. Maybe they *all* had…

The man's gaze turned sharply to the well house—a much more modern thing than the one on Lannie's property, with faux stone construction and a tall gated fence set closely around them. Holly saw it then—a security camera. Not the least bit out of place on this sternly official site, especially given the high use of this tiny parking area—never mind the discarded condom that was evidence of the favorite activity here.

The man said, "I should have known. Get out of here. Do it *now*." He ran to the cluster of trees, kicking through the sparse grasses to hunt his keys.

"Really?" she said uncertainly. "It's just the town's security system. They probably don't even look at it unless there's been trouble."

"Go," he said, dropping to his knees with a curse, risking his hands in the sticker-riddled ground cover. "If your friend has an inclination to talk, he'll find me."

Uncertainly, she lifted herself over the pedal, pushing on…looking over her shoulder at him, and catching a glimpse of movement on the street—a big SUV, silver against the sun and moving fast on the way out of town.

No. Surely not.

This was only a well house, for Pete's sake. It was a conversation by a well house with an innocuous-looking man at the edge of a sleepy, artist-filled Southwestern town where she'd just had freaking *ice cream*—

And a silver SUV accelerating toward them at ridiculous speeds, until Holly finally jammed her foot down on the bike pedal, flipping gears to cycle up into the fastest possible start and desperately hunting a trail from which she could leave the road.

Because yes, the vehicle slewed to a stop behind her and a door opened and slammed, and yes, the engine gunned again and gravel spat. The car came swooping in from behind, pacing her for a long, heart-stopping moment—

And then gently bumping her off the road.

There was nothing gentle about her landing—the bike tossed her like a wild thing, and while padded leather half-finger gloves saved her palms, nothing saved her from the impact, the roll and the bounce and the final skid into spiky grass and a cloud of dust.

She was still hunting her first breath when a hand grabbed her by the upper arm and hauled her upright, setting her on her feet once—and then when her knees promptly buckled, once again.

This time she kept herself there. "What is your *problem*?"

By then she could see the beefy man who'd dug his fingers into her arm. His neck was thick, his scalp shaved and sketched with precise tattoos over and behind his ears, and his expression was nothing but annoyed. "You shouldn't have run."

In retrospect, she should have just ditched the bike and taken to the grasslands. She could have outrun this one, surely, with her long-distance legs and his bulk.

Maybe she still could.

He shook her, rattling her teeth. "Cooperate." He yanked the vehicle door open and tossed her inside. She scrambled to clear her legs out of the way before he slammed the door, and he made it around to the driver's side faster than she thought he could—before she could so much as untangle her legs and make another break for it.

He shifted into Reverse and grabbed her ponytail, yanking her head down to the center console with such a sharp tug she had no chance to resist. "Wha! Ow!"

He deftly reversed the car to the well house, tucking them into the little parking zone and bumping up against the weaselly man's car with a solid impact. Holly tensed, ready to burst free of the front seat and out into the junipers—

The man cupped her head in one huge hand and bounced it off the dash, sparking fireworks against darkness in her mind. By the time she could see again, blood trickled down from inside her brow and her captor had jerked her door open to latch his meaty grip around her wrist. Her kicking and flailing didn't so much as slow him down; he sent her pinwheeling into the hard-packed dirt. She sprawled at the feet of another man—and found herself staring inches from pained gaze of the weaselly Core minion.

She rolled away from them both and came up to her knees—but at the sight of a gun, she hunched slightly and held both hands out in capitulation. "Okay, *okay*." Though she couldn't help but glare. "What is your *problem*? Do you really think no one is going to notice this?"

Only then did she realize that they were behind the well house, hidden by two vehicles and a screen of junipers. The man stood by the truck with his arms crossed and a smile that spoke for itself.

The Core minion started to sit upright, but a foot on his shoulder pressed him back down again. Holly took a second look at him, found him more battered than she'd first thought—his tidy suit coat torn and smeared with dust, his arm over ribs that must be broken and one eye already puffy and closed.

The other man from the silver SUV had worked fast. No hesitation, no mercy.

"She doesn't know anything," said the Core minion, and Holly stopped thinking of him as weaselly.

"She knows enough to talk to you."

"No," said the minion, somehow inserting a patronizing patience, "*I* knew enough to talk to *her*. And it's been a waste of my time."

"I *don't* know anything," she said, echoing the man who'd suddenly become her ally. Sweat trickled down her back; gritty dirt stuck to the road rash on her arms. "I don't even belong here."

The man with the gun didn't even bother to look at her. He jerked his head at his companion. "Deal with her."

Fear struck deep inside at those hard words. "No," she said. "No, you can't—"

They could. They would.

Holly reached past the dread and put life into her legs, pushing off in a desperate sprint for the road— the road and some witnesses and the benign little town of Descanso.

The beefy man snagged her arm and slung her around against the SUV grill, a slamming impact. But unlike the last time he'd caught her, she wasn't stunned by circumstance and she knew exactly what the stakes were. Even as her vision grayed from the impact, she rolled aside; she found her teeth bared and her fingers clawed and she slashed at his face when he grabbed for her. It gained her a fraction of space and again she lunged for the road.

But when the man cursed, it had nothing to do with her and everything to do a fast approaching truck engine and the skid of rubber on hot asphalt—her hesitation allowed the man to catch her up, cruelly impersonal hands in personal places, and toss her back behind the vehicles. He crouched at the fender of the SUV with his gun in hand, aiming—

Lannie's pickup truck slewed across the road and into the parking area. *Lannie! How—?*

The beefy man squeezed a calm trigger, popping gunfire into the sudden silence. The truck's windshield cracked spiderwebs of glass as the truck door opened and Lannie rolled out, coming to his feet shirtless and fierce and without hesitation. Another shot and he jerked without slowing; a third and Holly saw the impact, saw the blood already streaming. She clawed her way back to her feet and rammed her shoulder into the beefy man.

It was like hitting the SUV itself.

But his next bullet went wide, and he snarled something and shoved her hard. She sprawled, ungainly, and lifted her head in time to see Lannie coming on strong, his eyes piercing, his intent unmistakable...the *wolf* unmistakable, as human as he remained.

The man's nerve broke; he hesitated an instant too long and Lannie was upon him—Sentinel speed, Sentinel strength, Sentinel grace. From behind her, men grunted with effort, scuffling...another gunshot rang out and another curse, and then the second man ran past, yanking open the driver's door of the SUV.

All while Holly flattened herself out of the way, dazed disbelief at Lannie's speed and his strength replacing her terror. *Is this me? Could this have been me?*

A startlingly wry chuckle broke through her focus—the man from the Core, closer than she'd thought. She spared his battered face only a glance.

"You see?" he said, and she wasn't sure what that meant.

Lannie's opponent hit the ground with a jarring thud and Lannie pounced on him, hand gripping that thick, muscle-bound throat with the strength to rip flesh, closing around the man's windpipe with fingers gone white.

The SUV started, revved—shifted gears and bumped forward. Holly opened her mouth to cry a warning but Lannie already saw it—the bumper, coming his way with wheel-spinning acceleration. He sprang away, rolling—coming up with blood streaming across his chest, a snarl on his face, his eyes nothing like Holly had ever seen before.

And she'd thought him laid back. She'd thought him remarkably self-contained. She'd thought him more...

Human.

The passenger door opened and the beefy man crawled around to it, his face florid, still choking for breath. The moment his trailing foot left the ground, the other man jammed the car into Reverse, cranking back into the road with no regard for anyone else who might be on it.

The engine roared away, and silence settled around them.

Silence except for Holly's panting, Lannie's sudden exhalation...the Core minion's groan.

Holly pushed herself off the ground, suddenly aware of a thousand discomforts—the sweat in her eyes, the grit sticking to her skin, the road rash...the bruised bone and wrenched muscle. She swiped the back of her hand over her brow, smearing away sweat, and took a breath...deep, stabilizing.

"You okay?" Lannie asked, his voice rough. He knelt in the dirt, sitting back on his heels with the wariness of a man who was only just then beginning to feel—

"Oh my God," she said. "You're shot. You're shot *twice!*"

"Hell if I'm not." He looked down at himself, at the slightly pulsing flow of blood from the wound in solid muscle high to the side of his chest, and to the dark, obscene hole low over his hip, now hardly bleeding in spite of the clear trail already soaking the waistband of his jeans. The old knife wound again lay under an X of tape. "Hell," he said again, more fervently.

The man from the Core laughed, that wry sound

again. "Hurts to be the hero, doesn't it? Maybe now you'll wish you'd listened to me."

Lannie narrowed his eyes at the man, the wolf still glimmering behind them. "Maybe now I *will*."

"No, I think not." Something in his voice grabbed Holly's attention—she turned to him, and lost her breath all over again.

The wound in his chest had already soaked his shirt and left a trickle of bright froth at his lips.

"Don't take me the wrong way," he said, his breathing shallow and jerky. "I think your people are a menace. I'm not sorry to have worked against you all these years. But this…one…time…" He paused, and Holly wasn't sure he would—or could—continue. She resisted the urge to put a hand on his shoulder as she crept closer. He caught her gaze, just for an instant. "I think…we should have…*kryptonite*…"

"What?" She did touch him then, shaking his arm just a little. "If there's something we should know—"

"Holly." Lannie's voice came grim, and then again. *"Holly.* Best get away from him."

"He's dead," she said, realizing it. "He knows stuff we need to know, and he was only trying to talk to me, and now he's *dead*."

"And we'll deal with all that, but right now you need to get *away from him*."

She turned on him, suddenly furious for every possible reason, including the way he'd so casually run into the face of gunfire.

Although in truth, there had been nothing casual about it.

"Get away from him *why*?" she snapped. "Because he'll self-destruct? Don't you think he deserves a little

consideration? And what about the cops? Didn't anyone even *notice*—"

But she broke off, because the man had wiggled just
a little. Had...squirmed. She jerked her hand away, wiping it on her bike shorts even as his body made a disturbing shift—seeming to grow, seeming to shrink.
"Oh," she said. *"Oh."*

"They do that sometimes," Lannie said, his voice as
gritty as Holly felt. "When they're working alone, and
there's no one else to clean up after them."

"Holy wha, *why*?" She couldn't keep it from becoming a cry as she scooted away from the man, watching
him bubble and boil and writhe and...

Disappear.

Lannie said, "That's why."

She hadn't intended to whisper, but it came out that
way somehow. "Was that a Core working?"

Lannie moved as though to rise, grunted in pain, and
stayed where he was after all. "It was," he said, sounding strained. "Did you feel it?"

"I—no. What?" She knew she sounded like an idiot,
was suddenly too dazed to care.

"Some of us can feel those things." Still strained, his
breath catching, he added shortly, "It doesn't matter. We
need to get out of here. Can you drive?"

"But..." She looked at the empty space where the
man had been. Even the bloodstains were gone from
the thirsty dirt. "Won't someone miss him?"

"He was working on his own. Sooner or later, his
people will figure it out. Holly, we need to—"

She turned on him. "You should have listened to
him!"

"Maybe." He bent over slightly, his mouth tight.

"But my responsibility is to the pack. To *you*. Can you drive?"

She looked at him sharply for the first time since his arrival—seeing for certain that he no longer bled. Whatever affected his side, it clearly hadn't affected his ability to heal these terrible new wounds. "What are you even doing here? How—"

He laughed, though it carried a grating sound. "You called me. The moment you came across *him*." He nodded at the spot where the man from the Core no longer existed at all. "I was well on my way by the time you met up with the others."

Not Core. Not Sentinel. Outsiders.

"Holly," he said, and this time he made it to his feet, staggering a step to sway there. "The keys are in my truck. Get behind the wheel before someone stops to see if we're all right."

She did more than that. She spotted a handgun by the edge of the brush and rose to snag it up—unsteadily at first, but regaining her balance along the way. Knowing that like Lannie, her aches and pains would disappear more quickly than usual, if not at the rate of his.

So for now, she'd do what she'd seen Lannie do—ignore them. She dusted herself off and grabbed the gun, handling it gingerly as she stuck it under the seat. By then Lannie had made his halting way to the passenger side of the truck and seemed stalled there in spite of his urgency. She reached across the seats to extend a hand.

He gave her a sharp look, something unexpected rising behind his eyes once more—a challenge from a man who wouldn't be patronized, and from a Sentinel whose nature wouldn't allow weakness. Something in her expression must have satisfied him. After a moment, his hand settled in hers—firm, sticky with his own blood and warmer than she expected.

She didn't pull him up so much as she held herself steady against his weight—but when he settled into the truck seat, he tipped his head back against it with his eyes closed, his face paled, and she took liberties. She reached across him to finish closing the door and then to fumble at his seat belt, clicking it into place.

She hesitated there, studying him. Trying to see if she could discern where the man ended and the wolf began, and why that wolf so suddenly seemed clear to her.

Maybe it was him. Maybe...

It was her.

The sweat along his brow had dried; his face had regained its normal tanned complexion. The straight, strong lines of brow and nose and jaw stood out strongly in this light, his mouth tense but still well defined. The sudden faint flare of nostril should have warned her— his eyes opened, staring straight into hers with an impact that made her flinch. Clear, light blue rimmed with indigo, the pupils tight against sunlight.

The wolf crouched there.

Holly abruptly dropped back into the driver's seat, clicking her own seat belt into place and reaching for the keys. She cranked the truck around and pulled out onto the road, straightening up to speed just as another pickup approached town, the driver lifting his hand in a friendly acknowledgment. And just like that, Holly drove away from violence and death.

Her mouth still tasted bitter.

Chapter 12

Lannie blocked the pain with anger, ignoring his blood smeared around the white porcelain sink and the scatter of stained towels, the tub of open salve.

Already his flesh healed, just as it should. The lower wound was a through-and-through, a clean, high-speed round. The upper wound had been a bullet lodged in muscle against a high rib.

Had been.

Now that chunk of metal rolled from his fingers to clink beside the cold water faucet. Lannie closed his eyes and leaned against the sink and swore a lengthy litany, knowing himself pale, his limbs watery and his heart pounding.

But it wasn't hard to dredge up the anger.

I should have known.

Whatever had broken in him, however it had broken, it had left Holly open to a danger he'd only been

able to resolve with luck and brute force. It left *all* of
his people in danger—unable to count on him to back
them up unless they could do just as Holly had done
and instinctively send out their own clear cry for help.

If I she hadn't called out...

A soft knock sounded at the door, followed by a hesitant query. "Can I help you in there?"

Holly, awaiting her turn at the sink and the salve.
Ugly road rash, ugly bruises and not nearly enough
awareness of how much worse it could have been.

No wonder Kai hadn't been able to sense any Core
presence. The only man here had been running truly
silent. And they had an enemy, all right...

They just had no idea who it was. Or why.

You should have listened...

Except he'd told Holly the truth—his responsibility,
his deepest instinct, was to protect his pack. Not the
larger pack of Southwest Brevis as a whole, but his very
own people. And he'd warned Nick Carter that something was going on here. He'd already asked for help.
He'd even emailed the little man's contact information.

Now he'd have to face the truth that he couldn't protect his people as they deserved to be protected—as
they counted on him to do, whether they realized it
or not.

Never mind that Holly wasn't officially *his* any longer. She damned well *was*.

And she was all he had.

"Lannie?"

"I'll be out—" He cut himself off. He didn't mean
to sound so harsh. He wasn't used to fighting his wolf
back; he wasn't used to being broken. He took the snarl
out of his voice. "I'm fine." *Liar.* His fingers curled

around the edge of the sink as if they could dig right into the porcelain. "I'll be right out."

He lifted his head, forcing himself to meet his own eyes. Seeing the wolf there, and knowing how close to the surface it ran—how hard it would be, now, to keep the wolf running quiet.

Because being alpha was indeed about fighting for what the wolf wanted. And right now, the wolf *wanted*.

So many things. So many ways.

Holly.

His eyes gleamed back at him in the mirror, his features in no way relaxed. He took a careful breath, pushing himself upright against the fiery burn of healing wounds—pushing the wolf away.

For now.

He opened the door and gestured Holly inside. "Don't mind the mess. We'll get it later."

But he found her already nominally cleaned up— her face washed, the embedded grit gone from her road rash, her clothes wet and her expression uncertain. "I used the mules' hose," she said, and then added in a more normally wry tone, *"Refreshing."*

He couldn't help a small snort. No doubt, as that spigot ran only cold water.

"You look…" She eyed him up and down, a gaze that made his skin feel tighter than normal. "Wha! You look a lot better than I expected."

"Don't ask me how I feel," he said, meaning to keep it light, but failing. Damn. He grabbed up the jar of salve and held it out for inspection. "Here. This is Ruger's. Goldenseal, comfrey, mesquite…" And whatever mojo he put into the stuff. "It won't take much."

He wanted to offer to do it for her. He wanted to put

his hands on smooth skin and tend her hurts, and then he wanted to tend *her*, and to make her truly his own.

His hand wasn't quite steady as he gave her the jar. She flashed him a look as she dabbed her finger into the thick salve, looking down at herself as if she wasn't certain where to start. Finally she moved past him to flip the toilet lid down and sit, putting the jar on the side of the tub and choosing a spot along her elbow. When she spoke, her voice was carefully neutral—as if he didn't still loom in her space in this small room, not quite able to make himself back away. "The bike's in amazingly good shape," she said. "It really didn't do anything more than fall over."

"I'm not worried about the *bike*."

She found a scrape on her lower leg and smoothed the salve over it, more assertive with this lesser wound. "Well, I was. But now I'm not." She glanced up at him. "You give me crap about taking more bike rides and I'm out of here—you won't find me if I don't want you to." She glared up at him. "I won't be caged."

The wolf rose instantly to the fore, and Holly just as instantly stood to meet it, glaring back at Lannie from well within striking distance.

Striking, or...

The wolf growled within him, pushing him into instinct. *Want her. Take her, if she'll have it.*

He pushed back, finding it harder than it should have been. "Earlier, you asked about Jody."

She looked up in surprise, hand lingering on the outside of a sleek, toned thigh. "Right, and you didn't answer."

"I wasn't ready to." He leaned on the sink, simply because it suddenly seemed like a good thing to do.

She straightened, the salve forgotten. "And now?"

He reached past the turmoil of a wolf fully roused—protective, wanting…lonely and more needy than he could remember. "Jody came here with her team. They weren't a front-line team…but she was a front-line Sentinel. Or thought she was."

"She didn't play nice?" She tipped her head, curiosity betrayed.

"She had no patience for it." He watched her, catching the copper brown of her eyes—not so much holding her gaze as looking for every nuance of her response. "She had no patience for *them*. And at first she had no patience for the packing process, but—"

Understanding lit that gaze. "You connected with her. But…it wasn't real."

"It's never *real*," he said shortly. "At least, it's never as real as it feels. I know that. I know how to manage it. How to protect both sides from it. Or I *should*."

Her eyes narrowed, lashes shadowing them to darkness. "She used you."

The words startled him. "She fooled me," he said. "When she shouldn't have been able to. I thought I'd gotten through to her—that she'd embraced the need for teamwork. Turns out she hadn't."

"She *used* you," Holly repeated without hesitation. "She did what she had to in order to get what she wanted. Your approval. So what happened? You signed off on them, and she went out there and got everyone hurt. Or killed. Right?"

"Yes," he said, taken off guard. "She did. They all did. It was stupid and senseless. She wasn't ready and I should have known it."

She made a rude sound in the back of her throat and set the salve aside. "She *used you*," she said, as if she would get through to him a third time. "She wanted what she wanted. I bet she knew about the pack effect thing before she even got here. I bet she played you from the start—you never had a chance to hear her true song. I *bet*—" And she broke off, maybe a little startled at her own ferocity.

Lannie certainly was.

Not to mention his surprise at the effect of her words. The wash of relief.

Holly's expression gentled. "You never even considered that, did you?"

"No," he admitted. "But..." The teams with which he worked were vetted by the time they reached him. They met a certain criteria—they had the need, but they also had the potential. They had to earn the chance for redemption.

But Jody's team had been rushed. They had come in on the heels of a recently completed assignment, when Lannie had been reeling from the transitions. They had been an exception.

Maybe she saw it on his face. "Someone might have failed," she said. "But I don't think it was you."

He couldn't quite breathe. Not from the pain in his side or the faint tilt of the room around him, but just because his body seemed frozen, unable to absorb that single twist of thought.

And then he drew a sudden deep lungful of air, and another.

"Not," she said, and put her hand over his where it rested on the sink. "Your. Fault."

He flipped his hand over to capture hers. "It doesn't matter," he started, but she was having none of it.

"It *does*," she said. "Look what it's done to you!"

He hesitated and tried again. "It's *okay*," he said. Or it would be. "But that's not why I brought it up."

She frowned, and might have withdrawn her hand if he hadn't gently squeezed her fingers. Not so much as to trap her, but enough to surprise her, making her hesitate.

"I wasn't ready to trust myself," he said. "Damned sure not ready to trust the way you make me feel."

"Because you thought it was same old same old," she said cautiously. "*It's not real.* I heard you. That first time, there in the store. I just couldn't understand it."

She'd heard him.

One of these days, she wouldn't come as such a surprise to him.

Maybe.

He said, "I still had my pack sense then," and shrugged. "I'm not sure when it started to fade, or how fast, but I had it *then*. I wasn't taking any chances."

She stood, raising her head to meet his gaze—to hold it, as he'd been holding hers. "Now?"

"You know about *now*. You saw what happened at the conservatory. I have no pack, not any longer. No pack sense. What I feel for you is just what I feel for you."

One step closer; her breath trembled against his neck. She opened her mouth—and snapped it closed again, blinking, at the knock on the loft door.

Lannie didn't have time to so much as draw breath before the door opened and Aldo slipped inside.

"Lannie," he said, his voice a hesitant creak. He didn't even appear to notice what he'd interrupted; he had eyes only for Lannie, and an unhesitatingly sharp gaze at that—checking wounds old and new. "I need to talk to you."

Lannie grit his teeth, his jaw working. "Aldo. *What*?"

Aldo pushed the door closed behind him, so carefully, and came only a few steps into the loft. "I thought it was the pot," he said. "Because of how much. I've been spending a lot of time at that well house lately."

Lannie had no patience for riddles. "Spit it out, Aldo. Start at the beginning this time."

Aldo cast Holly a cagey glance, as if noticing her for the first time. "Maybe," he said, letting the word hang a moment, already groping behind him for the knob, "I should come back."

Lannie rode a renewed spurt of impatience all the way to the door, stiff-arming it closed over Aldo's shoulder and holding it there to look down at the smaller man. *"Aldo."*

Aldo snatched his hand away from the knob and held it out in front of him in exaggerated supplication. Lannie glared, hearing Holly's faintly uneven breathing behind him.

Finding himself unsuccessful, Aldo straightened; he became himself, and the remaining anxiety around his eyes was as honest as Lannie's anger. "I've been losing things lately, Lannie."

A few heartbreaking words, summing up the changes they'd all seen.

Lannie's anger drained away. He dropped his arm. "Yeah," he said. "I know."

"I'm not all that smart, maybe, but I'm *clever*, you know?"

Ragged in clothing, ragged in his hair and random with his shaving, Aldo was more than clever. He was, in his own ways, brilliant. He had just never been *wise*.

But Lannie didn't argue the point. He knew what Aldo meant to say. So he only repeated, "I know."

"The way things have been with our people these past few years…the ones we lost…you know we all felt those things. We all knew *someone* who didn't make it…"

"Yeah." Lannie spoke with understanding, but without excess. He didn't want to go there in front of Holly—the difficulties the Sentinels had faced over the past several years, the losses they'd had.

Aldo looked away from Lannie, a shine to his eye. "So I spent more time at the well house."

Right. He'd been upset. He'd smoked more pot than usual.

Aldo shifted uncertainly. "So that's what I thought it was. When my healing went strange after the fight. But I tried it again, and it didn't get any better, and I tried it again and I think it got even worse." He dared to look directly at Lannie then. "I didn't mean any harm, Lannie, I swear I didn't mean any harm!"

Understanding flushed over Lannie, cold and shocking. "Back at the well house. At the fight. When you suggested a healing and I said not to bother. *You did it anyway.*"

Behind him, Holly sucked in a breath, let it out on a low sound of dismay. "You did it anyway," she said, "and now that wound won't heal." Her voice rose. "Holy wha! You did it and now he can't find any of us!"

Aldo frowned, his mouth a tremulous thing. "What do you mean, he can't—?"

"Nothing," Lannie said, a harsh word that barely made it out through clenched teeth. His wounds throbbed with tension.

"Take it back," Holly said, coming up beside him with swift, urgent steps. "Whatever you did, don't do *more* of it. Take it back!"

Aldo pressed himself against the door, uncertainty writ over lined features. Lannie found Holly's arm and drew her back. "Never mind, Aldo," he said. "She doesn't understand. I do. I've already called Brevis— I asked for Ruger. He'll put things to rights. For both of us."

"Brevis," Aldo said, stiffening—not in anger, but like a wild thing about to bolt.

"They know I won't let them take you from here. Ruger will do what he can. The rest, we'll deal with as pack."

"As pack," Aldo repeated, grasping behind himself for the doorknob. This time, Lannie didn't stop him. Instead, he took another step back, releasing the older man. Aldo hesitated. "I'm sorry, Lannie. I didn't mean—"

"Yeah," Lannie said. "I know."

His words fell on silence. Aldo slipped back out the door and skittered down the stairs in quick, uneven steps.

Holly took a deep breath. "I'm sorry, Lannie. I'm so sorry."

Lannie closed his eyes, steadying himself. Not easy to do when she stood so close, scenting the air with her wounds, with the stress she hadn't been able to wash away. And then there was her underlying response to him, still lingering. "Ruger will do what he can."

She crossed her arms, a distinctly skeptical stance. "When?"

"When," Lannie said through his teeth, *"he gets here."* He moved past her to grab a shirt from the bathroom doorknob, closing it with a token two buttons and heading for the door.

Holly stood where she'd been, looking bereft. "Where…?"

He send her a glance of apology. "I can't—" and

ran out of words, trying again—unable to remember floundering not just for words but for thoughts. Too many sudden understandings, his blood still burning through healing, through his want for Holly…through a sudden burst of anger she was nowhere near deserving. He shook his head, another apology. "Just down to the store. I need to catch Faith up on the day—we've got dog food coming in. She'll need help." Help Lannie wouldn't truly be able to give her, not today. But he headed down the loft stairs anyway, knowing he wasn't fooling Holly and that he had little chance of fooling Faith.

To judge by Faith's expression when he stalked into the store, well she already knew it. "I called Javi. He'll be here in time to help with the order." She nodded at the several freezers tucked in beside the bagged dog food in the back right corner of the store. "I already moved the current stock into rotation, got the gloves out and the order sheet ready." She glanced askance at him, dropping her clipboard on the register counter. "We're missing a two-pounder of whole ground rabbit. I don't suppose you've had a midnight snack?"

"Check with the lamb chubs," he said. She had a right to be peeved—she was taking up the slack for him, and had been since Holly arrived. Not that they hadn't ever needed to make arrangements for Lannie's Sentinel work…but they normally had warning, and the time to do it. "The label colors aren't that different."

But Faith propped hands on hips to give him a narrow-eyed stare. "Look at you," she said. "Is that *more* blood? Have you been hurt *again*?"

Lannie turned on her, his simmering temper close enough to the surface to make her take a step back. *"Yes,"* he said. *"Yes*, in fucking fact I have been shot. *Twice.* And it hurts like hell. And I know things aren't convenient right now but they're happening, and I need you to *deal with it.*"

He'd never seen her eyes so big. He'd rarely felt such the fool, an alpha wolf going off on his own people in a way that wasn't the least bit alpha. And he'd rarely been as surprised as he was when she took a deep breath, pressed her mouth closed and lifted her face to look up at him more fully—especially not when she fearlessly reached up to tip his chin aside with two fingers, studying the old bruise that no doubt showed perfectly in the storefront light. She plucked his barely closed shirt away from his shoulder to peer behind the material at first one wound, and then the other.

Then she patted it gently closed again and said, "Okay, then. I'm gonna call on the twins, and the cousins, and fill out the schedule. You're off the roster until this is over. Whatever, exactly, it is."

He hadn't expected this sudden maturity. Or how it knocked the legs right out from under his temper.

She patted his shirtfront again, the faintest humor showing in her kohl-smeared eyes. "Did you think you were the only one who cares about pack, Lannie? Or did you just forget that you're as important to us as we are to you?"

He opened his mouth. He meant to say he was sorry, but he was too startled and too off balance and too weary in the wash of fatigue that filled in the places vacated by temper, and Faith got there first.

"It's okay," she said. "I know. Now. I've got this covered. And I can only suppress my natural smartassery for a few moments at a time, most of which you've already used. So go back to the loft. Or wherever."

He took a step back, more dazed than he'd been all day, and returned to the loft with a much quieter step.

Because while since Holly's arrival he'd been content to sleep as wolf in the barn or out beneath the stars, he was currently far too human to want anything but his own bed. To fall in it and heal and let the inner roil of desires and fears and ferocity settle into something more manageable.

Holly's murmuring voice reached his ear as soon as he opened the door. She sat at the tiny breakfast bar drinking a glass of ice water, eating peanut butter out of the jar and talking on his cell phone—and she lifted her gaze in a way that invited him to be part of the conversation. "I can't believe Kai felt that. I couldn't feel it, and I was right *there*. No, we're both fine. Just a…well, a minion, I guess." She listened a moment, watching Lannie as he went to kick off his boots and realized he'd never actually put them back on after cleaning up. "He was just…passing through. I'll have Lannie call you when he gets back, okay? And thanks for the shopping this morning. I needed that." She waited long enough for Lannie to break in if he really wanted to talk to Regan.

He shook his head. Holly murmured her goodbyes and placed the phone on the bar. "What happens next?" she asked, carefully enough to let him know just how off balance he'd left them both.

"Sleep," he told her, as if that was any choice. Now that he was coming down, he was coming down hard. Hard and hurting and needing time to recover.

She glanced at the bed somewhat wistfully.

"Share it with me," he said.

"A together nap," she said, so clearly tempted. But in the end she offered a rueful lift of her shoulder. "It's… been a big day. You need to *sleep*…and I need to think." She didn't even give him time to say it. "I won't go far. I won't take the bike. And I won't be gone long."

Not much left to object to. Especially not when he swayed on his feet, toes flexing against the plank floor just to keep himself upright without staggering.

She pointed at the bed. "Sleep," she said. "I promise. I won't even go out of sight of the barn. I'll take your phone." She scooped it up and displayed it for him.

And he nodded and let her go, because there really wasn't anything he could do to stop her—and if he tried, he'd lose the only scant semblance of *pack* he had left.

Alpha wolf. Alone.

Sitting on an old saddle blanket up the hill from the barn with the late afternoon sun beating down hard on her face and arms and shins, Holly knew that she wasn't totally safe here—or totally safe anywhere. If those thwarted killers from the SUV wanted to get to her, she wasn't particularly safe anywhere. But she was *close*, and that was what mattered for now.

Also, she was on a hillside with a good signal, where she could place a call.

"Marlee Cerrosa." The voice that responded to the number labeled *Brevis* came through clearly, a professional detachment in the tone. "Good afternoon, Lannie."

"It's not Lannie," Holly said. "It's Lannie's *phone*. I want to talk to someone in charge."

That professional tone was instantly infused with wariness. "Where's Lannie?"

"Sleeping," Holly said, without attempting to explain. She picked a pebble up from the fine, sandy soil and rolled it between her fingers. "This is Holly Faulkes. If I can't talk to someone in charge, I want to talk to my parents."

"That's actually not the way—" Marlee Cerrosa

stopped, seemed to consider her words. "Perhaps I can help you."

"Can you change what's happening here? Can you put me through to my parents?"

"I don't have that—"

"Then let me talk to someone in charge. Or I'm out of here. For good." Not right away, because she'd promised Lannie—this time. But he'd taught her how to maintain Sentinel silence, and she already knew how to run. Not to mention she had identification waiting in a locker half the country away and a bike to get her to that long-standing precaution.

Maybe Marlee Cerrosa heard the truth behind her words. "I'm not playing you, Holly. I can't reach Nick right now, and I don't have anyone else cleared to take this call."

"Mariska?"

Regret colored the woman's words. "She's in the middle of a field op. Helping Ruger, in fact, so we can get them both out your way."

"You know enough," Holly said, deciding it on the spot, the emphasis on her words coming from the abrupt motion of flinging her pebble down the hill. "You can tell *Nick*—"

"Southwest Consul," Marlee said, somewhat drily.

"—that he'd better figure out what's happening here and get some help over. Maybe I'll still be here, maybe I won't. But *Lannie* is here, and he's the one getting shot over whatever's going on here, and stupid weaselly little guy from the Core already died—"

"Shot?" Marlee interrupted her. "Did you say—"

"Shot," Holly said, interrupting right back, her fingers closing hard over the next little pebble. "Which is why he's sleeping it off. But he's not right, and we all

know it. He asked for help and you guys are dragging your feet. No wonder my parents chose to take us into hiding rather than risk Kai to you." The futility of the call struck hard at her; Holly thought briefly of simply hanging up on the woman and ending it.

It must have come through in her tone. "Holly—no, wait." A deep breath. "You don't understand. We're *not* dragging our feet. We're hampered because no one there can work with Annorah. She handles all our critical communications. But Lannie's never been open to communication from outside his current pack, not even on the phone—"

"And you know why!" Holly flung that pebble down the hill, too, watching it roll until it nested up against a cholla. "Or you should. If you had any idea what you ask of him, and what he just *does* for you—"

"Yes. We *do* know." Marlee seemed to collect herself. "I didn't mean to sound critical. It's just the way it is. It's not normally a problem, but right now? You can tell him that we've been in touch with the Core— they're emphatic that they have no interest in that area at this point, and we believe them. Your brother made sure of that. But they're evasive, too, and...we're working on it. There are protocols—"

Holly spat a quick imprecation at *protocols*. Then she said, "I don't care about your little problems. Lannie's sick, and Aldo is sick, and two men tried to kill me and *that's* what matters. What you do about it matters. Because Lannie's not the only one teaching me about the Sentinels. And I'm beginning to think I'm better off without you after all."

"Holly!" The desperation in Marlee's voice kept Holly on the line, if nothing else. "Listen to me. We're working on this. The information you're giving me will

help. But we have no intention of leaving Lannie out
there on his own—"

Alone? Holly made a noise in her throat, a satisfying thing that felt like certainty. "He's not *alone*, Marlee. I'm here."

"I meant—" But Marlee evidently couldn't find a
way to finish her thought in a way she wanted said out
loud, which meant Holly could figure those unspoken
words very well indeed. *I meant other Sentinels.*

Those who were truly of use.

"Just do something," Holly said, and hung up on the
woman after all.

He's not alone, Marlee.

Except Marlee was right. Lannie had backup in a
handful of Sentinel misfits and he had Holly, whose
brother was the most Sentinel of all, but she herself had
never even sought out her other. Had never wanted to,
and didn't even know how.

She wrapped her arms around her legs, uncomfortably aware of how quickly the raw, abraded skin had
faded to patches of healing tenderness—her own familiar healing combined with Ruger's salve. Such healing
would be even more profound, Lannie had said, once
she was initiated.

If.

Her parents had alluded to the earthy nature of the
Sentinel lifestyle—friends with benefits, everywhere
one looked. But Holly hadn't grown up in that culture,
and even if she had…

She looked at the stairs leading up to the loft where
Lannie slept.

But Lannie hadn't wanted her.

Correction. Lannie wanted her all too much. But
Lannie was a man who couldn't separate his physical

from his emotional. Still, she'd seen how deeply he responded to her.

Dampness prickled along the insides of her elbows, the creases behind her knees, reminding her that the sun ran strong here no matter how pleasant the air felt or how quickly the sweat dried. She looked down at herself—her hands, just as human as anything. Her ankles, and the shoes covering her feet. Her knees, one scraped along the outside.

Did she even have an *other*? Sentinels defined thickness of blood the old way—by the manner in which it was expressed. Lineage didn't matter; anyone who could take their other form was field level, and those who had no hint of it, no hint of unusual talent or skill, no ability to manipulate the earth energies around them—those were the light bloods. Just because strong blood tended to follow family lines didn't mean they had to.

She'd always known that much—because she'd always known Kai was the strongest of them, and she'd always believed herself to be of very little blood at all.

But Lannie seemed to think differently. And Lannie was the one who'd know.

Holly hugged her knees more tightly, closing her eyes—wondering what Lannie felt in himself when the wolf seemed so close to the surface. Wondering what it was like to reach for that difference, and to let it bloom into something that took him over. What would it feel like, the change? Now that she'd seen it, she could only call it beautiful—the tumble of coruscating light, the glimpse of motion and energy. The man, turned beast.

Something far more than beast.

Just as Lannie, as human, was far more than man.

Somewhere, inside her, did that impulse still lurk? She looked for it. Not even knowing what it was, she looked. Just for some sense of the unfamiliar—some sense of the *more than*. She invited it…tried to make room for it.

Resounding silence. She saw nothing. She felt nothing.

Nothing.

Lannie was wrong. She was no more than she'd ever been.

Holly stood, dashed away stupid tears, and picked up the old saddle blanket, striding back for the cool shadow of the barn with her plain old human feet.

But when she mounted the stairs to the loft, she did so with quiet care. With luck, Lannie was sleeping. She could replace the phone on the counter and go bask in the window area, lingering in the cool, indirect light and the soothing greenery, and beside the pleasant trickle of the fountain that Lannie had gotten just for her—even when he thought himself rejected.

Not the human part of him—she'd made that clear enough. But the part that meant so much to him. The part of herself that she apparently simply couldn't find.

She crept into the loft, hesitating to listen and hearing nothing but the deep breathing of a man exhausted.

At least, at first. But by the time she'd drawn and downed half a glass of water, that had changed. His breathing hitched; he shifted on the bed. She left the glass on the counter and moved to the unenclosed area that served as bedroom, watching him and uneasy about it. This was his space, not hers—no matter that he'd lent it to her. His privacy.

He sprawled on his back, his jeans riding low and his shirt abandoned to reveal a pure masculine beauty of form—dusted with hair, lean and tightly muscled, defined abdomen dipping into the shadows of his waist-

band. The wound over his hip looked good—clean and
healing, no signs of swelling or even of bruising. Torn
flesh, healing in the Sentinel way. The wound at the side
of his chest looked angrier—as well it should, from the
double insult it had endured. The older wound lingered
as it had been, its strange behavior now explained. Not
getting worse, and still not healing.

He twitched, pressing his head back into the jumble of soft pillows, dark brown and honey-laced hair
in disarray. His face changed—no longer relaxed, but
jaw tightening and dark brows drawn...lips ever so
slightly lifted. He made a deeper noise—it started out as
a threat, and abruptly turned to a gasp and a groan, and
he twisted to shove his face into the bedding, fighting—

She suddenly knew exactly what he fought. Because
somehow, she'd come to know this man just that well.
She breached the privacy of his space, already doing
just as he'd so recently taught her—reaching out. Not
with her hands—although she did that too, stroking his
shoulder and his side—but with the part of herself that
seemed to mean so much to him.

The part he'd taught her to share.

He sucked air, his body jerking with the sudden-
ness of it, and seemed to hold his breath. When he finally exhaled, it came through a long sigh. She could
just barely see his lashes flutter—then open wide, and
then she lost her opportunity to move away. He flipped
around and rolled right over her before she even saw
it coming—propped on his elbows, his body hard and
aroused against her, his gaze pinning her every bit as
much as his weight.

Only then did it occur to her that she'd made assumptions, crawling into his bed as she had—reaching out to the wolf while treating him as something less.

Only then did it occur to her that maybe she'd made a mistake.

Chapter 13

Lannie's pulse raged through every inch of him, settling strongest in the places he could least afford—making him hard enough to hurt, making him want her badly enough so he could barely even feel the disgruntled objection of fresh wounds.

"Hey," Holly said, with no attempt to hide her alarm. As if she could, with her lips brushing his chin and her own heart palpable though her chest, the song of her surging through his heart and brushing a tremulous pleasure along his nerves. "You're *awake*, right?"

He struggled for control. "What," he said, one word at a time, "are you...doing?"

"Get over yourself." It wasn't convincing, not with that breathless note in her voice. "You're not so irresistible that I couldn't help myself. I was just—" She squirmed, and he set his jaw against the feel of her breasts brushing his chest, the arch of her toned belly against his, the erotic tangle of their legs. She bit her lip and tried again. "You were in pain, dammit! I was just filling the empty places."

Filling the empty places. And indeed her song flooded through him, leaving no room for the static, soothing the wolf's lonely cry.

He pushed away, rolling over to throw his forearm over his eyes.

He had no business turning on her. No business resenting her for what they couldn't have simply because he didn't have the strength to let her go.

And still, when her hand skimmed over his arm to rest there, he couldn't help the bitterness in his voice. "Are you looking to fill the empty places in me? Or in you?"

Before he knew it, she'd pounced, straddling him—holding his shoulders and glaring straight down at his surprise. "What I *want*," she said distinctly, "is to make you pant for mercy. I want to see just a little bit of panic in your eyes when you understand that power I have over you and I want to feel you tremble when you come inside me." Her fingers curled over his shoulders, digging in just enough to let him know she'd done it. She leaned in close, her breath on his mouth—because suddenly he was straining for her. "*You're* the one who made it into some big deal, with *initiation* and *pack* and being too damned afraid of what it would mean."

"Well," he said, closing his eyes in some effort to regain control and then regretting it when the darkness only made it easier to feel every single place their bodies touched, every touch of her soft skin. "Well, *hell*."

"Don't you worry about it," she told him, every bit of that edge still in her voice. "I can give you almost all of that…and still keep you safe. In your heart, where it matters." Her voice grew rough and he jerked his gaze up to hers in sudden suspicion—seeing the gleam in her eye just in time that the splash of a hot tear on his cheek came as no surprise.

"Holly—"

"Shut up," she told him, pushing down on his shoulders as she bent to kiss him.

She wasn't gentle. She didn't mean to be gentle— that was clear enough. She meant to nip and clash and bruise her lips against his, and she meant to push and tug at him, her hand already slipping down his jeans to grasp him in a warm grip that was hardly gentle.

He thrust into that touch, a startled sound in his chest, and might have come within a stroke or two had he not flipped her over. If he wasn't already panting for mercy, he was damned well panting for more of her. "Holly—"

He had no idea how she got them turned around again, her mouth on his neck and biting, her fingers scraping over a nipple and turning his head inside out. Only then did he realize she'd unzipped his pants, that she cupped his balls and stroked the length of him and oh, *hell*, she had perfect teeth for nipping.

"Holly," he said, grinding down on his back teeth until the word barely made it out.

She turned her head, kissing the skin of his belly. Still holding him. "Can't I just *want* you? Can't you just want me back?"

She'd asked it before of him, and he had no different answer for him. "Not for us," he said. "Not *now*."

"Initiation," she whispered bitterly, sliding back up along his torso to lick his collarbone. *"Pack."* She made it all the way up, and he realized that she'd pulled off her shirt, and that her bra was a mere token layer of sporty material, easily pushed aside. His hands slid up to find soft, soft skin. Holding her so much more gently than he wanted as she slid over him and he discovered that bike shorts really, truly, left nothing to the imagination.

"Holly," he said, and in a way it was a plea.

"Lannie," she whispered against his throat, and another of those tears rolled down his neck, "I want to find myself. I want to know who I am. *What* I am." She breathed out a moan as he left her breasts to skim his hands firmly down her sides, holding her there as he just…couldn't…help it, thrusting up against her.

"So you think I should use you to fill my empty spaces," he said into her hair. "And you should use me to look for yourself."

She pushed herself up to glare down at him, her cheeks flushed and her hair spilling free of her ponytail to frame her face in disarray. "Stupid man," she said, anger snapping through the heat in her eyes. *"So* stupid. What I want, Lannie Stewart, is to find out who I am with *you.* I've got the nerve to see how that turns out…do you?"

Risk everything. Risk never getting beyond this moment. Risk breaking what he was, beyond anything that could ever be healed.

But there was only one true answer. One *possible* answer.

He bared his teeth at her, letting the wolf push to the surface.

She sobbed an exhalation of relief and he didn't give her time to relish it, threading his fingers through the silk of her hair to tug her up into a battle of a kiss. She didn't hesitate for an instant, fierce in her response— breaking away only long enough to pull the bra up over her head and push his jeans down until he kicked them off his feet. By then she'd found him with her mouth again, working him with lips and tongue until he pressed back into the pillow. He tried reaching for her and stopped short; his hands fell back to the sheets and grabbed hold as if they could save him from such an exquisite curl of pleasure, sweet shards of it tugging all the way into the core of him.

"Holly," he said. *"Holly—"*

In response she did something that made his back arch off the bed and his eyes squeeze shut and the snarl come out on his lip again. She laughed, and it sounded delighted.

That's when he knew. She'd meant it. She'd meant every word of it. What she wanted from him, what she'd wanted to do to him. *Holly...*

She crawled back up his body and he let her, his hands shaping her along the way—skimming with enough pressure to feel both soft skin and delightfully graceful movement. Every curve of her waist and hips, every shift of toned muscle in the body of a woman who worked in gloves and boots for her living.

When she lay fully over him, face-to-face, she licked his lower lip and sucked it gently into her teeth. "One," she said, not gloating so much as reveling in the way he'd panted beneath her touch, gasping her name. "And just enough of *two* to make me want you forever."

Not fair words. Not the way they tripped into his already pounding heart and through the spaces that had been clamoring for her for days. The wolf pushed at him—demanding and claiming her—even as the human knew this woman would be claimed only ever as she allowed.

"My turn," she said. "Time for *three*."

I want to feel you tremble when you come inside me.

He'd do more than tremble. He knew that now.

With the lightest of guiding touches, she slid down to sheath him completely, her face flushed and her eyes bright.

He drew a great shuddering breath, his hands clamping over her hips. A wash of light flickered at the edge of his vision, warming him from the inside out—and it came with the faintest music, a clarity still hovering in the distance. *There it is...* He grasped for it, yearning.

Holly bent over him, her hair brushing along his neck and collarbones and face, her assertion turned to a startled expression. She pressed a hand over her heart, and the other sliding low—cupping herself as he might have done. *"Oh,"* she said. "Is that—do you hear...do you *feel*—"

"—the rest of you," he said, breathless—trying to hold still while she adjusted, and knowing the sensation of initiation was different every time. It came according to individual...according to the couple. And because of that, he pushed slowly against her and added, "The rest of *us*."

Just like that, the mood changed. She'd been fierce—beyond fierce—and now she clung to him with uncertainty. She'd been driving, and now she hesitated.

Lannie easily flipped them around, once more on his elbows above her. Her hair splayed over the bedding in a gleam of black silk; brown eyes caught the light, gone from rich chocolate to something darker. She reached up to grasp his elbows, as if he were more lifeline than lover. Her flushed cheeks looked as much feverish as aroused, but there was no way to mistake the just-kissed look of her mouth for anything else.

He brushed his lips over hers. "Stop thinking so much."

"I wasn't," she said. "And then I suddenly was—*oh*!" Her legs tightened around him, as if he could possibly be any closer than he was, and he rocked into her again, just a twist of hips at the end of that short stroke. "Oh, do that again!"

He did, closing his eyes to focus on their inner landscape—scents of arousal, the sound of their bodies brushing together, their movement on the bedding, her soft noises of surprise each time he drew back and re-seated himself.

The song of her in his mind, filling all those empty places. Not just the places where the pack song should have resonated, but a place that had been so empty for so long, he hadn't even noticed it.

And the lights. An aurora of them, flickering around the edges of his mind, drawing shivers of pleasure through his body.

Her heels dug into his back and he growled in response, lost in heady pleasure—dropping his head to her throat and her collarbones, and shifting lower to find her breast with his tongue. She cried out, startled, arching in such a way as to completely change the angles between them—and that changed *everything*.

He grabbed her hips, jerking her closer and higher and raising up to come down over her, driving into her not with that gentle twist but with a hot and uncontrollable fervor. The music roared through him; the light bloomed from their connection to create a world of twisting color. He bent to her, catching up her mouth and leaning on one arm while the other roamed her body—her breast, her belly, the sweet crease from hip to groin, the damp folds where they met and joined.

She made a sound at that caress, a battle cry of sorts, and latched on to his arms with a clutching hold, a high growl in her throat as she received every thrust and every touch.

"Holly—" he said, and didn't even know what he was asking for, only that he wanted it so very badly.

"One," she gasped, just the barest hint of laughter behind it. Enough so he opened his eyes to look at her, to *see* her, to understand all over again just how much power she had—over his heart and now over his body.

"Two," she managed, if just barely, the humor mixed with a little snarl of pure focus. Her eyes closed and her head dropped back, her fingers digging into his arms. And, "Oh—the *light*, Lannie—"

The light, washing across them both as Holly spasmed around him...as her song filled him to overflowing and the climax gathering behind his balls exploded into his own song and his own shout, a thing wrung from him while he trembled uncontrollably above her.

She was still gasping with the aftershocks, but it didn't stop her from raising half-lidded eyes to offer him the most direct gaze of all, utter satisfaction on her face and a curl of a smile at the corner of her mouth. *"Three."*

Holly didn't think she'd ever breathe normally again. Or see normally, not with her inner vision still awash in the lingering aurora of initiation. Or *hear* normally, after the swelling depth of Lannie's shared song. She drew herself inward, humming throughout with the joy and completion, letting it dwell within.

Lannie looked down at her with his weight propped on his forearms and his hands framing her head, his own breath still right there on the edge of panting, the wolf not pushing his expression so much as lurking in his eyes and at the edges of his quiet voice. "Is that what you were looking for?"

"Mmm," she said, still luxuriating in sensation. She nudged her face against his loosely curled fist, let the sigh in her throat turn to a purr.

He tangled the fingers of his other hand in her hair, stopping her—startling her into better focus.

"You really want to know," she said, surprised at his tension, and at the fleeting vulnerability on his face, quickly shuttered by what was probably supposed to be anger.

But Holly could hear his song, murmuring through. Not anger...

Not yet.

"I really want to know," he said. "I *need* to know. Because—"

His voice bottomed out. He stared at her with narrowed eyes, just a moment too long. Then he released her, smoothed her hair against the bedding and rolled away from her to stare at the ceiling instead.

"Hey," she said, drawing her legs up and curled beneath, propping herself on one arm to rest her hand on his chest. Muscle twitched beneath it. He lay fully exposed and unconcerned about it, his erection fading, his abdomen still betraying the uncertainty of his breath. "What just happened?"

He sent her a sharp glance; she would have flinched had she not been ready for it. "Exactly what I told you would happen."

"Initiation?" she guessed, knowing herself wrong. Or, if not wrong, off track.

His hand came to rest over hers on his chest—closing over her fingers to flatten them against the plane of his pectorals. *"This,"* he said. "Just *this.* You gave me what I never had before." He closed his hand in a fist, scooping up her fingers along the way, forming them into a fist inside his own. "And then you took it away."

She heard it, then—the hollow quality of his voice. The grief.

"I didn't—" she said. And, "I don't—"

And then silence, because she didn't know exactly what she'd done and she had no idea how to fix it.

Lannie took a deep breath—a distinct rise and fall of his chest, a long exhalation. He smoothed her hand down again, his own a more relaxed layer with fingers intertwined. "Never mind. It was my own choice," he said. "I knew." Another of those deep breaths, and he brought their hands to his mouth together, brushing a kiss against her knuckles. "How do you feel?"

As if the amazing wash of light lingered invisibly inside her chest, filling her completely with arousal and satisfaction and a faint distant throbbing. And as if she hadn't changed at all…except that nothing else seemed quite the same.

But that, she thought, was how anyone would feel after being loved by this man.

She held her free hand up in the light of the window, turning it this way and that. She stuck her foot in the air, doing the same. She fell back against the bedding as he put a big hand flat across her belly, nearly spanning it with work-roughened fingers, and she shivered as he stroked downward to one hip.

"Don't push yourself," he said. "It takes time. Sometimes the changes are small, but they nearly always add up to something in the end." He ran his hand across her belly to the other hip, and then back up her side, the other hand still trapping hers against his heart.

She made herself ask what she feared, and hoped

he wouldn't—couldn't—answer. "What if it's too late? What if I'm too old?"

"You're twenty-four," he said, with no little amusement.

"Kai was fifteen."

Lannie's fingers followed the curve of one breast around to her side and down her arm—a light and careful touch. "So was I—and it changed my world. But it's not always like that."

"How old are you now?" She closed her eyes to shiver again as his hand returned along wrist and shoulder and moved on to trace her collarbones.

"What do you think?" he asked, amusement there. No hint of his anger or his grief, and Holly wondered if he'd let go of it or simply hidden it from her.

And she had no answer for him, suddenly realizing that his natural authority had superseded all the normal little clues as to age. "I don't know," she said. "I think I get a handle on you, and then you pull out the pack mojo and suddenly you're just *Lannie*. Then I forget to think about it."

He traced down her other arm, briefly cupped her breast. Owning her, with the complete assurance of his right to it. "Thirty-one," he told her. And he wasn't just owning her. He was *memorizing* her, here in the bright light of the loft and its the glorious window, every inch of her revealed.

She thought she probably should have been made uncomfortable by such scrutiny, but she responded to his touch without second thought. His hand traveled back down her belly and she shifted into it—and, when his fingers scraped into the dark curls at her groin, she opened her legs to him. He cupped his hand over her before moving to explore—gentle fingers, not quite yet meant to be arousing.

Memorizing her.

"It won't be the same," she told him, thinking not just about the pleasure and the astonishing energies that still played around in her body, but of that fleeting look in his eye.

"It'll never be exactly the same. That's one reason we usually take unfamiliar partners." He touched her with more intent, leaning over to brush lips and teeth against the round of her shoulder and eliciting an entire tangle of sensations, twitches of response and a deeper pleasure growing within. "Doesn't mean it won't be good."

Oh, she was pretty sure it was going to be good.

Really good.

He used one deft hand on her hip to turn her, gaining access to the back of her neck—only because she let him, and because his nibbling teeth quickly chased her instant flash of vulnerability. He traced the length of her spine, his hands firmly clasping her shoulders, then her torso…her waist and her hips. Claiming her, in a way he hadn't done before, simply by the way he handled her.

When he nibbled at the base of her spine, the tingling of his ministrations broke through to a throb of pure pleasure, and she released a shuddering gasp. He made his way back up to spoon her from behind, one hand teasing a breast and the other finding its way back to even more sensitive places. She pushed back against him and found him hard and ready and couldn't help but blurt, "Already?"

His breath gusted out into her hair. "When you do that? Always." His voice lowered as he pressed against her and she felt the tremble in it, knew him far more than just *ready*. But he managed to add, "Call it a Sentinel thing. Good recovery time in all things."

"Well," she said, squeezing her eyes closed as his fingers inspired exquisite response, "me too."

His response came through another gust of breath and another, harder thrust against her, where he held himself still with what seemed to be a great dint of will. "Good."

"Now," she suggested, offering an impatient wiggle.

She had no idea he could fill her so quickly. A hand shifting the angle of her hip, another quick movement to reposition her leg and make room for him, the mere hint of a guiding touch and he was *there*, fully seated, and she was clutching bedding and crying welcome. He bit her shoulder and he bit her neck, and she felt only sharp counterpoints of pleasure to the warmth already building inside her. "Oh," she told him, and sobbed just a little bit. *"Please."*

Instead, to her incredulous dismay, he stopped moving—the effort of it more than a tremble in him, already gone over to a shudder. "Holly," he said, and gasped into her hair at the same time he throbbed within her...involuntarily, leaving him striving for restraint that she didn't really want. "Holly," he said again, and this time she heard the faint note of desperation in his voice. *"Sing to me."*

"God, yes," she told him, and released that part of herself to him again.

He made an inarticulate sound—she thought something of a sob, something of pleasure beyond voicing—and freed himself back to her, driving into her hard and fast.

And then they both sang of release.

Chapter 14

Lannie knew when Holly rolled out of bed and shrugged herself into the shirt he'd left hanging on the back of the breakfast bar chair. He knew when she made her way over to the window. He heard the dabble of her fingers in the fountain water—her surprised murmur of reaction.

Surprise at what, he didn't know. But he'd find out. And he did know—or at least suspect—that Holly's affinity to water came as more than just a whim, whatever shape her other might take.

He'd come so close to blowing it. He might not be her pack leader, but he was still alpha, and with that came the responsibility to do what was best for those under his care.

That meant never telling her how it felt to experience her song swelling within him, filling places he'd never been touched before. Places lying dormant all this time.

It meant accepting the gift of that fleeting completion, and letting it recede in empty, gaping silence—one made all the more profound by the knowledge that he could no longer reach out on his own.

How greedy he'd been to accept that gift a second time. He thought he'd been prepared when it ebbed away again, but...

No.

He'd been wrong to think he ever *could* prepare.

So, yeah, he'd almost blown it. But now he would do what she needed—living in the moment and giving for the moment and then letting go, each and every time it came to letting go. Not as some noble sacrifice, but because she deserved that much after how the Sentinels had tangled up her life.

He took the deepest of breaths...the slowest. If his solitude could be fixed—*healed*—then Ruger would do it. Until then, Lannie's wounds weren't Holly's problem.

"I tried, you know," she said, as if she'd understood all along that his thoughts were of her, and his attention was on her. "Earlier, out on the hill. I thought how much it would have helped if I'd been able to draw on my Sentinel mojo outside town, and I thought...even if I can't make that change, maybe there's something lurking—the strength you have, the speed." She hesitated, and he opened his eyes to find her sitting cross-legged in his shirt and nothing else, looking at him. "I *tried*—but there was nothing at all. Nothing except what I've always been."

While Lannie had been sleeping. *Dammit.*

"You didn't have to be alone with that." He had to clear his throat of the lingering effects of passion—the unrestrained cries of completion, the struggle with emotion in the aftermath.

She dabbled her fingers briefly in the fountain, and her throat worked. "The thing is, I don't…I don't think I'm strong enough. Brave enough. Because…" She swallowed, hard; fading window light glinted off the spill of a tear on her cheek. "Because if I embrace it all now, then I have to look at what I lost all those years ago."

"Your brother," he said in realization. "The way your family could have lived."

"Who I could have been," she whispered.

He rolled from the bed, not bothering with the jeans, and padded to crouch beside her. "Holly," he said, cupping his cheek with her hand. "You're not looking for who you could have been. You're not looking for some *other* part of you. You're looking for who you *are*."

A frown flickered across her face; she put her hand over his and said nothing.

He took that hand and placed it on his shoulder. "Listen," he said, leaving himself unguarded. *"Feel."*

"I don't—" She stopped in clear frustration.

Of course she didn't understand.

Lannie explained it the only way he could. He reached for the wolf—*released* the wolf. He lost himself in the brief wash of invigoration, the joy of embracing the pure unmitigated other and the primal exhilaration of finding himself wolf.

Holly sat frozen, her hand on the neck of a timber wolf—her expression a mixture of awe and fear. She pulled her hand away, looking at it—flexing fingers in the wake of energies shared, experience shared. "Wha," she said. "Is it…does everyone…that was…" She shook her head. *"Wha."*

He dropped his jaw in a wolfish grin, lingering uncertainty betrayed only in the set of his ears. When she reached for him, he nuzzled her fingers, gave them a little lick and nibble, and then bounded back with head lowered and rump ever so slightly raised.

She laughed, but she climbed to her feet, heading to the kitchen to made herself at home with his cookie-jar jerky stash, taking a big bite from the first hunk and extracting several additional pieces. "Here," she said, tossing one his way; he snapped it out of midair. "We haven't actually eaten since breakfast. Did you even *have* breakfast? I should make something, but...yeah, that's not gonna happen."

She tossed him another piece, aiming it a little higher so he leaped to snag it and she laughed. Playing, in spite of it all.

"It's still early," she said, flipping him a final piece as she chewed hers. "But after this day, I think I can sleep some." She found her underwear and slipped it on, but didn't bother to trade his shirt for something of her own before she crawled back onto the mattress. "Come on," she said, and patted the bed.

He launched to it from where he stood, making her laugh again, and pawed the bedding into a pleasing nest before he stretched out full length, his paws dangling off the mattress. Holly curled up behind him, pulling a disarrayed quilt over them both. "Good night, Lannie," she said. "Maybe we can figure this all out in the morning."

Maybe.

But Lannie, like the wolf, would live in the moment, and for now that meant lying in bed with her hand resting on his side and her cheek against the back of his ruff. He sighed, rubbed his whiskers into the bedding, and relaxed, absorbing the subtle ebb and flow of the sweet song she shared with him as naturally as breathing.

For now.

They slept straight through to morning, more or less.

More, because it was a deep and satisfying sleep, relaxed and safe and somehow luxurious.

Less, because Holly dreamed. She dreamed of whiskers and claws and the wash of an internal aurora; she dreamed of pleasure and she dreamed of the desperate sounds Lannie made as they spiraled toward completion together. She dreamed, too, of a different kind of energy, something bursting and joyous, and not anything that belonged to her.

Holly wasn't surprised when she woke in a strange state of mixed sensations—profoundly sated, profoundly yearning, her body humming and restlessly aching at the same time. Though no longer from the bruises and abrasions of the day before, which had healed to a barely noticeable ache and faintly tender skin.

She was more surprised to find Lannie in perfectly human form beside her, tangled in the covers with his arm flung out over her stomach, one leg entwined between hers, and his posterior bare to the world.

It deserved a moment of admiration, that posterior did. She gave it its due. She followed the dip of his spine, the channel up his back to smoothly muscled shoulders, rounded biceps and the heavy arm weighing her down.

To think he hid all that beneath worn jeans and a series of muted work shirts, plaid and chambray. He hid it, too, beneath a laid-back walk, a habitually quiet posture.

Because an alpha didn't fight unless there was something worth fighting for. And then he became a force beyond reckoning.

She'd seen it now.

Holly slipped out of bed for a quick shower, and slipped into the cleanest of the clothes that had come with her. Something about this day made her want to feel prepared...solid in herself. The low-rise fire hose pants hung around her hips with familiarity; a short-sleeved shirt covered with tiny flower sprays gave her plenty of room to move, but snugged gently around her breasts and nipped in at her waist, the back tail hanging low. Long hair hung damply between her shoulder blades, swinging in a ponytail.

She was reaching for her sunscreen when Lannie made a noise and rolled over, all relaxed loose limbs and sleepy eyes.

It stopped her in her tracks.

Not the beauty of him, or how well his wounds had healed overnight, or his completely unself-conscious nudity—half aroused in his morning state and comfortable with it.

No, it was more the sense that she was seeing something rare in those half-lidded eyes—that these fleeting moments came as a gift of trust.

That just maybe, this was a part of Lannie that no one else had seen.

He rolled to his feet from the low mattress, snagging his jeans along the way, and padded into the bathroom still naked, not bothering to fully latch the door behind him.

Holly finished applying the sunscreen and went to

sit beside the fountain, reaching among the plants to offer them a light grooming.

She'd wanted so badly to get away from this place, and yet...suddenly she wasn't sure what she wanted to run from. This man who had taken bullets for her? Who had always, always, kept her needs in mind, even as he inexorably maintained his loyalty to his own people, his own nature? This man who had offered her everything of himself, and maybe yet a little more?

Maybe she wasn't running from him at all. Maybe she was running from herself. *Hiding* from herself.

She'd become particularly good at that.

"Hey," he said, standing over her—how he'd come to be there, she wasn't exactly sure. His skin gleamed, his jeans were only half-buttoned and hanging low, and he quite obviously hadn't bothered with underwear. "Did you do something to the shower?"

She frowned in bafflement. "Like what? It's not a particularly robust system to start with. You've got a pressure pump hooked in there, right? I can tell that much. I'm not sure, but what you need to flush things— what?" For he'd given his head a shake, and it stopped her short.

"It *was* kind of iffy," he said. "Not so much now."

"Huh," she said, and suddenly heard the faint echo of Regan's words, her surprise when her sluggish kitchen faucet perked up. She looked down at the burbling fountain, absorbing the clarity of that high mountain water. She thought of the difficulty of returning from Cloudview to Descanso, and how bitterly metallic her mouth had tasted outside construction areas.

She pushed to her feet, already moving for the sink. "Do you have any bottled water?"

"Everyone around here keeps a case stashed away," he said, watching her with those piercing, dark-rimmed eyes.

"How about the water Regan brought for the fountain? Any more of that?"

"Five gallons of it, more or less."

Holly cleared the counter, pushing away old mail, Lannie's cell and a handful of spice jars. She filled the space with every coffee mug he owned. "Can you get it for me? And get some from the mule trough—that's not softened, eh?"

He didn't respond so much as he simply went to work, out of the loft and back again. Within a few moments she had a counter of mugs labeled with sticky notes and filled with water from a variety of sources, and she'd pulled herself in tight to face the moments to come. "If this works…" She eyed the mugs with a dry awareness of how she would have viewed this moment only a week earlier. "It's either going to explain a lot, or just make it all that much more confusing."

At first she thought his silence was thoughtful—but when she glanced at him, she found his gaze so vacant that a stab of fear made her forget everything else. "Lannie!"

Not so much as a flicker of response. Just a man without any sign of Lannie's spark or Lannie's presence, standing between the stove and the breakfast bar and looking at nothing.

"Lannie," she said, more sharply than she might have dared had she not shuddered in his arms the night before. She lost her self-containment, her worry spilling out at him in a way that even she could feel.

He jerked slightly, blinking as his eyes came back into focus—the pure intensity of his personality again filling the kitchen. The contrast didn't reassure Holly so much as it terrified her. "Where did you even go?"

"Where did I...?" He frowned, considering her. "Nowhere. Why?"

"I beg to differ," she told him, asperity in her voice and her scowl.

He looked down at himself—his feet, his hands, his bare torso. "I think..." He cast her a narrow-eyed glance. "I was just empty."

"You were *gone*."

He murmured, "Nothing to keep me here," and then frowned. "That was a strange thing to say."

Fervent agreement didn't seem enough. "I think it's about time to make another call."

"To Brevis?"

"Yes. So they know it's serious."

"I'll send them an email." He nodded at his laptop. "But they already know it's serious. I wouldn't have asked if it wasn't."

Her scowl grew fierce. "Then why aren't they here?"

"They *will* be," he said. "When they can. It's not that easy, Holly. It never has been, and after the past couple of years we're stretched pretty thin."

She hazarded a guess. "Too thin." Too thin to protect their own people, even the people from whom they were asking the most.

Too thin, she realized, to allocate multiple resources to a single woman who now resisted coming back into the Sentinels.

Lannie didn't disagree, but he didn't go into it, either. He gestured at the mugs, fully focused again. "What's up?"

She stepped back and closed her eyes. "Pick one," she said. "And give it to me."

The faint scrape of ceramic against the countertop. His hand—warm and big and callous, a hand that had touched every inch of her body—steadied her at the wrist as a mug pushed into her grasp. She curled her fingers around it, but she already knew. *Flat, lifeless... barely there.* "Bottled water."

He had the game, now—he took away the mug, replaced it with another. *Mushy, slippery...the tang of salt.* "Your faucet. Through the water softener but not the reverse osmosis filter."

He offered a faint noise of assent, gave her another. She'd doubled up on some of the samples, even tripled a few, and now he'd given her a duplicate. "The bottled water again."

The mule water, the RO water... The water from Regan's well. Lannie gave her every mug in turn, and she identified them all—and realized she'd always done this very thing. She'd just done it on a deeply subconscious level, making decisions based her perceptions, quietly forming her own life in a way that honored this inexplicable connection.

Not inexplicable after all.

She wondered if her parents had noticed. She wondered if she ever would have realized, had she not come here...had Lannie not given so much of himself to her.

She opened her eyes and found him watching, his eye bright and the rest of him so intent that she took a step back. She didn't want this to mean so much. Not to her, not to him. "So, what then?" she asked. "Does this mean I'm a Sentinel *fish*? Because I don't want to be a fish."

He ignored that prickly moment and took the final mug from her, setting it aside to thread his hands around her waist and tug her close—up against his hips, all fiery where they touched and perfectly casual where they didn't. He nuzzled at her neck, and she couldn't help that small noise in her throat, or the rub of her cheek against his head; her hands quite naturally fell on his arms. "Didn't you know?" he asked, barely a murmur at her ear, which got its own nudge of a lick and nibble. "You're like your brother. Maybe not lynx, but cat."

She tightened her grasp on his arms, digging in just a little. "You *knew*?" she asked. "How long? Did you know just *looking* at me, and just didn't bother to tell me? How could you know when I don't?"

"Whoa, there," he said, bending just a little to get a better grip on her—scooping her up from behind, and doing it so deftly that she didn't even see it coming.

Maybe her legs had, because they curved quite naturally around his hips and crossed at the small of his back. Ceramic clinked as he lifted her to the edge of the counter.

"Don't try to distract me," she told him, and pushed herself against him as if it was a choice—as if she could have helped herself. *"Did you know?"*

His breath gusted down her neck. "Not at first. Not for a while. But now…it seems…ahhhh, *Holly.*"

Really? *Really?* She was worried about him, she was annoyed with him…she was all caught up in making the discoveries that would shape the rest of her life. And yet here he was, already struggling for composure in her arms, and here she was, gone from *I want breakfast* to *I want Lannie* in little more than a touch. Already she regretted her pants, and she certainly regretted his.

So of course she pushed him, shoving with the flat of her hands. "Is this what it's always like?" she demanded. "Initiation? When do I get to think of anything else but *you*?"

Lannie laughed, and it tasted as bittersweet as the filtered water—water that knew it should be good, but knew itself also somehow lacking. "No, Holly-cat," he said, wrapping her ponytail around his hand and clutching it tightly against the back of her head, the pull a painless but inexorable thing that tipped her face up, left her mouth slightly open and perfectly ready to meet his. "This has nothing to do with initiation."

He took her mouth, and she took his back, and she barely heard his next words—and then barely had the wits to realize he hadn't actually spoken them out loud.

This is us, *Holly-cat.*

Chapter 15

Lannie led the way down to the store, stiff and sore and absurdly sated. Not to mention greedy.

He wondered if Holly understood what she gave to him when they touched one another, and how she filled him when they came together. He wondered if he used her, or if he simply wanted her as anyone would, and the chance to hear her song came along with that. Even now, the ache from the emptiness crept back in, bringing that hollow feeling under his feet.

"You're really okay?" she said as they threaded the hall to the break room, where he dropped off another canister of coffee for Faith to ruin.

"If I unbutton my shirt to show you, are we going to make it to the front of the store?" He kept the words matter-of-fact, but when he stole a look at her from the corner of his eye, he found her frowning and thoughtful.

"No," she said, a wistful note in her voice. "I suppose not. I just find it hard to believe that you could be shot yesterday—*twice*—and now you're up and about. After all we did last night."

And that morning.

With the knife wound just as it had been for the past week and more—an aching, occasionally bleeding and entirely unnatural wound in his side.

He thought to catch her up against the counter to make his point, then thought again and kept his distance. "They weren't bad injuries. They'll heal normally from here on out." Lingering, but no more than inconvenience.

Holly made that noise in her throat…one that now seemed to him a particularly feline derision. "Right," she said, following him down the hall to the sales floor. "Bullets. Nothing significant about those."

"Well, look who's here." Aldo's voice rang out with a heavy-lidded sound that told Lannie exactly how the old coyote had started his day. "What have you been up to, boy?"

Faith popped up from behind the counter, looking hazy and rattled. She was missing one of her piercings and had forgotten her dramatic makeup altogether, revealing a surprising innocence to her features and expression. "Lannie," she said, as if she hadn't expected to see him here today at all. "I've got a new roster all worked up, and Javi is coming at noon. Plus it's Saturday, and that little girl group from Ruidoso is coming in to practice haltering and bridling Horace."

"Horace." Holly came to a stop beside Lannie, her hand just lightly brushing along the back of his shirt before it fell away.

"Horace," Faith repeated, nodding at the full-size fiberglass quarter horse standing stoically along the front wall. At the moment he wore a saddle, bridle and a pair of gloves on his ears.

Right. Little girls. He opened his mouth to ask her to handle it—a first—and didn't get the chance.

"Lannie," Faith said, with uncharacteristic hesitation. "Was there some sort of...*event* last night? Because I thought I... Well... And Aldo went straight to the well house this morning, and Javi sounded funny on the phone, and you look...well..."

"Yeah." Lannie felt Holly's surprise, and the sting as her faint, lingering song went silent. "We'll talk about it later. Everything's all right."

"Everything's strange as hell," Faith said, grasping at her normal asperity. "But never mind us. We'll just keep on keepin' on."

"You do that," Lannie said, more absent than short in his words as he considered how far the effects of the initiation might have spread, and whether he'd be fielding a phone call from Cloudview—not Kai, who did not noticeably use phones, but Regan, calling on behalf of Kai's little sister.

Kai's startled and currently silent little sister. Maybe he should have warned her how far the explosive energies of an initiation could spread. His toes curled inside his boots, instinctively seeking purchase with the world...not finding it. The world seemed to shift out from beneath him, but it didn't truly matter, not in the absence of the twining, variable songs that had anchored his very existence.

"Lannie," someone said, in a far distant place not worth attending, "are you okay?"

Words meant nothing in the absence of pack presence. Nor did the hand on his arm, a touch barely felt across miles. *Lannie, talk to me. Lannie, what's wrong? Lannie...Lannie...Lannie...*

Song burst into his head, warm deep notes of strength, twining vines of sharp, sparking worry...a sensual caress of heat. His feet felt the ground and he staggered hard, coming up against Holly's strength—his vision the last to return and her face the first thing he saw. *Worried. Annoyed. Determined.*

Before he knew it, Faith had steadied him from the other side. "What," she demanded of Holly in a low and accusing voice, "was *that*? Because it sure wasn't anything that happened before you got here!" A scuffle of noise, a slammed door, and Faith added a curse. "Where does he think he's going? I *need* him today!"

Lannie focused on Holly's face, on rich brown eyes shot through with faint copper and wide with concern. Gravity took hold again; his body had substance and weight. "Holly."

She ran her knuckles along his cheek. "You're okay, eh?" she said. "You're back."

"Back from *where*?" Faith grabbed Holly's arm, demanding. "What is going *on*?"

Maybe she'd forgotten Holly's last response to being pushed, but Lannie hadn't—and even as he saw the ire raising in Holly's eye and heard the dark anger of it in her clear song, he sucked in a deep breath and found himself fully involved again—standing in the feed store with grit under his feet, the scent of sweet hay and oiled leather in his nose, and the bright light of the early morning splashing in through the storefront.

"No one's keeping anything from you," he told Faith, short enough to remind her that he, too, knew she'd stepped over the line again. "We're still figuring this thing out."

"Right," Faith said. "While *I'm* still figuring out that there's a thing to figure out."

Holly released her temper with a sigh. "It's confusing. It's all *really* confusing."

"Because there's more than one thing happening." Lannie looked down at his own hand, opening and closing it much as he'd seen Holly do earlier. His hand, browned from the sun and his natural depth of skin tone, calluses at the base of each finger, bare of rings. *His.* How had he been so separate from it, only moments earlier?

Holly placed her own hand into it—strong fingers, graceful nonetheless, fitting through his as though they belonged there. He understood that unspoken worry—the message behind the gesture, as well as the one behind the slight swell in their connection. And because he didn't want to say it out loud and make Faith worry even more, he did what he'd never done and quite deliberately internalized his voice. *I'm here,* he told Holly silently.

Her eyes widened. "It's been you all along."

Faith snapped her fingers for their attention. "Because *I'm* still figuring out there are things to figure out!"

Lannie let his hand drop, taking Holly's with it. "A week or so ago—"

He wasn't surprised when Faith didn't let him finish. "When she got here."

He lifted his brow; it was enough to quell her again. "When Aldo got into that scrape at the well house."

Faith flicked a glance at Holly, crossing her arms and leaning against the counter. "Make it quick. I just saw a van pull into the lot out there, and it was full of little-girl faces."

Lannie did. "Aldo tried to heal me."

"Tried?" Faith said, her attitude bleeding away as she looked Lannie up and down, her gaze settling unerringly at the knife wound. "Oh, hell. So that's why he's been skulking around. He's finally sucked down enough weed so he healed you backward."

"That's what I thought at first." Just her scrutiny on the wound made him more aware of its underlying pain. "I don't think so any longer. I think Aldo's just—"

"—losing it," Faith said bluntly.

"Losing it," Lannie agreed.

Holly said softly, "And the pot was self-medication. The result, not the cause."

"What're we gonna do?" Faith looked away, her mouth flattened. In the parking lot just out of Lannie's view, the van doors opened and closed. *Little girls, impending.*

"Brevis healer," Lannie said, and cut Faith short when she lifted her head, protest in her eyes. "We have no choice, Faith. For both Aldo and for me. We'll have enough warning so you can take off for the day."

Holly shifted, her gaze catching the approach of a small troupe of girls in perpetual, chattering motion, and the attempts of two chaperones to modulate their excitement. "And there's the SUV guys—"

"Who?"

"The Core minion found Holly in town yesterday," Lannie said, short and hard, no time for mercy. "So did two men who killed him and went after Holly."

"When you lit out of here yesterday," Faith said, lowering her voice as the first of the girls trickled in, the bell jingling in cheery announcement.

"They shot Lannie," Holly said. *"Twice."*

"Lannie!"

Lannie shook his head. "I'm healing like I should

with these," he said. "But we still don't know what's going on. Only that our guy had information, and we didn't get nearly enough of it."

"They'll be back." Holly squeezed his hand again, only this time he thought it was involuntary. "Those men in the SUV. They won't leave it at that."

"I don't think so, either. I don't think they'll come here, but…Faith, you keep an eye out." Lannie raised his voice to a normal level as the group leader approached, looking simultaneously grateful and hassled. "That's why Holly and I need to go check into some things, while you hold down the fort here." He gave the assembled girls a casual lift of his hand. "Hey, girls. You here to put Horace to work?"

By some miracle they didn't mob him, though they did bounce on their toes and giggle and nod with enthusiasm.

"It's all yours." Lannie grinned at Faith, and told the girls to have fun as he headed out the front door, bringing Holly behind him.

She said, "But what are we going to *do* about all this? Sit and wait for Brevis? Sit and wait for those men?"

No. Not this wolf. Not when his people were threatened and confused and frightened.

He looked over to find her face awash in the sunlight, the copper streaks of her brown eyes shining back bright and strong beneath a faintly frowning brow and the determined set of her mouth. She'd asked the questions, but she clearly had her own ideas about the answers. "I'm of a mind to gather some information," he said. "And I need your help to do it." But he nodded over at the barn, and the mules, and the chicken and rabbit coops beyond. Faith would tend them, normally—or Aldo, if he hadn't run off—but Aldo was hiding and

Faith was busy with little girls, and daily life went on. "But before we go haring off…there're chores to do."

Holly looked at him with some disbelief—but then she laughed, and relaxed some with the doing of it. "Of course there are," she said, squeezing his hand a final time before she dropped it. "They're all depending on you, too, after all."

Yes. They were. They always had.

He wasn't about to let them down now, crippled alpha or not.

Holly dumped hay into the mules' second feeder trough, securing the slow feeder mesh over top and stepping back as the animals trotted freely from the darkness of the barn, ears flopping, and headed straight into their pipe corral paddock. Lannie moved with no hurry as he followed them out and secured the gate.

With the small animals fed and the mule water topped off, Holly grabbed an extra manure fork to help Lannie sift through the shavings of the generous mule run-in. Lannie looked extraordinarily peaceful as he gave an expert flick of the fork, and she found herself giggling.

He stopped to regard her, the question on his face.

Holly muffled the next giggle with the back of one hand and gestured at the barn in general. "All this drama going on around us, and here we are. Poop patrol."

"Don't knock it," Lannie said, but she thought she saw a smile in his eyes. "If more people had a chance to fling mule poop, this would be a quieter world."

"Right," she said, and thought he was kidding. He only nodded at her fork and they went back to work. She shrugged and settled into the work—and found herself settling also into the quiet underlying music between them. It hummed and waxed and waned…until suddenly they were done and she was sorry to discover it so.

And there was Lannie, standing close enough to wrap his hand around her waist and pull her in close, resting his face against her hair…doing nothing more than breathing with her until she relaxed and absorbed the scents of wood shavings and Lannie, and the juniper-scented air filling the barn. Barn scents. With Lannie.

"You see?" he said. "From here, I can…I *could*…hear them all." He pressed his lips to her temple, held them there…breathed out to warmly tickle her hair. "And now it's yours, if and when you want. If you can't find a fountain in the desert."

"Maybe you're my fountain in the desert." Holly clapped her hands over her mouth. "I don't know why I said that. I'm sorry. I'm not trying to…to change things. To…you know…mess with you."

His eyes, already darkened in this shade of the barn, nearly lost their unique brightness altogether. "I'm not the only one you're messing with, Holly-cat," he said, and abruptly hauled the wheelbarrow outside.

By the time he returned to her, stowing the emptied barrow along the wall and hanging the forks, her restlessness had returned.

"You said you wanted my help to gather information." She spoke before he even hesitated beside the run-in door. "What is it you want me to do?"

"What you've been doing all along," he said. "Even when you didn't know it." And he nodded at her hand.

Because of course she'd drifted over to stand beside the indoor trough, and of course while she'd bent to run her fingers through the water, and now stood here running her thumb across those wet fingers, absorbing the sense of the water.

She wiped her hand off on her pants. "Of course I wouldn't know it, eh?" she said crossly. "At home, this was my *work*. I was surrounded by water, not by your dry desert."

"The way I figure it," he said, as if she hadn't been cross at all, "we've got only one common thread to follow."

She took a step away from the trough, as if just to prove she could, and another...joining him at the gate. "I don't see it. We've got one guy from the Core spouting vague warnings and two mystery guys who stopped him from spouting vague warnings."

His look went piercing. "You're smarter than that," he said. "Unless you don't want to be."

She didn't even think. She shoved him, hard enough to set him back a step. "Don't you even...!" Except when he said nothing, his meaning struck her, and she blurted out words with no intention to do so. "You mean *all* of it—all of the little things that have happened recently."

"Ever since five men gave Aldo a beating just because he was hanging around where they didn't want him," Lannie said.

"The well house," she said. "And then they were at the tavern—"

"I thought they'd come with the Core," Lannie said. "But now it seems more likely our minion was working entirely alone."

"He said as much," she said, going back to the events of the day before—the details they hadn't yet talked about, simply because they'd needed time. To recover, to rest...

She made a sound of dismay. "I should have told you—*kryptonite*—"

Lannie looked as truly startled as she'd ever seen him; she didn't give him time to ask. "I can't believe I lost this!" She shook her head. "Yesterday, before those men came…the minion guy mentioned the lab theft again, and he called it—"

"—kryptonite," Lannie said.

"For both of us. Core and Sentinels. He said they were just testing so far, but…Lannie, there's something out there," Holly said. "There's some*one* out there. And it has to do with— Oh. Oh, I should have *told* you—"

Lannie seemed a little taller. A little more of what lived innately inside him along with the wolf, whether or not he could reach out for pack song. *Because,* Holly realized, *he is what he is.* Being pack crippled hadn't really changed that. It just changed how he could do it. It hurt him, but he was still Lannie.

Am I still Holly, then? Even if she took her cat. Even if she embraced being Sentinel.

She shook it off, all of it. "I should have told you," she repeated in a rush. "I just didn't want to argue over whether it was safe for me to ride out. But the first day I went for a ride, I followed my nose to another well house. And those guys were there—remember the truck from town? Denton Construction. They were…" She hesitated, looking for the word and finding it hard to think with Lannie looking at her that way, some strange combination of demanding and protective. "Inappropriate. No contractor can afford that kind of behavior in a crew—it gets around, believe me. But these guys didn't want me there, and they didn't care about the impression they made."

Lannie stood silent for long moments, the wolf gleaming from his eye.

"Lannie," she said, "I'm *all right*. This was days ago. And the point is it happened at a well house. Yeah? *Again!*"

He inhaled sharply, releasing it as he stepped up to her—*stalked* up to her—and then around her, his cheek against her head and gone again, his fingers tangled in her ponytail to capture her in a way that no longer startled or frightened her. He came around to face her again, tipping her head up to kiss her—firmly, thoroughly...most decisively.

Not about sex. Not about the instant flare of heat in all the sensitized zones of her body. No, this was a claiming.

But Holly was nobody's to claim, so she kissed him back with just as much intent, her damp hands still at her side and her feet most definitely grounded in reality. A solid strength, meeting his.

He drew back with the wolf strong in his eye and lingered there, meeting her gaze—reading it. Maybe it satisfied him, for he stepped back and released her, nothing of the morning's tenderness in his manner.

Only then did Holly tremble, a brief sensation of some lurking decision that had briefly risen to the fore and now subsided again.

Lannie said, his voice low but remarkably matter-of-fact, "I need to understand what you feel at these places. Then, and now."

"Fine," she said, as if her heart wasn't beating a mile a minute—from his touch, from the implications of it... from the implications of what she was about to do. *As a Sentinel.* "I'll do my best."

Chapter 16

There was no evidence of the construction workers at the Old Rider Ranch Road well house…just the makings for a chain-link fence off to the side. Holly tensed up all the same, her mouth tight and her nose wrinkled slightly with distaste.

Lannie pulled over to the narrow shoulder and gestured through the brand-new truck windshield, propping his wrist over the steering wheel. "Talk to me."

She cleared her throat. "It's *awful*," she said. "All bitter and sour at the same time." She swallowed hard. "We don't have to stay, do we?"

He put the truck back in gear and swung around in a U-turn. "Best not," he said. "If they were watching the one by town, they could be watching this one, too."

"Unless they're through with what they meant to do here," Holly suggested, and then her eyes widened. "What if we're too late?"

"I don't do *too late*." But Lannie reached the T-intersection and turned them toward town without hesitation. Not as fast as he'd flown down this road the day before, Holly's cry for help ringing strongly through his entire body, but fast enough so she grasped the seat belt crossing her body.

The Core minion's car was gone from the well house, and Holly made a sound of surprise.

"They clean up after their own," Lannie said, barely pulling off on the shoulder and leaving the engine to idle. "We both do. We can't afford exposure."

She closed her eyes and swallowed hard. "Bitter and sour and oh, just a little too much like maybe I just threw up a little bit into my mouth." She looked at him, dark eyes worried. "It's so much worse than yesterday."

"Something they didn't think we'd detect," Lannie said, grim as he drove back onto the road and into town—straight on to the ElkNAntlers at the other end of the building cluster, where he pulled into the empty parking lot and pretended he didn't feel the ache of lingering wounds as he slid out of the truck and slammed the door behind him.

Holly hopped down to follow, her manner uncertain. "They're still closed…"

"They are," he agreed. "But there's a frost-free back here." Just around the side, with an empty bucket beside it and a cluster of piñons crowding in close.

She gave the free-standing water hydrant an uncertain eye. "Honestly, I've got such a taste in my head right now, I can't really tell you—"

He grabbed the bucket and held it beneath the faucet as he pulled the handle up; water spewed out. He shut it off and offered her the bucket.

Hesitantly, she reached for the water—then thought

better of it, and simply wrapped her hands around the bucket instead.

But only for an instant. She snatched them away as if she'd been burned. "What have they *done*?"

Used the well house access to introduce something heinous to the Sentinels, that was what. *Kryptonite.* Whatever it was.

Holly had felt something of it from the start—had resented it, and blamed the Sentinels for its effect on her, and struggled to absorb it along with the changes in her life. She'd had no idea of the danger it truly represented.

Lannie couldn't undo any of that, or their belated response to it. He could only move forward. "The question," he told her, "is when did they do it?"

She looked down at the bucket with a kind of horror. "It could have been this bad all along."

Maybe, maybe not. "How much did your perception of the water in the loft change after last night?"

She released a breath of relief. "Not that much. It was easier to tell the differences in the water sources— more precision—but the differences weren't *stronger*."

Lannie emptied the bucket into the container flowers at the tavern's corner and replaced it beside the hydrant. "So yesterday kicked these people into gear." *These people.* Someone the dead Core minion had considered a mutual enemy.

"Yesterday," she echoed, looking a little dazed by it all. "Seems like ages ago. And just a little over a week ago…I was *home*." She shook her head. "How can I even make sense of all this?"

"Maybe you can't," he told her, bluntly enough. "Maybe you don't try."

"Right." She didn't sound the least bit convinced; her pack essence retreated almost entirely.

He sucked in a silent breath, hiding the impact of it from her. She had enough to deal with. "We've got one more place to check."

She met his gaze squarely, realization there. "Home."

Home. The land that was Lannie's refuge, and the well house where Aldo spent so much of his time. "We'd better go take a look."

Holly clutched the seat belt as Lannie cranked the truck into the feed-store parking lot, leaving it skewed across spaces. *Home.*

Or what passed for home at the moment.

She disembarked into the resulting cloud of dust as the girl group came dashing out of the store, each waving a little treat bag. "Animal crackers!" one girl squealed happily, and cries of "Cowboy lip balm!" and "Dog cookies!" bounced between them so quickly that Holly couldn't even tell which girl had spoken.

Lannie stopped short, and no wonder.

"Thank you, Mr. Stewart!" They giggled on the heels of their practiced little chorus, and Lannie shook the hands of the chaperones and welcomed them back anytime.

He waited only until the last door of their big van slammed closed and then grabbed Holly's hand, pushing into the store where Faith was already ringing up a big hay sale over the phone.

"Aldo?" Lannie demanded. Faith responded with an exaggerated shrug and a whirling finger pointed at her head.

Lannie strode for the back of the store, and Holly followed a hasty step or two behind. "Wait," she called to his back as he headed straight out the back exit and up the hill behind. *"Wait."* He halted without turning, and she put authority into her tone. "I don't want to go up there without…"

Cleansing. That was it. Too much of that taste in her mouth, in her head. Too much of it all surrounding her. But she couldn't quite say that out loud.

She didn't have to. Lannie reversed course, his brusque manner easing. When he reached her, there was no less of the wolf in his eye…but the human tempered it, reaching to run a caressing thumb over her cheek. "You need a break."

"Not much of one. But…I really do."

He took her hand and led her to the loft stairs, tugging just enough so she went up before him. Once inside that bright, private space, she found her own way to that which called to her—the happily burbling fountain, filled with clear, clean water from Kai's world. She sat cross-legged beside it, breathing in the clarity of it before she even thought about touching it. She didn't *want* to touch it, not as contaminated as she felt.

She didn't realize she'd closed her eyes until she felt Lannie lifting her hand and pressing a mug into it before he lowered himself to sit not beside her, but behind her—resting his long legs outside of hers, folding his arms around her waist. "Drink."

She didn't have to look; she knew the mug held water and that it was clear and cold, and that it, too, had come from Kai and Regan. She sipped it, feeling it all the way down—not just mouth and throat, but spreading in a wave of relief through her arms, her legs…all the way to her toes.

"Better?" he asked, leaning against the end of the couch and drawing her back with him. She didn't think of the ramifications of the gesture—how easy it had become to relax into him, trusting him, or how readily she gave him that power. Not even about how quickly her body warmed to him, when that's not why they were here at all.

Instead she took another drink, a deep one. When she felt it flush faintly through her body, she instinctively gave it a little nudge—and made a little "oh!" of surprise when that slow impression of internal cleansing blasted right out to the end of her fingers and toes. For an instant, she panicked—but with Lannie here and his arms around her, she found the courage to stop and examine the experience more closely.

Wow. Definitely better. Tingly and clean and just-woke-up fresh.

Fear turned to fierce curiosity and even exhilaration. Holly took another sip—deliberately slow this time, and savoring every moment of the sensation. The cool water, its passage over her tongue before sliding down her throat, her awareness of it in her stomach—and then her never-imagined ability to push that cleaning through the energy paths in her body.

Those, too, she had never imagined. But now they were there, clear as day, and if she was a little clumsy with them at the moment, she thought she wouldn't always have to be.

"Did you know?" she asked Lannie, secure against his chest, his big hands resting over her thighs in a touch that might have been called possessive but not overbearing.

At first she took his silence as a *no*, and then suddenly she realized it was simply just silence. She set the mug aside and turned within his arms. He stared blankly at the vine window, his eyes without any sign of the wolf...without any sign of the human.

"Hey," she said, on her knees before him. "None

of that." She patted his cheek lightly, and then a little more firmly, and then she took his face in her hands and kissed him—no bones about that one.

His mouth was still firm, still warm…but utterly unresponsive.

"Idiot," she muttered at herself. It wasn't her touch that he needed, as much as she'd suddenly grown accustomed to his. It was her song. Her *self.*

Because he needed something to hold on to, and he no longer had anyone but her.

Cautiously—finding it more natural than she expected in so short a time—she reached for the open feeling he'd taught her. Confident in herself after the initiation, and after their time together.

Too confident. His blank gaze confounded her.

"Hey," she said again, her hands flat against his chest, sliding out to the breadth of his shoulders. "Lannie. Come *on.*" Sudden fear assailed her. What if this time she couldn't help? What if she *could* help but simply had no idea how to do it? How close was Brevis to sending someone, and how close was the exalted Ruger to arriving? What if Lannie simply stayed this way, all his glimmer of wolf and human, all his absolute certainty of self, drifting away in a gaze of pale blue rimmed with indigo? What if she never saw that marvelous, terrifying piercing perception again? What if—

He blinked. Something indefinable changed in his gaze; his focus shifted from nowhere to here, to *her.* And frowned to find them face-to-face, his hands rising to land on her hips and settle there, thumbs caressing the crescent of bone and tightening against her as if maybe she was still the only thing keeping him here.

She had no answers for him—and she had too much going on to face the fear of what had just happened. She pulled from his grasp and climbed to her feet, snagging the mug along the way. "Do you really want to check that well house?" she asked, as if nothing had gone awry with either of them. "I don't think there's much question what we'll find."

He climbed to his feet, mulling his thoughts…keeping them to himself along the way. After a moment's apparent contemplation of her fountain, he shook himself off—a strange little lift of his head and shift of his shoulders that somehow perfectly evoked *wolf* rather than *human*.

He said, "We need to know. You up for it?"

"I'm fine," she told him, and meant it. For the moment, her head was clear, her mouth free of bitter tang. *Kryptonite.* Whatever it was, whatever it did. That would likely change as they approached the well house, but she could deal with it—and now she knew how to flush her system clean.

Just as she had so inadvertently done for Regan's well, and for the private well right here at Lannie's home and his store.

"Hey," she said to him, finding him in hesitation by the door and no longer taking those moments for granted as a benign thing. "*You* up for it?"

He didn't answer, but he led the way.

Lannie grasped the quiet threads of Holly's song— her offering, fading in and out as she concentrated on their upward hike, flaring with her worry and then, as they approached the well house, flaring with her distaste.

He didn't need to ask if she could sense anything amiss there. And it wasn't hard to understand her withdrawal, or why she'd again put up the walls he'd so recently shown her how to manipulate. "Hey," he said, as they neared the place—and then, when she glanced back, a quiet request. "Don't go."

If at first she didn't understand, the faint compression of her mouth and brow quickly cleared, and so did the strength of the personal song she shared with him.

Anchoring him.

"Okay?" she asked, standing hipshot along the steepening slope, the well house not far away. She looked perfectly at home in this world, her clothing so clearly chosen for practical durability and yet perfectly skimming the lean curves he'd explored so thoroughly the night before, her ponytail sliding over her shoulder to cascade down over her breast, her gloves crammed habitually into a back pocket.

He swallowed hard on the words and the longing that crowded his throat. "Fine," he said, and escaped the only way he knew how, tugging at the scant buttons he'd bothered to fasten in the first place. By the time he'd shucked the shirt, she held out her hand to receive it. He tucked his boots beneath a juniper and would have stepped directly into the wolf had he not seen Holly's wistful look.

"I keep looking for it," she said. "What there is about me that feels different. It comes so naturally to you... to Kai. I don't even know where to start."

"It's not about the difference," he told her, something inside him disappointed that she'd seen it that way. "It's about what's the most *you*."

"I don't—" She stopped herself. "Never mind. Now's not the time, eh? But...may I?" She lifted her hand, a request in gesture, her wistful song open to him. *May I touch you as you change?*

One more step of intimacy, her need to explore him

in that moment. One more gift of himself that he might never get back.

He gave it willingly, lifting his head in assent. Her hand fell warm and careful on his shoulder.

As naturally as breathing, he stretched into the wolf—not an effort, but a release. From human skin to canine pelt, from tough bare feet to tougher pads, from strength to power. From being Lannie to being Lannie released…with Holly's hand still on his shoulder, her fingers burrowing into thick fur and her sigh loud in wolf ears. "I have to admit," she said, "I'm not sure I truly believed it before I came here. Before I saw you and Kai. Maybe not even then. Maybe I have to rebelieve it every time I see it."

You won't find yourself until you believe, he thought at her, internal words that must have, in some small part, made it through—for she flinched, and worried her lower lip, and looked away.

He nudged her leg with a less than gentle nose, allowing himself a pinch of tooth.

"Hey!" She glared at him and he lifted a lip in return, turning his back to lead the way uphill. Aldo's scent pooled in the shadowed dips of ground; Lannie cast for the scent trail in instinctive response, already knowing that the old man had gone up but not come back down, and knowing that it had been some hours earlier.

Too many hours for a simple toke or two. Lannie trotted upward, long legs and long strides, and Holly scrambled to keep up with him, a mild curse on her lips and a sharp thread of annoyance in her song. Aldo's scent grew stronger, spreading strongly downhill from the well house.

Holly topped the crest behind Lannie with a sound

of disgust. "It's awful here, Lannie. Whatever they're doing, they've done it big."

But Lannie broke into a short-lived lope, rounding the back side of the old structure to find Aldo there, collapsed in a heap that seemed much smaller, on whole, than the man he was.

By the time Holly reached them, Lannie had taken the human again, a hand on Aldo's shoulder to tug him over.

"What happened?" Holly asked breathlessly, a convulsive swallow in her throat and her complexion gone not so much pale as just a little green, an uncommon sweat dotting her temple and upper lip. "Is he—"

She'd been going to say *dead*, but didn't seem quite able. Her song faded, barely discernible, as she protected herself—from the kryptonite so clearly seeded in the water through the well access, from her fear for an old man. Lannie clung to the threads of it, and to the feel of his bare feet against the hard-packed earth.

"Not dead," Lannie said. He patted Aldo's spare frame to come up with a careful little snack-sized zip-lock bag and the joint in progress, not even warm. "But this is nothing he's done to himself."

Holly made a faint feline hacking noise at the back of her throat. "It's this *place*," she said. "It's what they've done since last night."

"Aldo," Lannie said, closing his hand over Aldo's arm to jostle him, to no effect. To Holly he said, "If Aldo *did* feel it…if it affected him, but he couldn't understand what was happening…"

She understood more quickly than he expected, sympathy for the old man in her dark eye. "Then being who he is, he'd come up here to self-medicate. But *here* is where the problem is."

"There's no dementia," Lannie said. "No *Aldo's getting old*. He's been fucking poisoned."

"Poisoned," she agreed. "And he passed it along to you." She gave his side a meaningful look.

He didn't bother to follow her gaze. He could feel the ache of it—a constant presence, shot through with moments of sharper pain. And so Aldo had tried again to heal him, and again…each time making things worse.

And now Lannie had no pack sense, and now he clung desperately to keep even his sense of self. "We've got to get away from here," he said. "And *stay* away from here—until Brevis cleans this up."

Holly sat back on her heels, frustration welling so strong she wanted to burst with it—a familiar feeling in the wake of the day the Sentinels had ripped her from her life. "But *who*?" she said. "And *why*? Do you think maybe the Core—?"

Lannie tugged Aldo into better position, ducking his shoulder down to catch the older man up in a fireman's carry. "Not if our minion friend was right," he grunted, finding his balance beneath that burden and feeling every one of the physical insults of the previous day. "Doesn't really matter. Not our job, never was. Grab my phone."

She frowned, working through his shorthand until her expression lightened in understanding. "You want me to call Brevis?"

"Right here, right now." He shifted Aldo out of the way, presenting her with the pocket that held the phone. And what he liked best about the moment, about Holly's unhesitating determination and the immediate slide of her fingers into that front pocket, wasn't the familiarity with which she touched him, or the way her song reached him so clearly when she did. It was instead the matter-of-fact way she went about what could have been awkward and wasn't, and what could have been full of innuendo and wasn't that, either.

The sensation, for that moment, of being in complete unresisting accord.

Pack.

She'd been in his address book before. She found the number for Brevis Consul without hesitation, checked the reception bars, and held the phone high as she dialed. "I'll catch up with you. I don't dare get any lower than this—I'll lose them."

Truth to that. The town cell tower might reach through the gap to the farm store, but it just barely wrapped around this slope. "Don't hang on," he said. "I want us together." *All* of us. As soon as he reached the store, he'd have Faith call the others in the area, his small primary pack and all the scattered, light-blood Sentinels who on the whole simply went about their lives. They'd be just as vulnerable as Aldo had been.

As Lannie had been.

Holly's acknowledgment cut off into a greeting. "Marlee, it's Holly Faulkes," she said, already at a distance as Lannie stepped carefully, glad for his unusually tough feet but watching sharply for cactus and stickers all the same. Her voice faded as he headed down for his boots, Aldo an awkward and unresisting passenger.

He heard the growl of approaching vehicles even as Holly's call reached down to him—her song spiking alarm, her voice rising with it. He sent her what he could—*reassurance, intent, the wolf's ferocity on the way*—and rolled Aldo off his shoulder and onto a patch of shaded ground. By the time he reversed course and took his first loping stride uphill, he was wolf again.

Ferocity, on the way.

The underlying grumble of ATV engines cut away, leaving the sharp exchange of words—voices male and annoyed. Before Lannie even topped the crest of the hill, he heard Holly's spitting anger of response, her cry of resistance.

Felt her absence, as she retreated within herself, leaving him adrift between the moment he powered forward in full-speed lope and the moment his front feet again touched the ground.

He almost stumbled, and he almost shifted back to human...but with the well house in sight, three ATVs clustered around it and three men converging on the woman who fled them, he managed to keep his feet. And with the knowledge that these men were the unknown enemy—*Sentinel* enemy—he managed to keep his wolf.

There was no point in hiding it. Not if they already knew.

One of them saw him coming and shouted warning to the others—two of them looking familiar from the silver SUV and one of them from that very first fight, all of them just a little slow to react to the sight of a wolf low and lean and charging with a purpose.

"Shit!" cried the guy from the first fight, not made of any sterner stuff than he'd been when he'd taken on Aldo five to one. "It's one of them! They're fucking real!" He jerked the trigger on his gun, burying a bullet into the ground off to Lannie's side.

"Get the woman," the SUV driver snapped to the third man, and Lannie understood that to be exactly what it meant—they would control him with Holly's fate. She sprinted away up the final thrust of the hill, all flashing limbs and bouncing ponytail, the phone still clutched in one hand.

Lannie bent to speed, the powerful push and recoil of long legs, big paws slamming into the fine, gritty soil and thrusting away again. Another shot missed him, and a quick series of several more—and then the man from the first fight scrambled away as Lannie reached him, screaming in anticipation.

Lannie had better things to do with his teeth. This man he shoulder-checked with all his weight behind it, a rattling impact. The man's knee made a crunching noise, briefly bending sideways. The man himself might have still been screaming if it hadn't been for the solid impact of his head against the old well house.

Lannie ducked under the raised gun without slacking and latched on to the man's wrist with powerful jaws, anchoring himself there as his body slung around to face the other way before stopping.

This man only grunted…and if his wrist was ruined, he could still reach for his knife with the other hand. Lannie sprang away again, knowing the third man was still there somewhere—either going after Holly or bringing his gun to bear on Lannie. The unfolding scene turned suddenly surreal, a fine veil separating him from the reality of the fight, the men and the taste of human blood on his tongue.

That instant of hesitation cost him the flashing pain of a knife scoring his ribs, a mighty blow that sent him staggering.

Then he heard Holly scream—and when he realized she'd reversed course to come back into the fray. *You RUN!* he shouted at her—but if she perceived it, she showed no sign. And the third guy—the one most damaged on the previous day—the third guy made a mean noise of satisfaction, crouching slightly to meet her with a linebacker's tackle.

Lannie snarled in furious frustration and whirled to the greater threat—the man who'd rolled, his injured wrist tucked against his body and a big combat knife tightly to hand as he came up to face Lannie with no fear in his eye.

Lannie lowered his head and growled through dancing motes of shifting reality—but when he launched himself at the man, he missed the mark by a foot or more, and the knife scored down his shoulder. And when he landed, he staggered not because of the injury, but because the ground wasn't quite where he expected it.

The man saw it in him—not understanding, perhaps, but no less aware that he'd somehow gained an advantage in this fight. Lannie leaped away, clipping the corner of the well house he hadn't seen coming and staggering away—and then he might well have faced a final thrust of that knife if it hadn't been for—

Holly.

She hadn't come back from the hill unarmed, and the overconfident man who'd crouched to meet her fell away with a high cry, his hands clapped to his face and then jerking away with another, more agonized sound. Holly came on and only then did Lannie understand—and the driver never did, not until it was too late, and the length of healthy, bristling staghorn cholla in her gloved hand slapped into his side.

She snagged the driver's fallen gun and backed away, stepping into the white haze of Lannie's vision gone suddenly strange. Lannie heard his own puzzled whine, a thing infinitely wolfish. He knew the driver twisted and cursed, unable to free himself of the spine-studded cactus without injuring himself further, and he had a sense of motion when the other man staggered off to the side. He also knew when Holly crouched beside him, gingerly biting off one glove and then the other and spitting them out at her feet, full of broken spines and brittle-hooked cactus hairs.

But that was all he knew, and then the hazy lack of reality swallowed him whole.

Chapter 17

Holly did the unthinkable. She dug her fingers into the scruff of the massive timber wolf and she *tugged*.

More than tugged—she hauled at him, frantic to get him behind cover. Never mind the retreat of the invaders—they were bleeding and stunned and hurt, but they'd already audibly called for reinforcements, and they would be back.

But Lannie still stood blank-eyed, and she didn't have time for niceties. She tugged and hauled and yanked him, one stiff, unbalanced step after another. By the time she got them around the well house corner, she was smeared with his blood and light-headed with panting, her mouth dry and desperate for water.

But the bitterness of this place surrounded her, invaded her even through the newborn walls she'd erected, leaving no single place in her body untainted. The sense of musty old bones, an acrid tingling, and the faint hint of cramping in her stomach.

Get away from it. Get away from them.

Except she couldn't run with Lannie like this—still standing beside her with his head dropped not in threat, but sending his blank gaze over the landscape.

And she couldn't run while those men waited out there. As soon as they got a second wind, bound their wounds and reloaded their guns, they'd circle out and this scant shelter would be no shelter at all.

Something within her twitched with the sudden urge to go on the hunt.

She pushed the sensation away and grasped the lock on the well house door, giving it a futile tug. Not that she wanted to go in there—in fact, *going in there* closer to that poison was the last thing on her mind—but it was the only shelter they had. Thick old boards, weathered but still sturdy, dark corners and obscuring equipment and a doorway that would slow down these mystery enemies until…

Until Aldo woke and brought help. *Not likely.* Until Lannie came back to himself and knew what to do.

Not likely.

The lock was now a new one, shiny and stout in contrast to the old hasp through which it threaded. She pulled the scavenged gun from her back pocket and regarded it, and then the padlock. She had the feeling that shooting it off wouldn't be nearly as easy as it seemed in the movies.

And she had the feeling she might want whatever few bullets were left in this gun.

The wolf swayed beside her, his ears at dull half-mast, blood glittering in runnels down his dense coat. He was a parody of the powerful creature she'd seen running through Kai's woods, his movement so full of freedom that even the memory of it made her want to swell into—

Something.

"Lannie," she said, even knowing it would do no good. She looped an arm around his neck, pulling him closer to shelter. "I'm sorry. I didn't mean to duck out on you. I had to hide, and I…"

She'd hidden, all right. Every part of herself. Even from the man who'd been counting on her.

Why being needed by the man she'd declared *not her pack* suddenly felt like a privilege instead of a leash, she wasn't sure.

But prodding him wasn't going to fix things, and poking him wouldn't do it, either. She'd have to wake him from the inside out—with enemies looming, the poisoned well house at her back, and reinforcements nowhere near on the way because she'd lost the precarious signal as soon as she'd ducked behind this place the first time.

The men out there didn't care that she wasn't truly Sentinel, nor that she'd never meant to be. That she'd only just now gained access to the fullness of who she was, and hadn't yet begun to define it.

Resentment spun through denial and then fury and then panic. It hardly mattered how she felt about the Sentinels. Not now.

Define yourself fast.

Lannie released a long groan of breath and his body collapsed in slow motion behind it—haunches sinking, shoulders lowering, and head lolling on the ground— not unconscious, but simply a body that no longer remembered to stand. Not really Lannie anymore at all.

Holly breathed a curse she rarely used. This was her only moment—now, before the driver and his cronies had company, or before they got impatient and moved without it. Before they realized that Lannie was no longer any threat.

She took the wolf's heavy head between her hands and looked into half-closed eyes—Lannie's eyes in amber, still ringed with darkness and familiar in spite of their entirely wolfish nature. "Listen to me," she told him, so bold as to rest her forehead against his. "*Hear me.*"

She made herself vulnerable, pouring herself into him as best she knew how—unable to hear her own song, but knowing she'd done it because of all that came flooding back through the vulnerability—the poisoned well house, the ugliness seeping not just through the pipes but into the aquifer where it would infiltrate the land.

She cursed at the invasion, struggling to hold it back even as she kept herself available to Lannie, feeling it wash over her and sink into her and—

She broke away with a gasp, finding her fingers clutching hard into fur but no sign of Lannie's awareness. Before she could think too hard on the consequences, she did it again—flinging herself at him, shouting at him from the inside out—

The connection flooded her mouth with such bitter sensation that she wrenched herself aside to spit and crouched there panting and working up her courage.

After a long moment, she wiped the back of her hand across her lower lip and straightened—still crouching, but more purposeful, her eyes narrowed as she regarded the unresponsive wolf.

Surely, they didn't have much more time. Surely even if reinforcements weren't imminent—and she had no idea how long it would take them to arrive down this barely evident backwoods track—the three men would count their guns and their resources and start moving in.

But Lannie wasn't just unresponsive. It seemed to her that he was pushing back—as if he was somehow already full.

Because like her, he'd become vulnerable, right here at the well house where the poison dwelled? Because he'd been empty, and the poison had rushed in?

"I'm not *supposed* to have to know what I'm doing," Holly said to him, voice low and resentful. "Not yet. Not even if I had wanted to be here, dammit."

She licked dry lips and wished again for a glass of water—thinking of not so long ago when she'd swallowed deeply and washed herself clean from the inside out.

The wolf stirred. Nothing more than a shift in his breathing, a blink of his eyes.

"Really?" she asked him, as if he might even answer. "But that's just making things up. That's just *pretending.*"

Maybe not in this world. The Sentinels' world.

She took the wolf's head between her hands once more, hesitating only long enough to listen for sounds of incursion. Silence so far. She imagined the shouted threats weren't too far behind.

Nothing to lose, eh? She let loose her song to him, but not just that. She filled herself with the sensation of swallowing cold, cleansing water, letting it flow not just through her limbs, but out to Lannie. Resistance met her, and she didn't push so much as she existed—inexorable, persistent. Like water. She imbued her thoughts with the impact of piercing blue eyes, the touch of a big and work-rough hand, the warmth of a body bigger than hers and the gift of his vulnerability. The thrust of unfettered response, the tremble of desire, the harsh, startled gasp of uncontrolled passion.

The understanding of what she'd demanded from him during these days of turmoil and loss, and that he'd given it to her not just because of who he was, but of who they were together.

This is us*, Holly-cat.*

He had filled her in every way, even when she hadn't known she'd wanted it.

"My turn, Phelan Stewart," she told him. *"Lannie."*

She didn't have water, so she filled him with herself.

Hard ground and the scent of blood, a scrub jay scolding at a distance and fingers clutching his wolf ruff just a little too hard—

Lannie jerked, and flailed, and threw himself back against wood that creaked under the impact, flinging himself back to the human so much faster than was ever wise. His head smacked into the well house—*ground, well house, enemy nearby...HOLLY.*

"Holly—" he said, and took a sharp breath as her song filled him.

Not just hers. Faith, blithely humming along at the store, her concern a mere undertone. Aldo, dark and ailing. Javi and Pete, full of the Zen of physical activity, the occasional spike of humor. And all the rest, a gestalt of voices spread out over the mountains.

Staggered, Lannie froze there—shirtless, barefoot, bleeding from new wounds and throbbing from new bruises but *whole.*

Completely, entirely *whole.*

Holly watched him, her eyes huge and gleaming and...not exactly frightened, but full of *seeing*—as if she'd looked at something that might just be too big to comprehend.

What had she done?

He tried to form a question and failed. *Not the time for questions.* Not now. He drew her up close and felt mild surprise when she melted against him as if she belonged there. A moment of complete, indulgent comfort.

Hell yeah, he kissed her.

For that moment, she kissed him right back, her mouth finding his with an urgency that spoke of things unsaid and no time to say them. He tangled his fingers in her ponytail and held her there an instant longer than she would have stayed—but no longer.

"They're still here, Lannie," she said as soon as she could. And she might have been breathless, but she was as intent as he'd seen her.

Still the words didn't quite come him—too much song in his head, too much Holly in his hands. *What had she done?*

"Are you okay?" she asked, more urgent now, scooting back to regard him from her knees. "Do you remember what happened?"

"Fighting," he said, thinking of the whirlwind of it, the desperation, the being outnumbered and guns and *Holly.*

"Bad guys," she said. "There are *bad guys* out there. You hurt them—"

"We," he corrected her, a sudden flash of swinging cactus and the scream of response.

"We," she agreed. "But they've poisoned this place. And no one knows what's happening but us. And they're still out there."

He snapped into focus. "Did you get that call off to Brevis?"

She shook her head. "I connected, but I lost it before I could tell Marlee anything of significance."

"She know that we need help?"

"Pretty sure I got that much across," Holly said, her tone dry enough to make him laugh shortly. "But who knows—"

He shook his head. "Hours," he said. "If they truly understand. They'll sacrifice what they need to to get here."

She looked out over the mountain. "The aquifers," she said. "What if it's too late? What if it's *already* too late?"

"One thing at a time." He reached a dirty hand out to caress her cheek, holding his breath on the sweet, subtle thrill when she leaned into it, a deep sound in her throat. *Holly-cat.* "Thank you," he said. "I don't know how you did it, but—"

"You're welcome," she said, still in that throaty voice.

He could have stayed there for just about forever, simply touching her and feeling the pressure of her touch in return.

But those men were still out there.

She rested a hand on his thigh and it felt like connection, just as much as the clarity of song now slipping easily through the back of his thoughts. She asked, "Can you call for help? You know…how sometimes I hear you…"

She heard him. He'd never been certain. It put a hint of smile at the corner of his mouth, in spite of the moment. But it faded before he answered her. "They're all light bloods."

Aside from Aldo, the light-blood members of his pack had no natural craftiness, no wariness to their natures. They would, rather than calling Brevis, investigate. And they'd be hurt or killed.

She couldn't possibly understand the layers of the statement, but she understood enough. "Then we're on our own." She scowled, her head tipping as she listened for signs of movement from the men. "And they hate us. *Why* do they hate us?"

Us. It was enough for another brief smile. "For the same reason the Core tries so hard to obliterate us. We represent something they can't control or truly understand."

Holly's music tangled in frustration, bringing itself to his attention. "I keep trying. I keep looking for something *other* in myself, something that wasn't so clear before we—" But he couldn't help a little laugh, and she stopped short, offended. "It's not funny," she said. "Just because this comes so easily to you, you…you…*wolf*."

An ATV motor sounded in the distance—far enough away so human ears wouldn't have heard it. So Lannie just shook his head, short on time and words. "You've got me wrong, Holly-cat. And you've got yourself wrong, too. I already told you. Don't look for the unfamiliar. Look for the *more*." He wiped at a trickle of sweat gathering inside his brow. "They're coming. If I boost you up on the roof, can you give me a few covering shots?"

Startled, she glanced up to the roof, where the sun beat hot on curling old shingles. She took a breath, standing to wipe the grit from her work pants. "Boost away."

He took the gun from her, ejecting the fifteen-round magazine of the HK P30 to find it nearly full. "Count 'em," he said, smacking the magazine home again and shifting the safety on before he held it out to her.

"You've got twelve cartridges. Keep a couple back. This is the safety—don't shift it until you're ready to fire. And don't fire—don't give yourself away—until they react to me."

She nodded and took the gun back, and now the ATV was close enough so she lifted her head, hearing it— knowing as he did that maybe they'd run out of time.

"Holly-cat," he said, and nothing else. It was enough—just meeting the richness of her gaze in the shadow of the well house, seeing the glint in her eye and most of all, hearing the swell in her song. Hearing the subtle shift, the hint of blending that hadn't been there before.

She wiped fiercely at her eyes, jammed the gun in her back waistband, and put her hands on his shoulders, lifting one foot. "Okay," she said. "Boost."

He cupped his hands into a stirrup and timed his lift to her bounce, tossing her up just enough to get a good purchase on the crumbling shingles. She landed lightly, sinking against the pitch of the roof, holding position for only a moment before reaching back to lift the tail of her shirt and pluck the gun from her waistband. In the distance, the approaching ATV somehow grew no closer, and Lannie frowned, trying to make sense of it— and knowing how these mountains could twist sound.

By the time Holly reached the roof ridge and just barely peered over, Lannie had reached for his wolf— finding himself to be strong, reveling in the renewed completion Holly had given him. He waited for her to look back at him and nod, and then ghosted out along the side of the building, unnoticed at first by the men who'd forgotten to look for a wolf and instead waited for two humans to make their escape over the remaining rise of this mountain slope.

One man barely managed to sit his ATV and had no weapon in hand—the man Lannie had shoulder-checked and left lamed and thoroughly dazed. Another bled freely along his face—and though he had a gun and had it aimed, he most likely had only one working eye.

The driver remained their biggest threat, still red-faced with his anger. His injured wrist had been wrapped, but his gun rested awkwardly in his off hand; he wouldn't be able to drive the ATV and handle the gun at the same time.

They've got nothing, he sent at Holly, a focused internal voice. He felt her disbelief and added, *Hold your fire.*

He slowed to stand his ground before them. No threat in it, just his head held high, his eyes on the driver... waiting.

Because they'd been a bluff, waiting until their reinforcements could come, and the reinforcements hadn't. That distant ATV engine had growled to a stop, either lost or misdirected, and none of these men had the resources to aim at them or to pursue them.

Hold fire, he told her again, allowing himself to feel the fiery score of the new knife wounds, the aches of their encounter. *We're walking out of here.*

Not that these men wouldn't still be out here, working toward their goal. But they were no longer invisible. So when Holly's disbelieving resistance reached him, Lannie sent her reassurance, and he laced it with an alpha's command. *It's as much as we can do.*

That, she accepted—and Lannie turned away from the defeated men.

Except the driver didn't look at all defeated. He didn't look at all concerned. He looked...

Mean and hard and satisfied.

Lannie thought again of the bounce of sound between the mountain ridges and points and valleys, the way a canyon could swallow an echo and the way a slope could shift it.

Holly...! He spun back on the men, well aware that her song stuttered, easily able to read her surprise and alarm. Holly, out there on the roof and fully exposed to an enemy in the slopes around them. *Holly, out there on the roof—*

He sent her an immutable command, the alpha laced throughout. *Get down! Get OUT!*

He lowered his head and loped out toward the men, ground-eating strides and unmistakable intent. Silent, deadly and circling ever so slightly for an angle to take the driver down. *Drawing fire.*

A white hot stab of pain hit near his hip and sent him spinning. Holly's burst of ferocious song rang in his head—a wash of love yet undeclared, a burst of roiling blue-white energy—

Love and snarling, spitting defensive fury, the sense of a roiling bundle of fur skidding down the roof and landing on all fours with claws extended, still tangled in clothing but fast shredding free to RUN—

And then it turned out that the men in the ATVs could still wield their boots and a cudgel or two, and Lannie snarled back into action, all wolf.

All *alpha.* And not going down without the best fight he could give them.

Run, you Holly-cat, RUN.

Chapter 18

Holly panted beneath a juniper, blending perfectly there.

Knowing she blended, because of the reddish tan fur of her paws and the mottled black traveling up her legs. A twist of her head showed her the mere stub of a tail; a twitch of her cheek gave her...

Whiskers.

She didn't even know *how*—

She trembled at the memory of Lannie running for the ATVs, drawing fire—the sight of him tumbling to the ground. Sniper, in the mountain. *Sniper*, and he'd known—drawing fire from her with that stupid, bold attack. And still she might have readily been the next target, had she not somehow blossomed into energy and light and respun herself as—

Bobcat.

Holly-cat. Lannie had been right all along.

She'd rolled off the roof, torn her way free of claw-shredded clothing, and streaked into the woods where the ponderosa pines mingled with low-hanging junipers and scrub brush, dodging into cover in a way no human could hope to match.

And they had him. Until now, she'd had no idea that she'd woken from initiation with such a sense of him humming through her heart—but now the lack of it was a gaping inner wound. Not Lannie sleeping or distracted, but Lannie *gone*.

She found her paws shredding the ground before her—under scrutiny, they stilled. It was alien, this body. Bristling with energy, so keen to hear the smallest twitter of a bird, so alert to every hint of movement…the colors muted but not gone, the air vibrating around her whiskers, the breeze barely lifting the fur on her haunches. The bitter dead mustiness of the poisoned water seeped in through every one of those senses.

She had no idea how to get back to what she'd been. She was stuck in on a mountainside in a brand-new body, surrounded by men who had made themselves into enemies…and wailing inside at the silence from Lannie.

If this was only a hint of what it felt like to find a connection with someone, what had she been asking of *him* all this time?

She swore and it came out a yowl, which startled her into a dash for new cover, where she swore more silently and plastered her ears and whiskers back into ire. *Fine.* Think, *Holly-cat.*

Here she was. What was she going to do about the situation? What *could* she do about it?

Stalk them. That thought came unbidden.

These men were concerned about Sentinels for a reason. *I can do what they can't.* Stalk them. Find Lannie. *Watch* them. And they'd never know.

It wasn't as easy as that. She thought too hard about the first steps and put one foot wrong, and then another. Her stubby tail lashed, her ears flattened.

She liked that sensation—the fierceness of it, and the feel of the soft ear crumpling back against fur. She did it again, and flicked the ears, and then let them follow the faint sounds of the forest. They performed with perfect precision.

That was it, then. Quit thinking about it. Just do it.

Holly-cat slunk out of hiding and began to stalk.

She caught her bearings quickly enough. She hadn't gone far—and they hadn't gone anywhere. The three ATVs had become four, and three men clustered around a fallen wolf while the fourth sprawled in the seat of his ATV, a liquor flask in hand.

She circled in closer—quite close, with the men none the wiser and a clump of mixed juniper and piñon not far from them. Close enough to feel the faintest of responses from Lannie, and to see when the driver bent over to grab the fur beneath Lannie's wolf ear and lift his head to deliver a threat.

Surrounded by enemies and their guns and their heavy boots, Lannie responded with a quick slash of teeth. The driver swore and recoiled, and by the time Lannie hit the ground he was embroiled in clean, clear light—and then he was Lannie again.

Holly kneaded claws into dirt, a quick satisfaction. She sent what she could of herself to him, letting him know she was there, whole and well.

If he had enough awareness to reply, he didn't try. He lifted a face terribly bruised, boot marks already rising on his ribs and along his back. Blood pulsed from his leg—high on the outside, where the wound had been a quick in-and-out.

The driver's blood smeared his chin.

The fourth man put a hand on the driver's arm, stopping the raised gun. "Leave it," he said clearly. "You asked for that. And we have what we want—or we would, if you hadn't beat the crap out of him. We need him able to talk."

"Give it time," the driver said, derision in those words. "His kind heal fast."

The man who'd been in the bar—miserable, his hand held to his face and his body hunched with pain—said, "Cruz and I need a hospital. We can't do any good here. I'm gonna lose this eye if I don't get help."

The driver didn't offer any particular sympathy. "You've probably already lost it. You'll be compensated—both of you. I'm not sending you away while the other one is still out there...and while this one is still alive." He gave the man a meaningful look. "You're part of this now."

Holly? Lannie sounded vague and uncertain, a presence uncertain of itself.

Holly crouched more tightly under herself, both smaller and more prepared to move. She didn't know how to send words back at him, but she sent out an internal purr of confirmation.

Holly. He tried to roll to his side; an ungentle boot pushed against his shoulder and then rested there.

"See what I mean?" the driver said. "You think any normal man would be looking for trouble already?"

Holly pulled her whiskers back in a silent hiss. Lannie wasn't looking for trouble; he'd never been looking for trouble. He'd only ever been looking after his people, and now...now he was still trying to look after *her*.

Holly, get out of here. Those words came with a grunt of unvoiced pain, but they came clearly.

She didn't need words to say *no.* Surely he'd feel that stubborn refusal, twined as it was with fear.

She still had no idea what she was doing, or what she *could* do. She just knew she couldn't leave him like this.

Get. Out. Of. Here. Crystal clear, complete with the sense of clenched teeth—she could see it in him, from where she crouched in her cedar-scented cover and watching the tension in his jaw, wondering how these arrogant invaders could fail to notice it.

He didn't look her way—he so deliberately didn't look her way that Holly knew he'd located her. But he closed his eyes and his internal voice dropped in register and volume. *Please. Go tell the others—*

The others had Aldo. He might be unconscious on the hillside, but even that would tell them something. They'd find him, and he'd be such a mess that Brevis wouldn't know where to start. And if all the power of Brevis brought to bear—including, probably, Kai— couldn't pinpoint the presence of the kryptonite, then they had bigger problems to deal with.

I can help. She thought it as loudly as she could, exaggerating the sound of the words in her head. *What can I do?*

He flinched at the impact of her words. *Don't try so hard.* But he gave her no time to re-form her thoughts and try again. *Nothing you can do. I need time. Nothing critical here, just...too much.*

No kidding. It hurt just to look at him.

Brevis needs to know. They need to protect themselves. Get to Faith. She'll come through.

She hadn't thought of it that way. That this water would affect the strong bloods just as it had affected

Aldo, and just as it had affected her—and how quickly it had swept into Lannie once his guard was down.

Even now, the bitter nature of it pressed in against her, and only her natural instinct—a Sentinel affinity with water honed through years of work with all the subtle aspects of it—kept it at bay. She'd cleansed herself and she'd cleansed Lannie, and now she protected herself with a subtle pressure outward—not enough to create a flow of water energy, but enough to resist contamination.

But she'd done more than that, if she thought about it.

She'd cleansed Lannie of Aldo's broken healings. She'd cleansed his well—an unconscious effort already practiced on Regan's well. And while her Upper Peninsula neighbors needed filters on their private wells, Holly never had. Her clients called her magical, joking and meaning it at the same time, because when she came to address their balky water feature plumbing, it seemed she did little more than run her hands over the system.

This is far more than any water feature, and far more than any private well.

And the kryptonite already seeped back into a massive aquifer from multiple points of contamination, spreading out to affect the land above and below.

She wanted to help. And this was the one thing she could do.

She tucked herself together more tightly yet, squeezing her eyes closed and reaching out with her awareness—looking for the well house pump and piping, the sweet taste of iron casting and the sharp prick of the electric pump. All familiar things, never before labeled or even acknowledged.

The bitterness swelled up to engulf her, stunning

her with its intensity. It came burdened with the mustiness of old death, a slippery and clinging mucilage. She hacked against it and sneezed, then sneezed again.

Lannie's warning drew her fully out of the effort—no words, just alarm. She wiped a quick paw over her face and peered from her shelter—found the men in discussion and borderline argument. "I say haul him up, tie him off and get him talking. Why waste an opportunity to see just how much these creatures can take?"

Creatures? Holly froze in offense. *He's a man. He's a GOOD man. And you are NOT!*

But her silent affront didn't stop them, and the edges of Lannie's pain washed over her—an inadvertent sharing of something too big to contain, his song nothing more than a low rumbling sound that could have been growl or could have been groan. They dragged him across the rugged ground to an ATV, and Holly's pulse spiked in fear at the way his head lolled, at the way he gave no protest as they propped him against the front of an ATV and stretched his arms up, tying them to the grill guard.

The fourth man dug his hand into the hair at the top of Lannie's head and forced him to look up; Lannie's eyes opened without warning, and the man's smirk faded, replaced by surprise.

Holly knew what he saw in those bright blue eyes, made all the brighter by the indigo that rimmed them. She knew the look that could drill right through to a person's soul—she'd been challenged by it, reassured by it and loved by it.

The man released Lannie's head with a jerk of derision. "Glad to see you're with us," he said, and bent to jab a thumb into the darkest of bruises along Lannie's side. Lannie jerked, snarling against sharp lancing shards of pain that reached all the way over to Holly, and she knew the man a fool. Lannie, she thought, would not forgive this taunting.

"We've never had one of your kind alive before—and we've got some questions." He'd found his smirk, a thoroughly unpleasant thing on a face made of overly long angles and sharp edges—the brow too prominent, the nose a hawkish blade. "My friends aren't feeling kindly toward you, and they'd like to see just how close you can get to dead before you can't do your fast-healing thing."

"Tricky game," Lannie observed, though a fat lip made the words indistinct. "Question is just how long you can run it before you piss me off."

The man snorted, and the driver moved in to block Holly's view. "Don't play with him, Orvus. Just find out how much they know about us."

They'd kill him. They'd kill him, and they'd do it slowly. And the gaze that saw right through to her soul would dim, and so would something in Holly. The gaze that challenged her, and reassured her, and—

Loved her.

And there was nothing she could do for him except fix his world.

She flattened her ears. Fierce. Snarling inside. And she dove back into that bitter, deathly place, pushing aside the murky soup of it for clarity. Making of herself a filtering wash, a bubble of *what should be*.

Running out of breath far too soon…floundering… bobbing back up to the surface of her thoughts with a sneeze and another. Her eyes streamed and her nose ran and her stomach very nearly heaved.

Lannie's cry of pain broke through to her—a harsh thing, wrung from a hoarse throat. She bolted halfway from cover and stopped short, crouching, tail lashing—

saw that the fourth man crouched before him, one knee digging into the muscled curve of darkly bruised rib. Bright, foamy blood trickled from Lannie's mouth— a pained spasm of a cough, and he spit a mouthful of it at the man who would so happily break him down bone by bone.

And to Holly he said, *You were my anchor. Now let me be yours.*

Only then did she realize he'd cried out in part to distract from her—and then realized that he'd also defied them to distract from her. And she thought there was no way he could give anything more of himself and still survive.

And he looked her direction just long enough, just sharply enough, so she knew he knew it, too.

I won't. She wouldn't take that from him. She could do it without. She just needed to get her bearings—to find her way through this thing that no one had ever taught her to do, but that she'd somehow been doing her whole life regardless.

She backed slowly into the cover of her tangled junipers and drew herself tight. This time, she'd already found the well; she knew the taste of it and the feel of it and the sensation of finding her way down into it. She dove for it—not the slow descent of before, but an arrowing dive into toxicity, down as far and as fast as she could go before she expanded her awareness—

And gasped, floundering, finding it all too big and finding herself immersed too deeply to withdraw. She would throw everything she had and everything she was at it, and she would never find her way back—

She was drowning.

Not, Lannie said, a teeth-gritting sense to his words,

an awareness of coppery sweet blood and grinding pressure. *Not. On. My. Watch. In my pack.*

He filled her with pack song. Not just his song, but the sly and nimble dance of Aldo, the sharp, lurking resentment from Faith, the hint of a hundred distant songs all tumbling around together—far more than could be in this remote area, in his small home pack.

Everyone who'd ever been his.

He poured that strength into her, and she no longer needed to breathe. She no longer needed to hesitate, to find herself, to battle away the erosive toxicity in the water. She expanded with song, riding it like a wave— pushing it out through not just this well, but linking them all, pushing through them all with a shock wave of pressure that grew and grew and grew and only finally, far past the margins of the damaged aquifers, it faded and ebbed back towards her center.

Cleansed.

But she had no idea where she was. She'd spread herself so thin, so far—

Lannie's song.

It reached her, wherever she was.

Let me be your anchor.

She grasped it. She followed it. It grew stronger and so did she—until she opened her eyes to the searing, bright high-desert afternoon, squinting over grasses just beginning to green with the monsoon activity and a sky building clouds in the distance, and the clear, sweet bell of healthy water in the well nearby. And to Lannie, who looked all but dead in his bonds, no longer responding to the driver's goading with his cries but just hanging there.

Holly sprang up with a hiss-spit, finding her reeling satisfaction shooting straight to temper. *Mine!* she cried in the only way she could, a silent challenge of fury that erupted in a bobcat yowl. *I have had ENOUGH! Of! YOU!*

She emerged from cover with an awareness of claws and needle-sharp teeth, startled by her own surge of physical power, the speed with which she reached them. The one-eyed guy gave a shout of surprise, and they all whirled to her, unprepared for this new attack. She reached the driver and clawed her way up his body, all the way up to his face, clinging around his shoulders to sink her fangs wherever she could, as fast as she could. He screamed into her fur.

Lannie twisted into sudden motion and light and slipped his restraints to come up as wolf, instantly launched himself at the fourth man, his jaws going straight for the throat.

It was over just that fast. Lannie fell away and back into the human, spitting blood off to the side that was no longer just his own, wiping his mouth with a bare arm. The fourth man fell to the ground, his throat torn out. Holly sprang away from the driver, who fell to his knees with his hands covering his face, making noises that no longer even sounded human.

The one-eyed guy froze on his ATV. The other made an attempt to flee and dragged himself only a few feet away, thoroughly concussed and lamed.

Lannie bent, pressing his arm into his side, not hiding the pain and not quite giving into it. "Go," he told the one-eyed guy. "Leave your guns and get your people out of here." He spat again, his breath coming shallow and fast. "And remember—we might not know who you are, but now we know you're here. We stand together against you." This time, when the man hesitated, Lannie offered only a weary jerk of his head—a silent command. But he didn't need to straighten to put the alpha behind it.

And the man didn't need to be Sentinel to see it.

Moments later, four men—lurching and tipping or bungeed into place—rode away on two of the ATVs. The ATVs ran fast and hard, the sound bouncing around the mountains until it faded away.

Slowly, Lannie went down to his knees—bent over his pain, bent over his labored breathing…but watching Holly.

And Holly suddenly realized she had no idea how to make her way back to human. She made a surprised sound at that, looking down at the pads of one paw where shredded material still clung, and then back to Lannie. Her eyes grew big; her tail stuck out; her fur stood on end.

Lannie laughed, as quiet and pained as it was. "Holly-cat," he said, and held out one arm in invitation, "you need only come back to me."

One step, two steps…thinking of Lannie, thinking of the sensation of being woman in Lannie's arms, thinking of bare feet on dirt and her skin next to his.

Holly-cat, come back to me.

And she did.

Chapter 19

Sweet little bobcat, Lannie thought.

Holly had been fiery and fearless, bounding down the hill with a familiar feline grace and clawing her way up the driver's body—not so much accomplished as determined, that stumpy tail lashing.

And now she curled up in his arms, never having made it to her feet after finding her human again—not hysterical, not angry, not shaking from the impact of what she'd just been through. Just stunned and being with him, her breath warm on his shoulder, her skin soft against his, her loosed hair flowing like water over his chest and arm.

It worked for him. Though he didn't know just how much longer he'd remain upright, on his knees or not. Even in the midday heat, his jeans had turned clammy with blood and a cold sweat prickled the hair of his chest; the coppery tang in his mouth came as much from his own injuries as those he'd inflicted. His breath ran hot against his throat and didn't seem to do much to get him the air he lacked.

But through it all, the music of Holly's connection ran strong. Not just the notes she'd given him when he'd had nothing else to hang on to, but the fullness of a song—*her* song—intertwined with the pack.

He wondered if she knew it.

"Oh my God," she said. "I'm *naked.*"

His sound of amusement sounded as ragged as he felt, but she lifted her head to pin him with a narrow-eyed look. He nodded at the well house. "Dropped your clothes."

"*Shredded* them," she said, her mouth pursing—no doubt pondering whether to take her cat again. But Lannie…

Lannie found he needed her as human.

"*My* shirt," he reminded her.

She eyed the packed dirt between the ATVs and the well house, and rose to cross the distance with her head high, her rolling stride unaffected.

When she returned, she wore his shirt and her shoes, and carried what was left of her clothing. Her rueful expression turned alarmed at the sight of him, and he didn't have to wonder why. The world pulsed around him with a thrum of warning, and pain raged through his body in hot grinding aches and sharp unexpected spears.

Holly ran the last few steps and got there in time to make his descent to ground a gentle one. "Hey," she said. *"Hey."*

He thought he responded, but wasn't sure. He thought she held his hand, but couldn't quite tell. Familiar lips pressed his forehead and cheek and mouth, but he might have dreamed that. Then the hands and the lips and the murmurs of comfort left him to struggle with himself on the side of the mountain, but—

Never alone. Not with the song of her in his mind and soul, carrying him through passing time and the heat of the sun moving across his chest.

"Hey," she said again, eventually, this time with a hand on his shoulder—and not alone at that. *"Hey."*

This time, he might have growled, a lift of lip and barely slitted eyes.

"*Do* something," she said, and not to him. "He was holding them off for me...distracting them. He could have gotten away at any time—"

"Awesome," said another voice, deep and rumbly, and flat with its wry tone. "What the hell, Phelan Stewart? You think I don't have enough to keep me busy?"

"Hey," Holly said, her sharp tone with a warning now. "He called you people for help *days* ago—"

"Us." A light alto, a little husky and completely relaxed. *Mariska.* "You're one of us now, Holly. And Ruger will deal with this. Lannie will be fine."

"Eventually," grumbled the voice that was Ruger. "I do healing, not miracles."

"Give him room, Holly." Another voice yet, gentle and understanding. *Regan Adler?* Of course, Kai had felt the touch of Holly in the land. Of course he'd come.

Holly responded with a grim determination. "I'm not leaving him."

No, you're not. Whatever happened now, she'd be a part of him forever. "She's fine where she is," Ruger said, flipping open a container, rustling through its contents. "I'm just going to stabilize him, and we'll get back downhill. There," he added, a certain knowing tone in his voice, "you can clean him up all you want."

"Ruger." The faint sound of an impact accompanied those words.

"What?" He sounded aggrieved as glass clinked against glass, followed by the sound of pouring water. "She's *cat*. You know she's going to."

Someone laughed. It might have been Regan. And a strong arm slipped under Lannie's shoulders, raising him up and eliciting a growl of warning. "Yeah, yeah," Ruger said. "You hurt. I know. Drink this, and it'll be better."

Water, cool and tangy with herbs, slipped down his throat, spilling down his chin to drip on his chest. "Good," Ruger said matter-of-factly. "See you later."

Lannie opened his eyes to the sight of his familiar loft ceiling—rough-finished drywall waiting for paint. He had a vague memory of a body beside his, hand resting on his arm, warm breath on his skin. But he was alone now—darkness clung to the corners, and silence surrounded him. *Near* silence. The barely audible trickle of Holly's fountain put a twitch of a smile at his mouth.

He lifted his head enough to get a good look at himself—cleaned and bandaged and battered. But nothing looked worse. And for all the grinding ache of what had been done to him, the sharpness of it had receded. He didn't know whether to thank his body for that, or Ruger's potions.

Daring greatly, he propped himself up on his elbows, one cautious movement after the other.

Holly sat on the floor beside her fountain—legs crossed, back straight—looking out onto the mountains through his vine window, her fingers dabbling gently in the fountain.

"What time is it?" he asked, his voice creaky and the words as inane as they could be.

She must have known he'd wakened; she didn't so much as twitch at the intrusion of his words into silence. "Somewhere between really, really late night and really, really early morning."

"Aldo?"

"He's better already. Ruger worked on him, said he'd be back to making trouble in a day or two."

But something about her voice didn't sound quite right. "You okay?"

She laughed—just a huff of air, really. "I'm fine. I just have a lot to think about." She swiveled on her bottom to face him, putting her back to the fountain and clasping her hands around her legs. "You're fine, too. Or you will be. It's going to take a while, Ruger said. You cut it pretty close, eh?" She scowled. "You could have gotten away from them at any time."

"Not *any* time," he said. "I had to get my head back together. They didn't make it easy."

That they certainly hadn't.

She released a breath. "You wouldn't believe how many people are here. Half of them are out working the mountain and half of them are sleeping in town, which probably doesn't know what hit it. Kai's guarding the site. Mariska says come daylight they'll police it for evidence and then clean up. Whoever these people are, they aren't secret anymore." She frowned. "Though I don't know why no one seems concerned that they'll tell the world about the Sentinels."

"Because they haven't." Lannie dried for a deep breath and gave it up as a bad choice. "Because if they wanted that attention, they would have grabbed it by now. Because they were up on that mountain shooting at us, and now we have all the evidence of it."

"But they're still out there."

He was silent to that. Because, right. They were still out there. Fervent and probably completely undeterred, and with the resources to have pulled off a significant operation as their opening salvo. Instead, he asked, "The water?"

She smiled—a genuine thing, unfettered by the other concerns of the day. "Cleaner than it's ever been." She wrinkled her nose. "Problem is, now we don't know what it was in the first place."

"Kryptonite," Lannie said, and had to stop on a hitching breath, finding his way through an already encroaching fatigue.

Holly shook her head. "You cut it *too* close."

"Maybe. I had reason." He mustered enough of himself to look at her with the alpha behind it.

She absorbed it with a steady eye, a somber expression. And then she said, "I've got a problem, Lannie. You people ripped me away from my life, and my home. You took me away from what I'd always been and dumped me in the middle of not knowing who I was or where I was going, or what I might even turn into."

He nodded. They'd done that. They'd turned her inside out.

"I had so many decisions to make," she said. "Who I *wanted* to be, how I wanted to handle all of this. But it was all so much…I think really, the only thing I knew to do was to say no." She lifted one rueful shoulder. "No, I won't be a Sentinel. No, I won't stay here. No, I won't be in your pack. No, I won't—" she stopped on a deep and sudden breath, more like a hiccup *"—won't love you."*

He sat up the rest of the way, unheeding what it did

to the torn places within him, his arm pressing against his side. "Holly—"

"No," she said. "Just listen. I've put you through so much, and you've just *been* there. You've been *you* the whole time. You've been honest with me about who you are, every part of it. About how you felt. About what you wanted from me and needed from me. And I never gave you an inch, because saying *no* was the only power I had left." She tried again for a deep breath and seemed to manage it this time. "But I don't want to say no any longer, Lannie." She wiped her cheek against her shoulder, but it didn't do any good—another tear spilled down in its wake. "I want—"

But she stopped there, not quite certain enough of him and his silence.

Didn't matter. Lannie was certain. Details be damned, he was certain.

He held out one arm. "Holly-cat," he said. "Come to me."

And she did.

* * * * *

THE WORLD IS BETTER
WITH
Romance

Harlequin has everything from contemporary, passionate and heartwarming to suspenseful and inspirational stories.

Whatever your mood,
we have a romance just for you!

Connect with us to find your next great read,
special offers and more.

 /HarlequinBooks

@HarlequinBooks

www.HarlequinBlog.com

www.Harlequin.com/Newsletters

⟨H⟩ HARLEQUIN®

A *Romance* FOR EVERY MOOD™

www.Harlequin.com

JUST CAN'T GET ENOUGH?

Join our social communities
and talk to us online.

You will have access to the latest
news on upcoming titles and special
promotions, but most importantly,
you can talk to other fans about your
favorite Harlequin reads.

Harlequin.com/Community

Facebook.com/HarlequinBooks

Twitter.com/HarlequinBooks

Pinterest.com/HarlequinBooks

HARLEQUIN®

A *Romance* FOR EVERY MOOD™

**Stay up-to-date on all your
romance-reading news with the
Harlequin Shopping Guide,
featuring bestselling authors, exciting new
miniseries, books to watch and more!**

The newest issue will be delivered right to you
with our compliments! There are 4 each year.

Signing up is easy.

EMAIL

ShoppingGuide@Harlequin.ca

WRITE TO US

HARLEQUIN BOOKS
Attention: Customer Service Department
P.O. Box 9057, Buffalo, NY 14269-9057

OR PHONE

1-800-873-8635 in the United States
1-888-343-9777 in Canada

Please allow 4-6 weeks for delivery of the first issue by mail.